FEMINISTA

ALSO BY ERICA KENNEDY

Bling

ERICA KENNEDY

FEMINISTA

ST. MARTIN'S PRESS
NEW YORK

This is a work of fiction. All of the characters, organizations, and events portrayed in this novel are either products of the author's imagination or are used fictitiously.

FEMINISTA. Copyright © 2009 by Erica Kennedy. All rights reserved. Printed in the United States of America. For information, address St. Martin's Press, 175 Fifth Avenue, New York, N.Y. 10010.

www.stmartins.com

Library of Congress Cataloging-in-Publication Data

Kennedy, Erica.
    Feminista / Erica Kennedy. — 1st ed.
       p. cm.
    ISBN 978-0-312-53879-8
    1. African American women—Fiction.   2. Man-woman relationships—Fiction.
3. City and town life—New York (State)—New York—Fiction.   4. Chick lit.
I. Title.
    PS3611.E559F46 2009
    813'.6—dc22

                                                                    2009013191

First Edition: September 2009

10 9 8 7 6 5 4 3 2 1

To Gene Landrum, Robert K. Cooper,

Eckhart Tolle, Byron Katie,

August Gold, and C-Man for always

reminding me to look for the open space

ACKNOWLEDGMENTS

Thank you to the wonderful and patient ones: my editor, Elizabeth Beier; my agent, Ira Silverberg; and my love, Phillip Shung.

ACT ONE

The truth will set you free.
But first it will piss you off.

—GLORIA STEINEM

CHAPTER ONE

Sydney Zamora decided she'd had enough. She tossed her crumpled napkin on the table and pushed her chair back as her confused date watched in disbelief.

"Where . . ." he stammered. "Where are you going?"

"Home." She slipped into her coat and flashed a tight, angry smile. "Peace."

She was furious at him, at herself, at the world, really, but Quo was no place to make a scene. It was the überhip restaurant of the moment, the kind of New York it spot that had an unlisted phone number and a menu people called "creative." All the senior editors at *Cachet* had been raving that the Thai fusion fare was a-maaaaaaaaaazing, hype Sydney was disinclined to believe. It was never about the food at these places. It was about being seen.

And that was exactly what she *didn't* want now. Beating a hasty retreat through the dimly lit, ridiculously pretentious subterranean dining room, Sydney flipped up the collar of her trench and donned her plaid newsboy cap, tugging the brim down low. With her healthy five-foot-nine-inch frame, bronzed skin, and chocolate waves of hair falling just past her shoulders, she stood out like a penny in the snow at these trendy hangouts where most of the women were white, blond, and thinner than Darfur refugees. Her honey-brown eyes flicked about the room, on the lookout for Omnimedia employees. The last thing she needed was for this to get back to the office. Those catty bitches (male and female) gossiped about her enough.

She didn't see any of her colleagues, but Sydney knew nothing guaranteed safety in this stratum of the New York world. If someone on the waitstaff figured out where she worked, it was very likely that tonight's embarrassing debacle would be tomorrow's "Page Six" headline. On her own, she wasn't "Page Six"–worthy (thank God), but working for Conrad Drake, *Cachet*'s celebrated editor in chief, made everyone at the magazine targets by association. It would be his name in boldface, not hers.

That was just one of the negative outcomes that could arise from this rash act, and as she hurried toward the exit, a little voice whispered, *Go back.* But Sydney Zamora rarely took unsolicited advice, not even from her own psyche, so it was a call that went unheeded. Instead, she powered *forward.* She had already been pilloried by the *New York Post* once in her life, and the potential threat of having them publicly humiliate her again only strengthened her resolve.

Feeling like the odds were stacked against her, whether this was really the case or just her own interpretation of events, always brought out the fight in her. She was, in her own mind, a crusader, an avenger of justice, a voice for the disenfranchised. A childless, more tastefully dressed Erin Brockovich, if you will. Her biggest regret was that she had not followed in her late father's footsteps and become a civil rights attorney. It was a regret shared by many because with no class-action suits to fight, Sydney managed to turn everyone—her family, her coworkers, customer service reps at Verizon Wireless—into Goliaths against whom she felt compelled to wage battle.

So there would be no turning back now. Oh, no. If storming out of New York's trendiest boîte resulted in an embarrassing item on "Page Six," so be it. To teach Kyle (and every useless man he represented) a lesson, she was willing to martyr herself.

She nevertheless made an emergency detour when she saw their waiter standing directly in her path and practically sprinted the last few steps to the staircase as if she were a paparazzi-hounded celebrity trying to make her way out of the Ivy to a waiting SUV.

She still had one last leg to go before she was out of the restaurant and in the clear, but once inside the stairwell, she grabbed the railing and rested against the velvet-covered wall, suddenly overcome with fatigue. Lately, she had been feeling so drained. Some days she could barely drag herself out of bed before ten. She knew her emotional exhaustion wasn't about Kyle or her meaningless, soul-sucking job. It was about everything. And nothing.

She grew up believing she'd have it all. A Career with a capital *C*. A husband. Babies! She'd be the Enjoli woman, bringing home the bacon, frying it up in a pan, never never letting him forget he was a man! Who would've guessed the whole thing would turn out to be a scam, a cultural Ponzi scheme that would dupe every middle-class woman of her generation?

FUCK YOU, GLORIA STEINEM!

The only part of The Plan that had remotely worked out was that Sydney had (what some would consider) an enviable Career writing for *Cachet,* the glossiest of celebrity glossies. It was a soulless pursuit, but Sydney couldn't complain because it paid well (as most soulless pursuits did). She had always expected, even relished the idea, that she'd have to muscle her way to professional success, while assuming Fate would take care of her love life, but exactly the opposite had happened. The cushy *Cachet* job had fallen right into her lap through a bizarre confluence of events, and finding Mr. Right was turned into a punishing exercise that had pushed her to the brink of total exhaustion.

This extended fling with Kyle was pointless, but that was the point. Now that most of her friends were married and breeding, she needed ~~something~~ someone to do to pass the time. Kyle was a fuck buddy and, as such, not an impediment to her finding a real relationship and a breeder of her own. If, at any time, she met a serious prospect, she would drop Kyle without a second thought.

Trouble was, the guys she liked weren't husband material, and the men who were repulsed her. And she didn't subscribe to the "Give him a chance, he might grow on you" theory of dating either. Within five minutes of meeting a man she could tell if he was dateable or simply doable. Most of them were neither.

Now that her clock was officially ticking, dateable didn't even cut it anymore. She needed to find a *meaningful* relationship, a *marriageable* mate, a genetically healthy provider with motile sperm. It was a complete fucking drag.

She'd been telling herself she had time, plenty of time. As late as thirty-one, marriage and motherhood still seemed as far away as the moon, abstract concepts like IRAs or epidurals that she imagined she'd figure out when the time came. Well, she was thirty-three years old. The future was now.

The real kick in the ass was that she had spent her whole life striving to be independent! To not need a man, emotionally or financially, to make her whole. To never give her power away. All that Oprah shit. But if she wanted to have children the traditional way, she did need a man, didn't she? And soon. Reproductively, she was on orange alert.

That was the sick cosmic joke of it all.

CHAPTER TWO

If Sydney hadn't been so pissed, she might have become aroused when Kyle grabbed her arm and pinned her against the wall at the top of the staircase. "Sydney, what's wrong with you?" he said, as if he was in any position to question anything. "You can't just leave!"

Oh yeah? Watch me.

"We haven't paid the bill," he said, trying to keep her from squirming away.

She looked up at him angrily but tried to avoid direct eye contact. Those misty green eyes could be her undoing. "*You* haven't paid the bill."

Kyle released her arm and rested his hand against the wall. "Look . . ."

Hearing that one word come out of his disturbingly sexy mouth in that humoring tone made her that much angrier. She hated when men who were clearly in the wrong tried to turn things around to make it seem like the woman's fault! She knew what he was going to say. She was overreacting, being too emotional. She should calm down. Well, maybe she didn't want to fucking calm down. She was mad as hell and she had every right to be!

Since she'd landed the job at *Cachet,* every guy she'd "dated" made less money than she did. And for the same reason she always had a dollar and a kind word for a homeless woman but thought, *Drunk! Druggie! Loser!* when she passed a homeless *man,* she hadn't respected a one of them. Women had to work harder for less money all while trudging around like sherpas loaded down with guilt and self-loathing. Every time a guy pretended not to see the check a waiter had presumptuously set before him, she'd think, *If I can make it, why the fuck can't you?*

But she didn't need to respect someone to screw him. In her experience, the sex was way hotter when you didn't. Kyle was the male version of a dumb blonde, but the boy was a sexual savant, she'd give him that. It was amazing what he could do with just one finger. He was the first man ever to make her come from intercourse, which, being an all-around DIY girl, unnerved her at first. It still did . . . though not so much that she didn't give him the opportunity three or more times a week.

She usually lost interest in men around the eight-week mark, but, due to his sexual prowess, she'd kept Kyle around for six whole months. He wouldn't make it to seven. In the last few weeks, his liberal use of "let's" and "us" and "we," in addition to his persistent pleas that she go see *Spamalot* when his okeydoke Midwestern parents came to visit, was speeding up the demise of what had been a perfectly lovely and mutually beneficial meaningless relationship.

Had she asked him to take her anywhere tonight? Of course not. She preferred to order in. That way, she had distractions—the phone, TV, Facebook—to stave off boredom. Going out to dinner meant they had to talk for two hours straight.

But Kyle had insisted. Just as he'd insisted on ordering a celebratory bottle of Veuve Clicquot even after she told him she didn't like champagne. She never drank it. Not even on New Year's.

"I wanted to do something special for you," he said.

Then treat me to a mani-pedi, stupid.

The whole unnecessary show made her very uneasy, but, proving that she wasn't as much of a bitch as some people thought she was, she rolled with it.

And she was pleasantly surprised to find that the editors at *Cachet* weren't just hyping the place up. The food *was* a-maaaaaaaazing. (Not to mention light and healthy. She couldn't remember the last time she'd had a satisfying meal that fell within the draconian dietary parameters set by her nutritionist.) They had such a nice dinner that by the time Kyle handed over his credit card, Sydney was feeling guilty for giving him a hard time. Why couldn't she ever just let someone do something nice for her? Maybe she *was* as much of a bitch as some people thought.

She was on the verge of apologizing when she saw the waiter heading back to their table. Too soon. "I'm sorry, sir," he said, holding Kyle's toy Visa gingerly between his thumb and forefinger as if its impotency might be catching. "This card has been declined."

Kyle took the news much better than Sydney would have liked. A flushed cheek, maybe, a nervous laugh would have been nice. There was none of that. Kyle just gave a lame shrug, as though the situation had come about through no fault of his own, and slipped the card back into his beat-up leather wallet.

Years ago when Sydney had waited tables at Indochine, a perennially hot downtown restaurant, customers who found themselves in this predicament were usually so anxious to prove their solvency that they produced another piece of plastic faster than a card shark doing three-card monte. Not Kyle. He just sat there. When a viable form of payment did not seem to be forthcoming, the waiter actually had to give him a nudge. "Another card, perhaps?"

That suggestion fell on deaf ears. Instead of dealing with it like a man, Kyle looked helplessly across the table at Sydney, who, by that juncture, was checking her reflection in the small mirror that had come with her knockoff Balenciaga. She'd never been vain about her appearance, a trait that was becoming more of a liability than a virtue as she got older, and she didn't really care that her eyebrows needed a threading or that her skin looked oily. She was only using the mirror as a prop. As soon as she'd heard the word *declined,* she'd made herself look busy as a signal to both Kyle and the waiter that this little imbroglio should not involve her.

Her actions were apparently not speaking loudly enough. They both stared as she languidly applied a coat of nude gloss and pressed her lips together, distributing it evenly. When the waiter cleared his throat, Sydney looked up as if she was startled to find him there.

The unspoken question hung thickly in the air until Kyle was forced to put it into words. He could only get out two. "Can you . . . ?"

Sydney looked back down at the mirror, wiping away excess gloss with her pinkie finger. "Can I what, Kyle?"

"Get it?"

"Ummm . . ." She raised her eyes skyward, stared at the minimalist overhead lighting for a moment, then pinned him with a direct gaze. "That would be a no."

"This is my only card," he said, throwing the ball back in her court.

"Go to the ATM," she said, throwing it back in his.

Clearly, that was not an option either. Kyle settled back in his seat, pushed a chunk of dirty-blond hair behind his ear, and admitted, "I'm a little low on funds this week."

"This week," she said, refusing to let it go, "or this millennium?"

Kyle blew out a sigh. "This sucks, I know."

"You bet your ass it does, you little gigolo! *It's my birthday!*"

The cringing waiter scurried away to give them "a moment," and that was when Sydney decided she was jetting too.

In the six months they had been "together," Kyle, a struggling actor who on occasion worked as a server for Glorious Food, had not paid for a thing. Not a cab ride, not a movie, not a goddamned Frappuccino. At first it was, "Oh, I don't have any cash on me." Then "I lost my credit card and I'm waiting for the replacement." Or, for the last four months, "I'm just waiting for the residual check for that commercial I did."

By the time she realized he was the brokest of all her struggling-artist flings, she was hooked on the sex. And with his soulful green eyes, soft pink lips, and sinewy, nearly hairless body, he was too delicious to resist. Just thinking about the vee that formed on his lower abdomen made her forgive the fact that his "ends" were not "long"—as Jeffrey-James Eliot, her go-to gay, might say in a ghetto moment. Jeffrey considered it a sacrilege that Sydney paid for everything, but she was a modern woman with her own "ends," and she secretly enjoyed being in the power position. She always got to pick the movies and whether they'd order Mexican or Chinese, and whenever she called asking him to, say, make a midnight trek from the deep recesses of Brooklyn, where he lived in a row house with three roommates, to service her in her cozy West Village apartment and pick up a pint of Häagen-Dazs on the way, he always came. As did she. All things considered, it wasn't such a bad deal.

Tonight? Deal breaker.

"The one time," she said, looking him dead in the eyes to prove to herself that she could. She wasn't going to let him sweet-talk her and she wasn't going to be a slave to her own desires. She didn't need his magic fingers. She had the Hitachi Magic Wand! "The one time you say you're going to take me out and you pull this shit?"

A couple squeezed past them to get down the stairs, and Kyle pulled her through the doorway into the bar area. "Okay, I know you're mad," he said. "But I'll get it next time. I promise."

Sydney shook her head and sighed. "Oh, Kyle."

Didn't he get it? She had been a willing coconspirator in their post-modern arrangement, but there was always a bubbling undercurrent of latent resentment just below the surface. (On his part too, she sensed.) Tonight's eruption had brought it gushing forth like hot, molten lava, and there was no way to reverse the flow. It was the natural order of things.

Taking a step toward him, she put her hands on his flushed cheeks, gave him a long, soft kiss on the mouth, and whispered, "Sweetie, there isn't going to *be* a next time."

CHAPTER THREE

Kyle stood at the top of the staircase with a quizzical expression on his pretty face, fists jammed into the pockets of his army jacket, while Sydney continued her steady march toward the door.

A few purposeful strides later, she hit another roadblock. She stared at the tall man who'd stomped on the steel toe of her motorcycle boot, overcome with the familiar yet disorienting sensation of seeing someone you know you know but can't seem to place because they're completely out of context. Like when she saw her dental hygienist Rollerblading in Central Park.

When she finally made the connection, her normally husky voice came out in a squeak. "Trevor?"

"Sydney . . ." It sounded like the word was deflating.

He looked so different, Sydney thought as they gaped at each other with the bar activity swirling around them. He was thinner. He was tan. He had a sprinkling of hip facial hair. Where was the pasty, straightlaced Trevor she had dated for three years? And, more important, how the hell had he gotten into Quo!

"Wow," he finally said. "How long has it been?"

A lifetime, Sydney thought.

"You look . . ." He hesitated, struggling to find the right word, and Sydney fiddled with her hat, cursing herself for not looking her absolute best. But then she remembered: She was a size six. She let her coat fall open. *How you like me now, Trevor?*

"You look wonderful," he said.

She hated that he might think this was her A game, but she smiled anyway. She wasn't going to do the self-deprecating thing in front of him. Those days were long gone. And it was nice of him to say. Maybe everything that had happened was water under the bridge?

In the very next moment, she knew that was not the case. All of Trevor McBride's asshole tendencies came rushing back when he added, "You've lost a ton of weight!" And then a sucker punch: "Did you have *the surgery*?"

Sydney didn't know how long Kyle had been standing behind her, but out of the corner of her eye, she caught him flinch at the insinuation that she had once been morbidly obese. That annoyed her on general principle—what if she had been?—but as of three minutes ago, Kyle's opinion no longer mattered. (Not that it ever had.)

Keeping her eyes squarely on Trevor, she made sure her tone was light with just a hint of mockery when she said, "*Fantastic* to see you." Before she could escape, a woman appeared at Trevor's side and slipped her dainty hand into his.

"You find it, babe?" he said. The "babe" came very easily, Sydney noted. Babe held up her scarf and smiled.

"Look who I bumped into," Trevor said. "Sydney. Sydney Zamora."

"Aaaaaah . . ." Babe intoned, instantly recognizing Sydney's name, presumably from the many hours Trevor had spent trashing her.

"This," he told Sydney, "is Fabienne."

His voice remained neutral, but only, Sydney suspected, because there was no need to openly gloat. Fabienne spoke for herself. Even Kyle, who usually hovered in a state of semiobliviousness, was giving her an appreciative once-over.

Sydney was subtler, but in a millisecond, she had scanned Fabienne from head to toe like the Six Million Dollar Man. Lustrous hair that air-dried into perfect, shiny curls. Almost no makeup because skin that dewy needed none. A spray of freckles on the kind of nose you rarely see in real life, only in magazine ads that less fortunate women bring to their rhinoplasty consultations. A perfectly lithe body that was her birthright. Young. Twenty-seven, tops.

"*Allô!*" Fabienne sung, smiling beatifically as if she were running into a beloved former colleague down at the patisserie.

Sydney offered a faint smile and pushed the brim of her hat off of her moist brow. She had a "thing" about being touched, and kept an invisible perimeter around herself at all times, avoiding any place or activity—subways at rush hour, yoga on Saturday mornings, cuddling—that might lead to an unauthorized breach of that perimeter. Now trapped in the crowded bar area with random people brushing up against her from all sides, she was going into sensory overload.

When Fabienne leaned forward toward her, Sydney's internal alarm system began to blare. *Perimeter breach! Perimeter breach!* She thrust her hand out to create some distance, but Fabienne wasn't looking for a handshake. She put one hand on Sydney's shoulder and then quickly air-kissed her on both cheeks, a maneuver that left Sydney dazed.

As the French Personification of Bliss pulled her hand away, Sydney was momentarily blinded by the glint of a large but tasteful diamond ring on her fourth finger. Sydney looked up at Trevor. He smiled, baring his pointy incisors. "We're engaged."

The words hit Sydney like daggers. Inside she was reeling, realizing at that moment that it was possible to curl up into a fetal position while standing. Outwardly, however, she didn't so much as twitch.

"Congratulations," she said, forcing a big, fake smile. Then she grabbed Kyle's hand and struck back. "So are we."

CHAPTER FOUR

Max Cooper stood, disoriented, on an outdoor subway platform watching the N train barrel out of the station. He was supposed to get off at Fifth Avenue, but judging by the storefronts below, he was far from it. He walked down the platform until he found the station sign. Queensboro Plaza? He'd been so into the new N*E*R*D songs he'd imported into his iPhone this morning, he'd completely overshot his mark. Who knew one missed stop—or was it two?—would land you in Queens?

He pushed back the sleeve of his brown suede coat to check the time but let his arm fall without doing so. He was late, that he knew. Knowing how late wouldn't do anything to change that. Anyway, what would a few more minutes mean when he hadn't shown up to work in three weeks? They'd be happy he'd shown up at all.

He was just back from an unplanned European jaunt that started out in Madrid. He'd gone there chasing after a *muy caliente chica* who'd crashed one of his parties, convinced it was love. They ran off to Ibiza, and after two sizzling weeks together he told her, "It's been fun," and split. Since London was only an hour away, he decided to make a quick stop there and rang some of his old Oxford chums, one of whom dragged him off to his country house for a few days. Yesterday he was shooting pheasant in Wiltshire. Today he was in Queens watching rats scurry along garbage-strewn subway tracks. Ten minutes later, he was strolling down one of the most expensive blocks of real estate in Manhattan. Funny how life worked.

That strip of Madison Avenue, between Sixtieth and Sixty-first streets, was home to Harvey's New York, the ten-story flagship of the venerable luxury retailer that had seven stores in the United States and two in Japan. A favorite of the ladies-who-lunch crowd, their famously extensive designer shoe salon (it occupied the entire fifth floor and had been assigned its own zip code by the U.S. Postal Service) also attracted younger, downtown types, most notably Carrie Bradshaw.

With his music flowing at maximum volume, Max bopped rhythmically under the bright red awnings, giving only a cursory glance to the row of window displays that had been painstakingly designed by his overworked colleagues while he frolicked on the beaches of Ibiza. As he approached the main entrance, his slack posture straightened and his chest puffed out slightly. These little adjustments seemed to happen automatically when he got within ten feet of Tony Alvarez, the burly doorman. It was as if his own lanky body felt sorry for him and tried to compensate. Not that anything would change the fact that Tony's bulging arm had the same circumference as Max's thigh. Next to him, Max felt like a rag doll.

He was well acquainted with the intimidating contours of Tony's body, having made his acquaintance at a physical rehabilitation center where they were both having their knees treated for meniscal tears. (Tony's injury was an old one that had been worn down by years of "hooping." Max had been taken down by a snowboarding mishap in Stowe.) For several months Max had gone out of his way to avoid iron man Tony because working out any-where near him made Max's therapist realize just how lazy Max really was. When they finally did strike up a conversation one day, Tony said he'd been laid off from his job as a security guard, but luckily he still had "COBRA." Glossing over the fact that he had no idea what COBRA was (Max gathered it was not Tony's pet snake), he suggested Tony call the head of Human Resources at Harvey's. Tony had never set foot in the store, and he'd been on the job for two weeks before he learned there really was a Harvey. When he asked Max if he'd met the old man, Max told him with a straight face that he had. When Tony asked what Harvey was like, Max told him he was "kind of a dick," which was, in Max's experience, true.

Max felt no need to divulge further personal details about his relationship with the store's namesake. He knew Tony would find out soon enough the se-cret Max had never been able to keep for long: He was Harvey Cooper's son.

"What's that?" Max said, pulling out his earbuds.

"Nice tan," Tony repeated. He took a step backward and reached out to get the door for an exiting customer. Even when his back was turned, he seemed to have a sixth sense that told him when someone was on either side of the door. It was uncanny.

"Just back from Ibiza," Max said.

"Really? I'm just back from Atlantic City," Tony said, as if there was some correlation between the two. "Went with the wife. On the bus."

Max cracked a small smile. Most of the store's employees kissed his ass shamelessly or glanced nervously at the floor when he walked by. Tony, a man of real integrity, gave Max shit on a regular basis. "You win anything?"

"The wife did," Tony said with the rueful sigh of a married man who has accepted that he no longer has control over his own life. "But she don't share." He reached for the door out of reflex, then caught himself. Max considered him more of a friend than his employee (though calling him either would be an overstatement), and it was understood that unless Max had two broken arms, he would get his own door.

CHAPTER FIVE

Ranjit looked up from his notepad in disbelief. "You went to . . ." He could barely say the word. "McDonald's?"

"Uh-huh," Sydney murmured, looking around his office at anything and everything but her nutritionist. He'd always say, "You don't have to be perfect" when she admitted to cheating in their weekly meetings. But Mickey D's was not an acceptable slipup. In the gospel according to nutritional guru Ranjit Sagoo, eating fast food was akin to ingesting plutonium. Feeling his disappointed eyes searing into her, Sydney was happy to be interrupted by two quick raps on his office door.

"Sorry, Ranjit." His assistant, Deirdre, leaned in, her gigantic silver hoops swinging like pendulums. "Hilary's on the phone. She said you've been playing phone tag. She only needs you for a sec."

"Excuse me," Ranjit said, lifting himself from his modernist leather chair to grab the phone at his desk.

Sydney tried to eavesdrop to determine if it was a famous Hilary on the line. Ms. Swank? Possible. Ranjit had been her nutritional adviser during the filming of *Million Dollar Baby*. He was also the guru responsible for getting most of the Hollywood moms whose post-baby bodies were obsessively chronicled in the tabloids back into their size twenty-seven jeans weeks after giving birth. There was also the possibility that Mrs. Clinton was calling. Ranjit's reach was that far and that wide.

No matter who it was, Ranjit would never say. That was what Sydney loved about him. He wasn't a name-dropper. And given the caliber of names he had to drop, that made him a rarity in New York indeed. (She'd never forget when, years ago at a party, some guy had told her he could get tickets to a Bon Jovi concert because he knew one of Bon Jovi's roadies. Was that supposed to be impressive? She wouldn't have given a shit if he *was* Bon Jovi!)

She only knew about Ranjit's star-studded client list because she'd written a short piece on him for *Cachet*. When she'd shown up at his Upper West Side office for the interview, she could see why he was billed as a "life extension specialist." A Sikh Indian who usually rocked his crisp whites—shirt and turban—with a navy blazer and jeans, he was fifty-six but looked about thirty-five because he obviously practiced what he proselytized.

He'd peppered her with more questions that day than she'd had for him. What did she eat? How often did she exercise? Did she smoke? The answers—everything, never, and yes, a pack a day—sent him into a tizzy. "You don't just need to exercise to lose weight," he'd cried when she mentioned that was the only reason she wanted to. "You need to exercise to *live!*"

Oddly enough, Sydney had never thought of it that way. She'd always had an aversion to diet and exercise, and growing up tall with a body built for lacrosse, she tried to convince herself that she was just big-boned. Which wasn't easy when her mother would say things like "You have such a pretty face. If you'd just lose forty pounds, you'd be beautiful." That was what Vera, she of the corrupted empathy gene, called encouragement.

In her younger days, playing sports kept her in okay (in her mind) shape and Sydney had come to realize that keeping the extra weight on was just another fuck-you to the woman Sydney had not called "Mom" since Vera had left Sydney's father for Leo Weintraub, a partner in the law firm her father had to leave in shame. Liz, her spineless Judas of a sister, chose to move to Connecticut with Vera while twelve-year-old Sydney stayed behind in Scarsdale with their father, Reynaldo, a newly repurposed immigration lawyer whose clients saw more of him than Sydney did.

With Vera gone and her father either working or passed out from pro bono exhaustion, Sydney was free to stay up late, order pizza four times a week, and, in later years, have friends over to smoke cloves or pot in her room without fear of getting busted. That always led to a munchie binge, which would continue late into the night after her friends went home. And so began a lifetime of unhealthy emotional overeating that became epidemic after her father was killed in a head-on collision during her freshman year at Princeton.

By her mid-twenties, subsisting on cigarettes and fast food and too overwhelmed with her daily survival to work out or eat healthy, she'd blown up to unacceptable proportions—which was so depressing, she ate more. She didn't want to imagine what she'd look like if Ranjit had not come along to rescue her from a life of gluttony and sloth.

Apparently viewing her as someone in dire need of his services, he ended their interview by offering her a year gratis and didn't wait for her to accept the offer. He ushered her out to Deirdre, dumped two of his bestselling healthy-lifestyle books into her arms, and let her go with this: "From now on, you're going to eat right, you're going to live right, and one day very soon you're going to thank me."

Almost a year later (he hadn't mentioned when she'd have to start paying and she wasn't about to bring it up), she couldn't thank him more. With the loving guidance of her nutritional guru, she had sculpted her once-flabby body into a toned and svelte physique. She'd always avoided gyms—mostly because when she heard *gym,* she thought *Rocky*—but now she took classes five days a week at Clay, a swanky "healthy-lifestyle center" on Fourteenth Street that had state-of-the-art equipment, sleek locker rooms stocked with Aveda products, iMacs in the lounge, a Wi-Fi hookup on the roof deck, and a concierge on call who could do just about anything short of pulling a rabbit out of his ass. Sometimes Sydney stayed there all day because, really, what reason was there to leave?

Though she'd been initially motivated only by her desire to look good in a bikini, her physical transformation had been, in the end, as much internal as it was external. Now seeing her naked reflection did more than make her smile. It filled her with pride. Anyone could be born with skinny genes. The muscle tone in her back, arms, and legs was the result of her blood, sweat, and tears! She'd hit her goal weight last month and celebrated by taking Kyle to Miami, where, for the first time since infancy, she publicly rocked a variety of string bikinis without shame. Ranjit had been so proud of her, he'd given her a "You've come a long way, baby!" T-shirt to mark the occasion. Size small! And already she was backsliding.

"So you went to McDonald's," Ranjit said, calmly this time, as he slid back into his chair. "Tell me, why would you do that?"

Why would she not? The minute he'd banned her from eating red meat, bread, sugar, or anything fried, she felt as if her Technicolor world had gone gray. Now her mind ran a continuous loop of food porno. This morning she was almost mowed down by a FedEx truck because she was daydreaming about eating a soft, buttery croissant slathered with strawberry jam. That was this week's fantasy. Last week it was Krispy Kreme donuts, hot and sticky, just off the conveyor belt. And was it her imagination or had there been a rise in street fairs? A street fair meant *zeppoles,* the irresistible little fried, sugar-sprinkled dough balls that now, thanks to Ranjit, represented a perfect storm of banned foods!

"Well, the thing is, Ranjit . . ." Sydney squirmed on the sofa across from him. "I was feeling kinda down, I guess, and I've been so good, you know. I thought maybe I deserved a little treat."

Poor choice of words, she thought as Ranjit echoed in amazement, "'Treat'?"

Sydney shrugged. "What can I tell you? I was passing by. I said, 'Fuck it,' and went in."

Ranjit leaned toward her, his brow knitted with concern. "What were you down about?"

Sydney's body flounced forward and she felt as if she was about to projectile vomit her troubles at him, *Exorcist*-style. She wanted to tell him everything. About Kyle and the resurfacing of that useless prick Trevor and how every vague dissatisfaction had come together with painful clarity in that five-minute span at Quo and made her feel her life was completely meaningless.

And she would have spewed freely if she'd been paying Ranjit fifteen grand a year like the other rich dopes who relied on him. But, as a mooch, what right did she have? Besides, Ranjit knew her as a woman of discipline. Someone who'd cleaned up her act and had her shit together. Did she really want to ruin her rep and allow him to see her as a weak, whiny girl who was self-sabotaging with fast food just because she had man troubles?

Deciding the answer was no, she said, "I don't know."

"What did you have? Tell me." Ranjit closed his eyes and took a deep breath, trying to center himself for the hit.

"A Quarter Pounder, large fries, a Coke," Sydney admitted, staring at the red dot on his forehead. "And I asked for one apple pie, but they only sell them two for a dollar."

Ranjit opened his eyes and shamed her with his "I can see into your soul" stare. "So you ate two?"

Sydney smirked. "What do you think?"

"And how did you feel afterward?"

"Awful." She wasn't about to tell him she actually smoked a cigarette too, something she hadn't done in a year and a half. Or that she'd had three chocolate martinis the other day (at lunch!), since alcohol was also not Ranjit-approved.

"Okay. It's over, it's done," Ranjit said, his hand slicing through the air. "Just know that when you make a conscious decision to eat at McDonald's, when you give in to that impulse, you are choosing to live your life on the level of a primate."

"I know, Ranjit," Sydney said, bowing her head in shame. "I know."

CHAPTER SIX

H ey, Max!" called the cutie pie manning Marc Jacobs.

"Long time no see," trilled the raven-haired looker peddling Prada.

"We missed you!" gushed the new girl working Goyard, an innocent redhead Max was hungry to defile.

Shame his personal code of ethics forbade him from playing favorites or else he would've stopped to ask Red how much. Instead, he flashed her the same warm smile he'd had for all the rest and continued his brisk stroll to the elevator. The doors opened immediately, as if welcoming him back, and when he stepped off on the ninth floor, he was holding the pale pink business card of the stylish wedding planner who'd joined him on the fourth. Bypassing his own office, he went straight to Harvey's, whistling as he breezed through the corporate office suite.

"Hey, Norma," he said, greeting his father's longtime secretary, a fifty-eight-year-old woman who owned twelve gray cardigans and whose bun never faltered. "Can I go in?"

Typing at her meticulously arranged desk, Norma didn't look up. "Sure."

Max opened the door. He walked in. He walked out. "He's not here."

"Nope," Norma said, still typing.

"Where is he?"

"Lunch."

"He's having lunch with me."

"He *was* having lunch with you." Norma looked at him over her reading glasses. "Yesterday."

"We were supposed to have lunch on Wednesday."

"Today's Thursday."

Max scratched his head. *It was?*

Norma got up and grabbed his arm, leading him down the hallway like a child being hauled off to detention. "But your sister would like a word with you."

"Avery?"

"Do you have another sister?"

"Am I in trouble?"

Norma gave him a stern look. "Probably."

It never ceased to amaze Max how one short elevator ride could so drastically change his reality. On the first floor, he got nothing but love. On the ninth, he was Rodney Dangerfield. No respect.

Norma hustled him to the other end of the suite, where Remy Krysnecki was stationed outside Avery's door, answering the phone.

A perpetually tan twenty-six-year-old Staten Island native who had worked her way up from intern to Avery's executive assistant, a position she inhabited with great pride, Remy didn't speak, she chirped. "Avery Cooper-Fitzsimmons's office . . . please hold!" She smiled up at Max, her dimples as deep as gumdrops. "Max! Hi! Your hair's all gone!"

"I shaved it." He'd always wanted a crew cut, but he hadn't expected that shaving his mop of curls would be so liberating.

"Yourself?!" Remy marveled.

"Sure." Max bent forward. "Feel it."

Remy ran her hand over the half inch of brown hair that remained, her French tips almost scratching his scalp. "Oooh, it feels so . . ."

Norma cleared her throat, a cue for them both to halt the unnecessary chatter. "Sorry," Remy said. "Go right in!"

Max looked at Norma, who had always given him the creeps. She was holding on to him as if he was a suspect she was hauling into court and, given half a chance, he might bolt. Thinking about that for a moment, Max realized it was actually a scarily accurate analogy for what was going on here. And after being incommunicado for three weeks, he didn't expect Avery, the self-appointed judge, would be very lenient. What was she doing in the office, anyway? Thinking he'd apparently gotten some bad information (had he known she was going to be around, he would have been more stealthy in his movements), he looked to Norma for clarification. "I thought Avery was on bed rest."

Norma flung the double doors open. "She is."

Max stepped in slowly, surveying the scene. It was as if the curtain had been raised in the middle of a play's second act. The desk was gone. In its place was a large bed that had come straight from the Four Seasons, and in that bed was Avery Cooper-Fitzsimmons, thirty-nine years old, seven months pregnant with IVF-conceived twins, and still a multitasking dynamo.

Clad in navy silk pajamas with a matching satin headband holding her buttery blond bob in place, Avery had her bare feet propped up on a mound of pillows and pink foam toe dividers keeping her freshly painted toes apart. With two nurses buzzing about and a pedicurist in a white clinician's robe packing up, she didn't notice Max amid the fray until Remy rushed in with some papers and said, "Look who's here!"

"Maximillian Cooper!" Avery shot up, and one of the nurses promptly pushed her back down, securing the IV drip in her arm. Even in that prostrate position, her shout remained at the same healthy volume. "Where the bloody hell have you beeeeaan?"

Getting a better look at Avery's enormously swollen ankles and feet, Max recoiled. He'd seen bloated extremities like that before. On homeless people. He turned to Norma, who all of a sudden seemed to be the sanest person in the room. "What's with the accent?"

Norma shrugged. "She gets it from the hubby."

Waving at the back of the exiting pedicurist, Avery shouted, "Cheers, Suzy!"

"He's British," Max said, stepping aside for Suzy. "She isn't."

"She's going through a Madonna phase," Norma said. "This too shall pass." She rolled her eyes and followed Suzy to the door.

CHAPTER SEVEN

Sydney was so disgusted with herself when she left Ranjit's that she power-walked to the nearest Le Pain Quotidien, her favorite lunchtime spot, which was named for its delectable bread, and didn't allow herself to have any. Seated at a long communal table, picking at her mesclun salad, she buried her nose in an advance copy of Leslie Bennett's *The Feminine Mistake,* letting her eyes pass over the same paragraph four times—

The ultimate solution to the stress level felt by working women is not for them to give up their jobs in despair; it's for men to relieve them of their disproportionate share of the domestic tasks. Rise up—you have nothing to lose but your unjust share of the burden!

—before she realized she hadn't taken in a word of it. She was too riveted by the exchange between the two women seated at the next table.

"Patti?" one of them was saying. "She's a raging bitch. You know that thing she brought up in the sales meeting? Totally my idea."

It made Sydney think wistfully back to the days when she had so many great gossipy gal pals. She'd been close with six or seven women, and since she'd met all of them separately, each one plugged her in to a different social network. She had her dance-all-night party-girl friends. She had her more civilized let's-do-brunch friends. She had her Oscar party friends, a mixed group of women and gay men that overlapped with the loyal *America's Next*

Top Model watchers. She had her let's-commiserate-about-how-broke-we-are friends. She had her boy-talk friends, her work-talk friends, and, last but certainly not least, her you're-invited-to-my-summerhouse-anytime friends.

And now look at her. Eating lunch alone as she did most afternoons, with only her angry-woman books (she had more in her reusable tote) to keep her company.

When her many girlfriends began drifting, one by one, into lives of domesticity, Sydney had stupidly believed their relationships would remain relatively the same. She continued to e-mail them as much as she always had, until she noticed the response times getting longer and longer. Then when the belated reply eventually did arrive, it would be one line. And if the subject line was blank and the original message was not in the e-mail, she often had no idea what they were laughing out loud about.

And what a fertile bunch they were! Most of her friends seemed to conceive on their honeymoons, which Sydney later came to prefer after a few got knocked up unexpectedly with their longtime partners. With the honeymoon conceivers, she at least had the engagement period to begin the grieving process.

They all came flocking back after the baby boom settled, and for a time, she became a sought-after lunch companion for mommies in need of outside contact. But she stopped accepting invitations to these torturous chat-n-chews when she began to feel like she was reading from the same depressing script, only a different actress was auditioning for the part of the mommy. There was a limit to how much episiotomy talk one could take. And when were the mommies going to realize that those in the child-free community were not the least bit interested in their kid's potty-training issues?

Their eyes would glaze over with similar disinterest when Sydney talked about work, and once they realized she came with no scandalous as-yet-unreported celebrity gossip, they'd become palpably hostile. (If she only had a nickel for every time she'd uttered the words "Look, I'm not Perez Hilton.") By midmeal, the mommies would begin pestering Sydney about when she was going to settle down and join their baby-worshipping cult, a line of questioning built on the assumption that she would never know true happiness until she pushed a turkey-sized being out of the small (so she'd been told) orifice in her body that she wanted to remain that way. Deep down she felt there was some truth to that, and while she was beginning to admit it to herself, she sure as shit wasn't going to admit it to them! Screw them and their fertile wombs and their Baby Björns and their playdates! She wasn't childless. She was child-free, thank you very much. Free to sleep late! Free to jet off to Miami for the weekend and flaunt her newly toned, un-stretch-marked body! Free to be the focus of her own life!

And she didn't need the Mommy Cult to make her feel guilty or selfish for living the life they had all assumed they *would* be living ten years ago before the whole world turned upside down.

Marriage and motherhood had put every last one of her friendships on life support, and after having the umpteenth call ended with an abrupt "The baby's up!," Sydney decided it was time to pull the plug. And so she methodically erased the numbers of all of her former friends from her phone.

The gays (and Ranjit) were all she had now.

CHAPTER EIGHT

After a busboy from Binky's, the chic bistro on the seventh floor, set a small table next to the bed and laid out a place setting for one, Remy appeared carrying a mahogany tray table. She set it down on the bed, tucked a cloth napkin inside the V-neck of Avery's pajamas right under the tiers of bloated flesh that had once been a pointy chin, gave Avery a plate of olive oil and bread to nibble on, dismissed the nurses for lunch, then left the room, closing the door behind her.

Max had been there all of ten minutes and he was exhausted.

He pulled his chair out from behind the table, kicked off his Adidas, and threw his feet up on the bed. "Be careful," Avery said, his brightly striped socks giving her pause. "My toes are still tacky."

"To answer your question re my whereabouts," he said, moving his feet as far away from her tree trunks as possible, "met a girl. Went to Spain. Didn't work out. Now I'm back." He rocked back on the chair's hind legs and looked around the room, his eyes landing on the IV. "What's all this about?"

"Oh God," Avery moaned. "I'm dehydrated. I have toxemia. My cervix is loose . . ."

"Got it," Max said.

"This pregnancy has become so inconvenient!" She sopped up oil with a huge hunk of bread. "And now Simon's gone."

"Gone where?" Max asked, nabbing a piece of bread for himself.

"He defected. To Victor!"

"Oh, you mean he quit? That's not good." *Not good at all.* In theory, Max and Simon were supposed to work together as co–creative directors. In practice, Simon, a visionary metrosexual they had wooed over from Bloomingdale's a few years ago, did all the work. And then some.

"Did you see yesterday's *WWD*?" Avery said.

Max responded with a blank stare.

Avery pulled a copy from underneath a neat pile of magazines and papers on the other side of her bed/desk. Handing it to Max, she averted her eyes and pursed her thin lips in disgust as if it had an autopsy photo splashed across the cover. It was actually a picture of their competitor, Victor Takiopolous, a ridiculously stylish man with a handlebar mustache who owned the chain of smaller but edgier clothing and home goods stores called, of course, Victor. The headline: "Is Victor the New Harvey?"

Olive oil from a freshly dipped hunk of bread went whipping through the air when Avery threw her arms up and cried, "It's a disaster!"

On that point, Max was agreed. *Women's Wear Daily* was the fashion industry bible, and to have them even suggest such a thing, on page one, was a slap in Harvey's face. A bitch slap. *Harvey is probably shitting himself,* Max thought, not unhappily. He tossed the paper back onto the bed without reading a line of text. "Don't be so dramatic."

"His Chicago store is half the size of ours and doing almost twice the business," Avery said.

"I wasn't aware of that."

"Of course you weren't. Listen, love, you've always had a limited role in day-to-day operations because *we all know*"—she underlined the last three words with an air of exasperation—"this is not your thing."

"And because one of you is worth six of me," Max said obsequiously because (a) it was true, and (b) he hoped flattery might get him somewhere, namely out of this office and this conversation, which he sensed was headed for rocky terrain. "Even one of you on bed rest. Suffering from dehydration. And toxemia."

Remy appeared, nodding as if to say, *Ain't that the truth?*, and placed a plate of Binky's famous lightly grilled thirty-two-dollars-per-plate calamari on Avery's tray.

"I'm here against doctor's orders," Avery said, appealing to Max's brotherly instincts. The waiter set down Max's salmon, and when he speared into it without showing any sign of concern, she continued. "By this weekend, at the latest, I'm going to have no choice but to go home." Getting no reaction, she wheezed a sigh. "And you need to man the ship whilst I'm away."

Max had seen this coming, but he wasn't going down without a fight. "Me?" he yelped.

"Yes, you," Avery said firmly. "This renovation has been two years in the making. You know that. We have to debut the new women's floor before Victor opens his New York flagship. This is our turf, Max, we have to protect it!"

"Our turf?" Max mumbled. Were they putting on a production of *West Side Story* that no one had told him about?

"There's still so much to be done," Avery said, inhaling her calamari. "Especially now that Simon's not here. The renovations, the party . . ."

Her gums continued to flap, but Max could no longer hear her. He had put her on Mute. Feeling a migraine coming on, he massaged his temples.

Avery thought everything was so simple. That was because everything always had come easily *for her*. She'd been the most popular girl in school—pretty, scary smart, and the captain of every-fucking-thing. Still, somehow she managed to get everyone in every clique to like her, a hat trick that always awed him. She was practically running this operation before she finished business school, and now when she walked through the store, greeting employees by name, her loyal subjects treated her like she was the second coming of Princess Di. And, unlike Di, Avery would one day be queen of this vast retail empire.

Unless, of course, she dies in a fiery Parisian crash, Max thought, allowing himself a moment to hate her.

Realizing that the room had gone silent, he looked up. Avery was staring at him as if she expected a point-by-point response to everything she'd said in the last four minutes. What she got was: "Christ, woman, can't you find someone more . . . qualified?"

Max had never even made it into the line of succession, and being the Harry of the clan suited him just fine. He had his honorary position, stayed out of Avery's way, and never begrudged her the fact that she lived a divinely charmed life. So for fuck's sake, why couldn't she let him be?

"You're qualified," Avery said. "You have a degree from Brown."

"In philosophy."

"And a master's from Oxford."

"In hermeneutics."

"It's not that you can't do it. It's that you don't want to. Max, I'm trying to give you a chance here."

"A chance?" Max scoffed. "Are you under the impression that you're doing me some kind of favor?"

"Yes," Avery said bluntly.

"Do it from home," Max said, desperately trying to take the focus off of himself. "You live in that huge town house. Move the whole office there!"

Avery actually took a moment to consider the logistics of this.

"But the floor under construction is here," Remy pointed out. With a smile.

Avery nodded in agreement. Then she looked at Max the way he suspected she would one day look at her kids when they wanted to go out and play but they had homework to do. "Time to earn your salary, love."

CHAPTER NINE

My," Dr. Liessel said, surprised to find Sydney in the waiting room, flipping through a copy of *Wired*. "You're early."

Sydney was equally surprised to find herself there, on time and ready to talk. She had never really believed in the benefits of psychiatry, and two years of seeing Dr. Ellen Liessel had done nothing to change her mind (literally or figuratively). When you got right down to it, psychiatry was just an excuse for people to whine about their childhoods. And what good did that really do? The great thing about all the horrible shit that had happened in Sydney's past was that it was in the past. She didn't want to revisit it! She liked to move forward, always—to fix, not dwell—but the terrifying panic attacks she began having soon after her thirtieth birthday forced her to seek shrinkage. She had no choice.

Ellen Liessel had come highly recommended, but Sydney's first impression of the doctor, a tall fortyish blonde with a superb rack, was that she was too attractive to be a competent psychiatrist. They never really clicked, but Sydney stayed with her as penance for making that sexist and therefore self-hating judgment—though she still refused to call her Ellen, as she had been invited to do. (When she wanted to straight disrespect her, she just called her Liessel.)

She'd been coming in every two months for her Xanax fix, and every time, without fail, Liessel would give her the hard sell on becoming a regular patient, as if Sydney was some kind of junkie who was trying to detox on her own instead of going into rehab. Tired of the harassment, Sydney began deliberately arriving thirty or more minutes after the scheduled start time of their fifty-minute session, offering some vague apology as she rushed in, pretending to be out of breath, when in actuality she'd just been across the street killing time at H&M. Why should she get there at 3:15 on the dot? She wasn't looking to "explore the possible root causes" of the panic attacks as her headshrinker was so determined to do. She just wanted the Xanax. And it didn't take fifty minutes to write a fucking prescription.

Then, about six months ago, Liessel was linked in the gossip columns to Barry Goldman, a short, bald, cigar-chomping corporate raider who was known to be a destroyer of women's souls, and Sydney began to wonder if Liessel's hard sell wasn't just about drumming up business. She couldn't imagine who, particularly what *woman,* would trust Liessel's judgment after it became known that she was prostituting herself to a man whose ex-wife, his fourth, had thrown a drink in his face and screamed, "Wife-beater!" in the middle of the Waverly Inn and then offered regrets to Liessel because she had to go home and fuck him.

Although in another example of the oddball perspective Sydney had always had on life, it was that very thing that made her warm up to Liessel. Choosing to date a mongrel like Barry Goldman was irrefutable evidence that the "brainy, Harvard-trained beauty," as the columns had dubbed Liessel, was just as fucked up about men, if not more so, as any other single girl with issues. Armed with that intimate knowledge, Sydney felt she could confess to anything—murder, even—and remain morally superior.

And so, for the first time since their initial consultation more than two years ago, Sydney was here to vent for the full fifty. And that was all she was here to do. Vent. She wasn't expecting any brilliant insight from Barry Goldman's concubine, but after that horrific Kyle–Trevor double whammy last week, her preferred coping method—gut it out and keep it moving— hadn't been doing the trick. She just had so much to get off her chest and, these days, who did she have to vent to?

"So," Liessel said, readying a fresh legal pad.

"So . . ." Sydney fidgeted in an identical leather armchair that faced Liessel's, unsure how to begin a full session. She usually arrived so late, Liessel did some fast talking, then it was dope-dealing time. "Um, have you been to that place Quo?"

Liessel answered with a nod and Sydney thought, *Of course.* When you were Barry Goldman's piece, you'd been everywhere. And you never had to worry about picking up the check as Sydney had wound up doing that night. In the end, she felt the scare of being abandoned there with no money was enough of a lesson for Kyle. And why put herself in jeopardy of a "Page Six" flaying when she was just going to charge the whole thing on her corporate card anyway? Getting control over her self-destructive impulses was something she had been working on (not with Liessel, just on her own time), so she felt the entire scenario had worked out to her benefit in the end.

Kyle mistakenly thought her paying the bill meant she had forgiven him, and on the walk back to her place she had to explain that her announcement of their fake engagement was not her roundabout way of proposing to him. (He wished.) She let him come upstairs for the sole purpose of getting in one last angry fuck, but when it came time to kick him out as she planned to do, disturbing thoughts whipped up out of nowhere.

If she dropped him, who would help her compile her Netflix queue? Who would massage her sore feet after she played tennis? Who would she text when some randomly funny thing happened?

The horrifying realization that her fuck buddy had become her boyfriend—she hadn't even known!—was just the push she needed to get him out of her life. She hadn't explicitly told him they were finished—she'd just stopped taking his calls and blocked him from her Gchat. Allowing him to think they were having a temporary rift increased the chances that he would be sexually available if she wanted to bring him back into the fold a month from now, although she was growing more confident by the day that she would have gotten him completely out of her system by then.

The unpleasant feelings that had been stirred up by her run-in with Trevor were the bigger issue. And venting about him required the cloak of confidentiality only a shrink could provide. It had taken years to live down their spectacularly public breakup, and any mention of him within the general populace would get tongues wagging again. His name had not been spoken in forever, but Sydney knew from the occasional insinuating comment that people thought he was The One Who Got Away. In truth, he was The One She Had Gotten Away From. She never regretted leaving his chauvinistic ass. It was the way it all went down that had caused her so much humiliation and psychic pain.

Seeing him again had fucked up her head because it took her back to a period in her life that she wanted to forget. He only knew her as the needy, unfocused, overweight girl she was embarrassed to have been in the dark years after she'd dropped out of Princeton. She had long ago disowned that pitiable girl, and she looked upon any mention of that time as an act of aggression toward her. Trevor McBride was an act of aggression personified.

She hadn't seen him since The Incident, and flaunting Fabienne the Flawless Fiancée in her face was his way of letting her know that she had done him a favor by running out on him and that his life was a million times better without her. Announcing that she too was engaged (to a hot young piece of ass whose beauty rivaled Fabienne's) was her way of returning what Trevor thought was an ace.

Her life was by no means perfect, but that T-shirt Ranjit had given her said it all: "You've come a long way, baby!" Damn straight. Leave it to Trevor to pop up and in five seconds make her feel like shit. She'd been able to hold her own in his presence when it counted, but on the real, she was shook. The last she'd heard he was living in London. What was he doing in New York? Visiting? Had he moved back? Was he going to be mingling with people she knew? Were the chickens coming home to roost?

Running into that jackass had forced her to look back and question every decision she'd made in the last seven years. And wasn't that why she had stubbornly refused to become a regular patient of Dr. Liessel's? To avoid that kind of thing?

Thanks to Trevor, the last week had been all about reflection. And the big question she kept coming back to was, besides fitting into size twenty-eight jeans, what had she really accomplished in all that time? She'd completely given up on finding her "bliss" as she'd fully expected she would and, for the sake of comfort and convenience, settled into a job that meant nothing to her. She allowed people to think interviewing celebrities was as glamorous as they imagined, keeping to herself the ugly truth that lurked beneath the shiny veneer: She was whoring herself out to the Omnimedia publishing conglomerate, writing fluff pieces that made false idols out of undeserving celebrities, most of whom wanted to talk to her as much as they wanted to submit to an anal cavity search and felt little need to pretend otherwise.

With such a void in her professional life, finding personal fulfillment had taken on undue importance. She didn't want to be a failure on two fronts, but as things stood, wasn't she? She hadn't had a relationship that had lasted more than six months since her split with Trevor. Sometimes she wondered if she knew how to have a healthy relationship with a man. And could she be a good mother if she never learned?

She didn't want Trevor back, but she didn't want to see him—or his significant other—so blissfully happy either. And they were. Sydney had seen real joy in the flawless fiancée's eyes. That woman was radiating happiness. You couldn't fake that shit. It wasn't all due to Trevor, for sure. The capacity to be that joyful had to be there already. And that, Sydney had realized after days of involuntary rumination, was what had rocked her.

She didn't have that capacity. Her happiness was like a light coat of polyurethane spread out over a floor of chronic malaise.

After this revelation sent her tumbling down a rabbit hole of dwelling, she had a nightmare about Trevor and Fabienne spinning gaily in a field of lilies and another in which Fabienne cracked her over the head with a baguette. Last night she'd woken up in a cold sweat, thinking maybe Trevor had never been the problem. Maybe she was the problem. Maybe she had always been the—

"We have to stop."

Sydney looked up from the patch of carpet she'd been fixating on. She didn't really need to hear from the good doctor—as with any thorough regurgitation, she felt much better simply by spewing her neurotic tale of woe—but if Liessel expected her to show up for a full session ever again (she was thinking about it), now would be the time for her to offer some encouraging words. Sydney was hoping for something along the lines of "Don't be ridiculous. Of course you're not the problem. And don't let him make you feel that way. The bastard!"

Liessel chose to go another way. "We can talk about this more if you want to come back," she said, once again trying to get Sydney signed up on her active roster. "Maybe next week?" Sydney kept her game face on and Liessel continued. "But your feelings seem to be predicated upon the idea that Trevor and his fiancée are blissfully happy. Maybe you're seeing what you want to see."

"If you think I want to see Trevor McBride happy, you don't know the first thing about me," Sydney said. She almost asked to see the woman's license! "What I want, what I really, really want, is to see Trevor married to some fat chick with adult acne and halitosis. I want him to be miserable. I want him to pay for how he treated me, how he made me feel about myself, how he humiliated me."

"How did he humiliate you?"

"What business is it of yours?"

"I'm your psychiatrist."

"Has that been determined?"

"You've been seeing me for over two years!"

"For pills, lady!" Sydney sprang to her feet and gave the strap of her bag a violent yank, forgetting that it was filled with magazines she'd stolen from Liessel's waiting room. "The point is, men like him never pay. Okay? Especially not when the victim is a woman." Liessel scribbled out her usual prescription and Sydney snatched it from her outstretched hand. "Ask Anita Hill. Ask Nicole Brown Simpson! Oh, sorry," she said, hefting her bag onto her shoulder, "you can't. BECAUSE SHE'S DEAD!"

And on that note, Sydney stormed out of the office with no plans to go back (until refill time). She didn't need that quack anyway. She could take care of herself. She always had.

CHAPTER TEN

Good afternoon!" Remy said, bursting into Max's office.

Max looked up from his computer screen. Was it afternoon already?

Remy's purposeful hustle came to a halt when she laid eyes on the new chair that had been delivered while she was out. Handmade in Italy, it was shaped like a catcher's mitt and fashioned out of nautical rope. Lacking the vocabulary to discuss interior design, she fell back on the comment she'd made repeatedly since Max had begun redecorating: "Wow! I just love what you've done with the place!"

With Max's frequent absences, his office had become a makeshift storage closet, crammed with all the girls' stuff—clothes, files, Norma's knitting needles. On his first official day as acting head of operations, he had everything carted out, including the old furniture, which he could not tolerate on a regular basis, and stood in the middle of the empty room deciding "which way to go." By week's end, his office had been redone in all white with red accents inspired by the Townhouse, a boutique hotel he frequented in South Beach. The first piece he acquired was a white leather daybed that reminded him of the one on which he'd lain for countless hours talking to his childhood psychiatrist. As a desk he was using a white Ann Demeulemeester table, which he loved for its simple lines and nonofficey feel. He'd hung a plasma screen on the far wall, which he'd had painted bordeaux, and the room's focal point was a red lacquer coffee table that sat eight inches from the floor. But he still needed artwork, he thought, staring at the blank white wall over the daybed.

"So I'm just back from the printer," Remy said, trying to position herself in the catcher's mitt.

Max focused once again on his computer screen, where, for the last hour, he'd been engaged in a close game of Scrabulous on Facebook. Then he turned back to Remy, scratching his head. "Wait . . . wasn't I supposed to meet you there?"

"Yes," Remy said, flashing a dimpled smile. "But there's nothing we can do about that now!"

That's what he loved about Remy, Max thought, going back to his game. She didn't sweat the small stuff. If only he could get Norma, that old battle-ax, to fall in line.

"There were a couple of changes to the invitations, per Avery," Remy said. "This is the new card stock we'll be using." She laid the blank card on the desk. "And they'll send the new invitations for you to approve tomorrow!"

"Great," Max said, looking for a place to throw down his bingo. "What else?"

"You have to meet Benoit . . ." Remy glanced up at Max's wall clock. It was just two stainless-steel hands, more decorative than functional, and it took her a moment to figure out the time. "Like, now!" Max continued to stare at his computer screen, his brow furrowed in concentration, and Remy squawked, "Max!"

"Okay, okay," he said, rising halfway out of his chair. "I'm going."

Remy stood by the door, waiting to put him in the elevator before she took lunch, and squinted at the plain but expensive white tee he'd had her order in bulk from Fred Segal. "Max, there's a coffee stain on your shirt!"

Max glanced down at the hem, rubbing at the spot, and shuffled toward the door. He was known for spilling things on himself, but the beauty of working in a clothing store was that it never mattered. Remy appeared with a clean T-shirt in a flash, but it was a Harvey's private label, not the Fred Segal he (quietly as it was kept) preferred. "I don't like this cotton," he said, fingering it as she followed him to the elevator. And who cared about a small stain anyway? There were people being Madoff-ed out of their life savings! Some he knew personally.

"Just put it on," Remy insisted.

To make her happy, Max stripped off his shirt, turned it inside out, and slipped it back on. He always liked the look of exposed seams. It was at that moment, of course, that Norma turned the corner and saw him stumbling toward the elevator with his hairy torso exposed and Remy fussing over him as if he was an invalid.

"Now go straight to nine," Remy said, putting him in the elevator and pressing the button for the ninth floor as though he couldn't count that high. "Don't make any pit stops. You know how Benoit is!"

Ben-wha, Max thought, laughing at the way she always carefully pronounced the name of the famous (and famously petulant) Belgian architect. The first time he'd come to meet with Avery about designing the new floor, Remy called him Ben-oyt. He'd reeled back in undisguised horror and said, "Ben-who?" Remy was so embarrassed. After the meeting, to make her feel better, Max bid him farewell by saying, "Catch ya later, Benoyt!"

Mispronouncing a name was a small faux pas compared to the kind of gaffes Remy used to make daily when she started as an intern. She had recently moved out of her parents' Staten Island home, against their wishes, and she tried so hard to play the part of the "city girl" (even though she lived with a roommate in Queens) that Max got tired just watching her. By the time she became Avery's assistant, she had tamed her accent and, making the most of the store credits she earned for doing things Max couldn't be bothered to do himself, she was inching closer to her goal of becoming a Blahnik-wearing, cosmo-swilling *Sex and the City* stock character (she watched the show religiously in reruns, apparently unaware that it was no longer 2004). But there was always something that gave her away. Lipstick a shade too bright, hair a hint "mall," self-tanner a tad on the streaky side. Remy idolized Avery and Lulu Merriwether, Max's socialite ex, but Max wanted to tell her that they were who they were as a result of a lifetime's worth of experiences. No matter how hard she tried, she would never, could never, be them. And why would she want to be?

Poor thing, he thought. And as he ambled off the elevator, he wondered how he might go about giving her a raise.

CHAPTER ELEVEN

Sydney tripped down the concrete path to Victorian Gardens, Central Park's delicately named kiddie amusement park, keeping her fingers crossed that it would not be overrun with screaming children. She'd been summoned to go on the rides with her five-year-old nephew, Ben, because her sister, the oldest thirty-six-year-old Sydney had ever encountered, didn't do that sort of thing, and Liz's all-purpose nanny was visiting family in El Salvador. Normally Sydney would have begged off—while she had great affection for the little ones (provided they were cute, clean, and not seated next to her on a plane), random kids en masse annoyed the shit out of her—but she saw today's outing as the perfect opportunity to bring up the favor she wanted Liz to do *for her.*

She'd considered asking Liz to lunch to float the idea and went so far as to call her last week to make a date. Hearing her sister's chirpy voice-mail message brought her back to her senses. Theirs was a quid pro quo relationship of mutual dependence. Liz needed Sydney to help out with the kids, and Sydney needed Liz to run interference when their meddlesome mother was around. Asking Liz to get together for no apparent reason other than to enjoy each other's company would arouse suspicion. And Sydney didn't want to have her actions misinterpreted (always a danger with Liz). She didn't want to appear desperate, as if it meant too much. Because it didn't.

Reminding herself that she needed to play nice and act sisterly (whatever that looked like), she pushed through the turnstile and took it as a positive karmic sign when she found the park virtually empty. It didn't take long for her to find a new reason to be annoyed, though. No lines meant she'd probably have to go on every ride twice, and just looking at the flying swings was making her queasy. Glancing around, she spotted Ben sitting Indian-style, along with a handful of other kids, in front of a small performance stage at the center of the park, entranced by the ravings of a clown whose raspy voice and maniacal movements brought John Wayne Gacy to mind. Seizing the opportunity to put off her aunt duties, maybe get out of them entirely, she identified Ben's blind spot—the rock-climbing wall—and speed-dialed Liz as she crept in that direction. Without questioning why she was being asked to move from the bench in front of the spinning teacups (where Ben could see her) to another empty bench where he couldn't, Liz got up, grabbed the handles of Caleigh's pink Bugaboo, and started pushing.

Her sister's blind obedience was the most distinct way in which she and Sydney were dissimilar, though there were many others. With her fair skin, gray eyes, and wispy golden hair, Liz was the spitting image of their mother. Having inherited more melanin from their Afro-Cuban father, Sydney was dark all over. She'd been the café au lait sheep growing up in the predominantly white suburb of Scarsdale, but the thing that had made her the odd woman out as a child was working in her favor as the years rolled by. Her thirty-three-year-old skin was holding up wonderfully. Her sun-ravaged sister and mother wished they could say the same.

The lack of physical resemblance to their mother, coupled with the fact that Liz had an innate maternal attachment that Sydney did not share, added credence to Sydney's long-held belief that she was adopted. In her creation theory, her real mother was a smart girl who'd gotten knocked up in her teens and put Sydney—originally named Francesca—up for adoption so her baby could have a better life than a poor teenage mother could offer. And because her real mother hadn't been saddled with a kid at fifteen, she'd been free to pursue her dreams and become the dynamic, empowered, self-made woman she was meant to be. *Diane Sawyer, perhaps?*

Since the adopted thing never panned out, Sydney had come to accept the reality that she was stuck with a mother who disdained professional work, something she'd left to a series of increasingly successful, workaholic husbands. Sydney's father, Reynaldo, was Vera's second caretaker, and Leo Weintraub, her father's onetime colleague, was her third. She was currently married to hubby number four, a Chinese plastic surgeon named Li Wu. The family joke was that she'd married him for the free work, and as a result of all her facial "enhancements," as she called them, she was beginning to look like a Wu by birth, not marriage.

Beyond the suspicion that her mother was conspiring to keep the truth of her real parentage from her, Sydney believed she had been the victim of a *genetic* conspiracy. How else but through a divine mix-up could Liz have wound up with the gay genes? Sydney had always been the tomboy. Sydney was the rabble-rousing feminist. Sydney was the one who'd never had any interest in pleasing men. She even had an androgynous name! How dykey was that? There was no question that she would have made a fantastic power lesbian!

Liz? Nothing lesbianic about her! She wore pearls and insect-shaped brooches. She loved Jane Austen. She became faint at the sight of blood. Her name was Elizabeth Ann, for God's sake. Clearly they were both in the wrong tribes, and if Sydney could have easily righted that cosmic wrong, she would have done so a long time ago. Unfortunately, she only liked the *idea* of being a lesbian. The thought of actually getting near a foreign vagina made her ill. She was disgusted by her own half the time.

And so, despite having gotten halfway into the lesbian porn Kyle enticed her to watch, Sydney had been forced to accept the cursed hetero fate that would keep her weeding through the piggish male race, trying to find a good one, while Lizzie, the gene stealer, had a loving life partner, two beautiful kids, a country home sitting on two acres, and a sprawling Upper West Side apartment that had been featured last month in *New York* magazine's home-design issue. On a fundamental level, there was something very lopsided about that picture, and Sydney was on a mission today to straighten things out.

Lacking social graces, it was difficult for her to gauge what was an appropriate length of time to feign interest in Liz's banal chitchat before she introduced her agenda, but after babbling about a bunch of boring stuff—she had to go to Pottery Barn, Joyce had lost her debit card—Liz finally hit on something that was mildly interesting.

"So we ran into the Barries at the school auction the other night," she said, referring to Barry Kleinfeld, the wildly successful sitcom star, and his inexhaustible social-climber wife, Bari, whose children went to the same private school as Ben. Liz seemed borderline obsessed with Bari: what she wore, how much she weighed, her IVF treatments. "And, I mean, he really doesn't lift a finger. They have a full staff in New York and another full staff for the Hamptons house with a majordomo running each!"

Sydney continued bouncing Caleigh on her lap and listened. These were the kinds of stories Liz always told, about rich people and their rich problems, and like a horrific car accident from which you couldn't turn away, they both fascinated and repulsed Sydney.

"He and Joyce have become friendly, you know, since she started working on the AmEx account, and he asked if we were coming to their anniversary party. They're doing this recommitment-of-vows thing. And Joyce said, 'Well, when is it?' So he calls Bari over and asks her, 'Bar, when is the anniversary thing?' So she tells him it's the sixteenth and then he says, 'Is that our actual anniversary?'" Liz opened her mouth and drew in a breath as if that was the most scandalous thing she'd ever heard (it probably was) and marveled, "Bari didn't even get mad! She just told him the date. And then Joyce asks where they're having the party and he calls Bari back over and she says it's at their house. And he says, 'Which one?'" (Sydney almost added, "Ba dum bum!") Tickled to be retelling this story, which she clearly had done many times, Liz said, "Can you imagine? He literally doesn't have to do a thing."

"Well, he does do one thing," Sydney said, trying to control the anger she felt bubbling up. "He makes *hundreds of millions of dollars!*"

"Yeah, but that's from residuals," Liz said. "His show is off the air. All he does is travel around doing stand-up. He doesn't really *work*. That Bari, I swear. She caters to him like I've never seen."

Sydney was dumbstruck by the depth of Liz's naïveté, though she ought to have been used to it by now. Despite having a master's in elementary education, Liz hadn't worked a day in her life. After meeting advertising guru Joyce Livingston in grad school, the lovebirds were shacked up, in true lesbian fashion, within weeks. After graduation, Liz let her degree go to waste (and Sydney was a college dropout; how was that for irony?), forgoing even a part-time teaching job to become, at twenty-six, a full-time trophy wife to her rich, powerful, forty-two-at-the-time lover. Liz liked to say she didn't "work outside the home," but with more foreign aid(e) than most Third World countries, she didn't do much work inside, either. In addition to Elsa, her live-in nanny, she had a part-time manny (an Italian exchange student), a private Pilates instructor (a hot Scot), a five-day-a-week housekeeper (Brazilian), and, as of last month, Livingston & Lobell's newest client, a gourmet delivery service owned and operated by a South African couple, to deliver cooked meals to her doorstep every day. What she did all day was a mystery to Sydney, but she seemed to spend an inordinate amount of time returning shit to Baby Gap.

While everyone else was grappling with the intricate complexities of the real world (that included Bari Kleinfeld, who had to deal with people she'd never met calling her an "inexhaustible social climber"), it was like Liz lived her whole life in the hypothetical. She was always talking about some once-removed "Can you imagine?" situation like this Kleinfeld story or something she'd read about in the *Times* rather than her own issues, and her Pollyannaish perspective was infuriating.

"Why shouldn't she cater to him?" Sydney said, bouncing Caleigh with extra vigor. "He's paying all the bills, keeping her in the lap of luxury. What is she doing all day? *Yoga?*"

Liz was appalled by this statement, and understandably so, since it was a thinly veiled swipe at her. Sydney was attempting to hold her tongue, but she almost felt as if Liz was trying, in her passive-aggressive way, to provoke her. They'd had a similar disagreement a few months ago when discussing the impending divorce of Marvin Paul, the über-successful creator of *The Kleinfeld Show*. Having a purely conceptual view of money, Liz thought it was perfectly reasonable that he should give his environmentalist wife of ten years half of his $500 million fortune. After all, Debbie Paul had, according to Liz's warped perspective, "sacrificed" ten years of her life to be a devoted wife to Marvin, and she had "given" him three children. Sydney felt obliged to point out that Marvin Paul had given Mrs. Paul a wonderful life free of financial concerns that allowed her to travel the world, meet interesting people, and focus her energies on saving the planet instead of getting a real job like the other 99.9 percent of the world's population. And she hadn't "given" him three kids. They weren't ties or a Porsche she'd left in the driveway tied up in a big red bow. They were created fifty-fifty with her egg and his sperm. And while few in the history of entertainment had been able to leverage their creative genius to a level that came anywhere near the success achieved by Marvin Paul, any woman with a viable womb could have done what Debbie had. "Giving birth to someone's kids doesn't entitle you to millions" were Sydney's final words on the matter. "Just ask any rapper's baby mama."

Liz didn't speak to her for two weeks after that—as if that was some kind of punishment?—but Sydney couldn't afford to be so confrontational today. If she was going to convince Liz to do her bidding, now was the time to zip it. And she was trying. She really was. But . . .

"If I were making hundreds of millions of dollars, and my wife, who didn't have to work and had dozens of staff, didn't wake me up every morning by sucking my fucking dick, I would *beat* her!"

Liz reeled back, just *horrified.* Then she looked at Caleigh, to make sure her infant psyche had not been damaged by Sydney's heinous, politically incorrect sentiments. Sydney knew it was an incredibly stupid thing to say, but the story showed Liz for the infantilized ninny that she was, and Sydney couldn't contain herself. Liz obviously thought she was the Bari of her lesbian union, but she was, in fact, the *Barry.* All she had to do every day was wake up and breathe! But unlike Barry Kleinfeld, she hadn't earned the right to live such a pampered life. Who was *she* to talk about anyone's being catered to? She could actually learn a thing or two from a go-getter (however misguided) like Bari Kleinfeld, but that was not the conversation Sydney was here to have.

Feeling pressured to hit all of her prepared bullet points before Ben came running over and dragged her onto some nauseating ride, she abruptly cut to the chase. "I've decided to get married."

CHAPTER TWELVE

G lad you could make it," Benoit said, divalike.

Oblivious to the fact that he was fifteen minutes late for a meeting that was taking place one floor above his office (his wall clock was fifteen minutes slow), Max grabbed a hard hat and said, "No problem."

Formerly devoted to children's clothes, which Harvey's had stopped carrying, the ninth floor was being transformed into a cutting-edge women's department that would include an idea Max had come up with—the Jeanious Bar. There would be a wide array of jeans displayed on the wall as bottles of liquor were in a bar, along with denim swatches and styles from which customers could special-order custom-made jeans (for $350 and up). In truth, Max hadn't really come up with the idea. Every upscale department store and boutique had some variation of a jeanious bar. He merely suggested they get one too. But he had to take credit where he could.

That was one thing he had on Avery. She was a workaholic and smart as a whip, but she wasn't hip. She and her moneybags husband collected art, dined at stuffy five-star places like Daniel, and vacationed on Necker Island, which was privately owned by the billionaire Richard Branson, a family friend. A few years ago, at a boring family dinner Max felt the need to shake up, he'd told his sis that her ivory-tower syndrome was a blind spot that prevented her, and by extension the store, from staying relevant, and it would behoove her to get more in touch with the streets that her Tory Burch flats rarely touched. Trends trickled up, not down. Didn't they teach that at Wharton?

Avery's barbed comeback—"Isn't that what I have you for?"—kept him from ever bringing it up again.

He'd put off joining the family business for as long as possible for one simple reason: He didn't want to be anyone's corporate lackey. "You're just postponing the day when you have to pick up the briefcase," Harvey had been telling him since he was eighteen, an ominous prediction that sounded, to Max's ears, like nails on a chalkboard. His father had been working in his father's, Harvey Sr.'s, store from the time he could see over the counter. Then a menswear business in the garment district, the store was called Harvey & Sons, a harbinger of the lack of control Harvey would have over his own future. Especially since Grandma Ida kept producing girl babies, four in all. With every female birth, Harvey's fate as a garmento was further cemented until Grandma Ida had a hysterectomy and it became immutable.

Max could never decide if picking up the mantle without complaint was a sign of his father's strength or a sign of his weakness. Whatever the case, Harvey's heart was not in it. That was clear. To see his father devote his life to an all-consuming career he had never wanted was like watching him swim into a shark's mouth with his eyes wide open. And from that example, Max had learned an invaluable lesson: Live for yourself and live to the fullest. He wanted to visit every continent! Scale Kilimanjaro! Catch a seventy-foot wave! Ride a camel! And that was just for starters.

What he did not want was to fritter away the one life he had sitting at a desk under fluorescent lighting tapping out memos. It was that simple.

Or so he thought. The time eventually came when his last resort looked to be his only option. So, at thirty, he relented, accepting the position as creative director of Harvey's New York under the assumption that it was an honorary one. He was appalled when it became apparent that Harvey actually expected him to work! The hiring of Simon Leeds, who, as far as Max could discern, had no social life, went a long way in alleviating his day-to-day burdens (his highest priority at the moment was finding a new Simon before Avery returned), but as imaginative as Simon was, he became so obsessed with the goddamn windows he couldn't see the forest for the trees. Avery was plotting to destroy Victor, but in all honesty, she should have sent the effete clown a fully loaded gift basket. If not for the threat he posed, they never would have gotten into gear.

Now that Max was around every day and acting as the de facto boss, he had to restrain himself from volunteering ideas about how they could overhaul the store's staid image. Give Avery an inch and she'd take the length of a fucking football field. If he allowed himself to get sucked into the Harvey's corporate vortex, he'd never get out.

Keeping that in mind, he said little as he walked around the new floor-in-progress, and after a few minutes, Benoit's incessant prattle began to sound like white noise (albeit less soothing). Thankfully, everything seemed to be moving along apace, so there wasn't much Max needed to say.

Until it came to the matter of the fitting room. Why was it in the middle of the floor instead of off to the side where it should be? And why was it round?

"It's conceptual," Benoit kept saying.

No, Max was on the verge of telling this Belgian prick. It was dumb and impractical and a poor use of space. *Don't get sucked into the vortex,* he thought, literally biting his tongue. *Don't get sucked into the vortex!* He was here to cover for Avery for a few months and then he would be free. (He was already planning a trip to Morocco to reward himself for surviving the ordeal.) Showing Harvey and Avery that he was capable of doing anything other than lurk in the shadows would create greater expectations on their part. Today it was a fitting room. Tomorrow he'd be the VP of store operations in Dallas.

And, hey, what did he really know? They wanted to make the store cooler. Maybe plopping a huge, round spaceship of a dressing room in the middle of the floor instead of letting *the merchandise* take center stage would be just what the doctor ordered. Realizing it was too late in the game to change it anyhow, Max conceded the point by uttering words that were surely music to Benoit's ears: "You, my friend, are a visionary."

Then he tossed his hard hat on a makeshift table, gave Benoit a hard slap on the back, and got the fuck out of Dodge.

CHAPTER THIRTEEN

Married?" Liz sputtered. She stared expectantly, as if Sydney had just said, "So two guys walk into a bar . . . ," until she realized Sydney's announcement was not the setup to a joke. "To who? Kyle?"

Sydney saw Ben's head turn in their direction—Liz was practically shrieking—and she slid down on the bench, hoping to avoid detection. "God, no," she said, clutching Caleigh to her chest. "I dumped him."

"You did?" Liz pushed a wisp of bang out of her eyes. "When?"

"Two weeks ago." In response to Liz's probing look, she added, "He made me pay for dinner."

"He made you pay for everything."

"On my birthday."

"Oh."

"Exactly. That's why I say, 'Good riddance.'" Tired of Caleigh's squirming, Sydney dumped her too—back in the stroller—and stuck a bottle in her mouth, hoping she'd be quiet. "And let me rephrase. I'm not getting married, I've just decided that I want to. Like, I've set that as a new goal."

"You want to get married," Liz repeated slowly. "And you've set that as a new . . . goal?"

"That's right," Sydney said with the gusto of a politician stumping for reelection. "I'm moving on to phase two!"

"Phase two?"

"Hearth and home." Sydney gave a dismissive wave. "You know, all that. It's time."

Liz smoothed her knee-length corduroy skirt. "Actually, I don't know. Am I talking to the same Sydney Zamora who when asked at age seven what she wanted to be when she grew up answered, 'Not a housewife'?"

Sydney smiled at the memory. She'd said it in front of a group of her mother's friends, and she could still picture Vera's horrified face. In response to Liz's implication, she imagined she was wearing a similar look of horror right now. "Housewife?" she sniffed. "Who said anything about me becoming a housewife?"

"You," Liz said. "Isn't that what you mean by 'hearth and home'?"

Sydney checked to see if Ben was still occupied. She didn't have time to go around in circles about this. She'd made her decision and she was ready to swing into action. Where was the blind obedience Liz was known for? "I'm not going to quit working," she said, thinking it was so typical of Liz to automatically equate getting married with housewifery. "That's not even an option." Sydney saw Caleigh's eyelids fluttering to sleep and caught the bottle as it slid from her mouth. "I don't want to become an indentured servant."

"What does that mean?" Liz repeated with all the indignation she could muster. "*I'm* a housewife."

"No, you're a lesbian," Sydney said, trying not to laugh. "That's different." *Not by much,* she thought, but they were getting off message. She wasn't here to anger Liz, she reminded herself. She was here to get Liz on her side. And after talking out of turn about the Kleinfelds, she had a lot of ground to make up. "It's just that I don't think my career should be my primary focus anymore. I've spent twelve years of my life, *twelve years,* chasing a career," she said, attempting the sisterly thing. "Climbing that mountain. Now I'm at the peak and come to find out the view just ain't all that."

"But you started doing those other assignments," Liz said. "For *Elle*?"

"*Marie Claire,*" Sydney said. Her *Cachet* contract precluded her from writing for any magazine not owned by Omnimedia, Inc., but she'd secretly begun taking "issue-oriented" assignments because she found writing celebrity profiles so mind-numbing. She wrote under the pseudonym Nancy O'Reilly, a name Ben had pulled out of thin air.

"I thought you liked doing that," Liz said, her head bobbling around in confusion.

"My last story was called 'I Shot My Molester.'" Sydney looked at Liz accusingly, as if she had been the assigning editor. "The one before that was called 'My Boyfriend Gave Me Herpes.' I can get depressed enough on my own, knowhaumsayin'?" (But now that she'd realized "Nancy O'Reilly" could pull in enough dough to cover Sydney Zamora's taxes, quitting was out of the question.)

"Well," Liz said, "I'm sure those articles are helpful for a lot of people."

"Except the only person who matters," Sydney said. "Me." Knowing she'd be better off talking tax shelters with Caleigh than discussing career options with Liz, she tried to downshift the conversation to a level Liz could understand. "I always assumed my career would be my passion," she said. "But it's just a way to pay the bills. Maybe all this time I've been seeing things the wrong way. Maybe being a wife and a mother, raising a family, maybe that's my true calling."

"Most people's careers are not their passions," Liz said, a comment that made Sydney want to pummel her. As if she needed the lesbian of leisure to tell her that! Between the ages of twenty and thirty, Sydney had been a hostess, a waitress, an operator at the Paramount Hotel, a receptionist at a nonprofit agency, an English-as-a-second-language tutor, a photographer's assistant, a model booker's assistant, an assistant fashion buyer's assistant . . . She knew from passionless jobs. The difference between her and "most people" was that she'd been filled with a simmering rage all along, knowing she was capable of so much more. "Most people" got what they settled for. "Most people" were sheep blindly following unspoken societal rules, doing what they "should" instead of taking risks to create the life they truly wanted. Sydney had refused to accept her miserable fate as an overweight, junk food– and nicotine-addicted wage slave because she was not "most people." But she wasn't going to point that out because, despite being dealt a lucky hand in life, Liz was.

"I actually think becoming a mother might open me up to new career possibilities," Sydney said, musing about the life she envisioned for herself. "I could totally see myself becoming one of those mompreneurs who invents some baby-related gadget, you know. Like that stay-at-home mom who invented Baby Einstein."

Again waiting for a punch line and not getting one, Liz said, "Hmmm."

Watching the lines of puzzlement appear on Liz's forehead, Sydney wondered why she didn't do something about them. Just because she acted like an old lady didn't mean she had to look like one. And wasn't the primary responsibility of a trophy wife to stay pretty? Sydney was not one to encourage plastic surgery, because it never seemed to produce believable results, but she had nothing against nonsurgical intervention. All Liz needed was a little maintenance, and she could get anything done for free by their latest stepfather, Dr. Wu (as everyone in the family except Vera inexplicably called him). Sydney really didn't understand what Liz was trying to prove. Nor did she much care . . .

"Anyway," she said as Liz continued to puzzle, "I can't just sit around waiting for Mr. Right to magically appear. I need to make shit happen." And then she segued into the business of the day: "So who can you fix me up with?"

The frown lines deepened. "I'm not following you."

"What's to follow? Who can you fix me up with? Cough up some names!"

"Well," Liz said, avoiding eye contact. "I would have to think about it."

"Think about it now," Sydney demanded. "You and Joyce know a lot of people."

Two kids wearing party hats ran by, and Sydney's head swiveled in the direction from whence they came. She saw a HAPPY BIRTHDAY streamer going up near the concession area and more kids in party hats pouring in. "We have to get out of here," she said urgently. "Get Ben."

Startled, Liz said, "What? Why? You didn't even go on any of the rides."

"I'll make it up to him," Sydney said, snapping Caleigh into the stroller. "Let's go."

Liz sighed, and watching her shuffle away in her driving moccasins, holding her little pointelle cardigan closed against the breeze, Sydney wondered why she was so unfailingly obedient except when it came to helping her only sister find a baby daddy. After all the free child care Sydney had provided for Liz and Joyce, not to mention the countless times she had stood up to Vera when she tried to defame their lesbian love, she expected to get at least five fix-ups out of them. And the men had better be suitable candidates!

As Sydney pushed the stroller toward the gate, Ben skated toward her at top speed on his new Heelys, cocooned in a helmet, knee pads, and hard plastic arm guards that stretched from elbow to wrist. Sydney was thinking that Liz was a total worrywart who was raising him to be a wimp at the very moment that he tripped and fell facedown on the concrete at her feet, a mishap that did not change her opinion. A boy with two mothers and no father was coddled enough! It would be good for him to get a few bruises, get roughed up a little by life. Hearing the beginnings of a cry, she made no move toward him, acting as if the fall had never happened. "Hey, Benny boy!" she said as he stood up, wiping gravel from his palms.

Ben grabbed onto her arm and lifted his foot to give her a good look at his new Heelys. "Cool," she said, and continued pushing the stroller toward the front gate. Liz repeated that she needed to go to Pottery Barn (to get aprons, of all things) and, concerned that she would try to escape before implicitly agreeing to help with her manquest, Sydney aggressively rolled up on her as if she was about to do a drive-by. "Which Pottery Barn are you going to? The one over here?"

"No," Liz said. "I was going to go to the one near us."

"The one over here is better." Sydney didn't even know where the closest Pottery Barn was, but in this part of town, there had to be at least two in the vicinity. And she couldn't let Liz get away without some kind of verbal commitment. "I'll walk you," she said, remembering there was one on Madison, a block down from Harvey's. "Let Ben skate through the park."

"Hey!" Ben said when he realized they were heading to the exit. "We didn't go on any rides."

"I wish we could," Sydney said. "But Mommy has to go to Pottery Barn."

"Mom!" Ben whined.

Sydney looked away so Liz wouldn't catch her laughing, then she tousled Ben's hair and said, "How 'bout a cotton candy!"

"Yay!" Ben shouted and took off toward the vendor, skating gingerly now.

Liz, who ran a strictly organic household, gave Sydney a scolding look, and Sydney said, "Come on! I owe the kid." She paid for the sugary cloud and pulled off a bite-size blue tuft for herself before Ben skated up the concrete path. "Now, about the guy . . ."

"What guy?" Liz said, bending down to fix something in the stroller's undercarriage.

Assuming Liz was deliberately trying to defy her in retaliation for the cotton candy (or the Kleinfeld thing, or the "Housewives are indentured servants" crack), Sydney said, with emphasis, "The wonderful guy you and Joyce are going to fix me up with." Liz gave her a cockeyed look, but Sydney went on, bent on completing the day's mission.

"Now, I prefer someone tall, but I can do short as long as he's not more than two inches shorter than me. He should make more money than I do, but no one too rich because those guys treat women like employees. Somewhere between two and three hundred thou annually would be ideal. I don't mind someone who's been married—really, you know, that could be a plus—but definitely nobody who already has kids. Unless the kids are grown up and self-supporting." They came to the top of the hill where the path split off, and she pointed Ben in the direction of Pottery Barn. "Funny, funny, funny. Can't say that enough. I should've said that first because sense of humor is at the top of my list."

Liz didn't seem to be absorbing the information, but that was okay. Sydney planned on e-mailing the details to her later and cc'ing Joyce. She tried to think if there was anything else.

"Oh yeah," she said, thinking of the time-consuming nonsense one of her former friends had put herself through to marry an arrogant man who happened to be an Orthodox Jew (and whom the ex-friend was now divorcing). "I can do Jewish, but I won't convert."

CHAPTER FOURTEEN

fter lunch Max kicked back in Avery's office bed with the latest issue of *Complex* and a bowl of tiramisu. He had always viewed routine as his enemy, but now, in his third week of full-time employment, he'd gotten into a groove that was strangely . . . *soothing*. He wished he had some actual work to do, but his main function was to police everyone else in Avery's absence to make sure they were doing their jobs. *How would he know?*

Avery seemed to be doing a perfectly fine job of policing from the confines of her bed. She had a daily conference call and seemed to know exactly what every staff member was supposed to be doing every moment of the day. Max couldn't even remember half their names. There were just so many of them.

Norma and Remy seemed to be working in tandem to keep him on track, which had conveniently allowed Max time to continue with his office redecoration. Interior design was sort of a hobby, his apartment being his proudest achievement. (He modestly called it "his apartment," but at forty-five hundred square feet, the converted firehouse nestled under the Brooklyn Bridge was, by anyone's standards, a spacious house.) He'd gotten it for a steal, gutted the place, and redesigned every room, keeping only the brass fire pole. He'd slowly furnished it piece by piece over the years, hunting obsessively for things he envisioned and commissioning what he couldn't find. For three years, it had been his passion. Then one day he walked in, realized there was nothing left to do, and spiraled into a postpartum funk.

He never bothered to keep close track of how much he was spending until everything was done. Boy, was it a shitload! And contrary to what most people believed, he did not have an endless supply. The family's finances were always shrouded in mystery as his mother, Elizabeth, "Binky" to her friends, came from old money, which meant any discussion of it was verboten. Max hadn't even known they were any different from anyone else until he was about eight and a classmate told him his family was "really fucking rich." A few nights later he'd wandered out of his room in his PJs while his parents were having a party and found a gaggle of uniformed waiters ogling the paintings in the hall that his mother usually kept slipcovered. He'd asked them what they were looking at and he'd always remember how they'd jumped back, as if they'd been caught stealing silverware, explaining that they had only ever seen such paintings in museums.

The next day, Max went to his mother and put it to her straight. "Are we rich?"

She looked alarmed, but after a moment, she answered, "No."

"What are we, then?" Max had asked.

"Comfortable," she'd replied.

Her siblings weren't as tight-lipped on the subject. They talked about money a lot—through lawyers and court documents during the eight-year battle that ensued over her father's estate. She was the only family member who did not partake, and Max knew it deeply wounded her to see her family torn apart over something as transient as money. Then, when he was about seventeen, she developed a fascination with India and returned from one of her consciousness-raising trips talking in tongues about money burdening one's spirit and such. Well, duh. She didn't have to go halfway around the world to figure that out. All she had to do was look at her family. Or anyone on the Upper East Side! Max wasn't trying to contest her mystical teachings, he just didn't know why she had to find religion right before he became of age to inherit some bucks. He was willing to risk his spirit!

On his eighteenth birthday, she had taken him for lunch at the Colony Club and had him sign some papers. Soon after, he got the first part of his inheritance. A few hundred thousand dollars. Lowballed, there was no question. (His father's fiscal philosophy was as simple as a bumper sticker: Want money? Work for it.)

Max expected them to be horrified when he purchased a vintage Bentley with the money he received at eighteen, and they were. But it was his money and they couldn't argue with that. Anyway, he had an image to uphold. At Buckley, a private school he'd hated for its homogenized, close-minded preppy jock crowd, he'd relished his role as the artistic outcast. By fifteen he was sneaking out to the hottest clubs like Nell's or MK, wearing Duran Duran hair and smudged eyeliner. At sixteen he was shipped off to boarding school, a fate worse than Buckley. A fake suicide bid got him expelled after two semesters and he arrived back in the city on Christmas Eve, planning to ring in the New Year with the von Furstenberg kids, whose European sensibilities were better suited to his own.

In an attempt to get his parents to buy him the dapper tux he'd seen in the Versace window, he'd slashed his old one to ribbons. It was a Harvey's private label, and his parents read way too much into that. The next morning, he was at the breakfast table eating French toast when his psychiatrist, Dr. Smithers, appeared in the kitchen. "We're going," he said. "You can make a scene and it can be messy or you can go quietly. But going you are."

He checked Max into a psych ward in the Bronx for thirty days of observation, which after the initial shock wore off, wasn't so terrible. As one would imagine, it was filled with crazy, babbling people (Max was the only person not on meds), but it didn't take long to figure out whom to befriend and how to work the system. Max didn't care for his roommate, a thirty-year-old serial rapist, so he got the nut transferred to twenty-four-hour lockdown by fingering him as the culprit of a kitchen fire. His favorite person, hands down, was a middle-aged Dominican woman named Mercedes who sang Billy Ocean's "Caribbean Queen" all day while she rode an Exercycle. And then there was Joan, an old black lady who was just fantastic. "I may be crazy," she'd say. "But I ain't stupid." Every night Max sat with her while she watched "Mighty Joe Young," punching the air, chanting, "Get 'em, Joe. Get 'em, Joe."

His psych-ward stint made him a star on the private-school circuit, and when all the Brearley girls returned from vacation, they'd chauffeur up to the Bronx in packs, bringing the loveliest care packages (which were thoroughly appreciated by Joan and Mercedes). Max was actually sort of bummed when he was sprung early for good behavior because then it was back to the reality of school, which he thought was pointless. In the end, he graduated from a busted-down *Welcome Back Kotter* high school called Walden that was way uptown in Washington Heights. It was billed as a "progressive" school, which was code for "kooks only." From day one, it felt like home. It was where he met Duke, one of his closest friends to this day and the lead singer of their band, Gray Does Matter. (Duke loved the Bentley.)

The year of traveling after graduation was like dog years in terms of maturation, and when he was accepted to Brown (many strings were pulled), everyone thought he was on the road to becoming the proper Buckley boy he was meant to be. But he was drifting still. After graduation, he applied to Oxford solely to postpone his entry into the real world, terrified that he would never have a competent set of working skills. That fear intensified when he returned from England with another useless degree and a wife.

The family's surprise turned to delight as they got to know Eliana, a woman they believed would put Max's restlessness to rest once and for all. His mother insisted they have a celebratory family dinner, a formal affair at La Grenouille, and Max agreed. (Robbed of a wedding, his mother deserved that at least.) It was the only occasion in his life when he felt completely embraced and supported by his family, and he wished he could have fully enjoyed the night. But he was preoccupied with trying to intercept the envelopes that were being discreetly slipped into Eliana's hand. Max knew what was in those envelopes. He *wanted* what was in those envelopes. Eliana didn't need to know.

He was head over heels for his Italian bride, in no small part because, never having been to the States, the name Harvey's meant nothing to her. She was an innocent, uncorrupted by the lure of filthy lucre, and he wanted her to stay that way. But a few envelopes got by him. When they returned home (to the SoHo loft his parents had given them as a wedding gift), he had to explain why they had received seven checks from his relatives, some of whom he hadn't seen in years, each in the curious amount of $9,999.

Because that was the maximum amount one could give as a gift without being taxed, and this was a way to keep the money circulating within the family.

That night was the beginning of the end. (And she didn't even know about the other sixteen checks Max had stuffed in his coat pockets.) In record time, his blushing bride became enamored of the New York social whirl and the endless supply of designer finery available to her as Mrs. Maximillian Cooper, and just as quickly Max became disenamored of her. His paternal grandmother left him $2 million in her will (much to Harvey's chagrin), which he received right around the time Eliana began divorce proceedings. To save them both the headache of a legal battle (there was no prenuptial—at that time he believed in true love), he offered her, against the advice of counsel, a lump sum far more generous than she deserved, with one caveat: that she return to Europe so he would never have to see her again. The quickness with which she accepted was the final nail in the coffin of their brief union.

He squandered another chunk of change in a typical rich-kid move. He invested in an independent film. Never saw a penny in return. Never even saw the *movie*. He wasted more money doing another dumbass thing. Drugs. Every night was a party, and every night he picked up the tab. A short, rather painless stint at a Malibu rehab cured him of that habit. (The family wished his younger brother, an Oahu-based junkie, could say the same.)

It wasn't long before it became obvious that he was going to have to support himself the same way most people did—by getting a job. It also made him feel like an aimless loser not to have one. After four years in his figurehead position as co–creative director, Max knew Harvey was still waiting for him to "pick up the briefcase" and get serious about work. Getting him to fill in for Avery was partly a ruse to move him in that direction, but Harvey would have to have the patience of Job to see that come to pass. Joining the family business was the path of least resistance, and Max was only in it for the ducats. Sure, he wanted to do something with his life, but that something would be his passion, not his profession. He wished he could tell Harvey to shove it altogether, but as the rest of his inheritance, entirely from his mother, wouldn't find him until he was forty, that was an impulse he kept under control.

"If you hadn't sunk so much into that vanity project you call an apartment, you'd have that fuck-you money," Jack, one of the family financial advisers, often scolded him. But screw mutual funds! Why should he squirrel his money away? So he could end up like Harvey? An old man with a vault full of cash that he would one day bequeath to the Shoah Foundation? Money was meant to be spent so you could enjoy your life in the present. Who knew if they were going to be hit by a truck tomorrow? Granted, he was no Warren Buffett—despite coming from money, or perhaps because of it, his financial IQ was rather low—but Max considered his home a very wise investment. By now, he could sell his house for ten times what he'd paid and sunk into it. (Or, in the current market, maybe eight times.)

Even though the place was like his baby, he sometimes considered putting it up for sale. Not for the cash, but to escape the rich Manhattanites who'd descended upon DUMBO in the last few years as all the warehouses were converted to lofts and condos. He knew he was considered a rich Manhattanite in the eyes of most, but he would not categorize himself as such. He was a pioneer. A conquistador who'd put down roots in the city's coolest outer borough before it was fashionable. He'd settled in DUMBO when there was no one walking the streets after seven o'clock in the evening. When there was no supermarket or ATM within a ten-block radius. When there were no restaurants in the area and he had to go door-to-door, bribing all the restaurants in nearby Brooklyn Heights so he could get deliveries.

Now there was an overpriced gourmet market across the street, a noisy bar next door, and three sushi bars a block over. Last week the death knell had rung in his ears when he turned a corner and there was a Starbucks where there hadn't been one a week before. He had nothing against the Starbucks corporation per se. In fact, he thought their emphasis on corporate responsibility was more admirable than most. Its existence in malls, suburbs, and heavily populated urban areas was fine. It was the bourgeois element and foot traffic it would attract to his 'hood that concerned him.

But what could he do? Gentrification. It was a bit—

The bed shook, causing Max's eyes to flutter open. Seeing Norma standing over him looking like Kathy Bates in *Misery*, he shrieked.

"No more naps," she said, holding the magazine in one hand and the empty tiramisu bowl in the other. She yanked the comforter back. Max was in his boxers.

Red-faced, he jumped up and grabbed his trousers. "In Europe, everyone takes a siesta in the afternoon!"

"We're not in Europe," Norma said. She walked to the door and waited while Max hopped around, trying to get his pants on.

Max zipped up and hurried past her, his brand-new Adidas cradled in his arms. "Edison took catnaps. He said it made him more productive!"

"Well," Norma said, slamming and locking the door behind him, "that doesn't seem to be working out for you."

CHAPTER FIFTEEN

Funny, quirky, tall, high-earner' . . ." Joyce turned to Liz, eyes wide. "What is this, her recipe for a *man cake?*"

Liz continued using slow, circular motions to lotion her elbows. She hated it when Joyce brought her laptop to bed, and this was a perfect example of why.

"Wait . . . a Leo?"

"I told you." Liz sighed. "It was like watching a kung fu movie. Her mouth kept moving, but the dialogue never matched up."

"This is big trouble, Liz. I'm telling you. Keep us out of this!"

Joyce thought a lot of things were "big trouble"—the lobby renovations, the new neighbors, the clicking noise Caleigh's stroller had been making— so Liz took that assessment with a grain of salt. "She's my sister."

"She'll find something wrong with anyone we set her up with. You do realize that?"

"Who's to say?"

"I am!" Joyce turned away from her precious Gmail (she loved everything about Google and was mad she hadn't invested earlier, though she'd made plenty) and ranted directly into Liz's ear as if she might not hear her otherwise. "This is just another fly-by-night idea she's gotten into her head. Like when she looked into signing up for the Peace Corps. Or when she started taking voice lessons because she thought she could be a jazz singer. Or when she seriously considered becoming a surrogate for her dermatologist and his partner and got so far into the process that she was taking prenatal vitamins."

"Did wonders for her hair," Liz murmured, moving on to her other elbow.

Joyce tossed the laptop on the bed between them (as if it wasn't already, Liz thought) and got up to put on the flannel pajamas she wore year-round because she liked the bedroom to be a chilly sixty-six degrees. Not sixty-five. Not sixty-seven. Sixty-six. It was amazing, Liz thought, how the little quirks that made you fall in love with someone could come back to haunt you when it was too late to do anything about it.

"Your sister is not ready to be married," Joyce said, dropping her sweatpants and socks in front of the closet, where they would remain until Liz picked them up and deposited them in the hamper two feet away. "She doesn't know how to be vulnerable. She doesn't know how to put anyone else's feelings before her own." She disappeared for a moment, returning with a glass of orange juice—it would never occur to her to ask if Liz was thirsty—and plopped down on the bed without noticing the droplets that splashed on the duvet cover. "She doesn't know how to let the man be the man."

"Oh well," Liz said, tucking the travel-size bottle of Kiehl's lotion in her nightstand. "I can just imagine what she'd say if I told her that."

"She'd say, 'Like you dykes know anything about men!'" Joyce said with a laugh.

"Honey, please," Liz said when Joyce went back to checking her e-mail. "Do you have to?"

"Yeah," Joyce said. "I do."

Liz pulled out *The Starter Wife,* a novel she didn't feel like reading. (She'd gotten too far. She had no choice.) "You wouldn't understand. You don't talk to your sister."

"Because she's a drama queen, just like yours," Joyce huffed. "And, trust me, I'm the better for it. We all are!"

"What does that mean?" Liz said, whipping off her reading glasses. "That by maintaining a relationship with my only sibling, I'm doing some harm to our family?"

"No, Liz," Joyce said in that exasperated "don't be such a nag" tone that Liz did not appreciate one bit. "Maintaining a relationship and giving in to her every ridiculous demand are very different things. Don't let her bully you."

Liz slipped her glasses back on and cracked open her book at the marked page. "She's not bullying me."

"That's what you think."

"You don't know her well enough to know what a big step this is for her, Joyce. I mean, I can't remember Sydney asking anyone to help her do anything—all those years when she never had any money, she'd starve before she'd ask us. She made this clumsy request to be fixed up because she doesn't know how to ask for help. Do you know how many times I've watched her struggle to get her suitcase off the luggage trolley at the airport when there's some man standing right there who's more than happy to help? Asking for help doesn't even occur to her. Sometimes my heart just breaks for her."

"Mine doesn't." Joyce glanced over and caught Liz putting her glasses back on to hide her welling eyes. "She sheds no tears for you, Liz."

"She came to us for help," Liz said, snapping her book open. "That's big."

"Yeah, big trouble. I'm telling you."

"Yes, Sydney is a piece of work," Liz admitted. "She can be completely thoughtless and unbearable at times . . ."

"At times?"

"Do I really have to remind you of all the times she's been there for us?"

"Yeah, maybe you should," Joyce said. "I'm blanking on that."

Liz leaned her head back on the pillow and sighed. She'd once read that most people tried to re-create childhood dramas in their adult life so they could rewrite history and fashion their own endings. She'd recognized long ago that she was one of those people. She'd spent a lifetime playing mediator between her mother and Sydney. Not a get-together went by without Vera's finding a way to disparage Sydney's weight (even if she were a size two, Vera would still think she could stand to lose another five to ten pounds), her career trajectory, or, Vera's preferred bone of contention now that Liz's "lifestyle" was set in stone, Sydney's single status. And Liz had spent the last twelve years dancing the same dysfunctional two-step between Joyce and her mother.

But she'd never had to worry about Joyce and Sydney butting heads. Just the opposite. Sydney viewed Joyce and everything she had accomplished professionally with a groupielike awe. You'd have thought Joyce had cured cancer by the unnecessarily big deal Sydney made when Joyce was ranked number three on *The Advocate*'s 2007 Power Lesbians list. It was a nice accolade, and Liz was happy to see Joyce recognized by her peers, but Joyce couldn't have cared less about it. Did Sydney really have to take them out to dinner to celebrate? Liz hated to think that Sydney's high praise was meant to put her down as much as it was to lift Joyce up, but all roads were pointing in that direction.

And now that Joyce had all but said Sydney was a head case no sane man would want to marry, and Sydney was pining for the life she'd made Liz feel ashamed to be living, Liz was filled with such a sickening glee that she found herself defending Sydney with more conviction than she really felt.

"Who read Vera the riot act when she went around at our commitment ceremony telling everyone, 'It's not legal, you know. Lizzie can back out at any time'?"

Joyce knew the answer was Sydney, but her response was an annoyed grunt.

Then Liz reminded her of the time Vera sent Sydney a panicked e-mail after finding out how Liz had been impregnated with Ben: "Does the sperm donor have to be a gay too? Call me!" In response, Sydney sent her a three-line e-mail with "Serenity Prayer" as the subject line: "God, grant me the serenity to accept the things I cannot change; the courage to change the things I can; and the wisdom to know the difference."

"We never asked her to do either of those things," Joyce said, piling her wiry gray hair into a bun (another thing Liz couldn't believe she ever found attractive). "And she'll use any excuse to fight with your mother."

"Well, she babysits whenever we ask," Liz called out when Joyce stomped into the bathroom. "And you expect her to drive me and the kids out to the Hamptons in that monster Navigator whenever you want to take the seaplane." Getting up to surreptitiously adjust the thermostat right before Joyce arrived back, she added a pissy yet inaudible, "Big shot."

"Well, maybe you should get your license already," Joyce snapped, giving her pillow a hard punch. "And let's not forget that she gets to stay in our guesthouse for weeks on end. Last summer she rented it out to somebody for a month and didn't tell us!"

Liz couldn't think of a rebuttal for that (it was just so wrong), so she let it drop. She hated to argue with Joyce, and they rarely did, not about anything serious. She wasn't going to let this one go any further on account of

Sydney, who'd been a troublemaker since birth. ("Kick, kick, kick," their mother would always say. "That's all she ever did!")

"For the last time," Joyce said, curling up to her allergen-free pillow, facing the nightstand so she could see her BlackBerry the moment she opened her eyes, "I'm telling you, not asking you, to keep us out of this."

She'd try to stay out of it the best she could, Liz thought. But she had to come up with some solution. Sydney wasn't going to stop hounding her until she did. In the meantime, she refused to let this create a rift between her and Joyce. She had a rule that they should never go to bed angry, so even though she sort of was, she leaned over Joyce to bestow her usual good-night kiss.

She was relieved when Joyce (who, like Sydney, had trouble releasing anger) lifted her head from the pillow to meet her halfway. Until she realized Joyce wasn't looking to return her affection. She was looking at the thermostat. "Is it hot in here?"

CHAPTER SIXTEEN

The revolving door spun Max out onto Madison Avenue at five o'clock on the dot and he found himself face-to-face with the last person he wanted to see. Mitzi Berman.

"Maxi!" she squawked, her twang hitting him like a bullet right between the eyes.

"Mitzi . . ." he breathed.

A short, buxom pistol of a woman who had the expensively garish wardrobe of Ivana Trump and the brusque demeanor of a bookie, she eyed him as if he were a sunken treasure. Running her hand along the lapel of his navy pinstripe suit jacket, she said, "Don't you look dapper!"

"Thank you," Max said, offering a wan smile. As she took in his slouchy jeans, then his sneakers—after three weeks on the job, Casual Friday had begun to bleed into the rest of his workweek—he couldn't tell whether she disapproved. Her face had long ago been Botoxed into submission. "I'd love to chat," he said, lightly touching the sleeve of her pink bouclé jacket. "But I really need to—"

"You really need to talk to me is what you really need to do," Mitzi barked. "Walk me down to Chanel."

"Believe me, Mitzi. I'd like nothing more." He was about to tell her the truth—he was trying to catch the 5:10 showing of the new Charlie Kaufman movie at the Odyssey—but he knew that Mitzi, a woman who never took no for an answer, would just tell him to catch the next one. And he hated to miss the beginning of a movie, a certainty now. "So, Mitzi," he said, resigned to his fate. "How the hell are you?"

"Since you ask . . . couldn't be better! The *Times Magazine* is running a huge story on me next week. A cover!"

"Mazel tov," Max said, hoping to wriggle out of this without having to walk Mitzi to Chanel. Once there, she'd probably coax him into helping her pick out a few tweed suits. If he could just keep the conversation here on the corner, he could escape relatively unscathed. It was like the advice FBI profilers gave in case of abduction: Never let them take you to the second location.

"I do very well regardless," Mitzi clucked. "But, needless to say, come Monday business is gonna go through the roof!"

"You think so?" Max said, swallowing a yawn.

"Think?" Mitzi harrumphed. "I *know* so!"

Mitzi's booming business, which she seemed to look upon as more of a calling, was matchmaking. "The second oldest profession," she was fond of saying. Strictly high-end, she was employed mostly by hedge-fund gazillionaires and CEOs who were used to having everything vetted for them, including potential wives. As the unattached, thirty-five-year-old son of a prominent New York family, Max represented big game, and for the last two years Mitzi had been unsuccessful in her dogged attempts to bag him as a client.

He ran into her everywhere, it seemed, but in and around Harvey's, her favorite place to troll for clients, the risk of a collision was higher. Working full-time had made him a sitting duck, and he supposed he should consider himself lucky that he'd been able to evade her this long. But he'd been polite enough. He had to give her the slip. It was now or never. "Great seeing you, as always," Max said, looking for available taxis. "You should go inside and check out the new espresso bar."

"I'm meeting someone in there later," she said. "Awesome girl."

Max looked at her blankly, refusing to take the bait. No matter how many times he brushed her off, they always had the same conversation. "Why don't you let me fix you up?" *Not interested, Mitzi.* "I have a girl who'd be perfect for you." *Not interested, Mitzi.* The woman was like a human boomerang.

"But enough about me," Mitzi said, her brilliant blue eyes boring into him, vulturelike. "Word is you ditched Lulu. Fact or fiction?"

Although Mitzi's rat-a-tat-tat conversational style often caused Max to respond involuntarily (when he didn't want to respond at all), today he was on his toes. Getting entangled with Lulu Merriwether, a woman whose histrionic personality was well known to him, had been a grave error in judgment. Any chance he had to downplay it, he did. Knowing that feeding this morsel to Mitzi Berman would be more effective than putting up a neon billboard in Times Square, he seized the moment. "Fact."

Mitzi shot him a look of mock outrage. (But knowing Mitzi, it probably wasn't so mock.) "When did this happen?"

"Some time ago."

She stamped her navy pump on the pavement. "Why am I just hearing about it?"

"I sent out a mass e-mail," Max said, patience wearing thin. "Yours came back as undeliverable."

"Always the joker, this one," Mitzi said. "You know what would be funny? If we hooked up." She fluffed her poufy blond wig, Mae West–style. "Mitzi and Maxi. Imagine that!"

Max felt his cheeks color with embarrassment. The idea of hooking up with Mitzi Berman, who was sixty if she was a day, was unappealing enough. But it was Mitzi's little nickname that hit him where it hurt. In junior high he'd been so traumatized by the taunts of "Maxi Pad! Maxi Pad!" that he'd switched schools. Unbeknownst to Mitzi, just laying eyes on her took him back to the single worst year of his life.

"You know, Lulu and I were never really together," he said, pushing his agenda.

"That's not what *she* was telling everyone," Mitzi said, hoping to draw out more information. When that tactic didn't work, she switched gears. "Maxi, how did a nice boy like you get mixed up with a nutcase like that?"

"I ask myself the same thing," Max said, playing it close to the vest.

"I know a girl who would be perfect for you," Mitzi said with an air of finality.

"So you've said," Max replied, his mind whirring as he tried to plot an escape.

"Not her," Mitzi said. "She's off the market. Taken. Married. To a guy who knows what to do with an awesome girl when he meets one." She let this scolding settle in, then, playing both good cop and bad cop, followed up with some positive spin. "But I have someone else. This one? Better than perfect for you. Why don't you let me set you up?"

Max stifled a groan. How many times did he have to tell this Bette Midler doppelgänger that he wasn't in the market for a wife? And even if he were, he was quite sure this "better than perfect" item Mitzi was hawking in her daily special was not his Ms. Right. He already had one failed marriage under his belt, and the woman who would get him down the aisle again would certainly not be one to auction herself off to the highest bidder!

"My prices are going up," she shrilled, right on cue. "Get in while you can!"

Going up? Max thought with astonishment. Last he heard, Mitzi was charging fifty grand—plus a "marriage bonus"!—for her matchmaking services. And if the guy didn't find a wife within a year, there were no money-back guarantees.

For obvious reasons, the intermingling of marriage and money was a sore subject for him. He'd given his ex-wife (he still couldn't say her name, but he had progressed from calling her "that bitch") a lump-sum settlement because he didn't want to be reminded of his mistake by seeing her name on the monthly bills his accountant sent him. It had taken a long time and a lot of therapy to get past the anger and mistrust he felt toward women after that colossal mistake. But he had gotten past it. Only when he had this annoying, repetitious conversation with Mitzi Berman did those feelings resurface.

"Are you offering me a special introductory rate?" Max said, his voice taking on an unfriendly edge.

"Your sense of humor really is your best asset," Mitzi said, swinging her boxy purse. "It's a shame you don't put it to better use. You're thirty-six years old, Maxi . . ."

"Thirty-*five*."

"*Same diff.* I mean really, all kidding aside, aren't you tired of putzing around with all these randoms?"

Yes, as a matter of fact, he was, Max thought. But admitting that to Mitzi Berman would be like painting a bull's-eye on his forehead. This was her modus operandi, one he was sure she employed with all the men she was actively recruiting. She let you tire yourself out deflecting all of her invasive questions and then as soon as you dropped your guard, she hit you with a knockout punch. *Bam!* But he would not be taken down by the old Mitzi Berman rope-a-dope. Not today.

"Of course you are!" she cried, taking his silence as surrender. "Tired isn't even the word. Look at you! You're exhausted."

She was right, Max thought, feeling his shoulders slump. At the end of another long week of full-time employment, he was exhausted. And the intensity of Mitzi Berman's vampiric force field had just sucked the last bit of reserve energy out of his body. He had nothing left to fend her off when she linked her arm in his and said, "Come. Tell Mitzi all about it."

And before he knew it they were gliding toward Chanel.

CHAPTER SEVENTEEN

Seeing as she wasn't Mariah Carey or a Nickelodeon star, Sydney had every intention of exchanging her outdated metallic pink phone, an illegal freebie she'd gotten at a Motorola event, for black or gunmetal gray, but its girly color turned out to be its greatest strength. She could always spot it quickly, shining like a pink beacon from the dark abyss of whichever purse she had in rotation, today a black canvas hobo so gargantuan it could hold the tire of a small car.

Hearing its muffled trill while seated in a cab (she loved getting an SUV), she lifted the phone out of the darkness, and when the screen confirmed her suspicion (it was Liz), she let it go to voice mail. Texting was her preferred mode of communication. It made people get to the point and gave her the power to end the conversation at any time. (She shunned PDAs altogether, choosing to be somewhat inaccessible.) Waiting for the inevitable "where r u" follow-up text to arrive, she held the phone in her palm and stared at the picture on the driver's hack license, making a mental note to ask Abdullah Aziz (or was it Aziz Abdullah?) for the receipt.

Taking the subway was always faster when heading into the packed jungle known as Midtown, but that was only an option if the subway was running, and today the stupid N train, the only direct route to Harvey's, wasn't. It would probably cost twenty-five dollars to get to Sixty-first from her house, a sum she would have once considered blasphemous. She could afford to take cabs now, but any cab ride over ten dollars still went on her monthly expense report whether it was business or not. The problem was that her mental notes were usually unreliable. And you couldn't expense what you couldn't back up with tangible evidence. So she slipped the black elastic out of her hair and wrapped it tightly around her pinkie until the tip flushed red. If that didn't remind her to get the receipt, nothing would.

Watching the passing blur of people and stores on Sixth Avenue, she thought about how foolish she'd been to think she'd never have to worry about money again after signing her first contract with *Cachet*. Ha! She was making three times more money than she ever had in her life, and her shopping-bag-lady syndrome—the fear that she would wind up homeless, destitute, and alone—had only gotten worse. Now she actually had something to lose. She was so afraid that all her savings would just disappear one day that she refused to invest any of it. She had no idea what to invest in, and she was embarrassed to admit she didn't want to know. She'd tried to learn, by watching Suze Orman, but talk of IRAs, 401(k)s, and five-year ARMs made her head hurt. She wanted someone else to take care of her money so she wouldn't have to think about it, but how could she be sure the person she hired wouldn't Madoff her out of her life savings? She didn't even trust the bank! She was hoarding a wad of cash in a savings account (earning a mere 3.5 percent interest), and every few days she went online to make sure it was still there. She liked thinking she was just paranoid, but now millions of people had lost their homes—Ed McMahon, even!—the economy was completely fucked, she kept hearing the sickening words "Greatest Depression," and was there really anything President Obama (as much as she adored him) could do about it?

Even before the economy had gone belly-up, the thought of making the huge financial commitment that buying an apartment required gave her heart palpitations! But what was she going to do? Stay in her illegal sublet forever? She didn't want to be one of those stupid women who waited until they were coupled to buy a place. What if she never met her Mr. Right? What if she stayed single forever and wound up living in a crappy little rental with a bunch of cats instead of babies? (There was a woman like that in her building and it hurt to even look at her.) What if she had to go to a genius bank for sperm? How much would *that* cost? What if, after wasting all this time, she found out she couldn't have children? Then what?

At least once a week she had a daydream about running off to New

Mexico, where life would be simple and cheap. She had never been to New Mexico—she had never even met anyone from New Mexico—but somehow New Mexico had become her personal Mecca. In New Mexico, the weather would be perfect, the food would be amazing, neighbors would be friendly, and the men would be down-to-earth, manly types who drank beer right out of the bottle and could unscrew a sink pipe and find your earring, no problem. Best of all, she'd be able to buy a home in New Mexico. A real home. An airy stucco pueblo, with multiple bedrooms, lots and lots of closets, a backyard, and perhaps even a garden. And she'd have a car! A silver Mini Cooper. A convertible, so she could enjoy the weather.

This reverie always came to a sobering end when she thought about what the same money would buy her in New York. A tiny one-bedroom (in Brooklyn) and a year's supply of MetroCards.

It was this city, she thought, staring mindlessly out the window. In New York, the chasm between the haves and the have-nots was too great to ignore, and you never knew when something would rise up and slap you in the face, reminding you that you were in the latter category and that was where you would forever stay. Sydney could still feel the sting of the smackdown she'd gotten last week. Her friend Mira had invited her to a party, and Sydney had jumped at the chance, not bothering to ask whose party it was. Married but not yet breeding, Mira was one of her "terminally ill" friends and they had precious little time left. (As a way of coping with the mass defection of her social circle, Sydney had begun to pretend, when someone got engaged, that she had contracted a terminal disease, and when she got pregnant she had—peacefully and painlessly, of course—died.)

After grabbing a quick bite at Extra Virgin, they'd taken advantage of the mild April weather and strolled leisurely through the West Village, catching up and joking like old times. The party turned out to be on West Street and, knowing by the address that the apartment inside the nondescript building would be huge and expensive (the Hudson River view alone cost a million dollars), Sydney braced herself.

Apartment envy was a quintessentially New York affliction, and though Sydney prided herself on managing to stay, for the most part, above the covetous fray, there were people she'd kill for their apartments if she knew she could get away with it. In the bizarro world of Manhattan real estate, she was supposed to feel grateful to be illegally subletting a vermin-free one-bedroom in the heart of the West Village for the below-market price of $2,400 a month. And yes, her place was nice; she was comfortable there. But how was she supposed to appreciate its humble charms knowing that six blocks away there was a single woman, seven years her junior, living in an enormous loft that had a three-story window in the living room from which you could see all the way to New Jersey? Even though she'd tried to prepare herself, Sydney's knees almost buckled when she saw that window. It was like something inside a cathedral!!!

Mira was equally impressed, but she had no reason to be envious. She and Olaf, her nightclub impresario husband (asshole), owned a fabulous apartment of their own, as well as a summerhouse that had a pool and a tennis court. The party's hostess, a plainly pretty brunette dressed casually in jeans and cowboy boots, was a FOO (Friend of Olaf) about whom Mira had scant personal info, so Sydney decided a little detective work was in order.

They crept around, peeking into every bedroom and bathroom, speculating as to how she could afford such a place and why there was so little furniture (and nothing in the medicine cabinets). Maybe she was minimalist to the extreme, Sydney suggested. Definitely family money, they both agreed. When Olaf unexpectedly rolled in with his posse, a band of hipper-than-thou guys and their airhead model girlfriends who hung around him like a thick fog, it ruined what Sydney foolishly thought was a girls' night out. When he gave them the scoop on the party's hostess—she was the daughter of one of the richest women in America and the place was bare of furniture and medicinals because she actually lived in another apartment in the building—it ruined Sydney's *year.*

"So what is this place?" she asked, knowing the second the words left her mouth that she didn't want to hear the answer.

"Her spare," Olaf said.

Sydney left immediately, went straight to bed, and after tossing and turning all night, couldn't get up the next day till noon. Her spare? *Her motherfucking spare?* Sydney had no desire to be that rich. Every rich kid she'd ever known had been completely fucked in the head. She didn't even aspire to be average rich, but seeing that kind of obscene wealth up close made her life seem so small and insignificant. For the last month, she had been agonizing, *agonizing,* over whether she should waste three hundred dollars on a pair of fucking shoes! She compulsively saved her pennies, never splurging on herself unless she could write it off, and for what? To buy a tiny apartment that was the size of that spoiled bitch's linen closet?

She used to think that if she just had enough, she'd be happy. Enough money in the bank, a decent apartment, a little disposable income to go on a modest vacation or two a year. After reading a widely e-mailed *Times* story about $200,000 being the new $100,000, she had to ask herself what exactly constituted enough. Before she had finished grappling with that question, the paper of record ran a chilling piece about millionaires in Silicon Valley who didn't feel rich because they lived among people who had tens of millions. Before clicking to the second page, Sydney had to stop and pop a Xanax. The quest for "enough" was what got her out of bed every morning. It was what kept her going when she wanted to give away all of her worldly possessions and move to a tropical island and sell handmade trinkets on the beach. She didn't want to ponder the idea that "enough" was unattainable, that it was a constantly moving goal she might never reach. Because that would force her to confront the possibility that her entire life's course had been charted with a faulty compass. And why put herself through that when she could just self-medicate?

CHAPTER EIGHTEEN

From her perch on the leather settee outside Binky's, Liz craned her neck to scope out the escalator yet again. Still no sign of Sydney. She should have listened to Joyce, she thought. She should have just stayed out of it. *Too late now.*

There had been a few times when Sydney was supposed to meet her somewhere and then didn't show. No call, no nothing. "Oh, I forgot," she'd say, which might have been the truth. Sydney could be very spacey; she was completely disorganized and, most of the time, so focused on herself that everyone else existed in a distant haze. So instead of divulging the real reason they were meeting, Liz had lured her to lunch with the promise of a belated birthday gift. (The "it's better to give than receive" principle worked in reverse with Sydney.) To lessen the chances that Sydney would show up in those graffiti-printed sweats she loved, Liz asked to meet at Harvey's, the most upscale venue she could think of that would not arouse Sydney's suspicions. And knowing Sydney would be late, Liz told her to be there an hour before today's surprise guest was scheduled to arrive. After all that, Sydney was still late. And since she hadn't returned the text Liz had sent twenty minutes ago, she couldn't be sure if Sydney was coming at all.

Feeling her butt starting to go numb, Liz lifted herself from the settee and went into the ladies' room. (Only to wash her hands and check her lipstick. She didn't like to use public restrooms, even at an upscale place like Harvey's.) She'd been quite proud to have come up with what she thought was the perfect solution to this vexing conundrum Sydney had put her in. A solution that would both satisfy Joyce's well-communicated desire to "stay out of it" and hopefully help Sydney find some happiness as well. She, like everyone, deserved to be happy.

Although it really was odd, this sudden desire to settle down. Sydney had never talked about getting married, not as a girl, not as an adult, and when she turned thirty she wasn't bemoaning her single status. She told Liz she was upset because she hadn't yet accomplished anything professionally and she had to accept that no one would ever call her a wunderkind. (This was the kind of thing that would never in a million years cross Liz's mind.) Did this sudden urge to wed, she wondered, have to do with what had happened last month at their cousin Natalee's wedding?

Sydney was fond of telling people she didn't believe in weddings, which was her uniquely exasperating way of being contrarian and politicizing something that was, for everyone else, just a cause for celebration. She'd been a bridesmaid once when she was a teenager for their now ex-stepsister, and before the reception was over, Sydney had ditched her sea-green dress for jeans and sworn she'd never do it again. Since then she'd turned down every friend who'd asked her, but she said she was making an exception for Natalee because she really liked her. This made no sense—didn't she really like any of her friends?—but Liz had stopped trying to understand "Sydney logic" a long time ago.

At Nat's wedding, Sydney had been, in her words, "verbally assaulted" on the buffet line by the matron of honor, Cheryl, a woman Sydney had arbitrarily decided she disliked after their first brief meeting and thereafter cattily described as "a thirty-four-year-old mother of four with hips as wide as the Grand Canyon." Liz had been standing right beside Sydney when the alleged assault occurred, so she knew the true story, not the twisted tale Sydney began disseminating. Cheryl had simply said that after living with Chuck for seven years, Natalee should try to get pregnant right away. "Like on the honeymoon. Even if she succeeded in doing that, she won't give birth until she's, what, thirty-two? If she wants more than one kid, she's going to have to get pregnant again right away. At thirty-five everything bottoms out reproductively."

"I'm about to turn thirty-three," Sydney had said, "and I don't even have a boyfriend!"

In Sydney's account of what happened next, Cheryl looked over her shoulder and sneered, "I'm not talking about you, Sydney. I'm talking about Natalee and Chuck, people with traditional values. You'll probably get pregnant by some guy"—here Sydney would add, "Making it sound like that guy would be a bum I tripped over in the street!"—"decide you don't like him, kick him to the curb, and go off interviewing people with your baby strapped to your back." With a cutting look (according to Sydney), she added, "Assuming you even *want* kids." Then she walked away with her overloaded plate. When Liz pointed out that Cheryl was doing nothing more than stating biological facts, Sydney said, "I know. I just don't like the bitch." And the smear campaign began.

The only part of Sydney's version that Liz could wholeheartedly cosign was the overloaded plate. The sneer and the cutting look? She hadn't seen them. And while she couldn't remember the conversation verbatim, she doubted that Cheryl, a stay-at-home mother who lived in Dobbs Ferry, would use the phrase "kick him to the curb." As for the bum inference, Sydney may have been onto something there. Liz had assumed that Sydney would one day wind up with some random, inappropriate guy, and she imagined she wasn't the only one. Sydney dated the same guy again and again. Cute, young, starving artists. She claimed to be over that now, but a seven-year habit wasn't easy to break. More important, did she really want to break it? Sometimes Liz thought Sydney latched on to these boys as if they were stray cats just so she could complain incessantly about how useless they were—although they were obviously serving a very real purpose. With them, Sydney could have sex, companionship, and control without the threat of a serious commitment. Now all of a sudden she wanted to get married? She'd had a chance to marry a guy who had most, if not all, of the qualities she'd listed in her e-mail, and everyone knew how *that* had turned out.

As far as biological clocks went, Liz didn't think Sydney had one. She was wonderful with Ben and Caleigh—although she bought them too much "stuff" when all they really needed was her love and affection, both of which they got in heaps—but that was partly because Sydney was a big kid herself. (The last time Sydney babysat, Liz and Joyce had come home at eleven o'clock to find Ben, whose bedtime was eight, painting her toenails. Sydney's excuse? "He wanted to!") Her free-spiritedness made her a fun aunt, but would it make her a good mother?

Sydney had gone to great lengths to prove she wasn't anything like their mother, but where did Sydney think she'd learned to always put herself first? Sydney was proud that she didn't have the need to please, what she called "the woman's disease," and Liz supposed that was helpful when it came to a career. But being married and being a mom was about sacrifice. She wasn't saying Sydney would make an unfit parent, certainly not compared to the monsters who beat and starved their children or worse. It was just that Sydney had so much hostility toward their mother, she had never felt mothered herself. Having a child was bound to bring up a lot of unresolved issues. Liz prayed that Sydney had been discussing these issues with Dr. Liessel, but knowing Sydney, she was probably going just for the pharmaceuticals.

Sydney openly scorned their mother for choosing "trophy wife" as a career, but she would never admit that she felt similarly contemptuous of Liz for being "just" a mom because it didn't align with her pro-woman image. Still, Liz knew that in Sydney's mind, a housewife was, as she'd said last week, "an indentured servant," a person to be reviled. A successful career woman like Joyce, on the other hand, was someone to be revered. What would Sydney think if she knew her idol wanted nothing to do with her "bizarre man-quest," as Joyce was calling it?

And if Joyce found out Liz had gone to Vera for the money . . . oh boy. Vera was the last person she wanted to involve, but Joyce was so paranoid about identity theft that she combed the monthly credit card statements like a scientist looking for a new genome. And if Sydney found out their mother had financed the operation? God help them all!

But how could Liz turn her back on Sydney after she'd made a desperate cry for help? If she did, this huge step forward might turn into two steps back. Sydney might never open herself up to anyone ever again. Her little bubble would close in tighter and tighter until she . . .

Liz finished wiping her damp hands and reapplied her lipstick. She didn't even want to think about it.

CHAPTER NINETEEN

Returning from his late-afternoon candy run, Max came upon quite a scene unfolding in front of the store. A little boy who looked to be four or five was trapped in the revolving door. Cute kid. He was jumping around, pressing his face against the glass, laughing . . .

His mother was freaking the fuck out. "He's suffocating! He can't breathe! DO SOMETHING!"

Tony was doing something, Max thought. He was trying to free the kid. Now here were two maintenance guys rushing out with tools in hand to join the rescue effort.

The added manpower did nothing to quell the mother's panic. "Danvers," she wailed frantically. "Danvers, Mommy's here. *Mommy's here, honey!*"

Danvers? Max thought. Now he felt bad for the kid. He stepped back to the curb as onlookers gathered to rubberneck and reached into the small bag of chocolate-covered almonds in his coat pocket. After noticing his energy took a sharp dip every day around four, he'd made a habit of visiting Bloomingdale's candy shoppe. The fresh air and sugar fix did him good, as did the rush he got from sneaking in and out of the store like a thief. Although Avery had, on occasion, sent Remy into Bloomingdale's as a spy, she wouldn't be caught dead behind enemy lines. To her, the retail business was a war, and the Big Three—Bloomingdale's, Bergdorf's, Saks—were her enemies. If that was what Avery needed to tell herself to keep her competitive juices flowing, more power to her. Max didn't think it was that serious, al-

though he knew if word got back to Avery that he'd been spotted in an enemy camp (purchasing something!), he'd never hear the end of it. To conceal
his subterfuge, he always refused the store's telltale brown paper bag, choosing to carry his goodies in plain plastic. But he was evidently harboring
more deep-seated guilt than he knew because he instinctively pushed the
unidentifiable bag farther into his pocket when Polly Jin, the head of PR,
and her annoying assistant, Reginald, darted out of the store.

A sexy Eurasian with a smoking bod, Polly looked at Max . . . the
mother . . . the boy. And gasped. Her instinct was to go to the mother immediately, but she took the time to give Max the "What a useless fuck" look
Avery had perfected after many years of practice.

Max cocked his head, hitting her with the smirk he'd perfected in response to this look: *What would you like me to do, Polly?*

She turned and put her arm around the mother, something that hadn't
occurred to Max. Okay, well yeah, he thought. There was *that.*

"Don't worry, ma'am," she said soothingly. "We're doing everything we
can."

Jesus, Max thought. *This really is turning into an episode of* Grey's Anat-
omy. He wanted to go back upstairs, but he knew Polly would flip. And she'd
tell Avery. These humorless bitches were driving him nuts! Avery, Norma,
Polly . . . even Remy's effervescence was beginning to go flat under the added
workaday strain. What tight-ass Polly really needed was a good fuck, and
Max was in the mind to give her one. (But then he'd be shitting where he ate,
and he wasn't that reckless.)

As if he wasn't annoyed enough, Reginald sidled up to him. A twenty-
something, overly styled suck-up who wore shiny new pennies in his loafers (to
be ironic?), he was such a complete weirdo that he *wanted* people to call him
Reginald instead of Reggie. On an ordinary day, he was a jangle of nerves.
This minor crisis had him looking as if he was tweaking on meth. "Has this
ever happened before?" he asked, pushing his chunky black glasses (that were
currently in vogue but didn't work on him) up the bridge of his oily nose.

Max shrugged. "Not that I know of." He reached into his pocket for
another almond. "You really think he could suffocate in there?"

Max thought it was a legitimate question. The PR team did not agree.
Polly shot him daggers and Reginald rocked up on his toes as if Max had
just grabbed his ass, yelping, "Well, we don't want to find out!"

. . .

What a useless prick, Sydney thought, yanking the door handle to no avail. As a New Yorker, she expected rudeness on some level, but when a doorman could not get the door for a woman who plainly needed the door to be gotten, it was a blatant shirking of responsibility she found difficult to swallow.

Abdullah tried popping the lock. That only made the situation worse. Sydney continued to yank unsuccessfully and the asshole just stood there, watching, as if her struggle with the door was none of his business!

The door finally opened, and she was halfway out with her coat slipping off, her gigantic purse hanging in the crook of her arm, and the shopping bag that held four light sabers she'd gotten for Ben banging against her calves when the guy finally offered his assistance. As if she needed him *now?*

Fully out on the sidewalk, she took a moment to pull herself together, and their eyes met for a beat that lasted too long, an egregious visual breach of her perimeter that felt like a molestation. He seemed to be inappropriately close as she headed toward the door, forcing her to walk on a slight diagonal to create some personal space. My God, was he *sniffing* her?

A small group of people by the front door began to disperse, some going into the store, others walking away, and Sydney noticed a woman on her knees hugging a small child, like some bizarre nativity scene. Hovering over them was the cute Spanish doorman she usually saw here, blotting sweat from his brow with a handkerchief.

"There was a kid," she heard someone say. She turned and there was The Sniffer, all up in her grill. Since the regular doorman was on duty, she wondered if this misfit, whose sloppy attire seemed a perfect complement to his lack of professionalism, was a trainee. "There was a kid stuck in the revolving door," he said.

Sydney looked back at the mother with sympathy. She had once "misplaced" Ben at the Times Square multiplex when she'd taken him to see *Shrek.* Scariest four minutes of her life. (Liz never knew. Sydney plied him with soda and popcorn in exchange for his silence.) It was not a moment she wanted to relive, so she was happy to have her attention diverted by the extended blare of a car horn. Catching a sidelong glimpse of yellow, she did a split-second check of all her possessions. She had a constant fear that she'd leave something important in the back of a cab. Somehow she knew she would never be one of those people you see in the newspaper hugging the honest cabbie who found their priceless clarinet or what have you and turned it in to dispatch, asking nothing in return.

She turned to find that it *was* Abdullah blaring . . . but not at her. He was trying to alert the doorman-in-training, who'd left the back door wide open. After he hurried over and slammed it shut, the cab zoomed off, and Sydney noticed the rubber band wrapped around her pinkie. Fuck! Another ten dollars—twelve, actually—she was going to have to eat.

As the doofus of a doorman led the way to the door, Sydney's eyes fell on the cute royal-blue Adidas he was wearing. This obvious flouting of regulation made her wonder if this person was even affiliated with the store, and she glanced into her unzipped purse to make sure she was still in possession of her wallet. She'd heard about a scam like this on *Dateline!*

When she glanced back up, he had his hand on the door's thick glass handle, but instead of pulling, he had the nerve to say, "Haven't we met?"

Sydney was on the verge of saying, "Move." Instead, she just shook her head.

"You look very familiar," he insisted. He closed his eyes and tapped his temple. "Isn't your name . . . ?"

Oh God, Sydney thought. *The ole "You look familiar; isn't your name fill in the blank" line? How original.* She stayed silent, expecting he would open the door anyway. When he stood there waiting for an answer as if he was entitled to one, Sydney had to give him credit for boldness. What he didn't seem to realize was that in blatantly overstepping his boundaries one time too many, he had escalated what was, in Sydney's mind, merely an annoying encounter into a full-on confrontation. He wanted a response? *Great,* Sydney thought and gave him one: a condescending look that said, *Know your place.*

Undeterred, the brash trainee smiled at her in a manner that was openly flirtatious, causing an unexpected ripple of battle fatigue to skip over her usually impenetrable surface. Men could do and say anything they wanted to you, she thought, a sense of helplessness washing over her anger. And ultimately, what recourse did women have? Every day she had to endure being repeatedly leered and jeered at when all she wanted was to get to the gym or the drugstore to get her Xanax. She was powerless to prevent random street harassment, something that infuriated her to no end, but at Harvey's she ought to be safe!

"Isn't my name . . ." She trailed off, drawing her harrasser forward in anticipation. Then she smiled, allowing him to think his lame come-on was working. "None of your business? Yes, as a matter of fact, it is."

Since he was obviously incapable of doing the one simple task he was being paid (or trained) to do, Sydney pulled the heavy door open herself, and watching his face crumble, she walked inside, power reclaimed, with a smile coming up on hers.

CHAPTER TWENTY

Sydney downed her espresso in one shot and looked at the book Liz had placed on the table. "'Don't Be a . . .'" Reading the fourth word of the title, her head jerked up. "What is this . . . a gag gift?"

Couldn't be, she thought immediately. Liz had no sense of humor.

"It's a bestseller," Liz said with a level of enthusiasm that rivaled Sydney's annoyance. "But that's only the first part."

"First part of what?"

"The gift."

"Honey, this is no part," Sydney said. "Because this"—she slapped her palm on top of the book, which bore the off-putting (to put it mildly) title *Don't Be a Spinster: 101 Ways to Snag a Husband in Less Than a Year,* and sent it careening back toward Liz—"does not qualify as a gift." Talk about cheap! "But we can go down to the shoe department and I'll show you what does."

"Sydney, this isn't the real gift," Liz said, coyly adding, "it's a prelude to the gift."

Sydney pulled her jacket from the back of her chair and grasped the handles of her bag, preparing for departure. Since the "real gift" obviously had some tangential relationship to the offensively titled book, it was safe to say she wouldn't want that either. The best part of having Liz for a sister (and Joyce as a sister-in-law) was that they always gifted her with high-priced luxury items that she'd never buy herself. What happened to that tradition?

"Wait a second," Liz said. Sydney looked at her, but her body was facing the door. "The woman who wrote this? Her name is Mitzi Berman. She's a professional matchmaker. The *Times* did a huge story on her last weekend!"

Sydney played dumb. "And that pertains to me how?"

"She can help you," Liz said. "She has a ninety-eight point seven percent success rate!"

"Good for her," Sydney said, annoyed for many reasons, but at this particular moment because Liz was making it sound as though she had some rare disorder and this matchmaker was a doctor willing to give her an experimental, possibly lifesaving treatment. "But I don't need the help of a professional matchmaker. I'm not desperate."

"Sydney," Liz said, sounding as if she was the injured party. "I'm not saying that."

"What happened to you and Joyce fixing me up?"

"I thought this would be better."

"Sure," Sydney said. "For you and Joyce!"

"For you too."

"So Joyce *did* put you up to this?" Sydney cleared her throat to flush out the wounded quiver she heard creeping into her voice. "You two are so embarrassed to set me up with someone you know that you pawn me off on a professional. Is that it?"

"No, no," Liz said. "That's not it at all. It's just that . . ."

"Well, I'm sorry I asked." Sydney hitched her bag over her shoulder. "Trust me, it won't happen again."

"Sydney," Liz said. "Why are you so angry? You said you wanted to get married!"

"So what?" Sydney's head darted toward Liz as if she were a bird trying to peck her. "I say a lot of shit I don't mean! You of all people should know that!"

Liz glanced around at the well-heeled patrons, then spoke in her "Please don't make a scene" voice. "So you don't want to get married?"

"No," Sydney said quickly. "I mean . . . yes. I mean . . ." She stopped and tried to calm herself. *Breathe, girl. Breathe.*

Yes, she had told Liz she wanted to settle down, and she did. She had to before her eggs dried up. It wasn't a choice—it was a biological mandate! But she thought she'd go out on a few bad dates, ease into it. Saying you wanted to get married was one thing. Letting a professional matchmaker who supposedly had a 98.7 percent success rate fix you up with a man who might want you to be his wife and the mother of his children and move to the suburbs and drive a Volvo and sacrifice all your personal hopes and dreams for the good of the family was quite another! It was the difference between saying you wanted to bungee jump and looking down at a two-hundred-foot drop with a harness strapped to your back. *She had to get ready first!*

Sydney took another deep inhale and blew the breath out slowly. "I didn't expect you to go from zero to sixty in a week, okay?"

"Oh, I see." Liz reached across the table and placed her hand over Sydney's in a consoling gesture. "You're scared."

Sydney snatched her hand away. "No, Liz, I'm not. Are you?"

"Me?" Liz said. "Scared of what?"

"Scared that I'll get my shit together," Sydney said nastily. "Scared that I'll find someone and be happy. Scared that I'll have everything. A career and a family." Wearing a superior smile, Sydney fell back and draped her arm over the chair. "Who will you have to pity then, Lizzie? Who will you have to make you feel better about your empty little mommy life?"

"My life is not empty," Liz said with surprising composure. "And I'm the one who paid for you to meet with this matchmaker. So what are you even talking about?"

Sydney looked away, her cheeks burning with embarrassment, suddenly feeling as though she'd been stripped naked. She hated these out-of-body experiences, which she experienced almost exclusively in the company of Liz or her mother. (There were some buttons only immediate family members could push.) Even though she was the younger sister, she had always bullied Liz. On a few occasions, she went so far as to physically attack her. Of course, Lizzie, everyone's little darling, never fought back, which made Sydney feel like an evil puppy kicker. Sydney didn't mind being thought of as a bitch. She had a whole series of bitch-themed T-shirts, in fact. (Her favorite said, "You call me a bitch like that's a bad thing.") But compared to Liz, she felt like the devil. She minded that.

Sometimes she felt she played the troublemaker simply because, in her family, that was the role in which she'd been cast. One would have thought her relationship with Liz would have gotten better as they both matured, but in the last few years, as Liz became a stand-in for all the domesticated girlfriends Sydney had cut off out of spite, it had gotten considerably worse. Liz bore the brunt of Sydney's misdirected anger and contempt, and Sydney knew Liz had no idea where the hostility was coming from. Sydney would say the meanest things to her—the vitriol she'd just spewed rating about an 8 on a scale of 10—only realizing after the fact how awful and stupid she sounded. It was like that joke about the woman who goes to her psychiatrist, puzzling over a Freudian slip: "I was having breakfast with my husband this morning and I meant to say, 'Honey, please pass the butter.' Instead, I said, 'You've ruined my life, you fucking bastard!' What do you think that means?"

Sydney knew exactly what was fueling her hostility, yet she felt powerless to stop it. Guilty as she felt afterward, she rarely apologized for her "Freudian slips," choosing instead to pretend they never happened. And she didn't think something could be classified as a Freudian slip if it was, like, eight sentences and punctuated by a surly smile.

"Liz," she said quietly. A simple "I'm sorry" would have sufficed, but Sydney took a moment to craft a more elaborate apology and, in doing so, got sidetracked. "Wait, did you say you paid this woman?"

Ignoring the question, Liz slid the book back toward Sydney. "Read it or don't read it. I don't care. It's yours."

"Answer me."

Liz raised her cup and whispered into it. "Yes."

"How much?"

"Does it matter?"

"To me, yes."

"It's a gift. You can't tell someone how much you paid for a gift."

"You can and you will." To show her she meant business, Sydney stuck one arm in the sleeve of her coat.

"You can't keep running away from things," Liz said.

Sydney stuck her arm in the other sleeve. That was the second time in as many weeks that Liz had tried to "go there." There was a reason The Incident of Which They Dared Not Speak was called The Incident of Which They Dared Not Speak!

"Okay, okay," Liz said. "A thousand."

Sydney sucked in a horrified breath. "Dollars?" That could have bought her the new Balenciaga! "What are you, my pimp now?" Seized by another

Tourettic spasm, she went all *Pretty Woman* on Liz. "I say who, I say when, I say . . ." The sight of two women, one of whom looked familiar, staring from the next table abruptly halted the tic. She leaned across the table and snapped, "Looks like you're out a thousand bucks, then, sweetie. Because I am never, ever going to meet with that woman."

"That's fine," Liz said, looking over Sydney's shoulder. "She's here to meet you."

CHAPTER TWENTY-ONE

A big-breasted munchkin of a woman wearing a knit skirt suit in an eye-catching coral hue, Mitzi Berman beelined through Binky's with her torso slightly bent forward as if she was about to use her upper body as a battering ram. Given the heavy scent of her *parfum*, the clanking of her oversized gold jewelry, and the volume at which she greeted the waitstaff, Sydney was surprised she hadn't detected her presence sooner. Sydney vaguely remembered seeing her on the cover of a *Times Magazine* that had been discarded at Cafeteria, dressed like a fairy godmother and floating over the headline "The New Arranged Marriage," but the full live-action spectacle that was Mitzi Berman was truly a sight to behold.

"Never fear" were her first words when she reached the table. "Your fairy godmother is here." Sydney took that to be some sort of joke, but then Mitzi explained, "My guys call me 'Bewitched.' I twitch my nose and she appears." Sydney's head swiveled from Mitzi to Liz and back to Mitzi. Was this woman for real?

Liz immediately went into hostess mode while Sydney, still wearing her coat, crossed her arms over her chest in an act of nonverbal dissent and arranged her features into an expression that clearly telegraphed boredom. She'd stay and listen, but she couldn't promise much more than that. Which worked out perfectly because Mitzi did all the talking.

"My clients are educated, attractive, fit, professional men who are looking to be in a serious committed relationship that will ultimately lead to marriage. I'm not a dating service. I'm a matchmaker. I get people married."

And with just a twitch of the nose, Sydney thought, looking around the restaurant for something more interesting to focus on.

"Streets, airports, trains, I can pick up men anywhere. That's why I got into this business. Because every man I ever dated, I picked up. Including my husband, may he rest in peace. Twenty-six years we were married." A (very) brief moment of silence. "Check for a band, then start a conversation. You see a cute guy trying to hail a cab, say, 'Wanna share?' You have no idea how many hot guys I've gotten into cabs with. Even when I wasn't going in the same direction."

Sydney almost said, "Lucky none of them hacked you to bits."

"My success rate speaks for itself. I'm currently running at ninety-eight point seven percent. I've gotten over eight hundred men married, I have a thousand in committed relationships, and I currently have fifteen men smitten!"

Exaggerate much? Sydney thought, yawning openly.

"I'm riding such a wave right now that it's like, Whoa. It's raining men! I'm inundated! Awesome, awesome guys. I can't even tell you."

Sydney hoped her smirk conveyed what she was thinking. *Apparently, you can.*

"Unlike women, men know what they want. I stopped working with female clients. They're too high-maintenance. Needy!"

Translation: The men do the choosing. The women wait to be chosen.

"But if you're a hot woman and you're looking? You need to find me. Like, yesterday! The biggest group of women I have are just like you."

Ha!

"Between thirty and thirty-five. Gorgeous, smart, successful. Awesome."

Sydney uncrossed her legs and slid into a position more appropriate for watching *Monday Night Football*, thinking, *So awesome they need you, huh?*

" 'What's wrong with you? Are you desperate? You go to a matchmaker?' That's what people think at first."

And at second and third.

"But where you gonna meet men? Sitting on a bar stool like a desperado? I don't think so. Get friends, amateurs, to fix you up and you know what they're thinking? Well, he has a pulse, she needs a date . . . And forget about online! Little boys in a candy store, that's all that is. And thirty percent of them are married!"

Sydney sat up straight, shaken by the image "sitting on a bar stool like a desperado" had conjured. It was true that getting "amateurs" to fix you up was hit or miss. (That earned Liz a bitchy look.) And, aside from the 30 percent being completely unverifiable, it was also true that online dating was for losers. Maybe this woman wasn't totally crazy.

"Now if I set you up, it's a potential husband. *Paging Vera Wang!*"

Strike that, Sydney thought. This old bat was certifiable. She wished Mitzi would just shut up, but every time Sydney reached for her bag, thinking she was winding down, Mitzi just kept talking and talking like some kind of broken Chatty Cathy doll.

Mitzi on attracting a man: "Men are intimidated by beautiful women. Blondes especially. You have to send off the right energy. Approachable. It's like a taxi. How do you know it's available? The light is on."

Mitzi on seizing the moment: "How many times have you been somewhere and you smile at a cute guy, he smiles back, and then nothing. What are you waiting for? That could be your effin' husband!"

Mitzi on what men want: "Women want intelligence, a sense of humor, dependability . . . you know, a guy who calls when he says he's gonna call. What do men want? Looks. But I'll tell you something, twelve years ago when I first got into this business, all guys wanted was a pretty face. Now they want to be intellectually stimulated too."

Mitzi on the marriage timetable: "You should be on your way to knowing in three months and by six you should be shopping for a ring. I met a woman who was with a guy five years. No ring. FIVE YEARS! I said, 'Whaddaya think, in seven he's down the aisle?' Four days later she broke up with him. That's right! I *empowered* her to get out of the relationship."

Mitzi on chemistry: "Chemistry is that intangible. That 'ya never know.' Playful banter. I went out on a simulated with this one guy, boring as a bowl of lukewarm milk. Set him up with an awesome girl and bing, bam, boom . . . fireworks like the Fourth of July. They're married now. Two kids."

"FYI, I need to be somewhere at six," Sydney lied to hurry things along, and finally, after close to an hour of jabbering, Mitzi got down to the specifics of how her shady operation worked. "The guys get twelve dates over twelve months, but usually by the third introduction"—she made a Trumpian "You're fired" hand motion—"they're done."

"Like a twelve-date package," Sydney said, thinking this was way worse than trolling online. At least dating sites were democratic. This was some straight-up concubine shit! "Very romantic. And how much does that cost?"

Mitzi's response? "I talk now. You talk later." Then she continued with her spiel. "I go on simulated dates with all prospective clients. I do home visits. I spend weekends with them. They take me shopping. Because what they buy me is what they'll buy you. I mean, I know I give great date. But do they?"

Okay, that's funny, Sydney thought. *In a headlining-at-the-Tropicana kind of way.*

"Prices have gone up drastically because I'm being much more selective. I'm into a whole different level of man. High-net-worth individuals."

Here we go, Sydney thought. *The moment of truth.*

"You think a guy like that needs help getting a date? They come to me because it's potential wives they're seeking."

Seeking, buying. Same thing, right?

"If you think a man's gonna pay fifty grand just to jump in the sack, think again!"

Sydney's mouth plopped open. FIFTY THOUSAND DOLLARS? Holy mother of God, this *was* a call-girl operation!

"Where are you going?" Mitzi said when Sydney scrambled out of her chair, hurrying to get out of there before she got caught in a raid. "We're not done."

"Oh yes," Sydney said, rummaging through her bag for her iPod so she could go cruising through the store and ignore the salespeople. "We sure enough are."

Mitzi took a sip of tea and began chatting with Liz. "You didn't tell me she was a hostile participant."

"I didn't think she would be."

"No biggie," Mitzi said. "I get a lot of those."

"You do?"

Annoyed that they were talking about her as if she wasn't there, Sydney stood over the table with headphones the size of earmuffs clamped around her head, waiting to hear the answer before she hit Play.

"Sure." Mitzi waved for the waiter to refill her cup, deliberately avoiding eye contact with Sydney. "I have fathers, mothers, sisters, brothers some-times, dragging women into my office kicking and screaming all the time. But since she was already here, I thought . . ."

"I tricked her," Liz said.

"Yeah, I could tell something wasn't kosher." She dipped a fresh tea bag. "Very funky energy." Mitzi sat back to let the waiter pour the water, speak-ing to Liz through the cloud of steam rising from her cup. "So I guess you didn't have her read my book."

"I dropped the ball on that," Liz said.

"And if anyone ever needed to read it . . ." Mitzi gave Liz a sympathetic look. "But the fee is nonrefundable. You are aware of that?"

Liz looked up pleadingly at Sydney, who said, "I heard her." She sat down and slid the headphones onto the back of her neck. If this broad was going to talk shit about her, she could do it to her face.

Ignoring Sydney, Mitzi dunked her tea bag, smiling at Liz. "I get a good vibe from you. What's your situation? I don't see a ring."

"I'm not wearing it today," Liz said.

"So you're married?"

Liz gave her standard answer to that question. "I'm in a long-term com-mitted relationship."

People usually accepted that, but unsurprisingly, Mitzi didn't. "What does that mean?"

"It means I'm gay."

Not missing a beat, Mitzi asked, "Kids?"

Liz smiled. "Two."

Mitzi smiled back. "Mazel tov."

"Did you hear me when I said I have to be somewhere at six?" Sydney said, falling back on her lie to break up their lovefest. "How long is this go-ing to take?"

When Mitzi finally acknowledged Sydney's presence with a satisfied smile, Sydney realized she'd been played. Without saying a word to her di-rectly, Mitzi had reeled her back in, using the kind of subtle manipulation that was Sydney's bread and butter. Sydney returned the smile, game recog-nizing game. "I'm listening."

"So is that how you dress on a date?" Mitzi said, setting her tea bag on the saucer.

Sydney glanced down at her cashmere V-neck and holey vintage Levi's, the newly termed "boyfriend jeans" that she'd been rocking way before Katie Holmes (hated) and Vicky Beckham (loved) made them trendy. Just to needle Dame Edna, she answered, "Perhaps I'd wear jeans without holes."

"Perhaps? Nuh-uh." Mitzi forcefully shook her head, and one of her clip-on earrings popped off. (Sydney thought the wig might go too.) "Men want two things. Sexy and feminine." Taking her earring from the young waiter, she dropped her voice to a coquettish purr. "Thank you." She snapped it back on and nodded at a nearby table, her voice recovering its grating rasp. "And sexy is not that."

Sydney turned and saw a tarted-up woman whose bursting cleavage was being eyed hungrily by a man old enough to be her grandfather.

"That is the antithesis of sexy," Mitzi said. "You don't advertise and flaunt. You accentuate." She stared at the woman as if she was nothing more than an overinflated cautionary tale. "Believe you me, he's not marrying that. He's whatevering with that."

Whatevering? Sydney laughed out loud. This woman was, without question, a kook, but if the *Times Magazine* had done a cover story on her, she had to be doing something right. As they said, there was a fine line between brilliance and insanity. Sydney was never going to become one of Madam Mitzi's "girls," but with the intention of gleaning some helpful man-catching hints from her, she made a conscious decision to play nice. "I don't know, Mitzi," she said easily. "I never really considered myself to be very sexy or feminine."

"You think I needed that news flash?" Mitzi barked. "You're wearing an army jacket and combat boots. You look like you're shipping out to Iraq!"

The good favor Mitzi had earned flew out the window in an instant. "This jacket is Chloé and these boots are Prada!"

Without batting a false eyelash, Mitzi shot back, "So?"

You big-tittied old cow, Sydney thought, glancing down at her distressed leather boots. She'd gotten them at the Harvey's warehouse sale for seventy-five dollars! She'd stolen the coat from a *Cachet* photo shoot. They were two of her best scores! She wore them with pride!

"So . . . so I have my own unique personal style, Mitzi!" she said, spitting out the name like an epithet. "I'm hip. I'm stylish. People stop me on the street to ask me where I get my clothes, okay? I'll also have you know that I get a biweekly mani-pedi . . . in the summer. I wax. And, on occasion, I wear lacy lingerie. But I don't do 'sexy and feminine.' It's just not who I am. Got it?" Watching Mitzi drum her coral nails on the table, looking like she had just sucked hard on a lemon, Sydney took the edge out of her voice. She would not let this woman get the best of her! "I'm part fashionista and part feminist, you know? I'm what you might call . . . a feminista!"

"No, you're what I might call alone," Mitzi said, unmoved. "And if you want to change that, listen and learn."

Oh no she din't! Sydney turned to Liz, foolishly expecting sympathy. Liz was smiling from ear to ear.

"For dates one through three, no pants—"

"No pants?" All she ever wore were pants! "Not even a really cute trouser jean?"

"Listen," Mitzi huffed, frowning so hard her penciled eyebrows were practically touching. "These men are at the office all day around women who dress like men. So for dates one through three, no pants of any kind! Dress like a woman! That means a skirt that shows your legs, heels, makeup."

Skirt. Heels. Makeup. Each word felt like a white glove slapping Sydney across the face.

"And for God's sake, get your hair blown out. Ponytails make me crazy!" Her eyes flicked up. "I don't know what that bird's nest is you have on the top of your head!"

Sydney put her hand up to her postworkout bun. "I just came from the gym!"

"You never know when you're gonna bump into Mr. Right. Always be prepared!"

Sydney glared at her, so angry she was shaking. Who was this stupid woman to tell her anything? There was nothing wrong with how she dressed or who she was. Nothing! Any man would be lucky to have her! She could feel her chest heaving up and down, her nostrils flaring, and she was pissed that this woman could see she was pissed. Why should she have to get all sexed up to get a man? Fuck what men wanted! What about what she wanted? She was restraining herself for Liz's sake, but on second thought, why should she? Liz was the one who'd sicced this bitch on her. If she could tell Mitzi off and embarrass Liz in the process, all the better!

"Let me tell you something, lady," Sydney snarled, the decision to let loose turning her anger into pure adrenaline. Liz would disengage at the first sign of conflict, never giving Sydney what she desperately wanted. A fight! But this old bat was beckoning her into the ring. *You wanna rumble?* Sydney thought. *Bring it!*

And Mitzi did just that. "Let me guess," she said, interrupting before Sydney could get off her opening salvo. Gripping the edges of the table, she slowly pushed her heavily made-up face forward until she was so close Sydney could smell her musty old-lady breath. "You don't need me. Right?"

Sydney leaned away, smirking. She was annoyed that the words had been taken out of her mouth, but, yeah, that was the gist of it. *Now what, bitch?*

"You're too hip and cool and stylish for this," Mitzi said. "You're above it."

Sydney gave a haughty shrug. Correct again!

"Well, let me tell *you* something, girlfriend," Mitzi said, regarding Sydney with a creepy expression that was half smile, half sneer. "Having someone to love, cry with, talk to, share your life with, and grow old with? That's cool. That's hip. That never goes out of style."

Sydney instinctively opened her mouth to fire back, but no sound came out. She noticed an uncomfortable sensation swirling in her chest and then a strange wetness forming around her bottom lashes. Tears? She gulped hard and quickly swiped under her eye, flummoxed. She hadn't cried publicly since September 11, 2001, and that was only because she felt pressured to! First Liz, now her own body was betraying her?

"You think your shit doesn't stink?" Mitzi continued to heckle. "You think you're so unique?"

She let out a scoffing little laugh, and Sydney wanted to scream, "SHUT UP! SHUT UP! SHUT UP!" She wanted to claw her eyes out. She wanted to do something, anything. Fight back! But she had to remain perfectly still. One false move and she was going to blow.

"Well, I hate to break it to you, my darling," Mitzi said, pausing to dab her napkin at the corners of her coral mouth. "But I see your type every day. And I'll tell you what I tell all the rest." She dropped the napkin on the table, then, leaning close, delivered the knockout punch in a chilling whisper: "Lose the attitude, put a smile on that pretty face, and call me when you're forty and single."

ACT TWO

It is easier to live through someone else
than to become complete yourself.

—BETTY FRIEDAN

CHAPTER TWENTY-TWO

The Omnimedia building was forty-eight floors of steel and glass that stood on the corner of Forty-second and Broadway in the heart of Times Square. With the exception of the law firm on the forty-second floor, the offices were occupied by the magazines owned by Omnimedia, Inc., the largest publishing conglomerate in the world, and the building was a hotbed of media gossip. At almost any time of day, itty-bitty fashion editors could be seen puffing away outside, sporting stilettos and bare legs, even in the winter, and later the same painfully chic style mavens could be heard in the bathrooms regurgitating the food they'd consumed in the Frank Gehry–designed cafeteria. This despite the fact that an award-winning guest chef was brought in every week by *Dish* magazine, and on the whole the Omnimedia cafeteria served food as good as, if not better than, most restaurants'. Cuisine from almost any part of the world was available, but one thing was not. Garlic. The legend was that Mo Gubelman, Omnimedia's decrepit and rarely seen chairman, despised garlic, which was why many jokingly referred to him as The Vampire.

Sydney started out at Omnimedia as a temp. Two weeks after her twenty-eighth birthday, she registered with Omnimedia's in-house agency because she had gotten it into her head that she should be a writer. (One of the few careers she had not tried on for size.) A writer *of what* she didn't know, but she thought Omnimedia was the best place to find out. She bounced around at several of their twenty-five titles—*Dish, Sports Weekly,* and *Teen Gurl!*—and talked her way into writing a few sidebars (without attribution) before landing a three-month assignment at *Cachet,* the holy grail of celebrity magazines. Going in, all she knew was that she'd be assisting the magazine's executive editor, Myrna Bell.

All of five feet tall and as frail as an A-list actress, Myrna wore her short muddy-brown hair in a wet slick that made her look like Gordon Gekko breaking through the surface of a pool. Sydney was one of the few who knew why she refused to deviate from this unflattering, unfeminine do. She had a bald spot at the back of her head, and this was the only sure way to hide it. It was the female version of a comb-over.

Although she wore standard-issue power suits, Myrna always looked disheveled, even at seven A.M. when she arrived at work two hours before everyone else. Anyone with a working sense of smell could detect the stench of Marlboro Reds that engulfed her, but in a futile attempt to mask the lingering effects of her nicotine addiction, she doused herself in sickly sweet perfume, popped Altoids like M&Ms, and sprayed her office with Neutra Air after every chain-smoke.

The higher-ups respected and valued Myrna, a perfectionist who would move mountains to fix whatever seemingly insurmountable problem arose. By everyone else she was despised. Some even believed her former long-suffering assistant, Christy, had been sent into premature labor by one of Myrna's vituperative tirades. "Swear to God, Christy fell to the floor in Myrna's office and Myrna stood over her screaming, 'Get the fuck up! Get the fuck up!'" Elena, the office gossip, had said. "They took her out on a stretcher. It was vile."

Having encountered her fair share of bad bosses, Sydney had learned, through trial and error, the best way to deal with them: Get your work done and agree with everything they said, no matter how stupid or illogical. "Yes, Myrna" became her mantra. She felt like a geisha, but knowing that if she got on the wrong side of Myrna Bell she'd be banished from the Omnimedia universe, where she hoped to parlay her temp job into something bigger and better, she decided that was the best way to play it.

Seeing Myrna every morning, her sallow complexion perked up with just enough rouge to keep her from looking like a corpse, was, for Sydney, like seeing the ghost of her future. The woman was pitiful. Forty-something, divorced, childless, dateless, friendless, and always so frazzled she seemed to be one bad day away from hospitalization. She was a jarring daily reminder that Sydney needed to get her shit together and she needed to get her shit together fast. Every other assistant at the magazine was fresh out of college. (And they were full-time employees with health benefits.) At the rate Sydney was going, she would still be a temp at forty, the mere idea of which made her want to slit her wrists. In New York, "What do you do?" passed for "Hello." If she wanted to be able to honestly say, "I'm a writer," she needed to get a move on because writing a few sidebars wasn't cutting it.

Who would have guessed that her big break would come in the form of . . . a big break? One of the regular contributors, a ditz with connections named Andrea, called at five o'clock on Grammy night from the St. Vincent's ER, where she was waiting to have her banged-up arm examined after a bicycle mishap. There was no way she'd be able to cover the two afterparties she'd been assigned, she said. But she couldn't reach her assigning editor and she was terrified to tell Myrna, who she and Sydney both knew would not give a rat's ass about a possibly broken arm and a few bruises when she had next month's pages to fill.

"Don't worry," Sydney assured her. "I'll take care of it."

Without telling Myrna, she went to both parties in the same clothes she'd worn all day and gave Andrea's name to get past the PR brigade. It had always pissed her off that contributors like Andrea were paid five hundred dollars or more just to cover one celebrity party when she had to spend fifty hours a week trapped in Myrna's purgatory and she only made nine hundred a week before taxes. Especially since Andrea, who was known to be too lazy to use spell-check, only had to write up two hundred fifty words on each party. That was one freaking paragraph! How hard could that be?

Not very, as it turned out. Sydney and the photographer (a freelancer she wound up sleeping with for a few months) roamed like wolves, accosting as many celebrities as possible. Writing up the stories was a breeze. Sydney read *Cachet* front to back every month (mostly during Myrna's long, boozy lunches, which she looked forward to the way a coed anticipates spring break). Using party coverage from the previous month as a template, she wrote both stories in under an hour. She had them on Myrna's desk by eight the next morning.

Once Myrna said they were up to snuff, Sydney admitted that she'd written them. She told Myrna the whole story, casting herself as the hero ("I knew how crucial it was to have that coverage, Myrna") and hanging

Andrea out to dry by making her injuries sound less serious than they were ("She sprained her ankle or something").

At first, Myrna didn't know what to make of this peculiar turn of events. She trained her glassy eyes on Sydney and it was probably the first time in six months that Myrna had ever really *seen* her. Then, as if too much time had been wasted on such pettiness, she snapped, "Fill out a requisition form so you can get paid."

And Sydney's career as a celebrity journalist was born.

By the time her thirtieth birthday rolled around, she had been writing for *Cachet* for eighteen months but hadn't moved beyond doing party coverage—at the rate of a dollar per word while everyone else got two. She was still temping for Myrna as well because Christy, surprise surprise, never came back. She thought she was finally establishing herself in a career, but she was still just a glorified office temp. Now she was a thirty-year-old office temp.

She was so freaked out about the Big Three-Oh that she woke up on her birthday covered in hives. She was sharing a tiny shoebox of an apartment in the East Village with a girl she didn't particularly like, and the loft bed in her room was so close to the ceiling it was like sleeping in a coffin. She'd lain there that morning wondering how her life had gotten so off track and wishing she really was dead.

She'd grown up watching *Wonder Woman* and *Charlie's Angels*. She sat in the stands when Katie Himmel, her eleven-year-old classmate and the only girl playing in the Upper Westchester Little League, pitched a perfect game. After Mary Lou Retton stuck two perfect tens, she wanted to be a gymnast! After Sally Ride went into space she wanted to be an astronaut! Anything was possible! She would have a Career with a capital *C*, not a lowly job. Her work would be her passion, and since she'd be doing what she loved, naturally the money would follow. (It went without saying that this professional success would manifest by the ripe old age of thirty.)

Well, the problem with believing anything was possible, she very slowly came to understand, was that you ran the risk of never doing anything at all. Sometimes she thought, in a strange way, life was so much easier for people with no options. If you lived in some dead-end town, you got a job down at the mill, married someone you'd known all your life, pumped out a few kids, and called it a day. (At least that was how it happened in *Norma*

Rae.) You didn't sit around thinking, *I could have been a documentarian or a forensic psychologist or a sitcom writer . . .*

That was exactly what Sydney had wasted a decade doing, and at thirty she was still doing it. She spent the day in mourning, curled up on the lumpy futon in the living room watching a Julia Roberts marathon with a wad of one-ply toilet paper in her fist, all phone ringers turned off. When she heard her annoying roommate coming in, she crawled back into her coffin and cried. The only thing she had to celebrate was that her birthday had fallen on a Saturday so she had two days to wallow in peace.

By Monday, the depression had not lifted in the slightest and the hives were still slightly itchy. In no shape to deal with Myrna, she called in, praying to get voice mail.

Myrna picked up on the first ring. *"And?"* she snapped when Sydney told her about the hives. "Put on some cortisone cream and get in here ASAP!"

Sydney shuffled in at noon, looking godawful. Myrna, in her corner office having what was likely her tenth Marlboro Red of the day, greeted her thusly: "Where the *fuck* have you been?"

"I had to go to the drugstore and get the cortisone cream," Sydney told her. She also had popped some Claritin and fallen asleep for an hour when she got back.

Myrna took one last drag, stubbed her cigarette out in the ashtray, and pulled a can of Neutra Air from her bottom drawer, spraying three quick bursts over Sydney's head. "That took three hours?"

"No," Sydney said quickly so she could close her mouth and wait for the cloud of antiseptic mist to dissolve. She and Myrna played these little games of chicken a dozen times a day. Letting Myrna see she was bothered in the least would be an act of surrender. "But then I had to go home and actually put the cream on."

Myrna glanced at the ashtray, a silent rebuke to Sydney for not grabbing it. One of her menial duties was to keep Myrna's ashtrays spotless at all times (and hidden when not in use), a full-time job unto itself. In New York it was against the law to smoke in any public space, including office buildings, and since there was no shortage of staffers willing to drop a dime to the city's health department, Myrna was raided regularly by city inspectors, who issued citations if they saw so much as an ash. Since Sydney had been serving under her despotic regime, Myrna had amassed more than five thousand dollars in fines and she'd spent more in lawyer fees trying to fight them.

"Yeah, well, they were expecting you in Human Resources over an hour ago." Myrna took another cigarette out of her silver case. "I'd get the fuck up there if I were you."

"Human Resources?" Sydney said. That spelled trouble. "Why?"

Myrna blew two streams of smoke out of her nostrils like the dragon lady she was. "You'll see."

CHAPTER TWENTY-THREE

ucking Myrna, Sydney thought, stabbing the button for the elevator. After all the shit she'd taken, the bitch had up and turned on her!

Riding down from the thirty-seventh floor, she racked her brain trying to figure out what Myrna could have fingered her for. By the time she reached the fourteenth floor, she'd given up. It could have been anything. She and Myrna had found a rhythm in working together but, bottom line, Myrna was crazy. And crazy people did crazy things. Myrna was paranoid. She sought revenge for imagined slights. She shifted blame. She lied.

Sydney was expecting to speak to Laura, the head of Human Resources, who had interviewed her to become an in-house temp, but the receptionist on fourteen told her Laura no longer worked there. The woman directed her to the conference room, and as soon as Sydney got a glimpse through the glass walls, she started to feel itchy again.

Waiting for her were four very official-looking executives she had never seen before. It didn't take four people to fire a temp. Something was definitely up.

She entered slowly, braced for an inquisition, but each person seated around the table introduced themselves pleasantly. Too pleasantly. As if she was a foreign leader and they were meeting for peace talks.

A young assistant entered. "Water, coffee, tea?" she asked only Sydney, who was so weirded out she just said, "Yes" without specifying which one. The assistant kindly brought all three.

The only woman among the four spoke first. "Zamora," she said, awkwardly trying to break the ice. "That's a lovely name. What is the origin?"

"My father was Afro-Cuban," Sydney said, feeling an ignorant comment coming on.

"Aah," the woman said, doing an uncomfortable smile-and-nod. "I love Cuban food."

The man in the navy suit had the good sense to step in before she said anything else. He cleared his throat and began. "Myrna says . . ."

Oh God, Sydney thought. Why did anybody listen to her?! Was she the only one who could see that Myrna Bell was in dire need of psychiatric treatment and a thorazine IV drip? She didn't care if they fired her as Myrna's assistant, but she liked writing. She wouldn't go so far as to say she'd found her bliss, but she couldn't keep jumping from job to job. Love it or hate it, she had to make this work. No more fucking around.

Sydney mentally flipped through all the minor transgressions she'd committed while in the employ of Omnimedia, Inc.: Maybe they'd found out that she'd been borrowing things from the fashion closet? When she had to cover parties, she stayed late, swiped some designer duds (whatever she could squeeze into), and changed in the bathroom at the ESPN Zone next door. Then she'd come in early the next day to put the clothes back exactly where she'd found them. All right, so there were a few things she hadn't returned. But that was only because they'd gotten all smoky and she'd taken them to the cleaners! And, okay, maybe they were still in her closet, but she had every intention of bringing them back!

But what could they really do other than fire her? Garnish her wages? Charge her for theft? Not likely, but . . .

Oh no, she thought with a jolt. The requisition forms! How could she have been so stupid? She'd paid herself eight hundred dollars for a few stories when she should have gotten only five. Just a couple of times. Myrna never looked at those sheets. She just signed them. The money was there for the taking. Sydney didn't think anyone would notice. *It was a lousy three hundred dollars!*

They would definitely want the money back. And she'd get fired as Myrna's assistant. And she'd never be able to write for any of Omnimedia's other magazines!

". . . you are a very talented writer."

Sydney had forgotten the first part of the sentence, but hearing "you" in such close proximity to "very talented writer" startled her. *"What?"*

"Myrna says you are a very talented writer," Navy Suit repeated.

She must have blinked ten times, then, almost to herself, she murmured, "Myrna said that?"

"Yes," he said. "She seems to be very fond of you." He looked around. "And we know Myrna Bell is not fond of many people." They all shared a knowing chuckle at Myrna's expense, but Sydney's fear of Myrna ran so deep, she instinctively kept her expression blank.

Now she was really thrown. She was obviously not in trouble, but what would these people want with her? Her mind racing, she picked up only bits and pieces of what was being said.

"You will have the freedom of an independent contractor, but you will have all the perks of a salaried employee," Navy Suit was saying.

"Full health benefits," the woman chimed in. "Including dental!"

She thought they were offering her a full-time job as Myrna's assistant until the man in the polka-dot tie said, "You'll work from home."

"All your expenses will be reimbursed," Navy Suit assured her. "For work-related travel, you are guaranteed first-class tickets, when available, and four-star accommodations."

Work-related travel? Hadn't the other guy just said she'd work from home? And first-class tickets? To where? She had never even considered flying first class, it was so far outside the realm of possibility.

"Hold up," she said before they went any further. "I don't understand."

The man in black, who had not said anything so far, opened a folder that was on the table in front of him. There was something about him that was different from the others. It was like the game "What's wrong with this picture?" Him. He didn't belong. He was dressed better, slicker, and while the rest were overly friendly, he was the opposite, exuding a quiet but deadly vibe. He passed the document to Navy Suit but still did not speak.

"I'm sorry," Sydney said hesitantly. Looking at the man in black, she asked, "Do you work here?" The others had given their titles when they introduced themselves. He had not. Was he a cop?

"In the building, yes," he said crisply.

"At Omnimedia?"

"No," he said, failing to hide his annoyance that his cover had been blown. "I'm a lawyer."

"A lawyer," she mumbled, scratching her arm through her sweater. "At which firm?"

"Cromwell, Whitney, Harrison, Zinterhoffer, and LeBoeuf," he said, the name rolling off his tongue as effortlessly as his Social Security number.

A lawyer was just as bad as a cop, Sydney thought. Worse, maybe. And Cromwell, Whitney, Harrison, Zinterhoffer & LeBoeuf was the high-powered law firm on forty-two that handled Omnimedia's legal affairs. Why would one of their lawyers be here? Then again, why was she here? Why were any of them here? WHAT THE FUCK WAS GOING ON?

"They do all our contracts," Navy Suit said, reading the confounded expression on her face. He was obviously trying to regain control over the conversation, and he got her undivided attention when he said, "We're offering you a yearlong contract to write for *Cachet*." He handed her the document. It was a "deal memo" that already had her name printed in the place designated for "author." "Seventy-five thousand dollars per year. Guaranteed."

Sydney's eyes darted around the page, catching random legal jargon. *Pursuant. Perpetuity. Ancillary. Thereto.* She'd heard about these contracts. The perks were legendary. Every writer in New York—or anywhere—would kill to have one. Especially with *Cachet.* As far as she knew, they had only five contract writers, all guys in their forties and fifties who'd raped and pillaged their way to the top. The two words racing through her mind slipped out. "Why me?"

They all chuckled and exchanged looks, the way they had when referencing Myrna. Navy Suit folded his hands on the table. "Like I said, Myrna thinks you're a very talented writer." He chose his words carefully. "We all do. We'd be lucky to have you."

Something was wrong here, Sydney thought. Very, very wrong. Horns were going to sprout from this man's head any second. And there was probably a tail hanging out of the vent of his blazer. This was exactly how they got Keanu Reeves in *The Devil's Advocate*!

And wasn't that what large corporations were? Evil, soul-sucking entities? If the devil were roaming the earth he'd be a Fortune 500 CEO. Or maybe a lawyer at Cromwell, Whitney, Harrison, Zinterhoffer & LeBoeuf.

She was obviously about to enter into a Faustian bargain of some kind. There could be no other explanation for why this *contingent* had assembled to coax a temp with limited writing experience into signing a cushy, perk-laden contract to write for one of the most well-known publications in the country. Her eyes swept the room in search of hidden cameras until it occurred to her that this was the kind of paranoid thinking that went through Myrna's mind every day. *She's getting to you!*

Sydney flipped through the pages of the contract to stall. Everything looked fine. Everything they said sounded better than fine. And this was guaranteed money. In the ten years she'd been on her own, she'd never had any kind of financial security. The most she'd ever made in a year was thirty-four thousand dollars gross. In New York that put her near the poverty line. Last year she'd made only twenty-nine. And she had two years' worth of income that she had yet to pay taxes on!

Signing this contract would mean she'd never again have to dump a Zip-loc bag full of scrounged-up coins into the Coin-O-Matic to buy groceries. She could take cabs when it rained. She could get her own place! In a neighborhood she actually liked!! She could realize her dream of getting a real couch from Crate & Barrel!!!

She looked up. They were all waiting for her to say something. They were about to hear, "Do you have a pen?" when, suddenly, a little voice whispered, *Why accept the first offer?* For whatever reason, they really wanted her to sign this contract. She had bargaining power. And the time to strike was . . .

"Chad Pennington gets a hundred and fifty thousand," she heard herself say before she had fully thought through her strategy.

There was an awkward silence, which was quickly filled by the lawyer. "We cannot divulge the specifics of Mr. Pennington's contract."

For a long, tense moment they stared at her, and she stared at them. A few seconds longer and they would have had her signature on the dotted line. But Navy Suit piped up. "We are prepared to offer you eighty-five thousand. Same terms."

"One hundred." If they could do eighty-five, they could do a hundred.

Navy Suit straightened his glasses, looking around the table with bewilderment. "Ninety," he coughed, as if he was hocking up phlegm.

Sydney pushed the deal memo across the table. "Sorry," she bluffed, her heart fluttering. "Can't do it."

Navy Suit looked at the lawyer, both of their jaws set tight. Navy Suit got up. "Excuse me." He no longer sounded pleasant.

Where was he going? Sydney wanted to yell after him, "Come back. Ninety is cool. I'LL TAKE IT!"

But he was gone. In his absence, no one spoke (to her) and she felt hives popping up all over her body like popcorn. A few minutes that seemed like an eternity later, she heard the door open behind her and then Navy Suit sat back down at the head of the table.

Without preamble, he said, "We can offer you one hundred thousand dollars. Same terms." He spoke very slowly, as if he wanted to hold on to the words as long as possible.

"And that is our final offer," the lawyer felt the need to stipulate. Devilishly.

Sydney was frozen. Was this really happening? Was it an elaborate practical joke? Maybe she was hallucinating. Maybe she was having a psychotic break brought on by Myrna's unrelenting abuse. When men in white coats didn't rush in, she opened her mouth to say something before they rescinded the offer. Stammering incoherently until she could form words, she practically squealed, "I accept!"

She had no idea how or why such good fortune had come her way, and at that point, she didn't fucking care. Her whole life was about to change for the better, and as soon as she was alone in the elevator she burst into happy tears, thinking, *Finally . . .*

CHAPTER TWENTY-FOUR

The *Cachet* receptionist was a forty-six-year-old black woman named Antoinette who wore her auburn hair in neat, impossibly thin dreadlocks. Her usual greeting was an ebullient "Hey, girl!," a violation of office protocol that had endeared her to Sydney. Today, though, when Sydney stepped off the elevator, Toni's first words were uncharacteristically brusque: "You here to see Myrna?"

It was an odd question (that sounded more like an accusation) considering the only reason Sydney ever came to the office was to see Myrna. And why was Toni speaking in a hush, Sydney wondered, nodding at her hesitantly. They were the only two people in the reception area.

"I don't think she's here," Antoinette said, punching an extension into her twelve-line phone.

Sydney couldn't imagine where else Myrna would be. She practically lived at the office. And they had a standing lunch appointment every Thursday at one. There was no way she could have forgotten. But waiting at Antoinette's glossy white station, watching her whisper into the receiver, Sydney actually felt a guilty sense of relief that they weren't going to have their usual chitchat today. The exchanges about their weight-loss struggles and victories were becoming awkward since the victories had been all Sydney's of late. She'd not only reached her goal weight, she'd transformed her body, adding muscle tone and streamlining her figure with the help of Pilates. Antoinette, on the other hand, kept gaining and losing the same fifteen pounds, and no matter where she was on the scale, her whole body seemed to droop from fatigue.

"Somebody is coming out to get you," she said, replacing the receiver.

"Somebody who?" Sydney always went straight back to Myrna's office. She only stopped at reception to talk to Antoinette. "What's going on?"

"All I know," Antoinette said, looking around as if she might get busted for trading state secrets, "is that they had me call 911 a while ago and some EMS people showed up. But I never saw them come out."

"You called 911?" Sydney looked at the frosted-glass doors that led to Cachet's inner sanctum. "For Myrna?"

"That's what I heard somebody saying."

Sydney's first thought was, *Omigod, somebody stabbed Myrna!* Her second was, *Oh shit, Myrna stabbed somebody!* Neither scenario was implausible, but then the cops would be there. "So they're still here?" She continued to stare at the doors. "The EMS people?"

"They could have gone out by the freight elevator," Antoinette said quietly.

Myrna had been diagnosed with adult diabetes last year. It could have been that, Sydney thought. But she seemed to have it under control. "So," she said, turning back to Antoinette, "what do you think happened?"

"I was hoping *you'd* find out," Antoinette said, slipping into her "Don't come to me with any nonsense" sista-girl voice. "Nobody will tell me shit."

That didn't surprise Sydney. Even to those dangling from the bottom rung at *Cachet,* Antoinette Davis was no different from the cleaning lady or the mail-room guy. The service she provided was very necessary, but it was one that no one respected. To them, she was just another cog in the wheel that went unnoticed as long as the wheel kept spinning.

Antoinette had been hired three years ago, right about the time Sydney signed her first yearlong contract with the magazine. Liz was the first person Sydney had called with the extraordinary news after that surreal meeting with HR. Martha Stewart wannabe that she was, Liz managed to reorganize the birthday party that Sydney had made her cancel, and that night she showed up at her favorite restaurant, Havana Central, giddy as a Powerball winner. There she joined Liz, Joyce, and a bunch of friends for a raucous celebration in the back room, where she downed mojitos until she couldn't see.

It wasn't until the next morning that the looming question—how had this dream job fallen into Sydney's lap?—was answered. A story ran on page one of *The New York Times* about the class-action suit that had been filed against Omnimedia, Inc. A group of black and Latina female employees were claiming they had been unfairly denied promotions due to discriminatory practices. Sydney had worked on four different floors in the building and most of the black or Latino employees she encountered worked in the mail room or at the security desk in the lobby. And they were all men.

The lawsuit had spurred the *Times* to do an investigative report on the lack of diversity in the magazine world, what they called "the glossy ceiling." They broke down the percentages of nonwhite staffers at every major magazine, to shameful results. All of a sudden, the conglomerate's burning desire to add the name of an Afro-Cuban, Portuguese, French, Irish female writer to the masthead of their highest-profile title made perfect sense. The article said that of the 203 staffers and contributors listed on the *Cachet* masthead, 6—or less than 3 percent—were people of color. After going down the phone list and ticking off every person of color, Sydney realized she was the sixth. That meant they had included her in the tally before she'd even signed the contract or, depending on the reporter's deadline, maybe even before they had come to her with the offer.

Naturally, Liz was horrified. "You're a token!" she cried when she woke Sydney up to tell her the news. "Reparations" was how Joyce succinctly summed it up. As an expert on corporate images she thought it was a smart, if superficial, move on Omnimedia's part. Sydney was a "good-faith hire," she told them. It wouldn't help Omnimedia when they went to trial because the affirmative-action hiring spree happened after the fact. (In addition to Antoinette, there were other women of color sprinkled throughout the building, mostly in lower-level positions—including a Peruvian "little person" in the mail room who killed three birds with one stone.) But, Joyce said, having a woman of color in a visible position showed they were serious about making changes, and it would be a step toward burnishing their tarnished public image.

In theory, Sydney didn't mind being a token with a six-figure salary. In practice, the situation proved to be more problematic. Everyone at *Cachet,* as well as those in the insular publishing world, knew why she had been hired. She hadn't earned her coveted spot on *Cachet's* short list of contract writers. It had been handed to her because she had a vagina and caramel skin.

That sat well with no one, least of all Sydney herself. She had always been a hard worker, the honor student who volunteered for extra credit. Smarts and ambition were all she'd ever had. That combination was supposed to be more than enough. It was supposed to be her winning ticket. While other girls dreamed of fairy-tale weddings, she dreamed about being the beautiful, commanding woman in the navy pinstripe suit in the "woman for president" Donna Karan ads. But all the ambition in the world didn't amount to anything if you didn't have tangible goals. Desperate as she was to be successful, she'd floundered for a decade like a fish washed ashore because she had nothing to be successful at.

The irony was she'd finally gotten the fab, well-paying Career for which she'd always hungered without accomplishing anything. She'd simply been a double minority in the right place at the right time. For that, she was looked upon with scorn by everyone in the office, who for the previous eighteen months had known her as Myrna's oppressed temp.

The most unlikely twist to the story was that Myrna, a woman Sydney had once feared was giving her an ulcer, became her mentor, her ally, her protector. Which made Sydney even less popular around the office.

"Don't feel bad," Myrna said (in a demanding, not sympathetic, way) when Sydney lamented the awkward spot the act of tokenism had put her in. "And don't apologize to anyone. Ever."

Myrna, a college dropout as well, had started at Omnimedia as a secretary in 1991. Now she was second in command to Conrad Drake, a Connecticut WASP whose severe lockjaw made his speech nearly unintelligible. He was a bit eccentric, but Sydney had no beef with him. Besides Antoinette, he was the only one who was consistently friendly to her. But Myrna, who referred to him as "that fucking phony," advised her not to be taken in by his charms. Myrna never let Sydney forget that Conrad was one of "the men upstairs." That was what she ominously called the top brass, as if they were a band of angels gone bad.

"The men upstairs," she'd explained after the lawsuit had become public, "knew you were controllable." Myrna had suggested two other women, one black and one Asian, both of whom had solid writing and reporting experience, but both were shot down. "The men upstairs found out the *Times* story was running and they needed to pull the trigger right away. Those other two would have gotten lawyers to look at the contract. It would have taken too long, and once the story broke, forget about it. They'd have known exactly what was up and they'd be asking for the moon. Instead they chose you, a walking rainbow, and they got you cheap."

Cheap? Sydney was kicking herself for weeks after hearing that. She thought she'd done so well! Then Myrna told her Chad Pennington made $250,000 a year. That didn't include the $400,000 he'd made last year from movie options on two of his rich-people-turn-murderous stories.

Sydney was floored to hear that "the men upstairs" wanted her to continue writing for the "Scene & Heard" section. They were willing to pay her $100,000 a year just to supply the few paragraphs of text that ran—but that no one ever read—under a page of celebrity photos? That was a serious bump up from a dollar a word!

Myrna, however, wouldn't hear of it. She got Sydney feature assignments, a page here, two pages there. Then she secretly edited all of Sydney's stories (which was not her job) and had Sydney make changes before anyone else laid eyes on them. Every week, at Myrna's insistence, they met for lunch at Binky's. (Myrna never ate in the cafeteria because she was paranoid about eavesdropping, and at Binky's she always had the "godfather table" in the back room.) Their lunches were ostensibly to discuss Sydney's stories, but most of the time Sydney listened to Myrna vent about things that had absolutely nothing to do with her. The lunch would begin with Myrna jabbing herself in the side with her insulin right at the table without taking a pause from her ranting. Then, once she got sufficiently tipsy, she'd start railing against the patriarchy, spewing conspiracy theories and repeating lines Sydney had heard a dozen times.

"You think these *white, heterosexual males* all earned their places in the boys' club?" she'd gripe, launching spittle into Sydney's face. "Think again. Half of these guys you read about in *New York* magazine, these so-called star executives, got there on hype and connections. You know how I got where I am? *By working my narrow ass off.*"

You cannot become like Myrna Bell in any way, shape, or form, Sydney silently repeated as she sat in reception, mindlessly paging through the latest issue of *Cachet.* The chanting of her personal mantra was interrupted by the catty voice (male and similar to Jeffrey's, oddly) that had been popping up much too often lately: *Sign up with Mitzi Berman and maybe you won't.*

She slammed the magazine closed—*zero chance of that happening!*—and found the beady eyes of Renée Zellweger, patron saint of the romantically challenged, staring back at her. Mocked at every turn!

She tossed the magazine aside, and a strange noise that was a cross between a groan and a whimper escaped from her throat as she turned her limp head toward the doors that led to *Cachet*'s inner sanctum. She'd been waiting in reception for a good ten minutes. Bodies kept passing by on the other side, but the mysterious somebody still had not come out to fetch her.

Every time she came here she thanked her lucky stars that she didn't have to work out of this office. Myrna fed off the office politics, the backstabbing, the machinations of which Sydney wanted no part. As long as she stayed out of the battleground, she could continue to do this job, she told herself. She had to. This was not another low-paying, dead-end job she could just up and quit. She'd hated being a wage slave, but the advantage of those jobs was that she always had an out. When she got sick of answering phones at a nonprofit, she gave them no weeks' notice, deciding one Friday that she wouldn't be back. When a boutique manager yelled at her for coming back late from lunch, she called him a eunuch and stormed out. What did she care? She could temp or collect unemployment (if you knew how to work the system, and she did) until she found another gig. The knowledge that she wasn't permanently tethered to any of those pointless jobs was the only thing that made them tolerable.

But how could she quit a $100,000-a-year job that required little time and even less effort? Her contract was up for renewal at the end of the month and Myrna was getting her a bump up to $125K. For two more years. That should be a cause for celebration. So why did thinking about signing the new contract make her feel as if someone was holding a pillow over her face?

She stared up at the huge silver letters that spelled out CACHET hanging on the wall over Antoinette's desk. She had to make the best of her situation and accept the fact that no career would give her life meaning. She was never going to be the woman in the Enjoli commercial. She had to come to terms with that and move on. To phase two. Finding someone, having a family; that would fill her up with genuine happiness. How could it not? Everyone she knew who had children said the same things. *I never knew I could love another person this much. I can't imagine my life without them. Why did I wait so long?*

Sydney felt the same kind of primal love for Caleigh and Ben, and they were only her niece and nephew. She'd been in the room when Ben was born, and holding him in the first minutes of his life, she'd felt a sense of elation that she had never felt before or since. What did a career—whether big or little *c*—mean next to that?

And she had no right to complain. There were people in the world with real problems. Life-or-death problems. *Starving African babies, starving African babies, starving African ba . . .*

She abruptly stopped chanting her reality-check mantra, realizing she didn't even have to take it that far. There were millions of women who felt they had to choose between having a family and having a career. There were millions more who couldn't even afford the luxury of entertaining that question. She didn't have to make that Hobson's choice because she was basically working part-time already. Though utterly meaningless, this job was the perfect setup for her. And because she was the company token, they'd never get rid of her. She was safe.

CHAPTER TWENTY-FIVE

Kimberly Nash stuck her pretty little head through the glass doors and called out, "Sydney?"

A cool, willowy blonde whose hair and eyebrows were so fair she was borderline albino, Kimberly was the assistant to the British hotshot who'd recently been hired as editor at large. Sydney didn't care for either of them. "Hey, Kimberly," she said, faux friendly, giving the curious Antoinette a final glance. "How are you?"

Holding the door open, Kimberly responded with an obligatory "Pretty well," then cut Sydney off when she tried to inquire about Myrna's whereabouts. "So I hear you're doing the story on Brett Babcock."

Sydney held up two crossed fingers. "We're like this."

"I love him," Kimberly said, a sentiment that was contradicted by her blandness of tone. "What's he like?"

"Short."

They continued to make forced conversation as they made their way down the long main hallway, passing *Cachet* covers of Nicole Kidman, Julia Roberts, Catherine Zeta-Jones, and Ben Affleck. It was known as "the Farrah hallway"—even though Farrah Fawcett had never been on one of their covers—because Gary, a senior editor who had interviewed her in her heyday, said she had a hallway in her Malibu home lined with more than a hundred pictures of herself. Nearing Myrna's office, Sydney could see that her latest assistant (she'd had over a dozen since Sydney had vacated the post) was not at her desk. When they got closer, Sydney could tell the desk wasn't just temporarily unoccupied. It was completely cleared out. Then two maintenance men came out of Myrna's office, carrying the beige, cigarette-burned sofa on which Sydney had sat so many times.

Sydney's heart began to thump, her body intuitively reacting before her brain could fully process what was going on. "Where's Myrna?"

Kimberly stopped at Myrna's door and turned to face Sydney. "Gone," she said, her ice-blue eyes aglow with schadenfreude. "They took her out on a stretcher. Considering what she did to Christy, it looks like things have come full circle."

"Oh, shut up. You didn't even know Christy!" As Kimberly's eyes twinkled with ooh-you're-so-busted delight, Sydney took two steps backward as if she might be able to rewind the last three seconds and give it another go. Jesus, how had she let *that* slip out? She had just handed Kimberly (and everyone in the office to whom the dumb bitch would immediately repeat the remark) a reason to openly hate her!

Watching Kimberly slither back to her cubicle with a wicked smile on her face, Sydney thought it would be wise to make tracks and find out the details of Myrna's demise later. But that message was slow in traveling from her brain to her feet. She stood immobilized, staring into Myrna's stripped office, until she heard the obnoxiously accented voice of Kimberly's boss, Gareth Oglethorpe, an excitable thirty-nine-year-old fellow who may or may not have been on coke. He was British and gay, which, according to Myrna, made him "double gay."

"Cindy!" he trilled, speeding down the hallway. "Cin-deee!"

Sydney looked around to see where this Cindy person was.

"There you are," Gareth said, ushering her into Myrna's office—or rather, Myrna's former office. Looking around, Sydney felt as if she was walking into the home of someone who had just died. The shelves were bare, there were four indentations around the dusty patch of carpet where the sofa had been, and languishing in the corner were two cardboard boxes filled with Myrna's things. (Sydney could see two cans of air freshener and three ashtrays sticking out of the bigger one.)

Gareth leaned against the mahogany desk, the only piece of furniture that remained, and clapped his hands together. "The Raven is a go!"

The Raven was a bizarre rock star that Myrna had been negotiating to get on the cover of *Cachet* for months. But first things first. "Where's Myrna?"

"Oh, that," Gareth said, fiddling with the gold signet ring that was engraved with his family crest. Along with that snobbish adornment, he invariably wore skinny black suits, short mod boots, and his brown hair in a so-retro-it's-cutting-edge shag. He was obviously going for a Beatles look, but due to his unfortunately pronounced bug eyes, Myrna called him The Beetle.

"She's gone," The Beetle said.

"I see that." Sydney almost lowered herself into the chair until she remembered there was no chair. "Gone where? What happened? Is she in the hospital? *What?*"

"Apparently, Conrad found her this morning hiding under this desk," he said, knocking against its wood surface as if he hoped his good luck would continue. "And when he tried to go near her, she sprayed him in the face with air freshener. The emergency people had to come in with masks and tranquilize her."

Sydney's mouth fell open. *Tranquilize her?* She wasn't an elephant. Myrna weighed ninety-eight pounds!

"Bonkers, that one," Gareth added.

Sydney pressed her hand against her open mouth and gasped. Oh. My. God. It had finally happened. Myrna had officially cracked up! "Where is she now?"

"Dunno," Gareth said with an emotional distance Sydney found appalling. Naturally, he didn't like Myrna. No one did. Even Sydney, Myrna's protégée, wouldn't go that far. She had a deep *appreciation* for everything Myrna had done for her and she felt tremendous pity for the woman, but there was no way Sydney could ever genuinely like her when, in exchange for Myrna's protection, she still had to endure occasional and completely random acts of abuse. (She'd seen Hedda Nussbaum on *Larry King* and it was scary how much she identified.) Nevertheless, Myrna was still Gareth's colleague, and just a few hours ago, she had been hiding out like a hunted animal under the very desk he was leaning against. Surely he felt a small dose of compassion for her?

"You'll be reporting to me until further notice," he said, getting back to business. "Where are we with Brett Babcock?"

Sydney felt awkward standing in front of him in the empty room, and she couldn't switch off her thoughts of Myrna just like that. Had they fired her? Was she on a leave of absence? Was she at Bellevue? Then her survival instincts kicked in. What did this mean *for her*? She was completely unprotected in enemy territory!

"I, um, hung out with Brett twice," she said, pulling it together. Gareth was her boss for now. He could make things difficult for her. And if Myrna had told her once, she'd told her a thousand times: Always look out for number one. "Or 'The Babcock,' as he calls himself," Sydney said. She was trying to lighten things up, but Gareth remained expressionless. "Got really good, colorful stuff. I have one more hang scheduled for next week. A night on the town."

"Did you get him on the record about Nicolette?"

"Um, no," Sydney said in a tone that made it clear she was thinking, *Duh*. That *did* cause Gareth's expression to change, and she quickly adopted a more agreeable tone. "A condition of the interview was that he wouldn't be questioned about Nicolette." Trying to be deferential, she said, "Wasn't it?" (It was.)

"Yes. It's still a pending legal matter," Gareth said. "But that doesn't mean we shouldn't try, does it?"

Sydney noted the "we" with annoyance. Did he have any idea what Brett Babcock was like after five rum and Cokes? Let Gareth fucking try!

"It's the money quote," Gareth said. "Get it."

Sydney didn't take kindly to his patronizing, but the unnatural way *money quote* rolled off his arrogant tongue made her feel she had the upper hand in a way. Myrna and Conrad always said that, but it was obviously not a term Gareth would use. He sounded like the new kid on the block trying to fit in by casually saying "wicked" when everyone in his old neighborhood said "excellent." Seeing this chink in his mod armor reminded Sydney that he was still feeling his way around—not just at *Cachet* but in New York— and she filed this observation away, hoping to somehow use it to her advantage at a later date.

"Now, about The Raven . . ." Gareth spent several masturbatory minutes talking about the shock and awe this exclusive would cause in the industry, while Sydney attempted to look psyched.

The Raven was a long-haired androgynous rock star who had been enormously popular in the late eighties when he went by the name Randy Lee.

After a string of hits and starring in a semiautobiographical movie that became a cult hit, he disappeared and resurfaced as a she. Adding to the weirdness, his people issued a press release saying the artist formerly known as Randy Lee would thereafter be known by the female symbol. Just as people were getting used to that, another press release was e-mailed to media outlets: ♀ was now going by the name of The Raven in a nod to his/her Native American heritage (which no one had ever known about). It was rumored that The Raven was on his/her way to becoming a full-fledged woman, but no one knew anything for sure because he/she never spoke to the press (except through releases) and stayed holed up in New Mexico on his/her property, which was designed to look like a Native American reservation.

"It's quite a coup," Sydney said, humoring Gareth. "I can't remember the last time I saw an interview with him."

"HER!" Gareth's arms flew straight up in the air, and Sydney thought she heard a seam in his Prada suit rip. "Don't ever call him her . . . I mean her him. He hates that!"

"She."

"She hates that!" He looked at his watch, then propelled himself toward the door. "I have a lunch. Walk me downstairs."

Sydney tried to keep up with his brisk pace as they walked back toward reception. "What happened to Chad? Myrna told me that if it ever happened, he was doing it."

"He's off," Gareth said, walking past Antoinette as if she were invisible. "You're on."

Sydney couldn't imagine why a switch like that would be made. Chad was Conrad's golden boy. They would never take a story away from him. Especially not one they'd been desperate to get. "Is Chad on the outs with Conrad for some reason?" Sydney asked, hoping it was so.

"No," Gareth said crisply. He pressed for the "lift," and Sydney glanced at Antoinette. She couldn't fill her in with Gareth right there. She mouthed, "I'll call you" and followed Gareth into the elevator. "So why'd he get kicked off the story?"

"He didn't get *kicked off*," Gareth said, indignant on Chad's behalf. Sydney stared at him, awaiting a more definitive answer, and he cryptically responded, "Our hand was forced."

"And that means what exactly?"

Gareth looked up and, seeing that they'd be trapped in the elevator together for another twenty-six floors, his hand was forced once again. "The Raven requested a woman."

"Hmmmm," Sydney said, pleasantly surprised. The Raven had managed to do what Myrna, in three years, could not. Get her a cover. Sydney had friends who would've given their virginity to Randy Lee back in the day. Even Liz had had a thing for him. (In hindsight, Sydney wondered if the lesbian in Liz had been attracted to the woman in him.) Sydney had never really seen the big deal, but she was beginning to feel a kind of sisterly solidarity with the eccentric tranny. And despite her professional disillusionment, the challenge of writing a cover story gave her a little charge. "Does she have an album coming out?"

"Her first in six years," Gareth said, restlessly tapping his foot. "It's perfect timing. It's going to be the July cover. Our music issue."

"July?" The magazine had a two-month lead time, and it was almost May. That was cutting it close. "When's the interview?"

Gareth repeatedly pressed the already lit button for the lobby. "I don't know."

"Where's it going to be?"

"I don't know."

Suddenly realizing this assignment might enable her to make an all-expenses-paid pilgrimage to Mecca, Sydney asked eagerly, "You think I'll get to go to New Mexico?"

"I don't know," Gareth said, peevishly this time. "The Raven is cagey about everything. We're hoping for a day of beauty at a spa to be determined."

"A little female bonding," Sydney said, thinking this might actually turn out to be fun. "Sweet."

Gareth shook the heavy flop of fringe out his eyes, looked at Sydney appraisingly for about five seconds (which was an uncomfortable length of time when you were alone in an elevator with someone, especially someone you didn't particularly like), and said, "Have you ever thought of dying your hair black?"

Sydney couldn't have more been more surprised if he'd said, "Drop and give me fifty!" She backed slowly into the opposite corner, almost frightened. "No."

"Well, Conrad thinks you should have it colored and blown out very straight. Possibly have some extensions put in." The words came tumbling out at a rapid clip because, obviously, it was something he'd been instructed to address and he just wanted to get it over with.

More baffled knowing this was not just random weirdness on Gareth's part but a mandate that had come down from on high, Sydney said, "Why would Conrad have any opinion whatsoever about my hair?"

"Because we told Anya, The Raven's publicist, that you were part Cherokee." The doors opened and Gareth rushed out as if he'd been in an underwater chamber and needed air.

"Cherokee?" Sydney rushed after him. "I'm not Cherokee!"

Gareth glanced over his scrawny shoulder. "Don't tell The Raven that."

"I don't understand," Sydney said, scurrying behind him. "Why would you say that?"

Gareth stopped by the front doors and looked at Sydney as if he was angry that she had ever been born. "First she requested a woman. Then it was a colored woman."

Hearing the words *colored woman* made Sydney's upper body spasm as though she'd just been shocked by a defibrillator. Gareth obviously didn't know that was an offensive term or else he wouldn't have let it cross his lips. *Was that some British shit?* Whatever the deal, she marked it as exhibit B and added it to her mental file of grievances so she could Don Imus his ass if need be.

Gareth registered her sudden reaction with a confused squint, then spoke faster to get past the awkward moment. "Then it was a woman with Indian heritage," he said. "This whole thing has been like a hostage negotiation! We had to acquiesce to all of her demands!"

"Wow," Sydney said. "She was that specific?"

"Yes. We offered Meenal Singh and they said no. Wrong Indian."

Sydney tossed that statement into the file (it wasn't patently offensive, it just *sounded* wrong), bristling that she was third choice after Chad and Meenal. "Meenal doesn't even work at *Cachet.*"

"She is employed by Omnimedia, Inc. And she has done covers," Gareth said, getting all pissy. "We've been working on this for five months. You have no idea what this she-male has put us through!"

No, *Myrna* had been working on it for five months, Sydney thought.

He'd only been at *Cachet* for three. "Fine, Gareth. I'm a woman of a lot of colors. But I'm not Cherokee."

"Pretend you are." A town car pulled up, and when he saw the OGLE-THORPE on the card in the window, he hurried outside.

"What if she tries to ask me something, I don't know . . . Cherokee-related?" Sydney said, walking up to him as he stood on the curb waiting, like the entitled prick that he was, for the driver to open the door.

"She won't," he said. "And we only told Anya that you had Native American ancestry. But maybe you should study up on it." He looked Sydney up and down as if he was sending her out on a spy mission from which he doubted she'd come back alive. "Just in case."

The driver stepped between them as if he was a bodyguard and Sydney was a stalker, obviously taking nonverbal cues from Gareth because how did he know *she* wasn't Oglethorpe? Gareth slid inside, taking a call on his buzzing Vertu, and Sydney shouted quickly at his back before she had the door slammed in her face. "Maybe I should get, like, a little beaded headband and stick a feather in my hair!"

She didn't think he'd heard her until the window lowered an inch and he blinked up at her through the narrow opening. "You don't think that would be too much?"

Sydney rolled her eyes. "I was kidding."

"Yes, of course," Gareth said, lowering the window a little more. "It's just a psychological thing. He wants . . ." He banged his fists on the back of the front passenger seat three times, snapping at himself, "She, she, she!," and the driver looked at him in the rearview the way people often looked at Myrna. "She wants to believe you'll feel her pain. That's all. Now finish up Brett Babcock," Gareth said, looking up at her with his bulging beetle eyes. "Then this should be your top priority. Your only priority. Do not go anywhere. Do not make any plans. Have your mobile in your possession and fully charged at all times, Cindy. The call could come at any moment!"

Nodding, Sydney (aka Cindy) said, "Right. Stay ready." Thinking she should show a little enthusiasm she added, "My first cover. I'm excited!"

"Screw this up," Gareth warned, "and you'll never get another." And with that, he leaned back and out of view, signaling to both Sydney and the waiting driver that the conversation was over.

CHAPTER TWENTY-SIX

You told her what?"

"I wasn't interested."

"Well, then, you are a damn fool. If that was all it took for me to meet a rich man, I'd be kissing that bitch's ass!"

"Jeffrey, the men pay her fifty thousand dollars. It's a form of prostitution!"

"All marriages are a form of prostitution. You're either fucking for money, jewelry, or a new dishwasher. Get real!"

"What decade are you living in?"

"You hate it when I'm right."

"Right? You sound ridiculous!" Sydney walked away from the table, leaving Jeffrey to deal with the bill, and stormed past the restaurant's owner, a friend of his, without saying good-bye.

A minute later, the restaurant door flung open. "*You* sound ridiculous," Jeffrey said. "Acting like you don't need this woman's help!"

Sydney started up the block. "I don't."

"Well, I do," Jeffrey called out. "Does she deal in queers?"

The sound of the squeaking microphone got everyone crowded into the Milk Gallery to look around. The evening's host, an L.A.-based trophy wife wearing a tight white sweater that accentuated her big fake boobs, stepped onto the small stage holding the mic. "Thank you for coming tonight."

"Those are the biggest nipples I have ever seen!" Max said.

Duke got on his tiptoes. Looking schlumpy as usual in dirty jeans, a thrift-store sweater, and beat-up Vans, he would characterize himself as "groovy," though everyone else would go with "weird." Tonight he was really feeling himself because a roaming photographer had asked to take a picture of him wearing his new accessory: a pair of clear plastic safety goggles that he'd bought at Home Depot for $9.99. A celebrity in his own mind, he was sure that he would ignite a new trend. Too bad they weren't at all functional. He lifted the glasses to get a better look at Trophy Wife's tits.

"Not her," Max said. He pointed at a nude photo on the wall that was dividing the room in half. "That."

"Yeah," Duke said, moving in close. "Sexy . . ."

"And thank you to all the photographers who have allowed us to auction their prints for tonight's event," Trophy Wife said.

"Sexy?" Max frowned, but he couldn't take his eyes off the picture. "Deformed is more like it. She's all nipple, no breast!"

Duke looked around. "You think she's here?"

Max stared at the black-and-white photo. The model was artistically posed outdoors on a huge boulder, her face hidden from view. "Unless she's parading around topless, how would we know?"

"All proceeds from tonight's auction will go to the Mammogram Awareness Project," Trophy Wife said in closing. "Bidding is open until ten." She exited the stage to light applause.

"She told Vera, you know."

"Who?"

"Liz! She told Vera about the whole thing." Even the crying bit, Sydney thought, trying to mentally erase that mortifying moment in her personal history. "By the time I got out of my massage, which was a total waste because all I could hear was Mitzi Berman's voice taunting, 'Forty and single! Forty and single!,' I had five missed calls from the crazy woman who claims she birthed me!"

"Sydney, the adopted thing never panned out. Isn't it time you accepted that Vera is your real mother?"

"There's no video! And I've never seen a hard copy of my birth certificate."

"Well, she's crazy and so are you. There's *that* link."

"I'm not Vera crazy, though," Sydney said, looking for Jeffrey to cosign, which he didn't.

"So what'd she have to say about Mitzi?"

"She said I needed professional help."

"See. Crazy recognizes crazy."

"Jeffrey, quit it. Really. I hate that you, like, idolize her! Be on my side!"

"What can I tell you? I've never met a diva I didn't love."

Realizing she was never going to win this battle, Sydney ended talk of Vera with a disgusted sigh. Her diva mother was the primary reason that Sydney was so vehemently opposed to this vulgar endeavor. It was exactly the sort of thing Vera would do!

If Vera Fischbein Zamora Weintraub Wu (nee Deveraux) ever found herself separated from her fourth husband, Dr. Li Wu—and according to the law of averages that should be happening any day now—she'd be ringing up Mitzi Berman in no time to have a new sugar daddy lined up by the time the divorce papers went through. With no man, there was no Vera. Marriage was her vocation, trading up her forte.

Never having had a real career herself, Vera held women's professional accomplishments, no matter how stupendous, in low regard. "Not married, no children. Some even say she's a lesbian," she'd lament about Condoleezza Rice (and later Oprah), managing to indirectly knock both of her daughters with one snipe. Amazingly, Sydney had nabbed the one job that did make her mother somewhat proud, though only because it was a glamorous one that separated Vera from A-list celebrities by a single degree.

Sydney would never be a real success in her mother's eyes as long as her ring finger was bare, but that was Vera's hang-up, not hers. Marriage was not an accomplishment. When were women (most of whom felt that way, whether they'd cop to it or not) going to get that through their heads? Crossing the finish line in a marathon. Becoming a cardiothoracic surgeon. Winning an Oscar. Those were accomplishments. Getting married was just a (hopefully) happy fact of life.

Ditto for having kids. There was no achievement in doing what any menstruating teenager could do. The achievement was in being a *good* parent, and just because every parent wanted to think he or she was didn't make it true. Vera thought she was a good parent. She wasn't. People who cursed at their kids and beat them in supermarket aisles thought they were good parents. They weren't. The parents on *Intervention* who let their junkie kids live at home and continued to give them money knowing damn well where they would spend it believed they were doing it because they were good parents. Were they? Last week, Jeffrey had forwarded to Sydney a video of a woman who was in police custody after leaving her four-year-old locked in a hot car while she went into Wal-Mart. For three hours. "I love my children," she wailed repeatedly about her dead son and his three surviving siblings, who would presumably wind up as wards of the state of Mississippi. "I'm a good mother! I'm a good mother!" As Jeffrey noted in his e-mail, "No, bitch, you ain't." Rich, poor, black, white, Bugaboo or no Bugaboo, no one knew if she had been a good mother until her kid had grown up to be, at best, a happy, healthy productive member of society or, God forbid, a serial killer. (Which terrified Sydney when she allowed herself to really think about it. So she tried not to.)

Sydney's sudden and intense desire to get hitched was purely perfunctory. She needed a man to make babies, and the clock was ticking. Of course, there were other ways to reproduce, but only a fool would choose to go it alone before she had exhausted more convenient options. At least that was the way it had been laid out in The Plan. If any good had come out of this meeting with Mitzi Berman, it was that Sydney had been forced to examine her long-held beliefs about the legal institution of marriage. And she was left wondering if she really needed it at all.

True, she had told Liz she wanted to get married, but she had been speaking euphemistically, hadn't she? She didn't really mean married as in *married*. As in "put on a poufy white dress, walk down an aisle, and pledge eternal love" married. She meant something more along the lines of "be in a committed relationship with someone who is going to love me, support me, make me laugh, be a good father to our children, and assemble the shit we get from Ikea." She was looking for more of a hus*friend* than a husband.

Naturally, she would expect a ring from the besotted man she eventually allowed to impregnate her. And she wouldn't mind going on a honeymoon. Or receiving a few congratulatory gifts. But she didn't need a ring to *prove* anything. She didn't need anyone to call her Mrs. And she for damn sure didn't need or want anything resembling a fairy-tale wedding. Every time she watched *Bridezillas* (who could resist?) and the inevitable moment came when the psychotic 'zilla demanded to have "the fairy tale" or "feel like a princess," Sydney always wanted to scream, "HAVE DI AND MASAKO TAUGHT YOU NOTHING?"

And now that the marriage had become a political issue, with conservatives embracing it as theirs alone, it seemed so uncool, so Elisabeth Hasselbitch. At the same time, oddly, the media's obsession with celebrity weddings (and subsequent quickie divorces) made marriage seem overly trendy, like a soon-to-be-out-of-date fad you'd one day be embarrassed you'd fallen for.

What did reciting vows in a church and signing a piece of paper even mean when divorce was always an option, one that more than 50 percent of couples who vowed "till death do us part" exercised? Either you were committed or you weren't. If there was nothing binding you to another person and you chose to be with them day in and day out, year after year, wasn't that the ultimate show of commitment? Why was it universally accepted that divorce was synonymous with failure? If two people divorced after ten years but they were happy for nine of those years, that wasn't a failure. *It was a success for nine years!*

"Forever" was the problem. "Forever" was what tripped people up. "Forever" was what broke people up. "Forever" was what suffocated people and sent them running for the exits. "Forever" was a fairy tale, and Sydney was a realist. She didn't need "forever."

And she didn't need Mitzi fucking Berman.

"Incoming," Duke said.

The next thing Max knew, his model ex was upon them. All in one motion, Natasha whipped her lustrous blond locks out of her face and kissed him hard on the mouth. Ignoring Duke's poked-out lips, Natasha wrapped her arms around Max's neck and, in one gushy breath, said, "I've been looking all over for you, bunny! It's crazy in here! Wish I could stay and chill, but I just found out I have to fly to the Maldives tomorrow for a shoot. Call you when I'm back. Love to Avery!" She went in for another lipsmacker but pulled up an inch from his face. "Oh, and can you put the new Luella bag on hold for me?"

The sweet warmth of her breath made Max remember what it was like to have her, and he briefly considered following her to the Maldives. Then he remembered what was stopping him. Work. He leaned into her kiss this time, lusting for more, but in a flash, she was gone.

"Like gangbusters," Duke said. He lifted his goggles and waved at her back. "Ta-ta!"

They watched her go, both thinking what every straight man thought when they saw Natasha Vitalenko: *That's one sexy piece of ass.*

Max shook his head in disbelief. "Can you believe when I met her she was a hostess at Coffee Shop?"

"What I can't believe is that you get her a trainer and an agent and then once she gets a Victoria's Secret contract, you dump her." Once Natasha's perfect denim-clad ass was no longer in sight, Duke clamped the goggles back over his eyes. "Insane."

"What can I tell you?" Max said, bending down to scribble a bid next to a photo. "My work was done."

"Dude, you know what I wouldn't do to get a piece of that. Natasha is every guy's fantasy."

"Physically."

"Right. I don't know how you can get bored with a chick who looks like that."

"Very easily."

"So," Duke said, scoping out the room for chicks, "who's your next pet project?"

"I don't know," Max said. "But I need one to take my mind off the fact that I have a full-time job."

Sydney and Jeffrey had been bickering for three avenues and she just wanted him to shut up. She loved him to death, Lord knows she did, but he was a constant reminder of what she didn't have. Girlfriends. A gay man was the next best thing, but there were some voids Jeffrey could never fill.

At a time when there were at least half a dozen celebrity pregnancies in full swing, he had neither the ability nor the interest to play the "Vaginal or Cesarean?" guessing game. There was no need to send him an urgent text when she unearthed a bargain gem on the sale rack at H&M or fire off a "tell a friend" forward to get a second opinion about boots she found on Zappos. (Some women might do the latter, but Sydney wasn't that kind of fag hag.) When it came to playing "If David Beckham was my husband," Jeffrey was more than willing.

If David Beckham was my husband, I'd find a way to forgive him after he slept with his assistant and she blabbed to all the tabloids about it. If David Beckham was my husband and he wanted his entire low-class Cockney family to move into our mansion, I'd deal. If David Beckham was my husband and he slapped me, I wouldn't call the cops . . .

But most of those things took on an entirely different connotation with Jeffrey, a point that was driven home the moment Sydney heard herself say, "If David Beckham was my husband, I'd let him fuck me up the ass."

And, most annoyingly, Jeffrey didn't have the perspective to see this Mitzi Berman thing for what it was. Wrong on so many levels.

"We all know how hard it is to find a man, gay or straight, who wants to commit," he was going on and on. "Mitzi Berman has found those men. She's done the legwork. She's done background checks."

Sydney let Jeffrey chatter on, refusing to admit that she'd been second-guessing her decision to blow Mitzi off. She was her own person and she would never compromise her values or integrity for any man. How could it hurt to go out on a few dates just to check it out? The problem was that it would have been impossible to keep something this salacious on the q.t. Anything Liz knew, Joyce, who knew a lot of people, knew. And there were people Sydney didn't know who knew her from her byline. She could just imagine the cocktail-party chatter. *Did you know that Sydney Zamora . . . she writes for* Cachet *. . . you know, the sister-in-law of Joyce Livingston . . . you know, the advertising guru . . . I heard she's using a professional match-maker . . . yes, the one from the* Times!

After her run-in with Mitzi, Sydney had actually called Mira from the changing room at Harvey's spa, while still in her robe and slippers, to get her take on it. A face-to-face would have been preferable so she could read Mira's reaction, but ever since marrying Olaf, Mira had become one of those overbooked New Yorkers who penciled you in for dinner six weeks in advance. Still, after being used as a platonic booty call last month, she'd pathetically reached out to Mira again, knowing full well that she'd have to suffer the further humiliation of waiting a week to get a return call.

It had been ten days. That call had still not come.

Not that Sydney cared. Less than twenty-four hours after she'd placed the call to Mira, it had become a moot point. She would have never been able to convince Mira that professional matchmakers were the next big thing and that she, Sydney, would be heralded as a trailblazer for venturing down this unbeaten path because Sydney couldn't even sell herself on the idea.

And Jeffrey couldn't sell her either.

"The fact that they pay her so much money just proves that they're serious about it. Get with . . ." He trailed off as they passed a darkened store window and, like Narcissus over a pool, he became entranced by his own reflection. As usual, his outfit was meticulously coordinated. His black lace-up shoes were polished to a high shine. (He didn't "believe in" wearing sneakers, and the pair he had for the gym were Gucci.) His pants and sweater, both black—and both too tight, Sydney thought—were obviously meant to give his brightly striped velvet overcoat center stage. And though it was eight o'clock at night and completely dark, he was wearing Fendi wraparound shades, which made his moment of reflection that much funnier. "Get with her," he said, picking up where he'd left off once they were past the reflective surface, "and you can put an end to all this accidental dating."

"Accidental dating?"

"Sydney, what else can we call it? You met that one guy, what's his name, at a coffee shop. He puts extra whipped on your latte and, whoops, you're dating him?"

"Caleb was a baristo slash painter slash aspiring cartoonist!"

"Slash not really husband material," Jeffrey said. "Come on, Sydney. He painted *houses*."

"Well, excuse me for not being a dating snob!"

"Don't look at me like that," Jeffrey said, sucking his teeth. "Just because I want a man with a job, a home, and some goals. And didn't you meet that other guy at a coffee shop too? The screenwriter."

"Oliver," Sydney said, remembering him fondly. Skinny with long dreads, he had a Lenny Kravitz thing going on (except he wasn't a midget). They'd shared an outlet a few times at the Starbucks on Christopher Street, and then one day when he went up to the counter, she snuck a peek at his laptop screen and saw . . .

INT. HALLWAY—NIGHT

A man approaches a body lying facedown in a pool of blood.

It was the best opening line a guy had ever used on her.

"Maybe you should stop hanging out there," Jeffrey said. "Successful men don't hang out in coffee shops in the afternoon."

"I don't go there to pick up men. I go there to work."

"No, you pick up men on the subway," Jeffrey said. "Remember the guy who played the violin on the platform at Grand Central?"

"Yeah," Sydney said, remembering him less fondly than Oliver. "I wonder whatever happened to him."

"I tossed the poor bastard a dollar last week!"

Sydney gasped. "He's still there? God, he went to Juilliard!"

"And let's not forget the one you found on Craigslist."

"New York City Tech Guy?"

"Mmm-hmm," Jeffrey said, twisting his lips. "Came over to clean your hard drive, next thing you know"—he thrust his hips back and forth—"he was cleaning your hard drive!" Finally, Sydney laughed. "And then there was the *artiste* with the windowless lair."

"Leave Socrates alone."

"Sydney, that's exactly my point. Nobody named Socrates is ever gonna make any money."

"What does his name have to do with his career prospects? That's the stupidest thing you've ever said. And that's saying something."

"Stupid but true. What do you even see in these boys? A man with no money repulses me."

"Well, Kyle was—"

"I don't mean Kyle. I know why you were with that tasty little piece of ass. I'm actually sorry it's over. Now I won't be able to look at him and fantasize." He sighed. "But the other ones weren't even that cute."

"To you. Maybe I'm not as shallow as you and everyone else you know in New York, Jeffrey. Did you ever think about that? Maybe I don't judge a man on his looks or his bank account. Maybe I judge him as a person."

"Oh, right," Jeffrey said. "You're definitely the least judgmental person in New York."

"I didn't say in New York. I said of the people you know. It's not hard to lock down that spot. And, by the way, Socrates' apartment was really cute."

"The hell it was."

"How would you know? You never even saw it."

"*Bitch*," Jeffrey said, stomping his boot on the pavement. "It had no windows. That's how I know!"

"He was a photographer. It was like his darkroom!" Sydney cracked up, seeing the ridiculousness of this statement now. But for the two months that she'd been sleeping with Socrates, it somehow seemed completely logical. "And for your information, New York City Tech Guy was . . ."

"Lordy," Jeffrey said. "What was the boy's real name?"

Sydney took a second to think about it, and Jeffrey frowned at her. "You can't remember?"

"Wait a second. It's coming to me." Spotting a herd of smokers congregating on the sidewalk up ahead, she stepped up the pace, desperate to get to the oasis that would provide a diversion from this conversation!

"*You slut,*" Jeffrey teased (as she knew he would).

Sydney jabbed her finger in his face and shouted back, "Franz Ludwig!" *Thank God,* she thought. If it hadn't come to her she would have obsessed about it all night. And she would have felt kind of slutty.

Jeffrey weaved through the crowd, making an exaggerated show of waving away the smokescreen, with Sydney nipping at his heels. "Franz was also a stand-up comedian," she reminded him. "Smart, funny, and he rode a motorcycle. Did we not go see him at Caroline's? And did he not kill?"

CHAPTER TWENTY-SEVEN

Sydney wasn't sure what this auction was benefitting, but glancing over Jeffrey's shoulder, she kept seeing breasts, breasts, and more breasts.

"The hello challenge?" he said.

"Yeah," Sydney said, taking her eyes off the boob show to gauge Jeffrey's reaction as she tentatively made a somewhat embarrassing admission. "It's an exercise in Mitzi's book."

He took two mushroom-covered crostini from the server's tray. "You're reading it?"

Sydney shrugged, trying to appear casual. She didn't want to admit to reading the stupid book, let alone practicing the techniques, but Jeffrey was making her sound like a victim of her own self-destruction. She couldn't have that. "I mean, Liz gave it to me. I figured there might be some helpful tips in there. As long as I'm not expected to use them on Sumner Redstone, why not?"

Jeffrey wiped his mouth with the cocktail napkin. "Who's Summer Redstone?"

"Sum*ner*," Sydney said. For someone who mingled with the rich and famous for a living, there was so much Jeffrey didn't know. "He's a very rich, very old man who not that long ago married a woman half his age. A woman he probably met through Mitzi Berman."

"Okay," Jeffrey said vaguely. "So what is this exercise?"

"You're supposed to say hello to three guys a day. Just hello." Sydney scanned the crowded room. "Mitzi says to start on the nerds. They'll love you for it."

Jeffrey nodded. "Good exercise to get you outside of your invisible perimeter."

"Well, I said hello to a guy on line at Whole Foods today and then his wife walked up and gave me a dirty look. I forgot to look for the ring. That's the first thing you're supposed to do."

"I would think so."

"And then yesterday I said hello to this cute guy on the subway and it turned out that one of his legs was shorter than the other. Like, I'm talking *a lot* shorter! He got off at my stop and wobbled after me for two blocks."

Jeffrey put his hand up to his mouth to keep from spitting out his second crostini.

Sydney laughed with him, happy they weren't fighting anymore. "I haven't met my quota for today," she said, methodically scanning the room, section by section. It was a very hip crowd. She probably wasn't going to find a nerd to practice on. Maybe it was time to upgrade to a viable prospect?

"Okay, this I need to see," Jeffrey said. "But I'm picking the guy."

Sydney gave him a wary look. "Are you now?"

"Your aim is off," Jeffrey said. "And it's only practice, right?"

Automatically going into the confrontational mode she defaulted to whenever someone tried to take control out of her hands, Sydney said, "And what am I gonna get if I allow you to do this?"

Jeffrey screwed up his face, looking like he'd just gotten a whiff of something rank. "A man, hopefully!"

"Bidding's ending in five minutes," Trophy Wife announced, and not a moment too soon. Max did not want to get pulled into another of Duke's ill-fated tête-à-têtes—he was presently sending his worst "Let's party" vibes to a woman across the room who would probably turn out to be a lesbian, married, or revolted by him—and now he had an excuse to make himself scarce.

He circled the room, placing last-minute bids on the photos he was watching, wishing Duke could learn to limit his obsessive flirtation to the drunk women who hung around until three in the morning in the smoky little clubs where Gray Does Matter gigged. Duke had an amazing voice and a magnetic stage presence, a seductive combination that helped him pull more than his fair share of chicks. He had a few groupies even. (Skanks, if you asked Max, but to each his own.) Duke's problem was that he struck out way more than he scored, his win-loss ratio decimated by a fatal flaw that bedeviled many creatively endowed people: He was inept at ordinary social interaction. Lacking the critical perception to see this, he always went down swinging, and it pained Max to watch.

Coming to a full revolution, he could see that Duke was no longer in their original chill spot and that the room had become so congested it was hard to see beyond the immediate ring of minglers surrounding him. Thinking Duke could probably use a few more minutes to flame out, Max stopped briefly to chat with a friend of a friend he would have otherwise pretended not to know, planning to do another lap if necessary. But the crowd shifted and he found himself standing directly behind the unfortunate recipient of Duke's vibes. It must have taken him all this time just to make contact because as Max hung back, tuning out the guy aggressively chatting him up, he heard the woman say, "Hello."

"Whassup," Duke said, playing it cool.

"I just had to tell you," Max heard the chick say. "Love the glasses!"

Well, Max thought. That sounded promising. Perhaps this was the one time out of a hundred that Duke's hunch turned out to be right? Abruptly ending the one-sided conversation he was in, Max slowly turned around. This he had to see.

"Thanks," Duke said.

Max gave an encouraging nod, thinking, *Good. Keep it simple.* But there was still a distinct possibility that this chick might go running from the room in another thirty seconds. The only sure way to tell if Duke was hurtling toward disaster was to get a look at the woman's face, and from Max's vantage point, he couldn't. Looking for an opening in the crowd that he could slip through and advance his position, he realized the large, fabulously attired man standing a foot to his right was with Duke's mark. When he saw the guy press his lips together as if trying not to laugh, Max got a bad feeling. He shuffled around to the other side, pretending to look at some photos, and snuck a peek at the woman's profile. And what a lovely profile it was! She was much too attractive, stylish, and clean to be interested in a schlub like Duke. Sizing up what was going on, Max turned away, hoping to spare Duke the added embarrassment of having him witness the brush-off that was surely coming. And then his worst suspicions were confirmed!

"I could use a pair of glasses like that," the mark said, her mockery disgustingly blatant. "There's some carpentry I've been meaning to do in my apartment!"

Max didn't want to get involved, but hearing the sound of pelting laughter, he thought, *Shit!* Now he was. He couldn't let this heartless woman or her snickering sidekick mock Duke to his face, and he needed to intervene quickly before Duke came back with some awful double entendre like, "I'll be happy to help you 'drill some holes.'" Max stepped between Duke and the little bitch—who looked better head-on than she did in profile—and, just to throw her off, said, "Have we met?"

Reflexively, she said, "No." Max could almost see a wall going up in front of her. But then her big, black buddy gave her a nudge and whispered something that sounded like "Practice makes perfect." Whatever that meant, she didn't like it. Her luscious lips tightened in anger, her nose scrunched up in annoyance, and she glanced at Max with her pretty brown eyes narrowed to slits. And that was when Max recognized her. They *had* met.

Her eyes fell on his sneakers, and then she looked up with a glimmer of recognition. "Oh yeah," she said, sounding none too pleased. "You're that *doorman*. From Harvey's."

Duke snorted, vicariously affronted. Max just stood there, perplexed. Doorman? He thought back to the day they'd met, how rude she'd been to him, and . . . *Oh man!* He laughed to himself, then he laughed out loud, letting out such a hearty guffaw that the aggressive chatter-upper he'd just blown off turned around to see what was so funny. She thought he was the doorman? How brilliantly, brilliantly absurd!

"He's not—" Duke piped up when Max didn't immediately set her straight. A quick backhand to his fleshy abdomen shut him up.

Duke would have given anything to have Max's name and connections (he said so often), but that was because Duke had no idea what it was like to be known your whole life as someone else's son or grandson. "His family owns Harvey's" was like the "Jr." or "III" at the end of "Maximillian Cooper." No one saw him for who he really was. Not even his own family, all of whom expected that he would wind up working in the position he was trying to escape right now. Growing up, there were times when he felt as if he didn't even exist, except maybe as an image in someone else's head. When he felt more like a hologram someone had projected onto a blank wall than a flesh-and-blood person. His first trimester at Oxford was the best three months of his life because no one knew. By second trimester, everyone did. And before long, this sexy little bitch would too.

"If memory serves, your name is . . ." He cast his blue eyes around the room, stroking his stubbly chin, then met her angry stare head-on. "None of my business, right?" He swept his hand in Duke's direction. "None, meet Duke." His hand sliced back toward her. "Duke, meet None."

Hearing her nervous laughter, he felt vindicated for how stupid she'd made him feel that day. Not to mention how she and her friend had tried to humiliate Duke. But when she began to speak, she didn't sound contrite in the least.

"My name is actually Sydney," she said, looking at him as if he were a maggot she'd just found in her sink. "And in my own defense, you were playing me kinda close. I don't know if that was your first day or something, but I could have spoken to someone and made sure it was your last. But I didn't. So you're welcome."

Wowza, Max thought, feeling some instantaneous action inside his briefs. A feisty one. That was always a turn-on. Smiling to let her know all was forgiven, he said, "Well then, I'm eternally grateful. My name is Max, by the way."

"Nice to meet you," she said, shaking his outstretched hand so briefly it was more of a grazing. Then she added, "This time." She glanced down and Max was surprised to see a smile—the hint of one, anyway—crossing her face. "Look." She put her sneaker toe-to-toe with his and Max saw they were wearing the same blue suede Adidas. "I bought them at Harvey's after I saw you wearing them."

Captivated by the softness of her features now that she was no longer sneering, Max said, "Did you?"

"I always go for men's sneakers," she said, almost friendly now. "Better colors. I'm lucky that I have big feet."

"So do I," Duke interjected. "And you know what they—"

Max coughed loudly and pointed to the farthest corner of the room. "Isn't that Chloë Sevigny?"

Duke hopped in the air. "Where?"

"There," Max said, shoving him in that direction. He turned his attention back to his new crush and resumed the flirtation. "I'm flattered to be your style icon, Sydney," he said, achieving his aim of making her laugh.

"I usually just shop the warehouse sale," she said. "This was my first full retail purchase."

"Really," Max said, his innate charm oozing out like honey. "All because of me?"

"Well . . ." She tilted her head and smiled.

They both seemed to have forgotten that her overdressed shadow was hovering just outside their orbit until he made himself known. "Jeffrey-James Eliot. The makeup artist," he said, as if there were only one. "So nice to meet you." He took Max's hand in a firm grip and said, "Now, what kind of discount do you get at Harvey's?"

Max laughed out of surprise. It was a question many wanted answered, but he couldn't recall a time when he'd been asked so bluntly. And by someone he'd only just met. Most people danced around the subject, trying (usually poorly) to conceal their true motives. It took a moment before Max remembered why Jeffrey hadn't felt the need to do that: He thought Max was the doorman.

Which was sort of silly, wasn't it? Max considered telling them the truth (that he was the creative director; he never volunteered that his family owned the store), until he was overcome by a visceral memory of his days at Brown when he fancied himself a thespian. Senior year he'd been a featured player in the massively popular campus soap opera *Cereal*, staged every Friday night by a wacky drama clique, and he loved the preshow jitters, the rush of getting a laugh. That summer he signed up for drama classes, convinced he'd found his calling. By fall he'd gotten over the acting bug. He wasn't good enough to make a go of it, and he didn't have the commitment to live the actor's life. But for a short spell, he'd felt a genuine, burning passion for something. That was what he missed.

And there was something refreshing about Jeffrey's directness and, less so, about Sydney's rudeness. Neither would have spoken to him in such a manner had they known his true identity. This might be a fun little *social experiment*, he thought. Anything to distract him from the monotony of work!

"What kind of discount?" he said, stalling as he tried to figure out how he was going to play this. There was no simple answer to that question. For him it was 100 percent, but when it came to the ladies, his clout was as much a curse as a blessing. He wooed chivalrously, taking great care in choosing the perfect gift for a woman, but gratitude inevitably turned into expectation. It wasn't a question of if but when the temporary object of his affection would begin bugging him to procure all manner of merchandise, dropping hints around Valentine's, her birthday, Christmas . . . When you were Harvey Cooper's son, it was never the thought that counted. How soon and how much a woman harassed him for free shit was usually an accurate predictor of how long a relationship or, more often, an infatuation would last. After sexual relations ceased, most women were demoted to 20 percent discount status—assuming, of course, there were no feelings of ill will. (The residual benefit of his enviable position was that no matter how abruptly he ended things, there never were.)

Still not sure what number he was going to pull out of his chapeau, he said, "Well, that depends, Jeffrey."

"On what?" Jeffrey said.

"Who's asking."

Jeffrey put his hand on Sydney's back and pushed her forward. "She is."

"Jeffrey!" she said, and they got into one of those little slap fights women only have with their gay friends.

Wanting her full attention back on him, Max said, "Well, are you?"

"Well, yes," Sydney said, giving Jeffrey a look. "I guess I am."

Max gave it a moment's consideration. He was going to say 40 percent, a higher than normal starting point, but then she tilted her head and smiled that mysterious smile. "Fifty," he said.

Jeffrey reacted to that utterance like a man possessed. His arm seesawed into the air, and his whole body arched as if he was about to go into a back bend. Adding to the impression that he was catching the Holy Ghost, he began speaking in tongues. "What you say!" he shouted as his raised hand curled into an exalted fist. Max had no idea what that expression meant, but he knew Jeffrey was happy because, in addition to the quick jig that accompanied his nonsensical shout, he let out an orgasmic moan that Max, as a heterosexual man, hoped never to hear again. When he recovered from the possession, which had Sydney in hysterics and Max in an uncomfortable state of confusion, he asked for confirmation. "You can get *fifty percent off*?"

It dawned on Max that a doorman wouldn't have that much juice (he had no clue), and he chided himself for breaking character. "Yeah, well . . ." he stammered. "I, uh, have my ways."

"Even on sale merchandise?" Sydney said, obviously trying to contain her excitement.

"Even on sale merchandise," Max confirmed. He slipped a flyer out of his jacket pocket, went over to the wall, and, using a pencil dangling next to a photo, scribbled on the back. He turned around and handed the flyer to Sydney. "That's our band. We're playing next weekend." She flipped it over and saw the number on the back. "And that's my cell. Use my discount anytime."

Sydney held her hand high, wiggling her fingers. *"Gimme some!"*

Jeffrey gave her a high five and quoted his favorite person in the whole wide world (Posh Spice). "This is *may-jor.*"

"And you thought I had no game."

"That little head tilt. Was that in Mitzi's book?"

"Not even. I came up with that all on my own!"

Jeffrey looked impressed. "There's hope for you yet."

"Kudos to you too. I saw you restrain yourself when he called you Jeffrey."

"Only because I knew there was going to be a payoff at the end. Do people call Sarah Jessica Parker 'Sarah'? Do they call Mary-Kate Olsen 'Mary'? My name is Jeffrey-James, people," he shouted to no one in particular. "Call me by my name!"

"I was very honored when you let me start calling you Jeffrey," Sydney said, smiling as she rooted around in her bag. It was so funny when he got all worked up over dumb shit like that. (Which was why she'd brought it up.)

"Lucky he didn't call me J. J., 'cause then I would've snapped."

Sydney pulled out her phone and flipped it open. "When he said fifty percent and you went into that little dance? I swear, I thought I was gonna lose it."

"Well, you saw, I *did* lose it. Shit, I don't care. Happy is as happy does." Watching Sydney open a new entry, Jeffrey began to nod. "Uh-huh. Lock it in there right now. *And put it on speed dial!*"

"Half off! Even on sale merchandise?" Sydney was so giddy she hit the wrong buttons and ended up in the calendar. "We won't even have to wait for the warehouse sale! Can you imagine?"

Swiping another nibble from a passing tray, Jeffrey said, "I couldn't be happier right now if we heard about another Republican senator gettin' caught with a dick in his ass!"

Sydney threw her head back, howling, and almost dropped the phone.

"See where a little flirting can get you?" Jeffrey said. Then he shoved a shrimp puff in his mouth whole.

"I know," Sydney said, wiping a hysterical tear from the corner of her eye. "And it was so easy!"

"Yeah, well, you better keep it up, missy," Jeffrey said, fake-smiling at someone across the room. "Don't slip back into your normal, 'Stay back, you're invading my personal space' self. That cute little white boy needs to become our new best friend."

"He will," Sydney said. "Trust. Because there's 50 Cent and then there's"—she held up her phone so Jeffrey could see the entry—"Our boy, Fifty *Per*cent!"

"But we'll just call him Fiddy!" While they were both doubled over with laughter, Jeffrey tried to catch her out. "So you *do* think he's cute?"

Getting back on defense faster than Kobe, Sydney deadpanned, "Who? Safety Goggles?"

"You know who."

"Let's go," she said, yanking Jeffrey toward the door. "There's nothing more we can achieve here."

"You know he's cute," he teased. "And I'll put money down that in a hot minute S and M will be spotted sitting in a tree k-i-s-s-i-n-g!"

Sydney frowned at him. "What are you, twelve?"

"That was my *Gossip Girl* impersonation."

"It needs work."

"I'm not saying you shouldn't make him your new boy toy. I mean, you have an opening now, right?"

"Didn't you just lecture me about the futility of accidental dating?"

"I did. But we can make an exception for him." They passed the table in the lobby where a cluster of people were writing checks and handing over credit cards to pay for their auction wins, and Jeffrey chose that moment to suggest, at an embarrassing volume, "Kiss him, fuck him, lick his balls if you think it might get us to seventy percent!"

Sydney shot him a hateful look, which he didn't notice because he was too busy laughing. "You know what, Jeffrey?" Her eyes brightened and she pressed her hand tenderly against his shoulder. "We've really come full circle tonight." Her expression turned hateful again and she shoved him. "You're back to prostituting me."

"Now, you can touch me, but don't touch the coat, babydoll!" He twisted the sleeve to get a look at the spot she had touched. "Did you have food on your hands?"

"I hope so."

"You know why you're so mad?" He wagged a manicured finger at her. " 'Cause you sent Kyle packing and that tasty lil sex machine was your stress reliever. Better get yo' ass to yoga."

Sydney looked straight ahead and said nothing, taking her irritation out on Max's flyer, which she was slowly crushing in her fist.

Stonewalled, Jeffrey went back to, "You know he's cute."

"Whatever," she snapped. "He's not my type." She marched to the front door, banged it open, then glanced back, realizing that Jeffrey was no longer by her side. And there he was in the middle of the lobby, hand on hip, lips poked out, head jutting attitudinally to one side. Sydney knew that pose all too well. He was about to read her.

"Not your type?" His head rolled to the other side. "Is that what you just said?"

Throwing as much shade as she was catching, Sydney said, "You heard me."

"Honey, he's a doorman slash musician," Jeffrey said, stalking toward her as if they were in a saloon, about to have a gunfight. "He's *exactly* your type!"

Sydney let him see the crushed flyer in her hand before she sent the crumpled ball sailing into the trash can in the corner. "That *used* to be my type." Then she struck a diva pose of her own and made a promise she intended to keep. "Not anymore."

CHAPTER TWENTY-EIGHT

As the clusterfuck raging in women's shoes slowly came into view, Sydney felt her hands ball into fists. Myrna hadn't been gone a week and already Gareth was treating her as if she was a second-rate freelancer. She hadn't done party coverage in two years! And if there was one party she didn't want to cover, it was this one.

At the top of the escalator, she was greeted by a huge photo of Lulu Merriwether, the party's guest of honor, a frail fauxialite of thirty-two with a nose as thin as a pencil. It was all Sydney could do not to whip out a Sharpie and deface it.

Harvey's had closed to the public an hour ago, clearing out the hoi polloi so Miss Merriwether and her fellow fauxialites could have the run of the place. Although it was the harried black-clad salespeople who were doing all the running. Sydney watched them scurrying from one rich bitch to the next, taking the overpriced shoes that dangled from their fingertips while sharply dressed men stood by idly, knocking back champagne to stave off boredom. And amid this controlled chaos Lulu Merriwether was gliding around with a diamond tiara, probably real, atop her expensively blonded head.

Even if Sydney hadn't had a personal beef with Lulu Merriwether, she would've hated the bitch on general principle. The daughter of a billionaire (that alone was enough to provoke Sydney's contempt), she was known only for being photographed at the "right" parties wearing the "right" clothes until, to Sydney's abject horror, she became a bestselling author three years ago. Her debut novel, *Confessions of a Park Avenue Princess,* an overhyped roman à clef born out of the "bored rich women who write books so they can be feted for something other than being the wife or daughter of someone who has actually done something" trend, was such a hit that it spawned a series. The follow-up, *Park Avenue Princess Ties the Knot,* had done even better. Sales were no doubt helped by the splashy, ass-smooching profiles that ran in almost every major women's magazine when Lulu married Carter Bailey, himself an heir to a media fortune (on his mother's side) and the "crown prince" of some obscure European principality that had banished its monarchy a hundred years ago, which conveniently made Lulu a real-life princess (for press purposes anyway).

And she surely wasn't going to relinquish her suspect crown princess title, even though tonight New York's high and mighty had gathered in Harvey's massive shoe department to celebrate the publication of *Park Avenue Princess Gets Divorced,* the third installment in the series. Lulu's nasty court battle with her now soon-to-be ex-husband was at a fever pitch, and the book's shrewdly timed release had many wondering if their mudslinging was just a Suri Cruise–type ploy to bring attention to the book. Sydney wasn't wondering. She was sure of it. Lulu Merriwether's success was hype, nothing more. And now, thanks to Gareth, she had become part of the bitch's hype machine.

Gareth had left her a message only a few hours ago that she had to cover the party, and she hadn't liked his tone. It wasn't a "Someone else was supposed to do it but there was a mix-up so help me out here" kind of plea. It was a "You work for me so do as I say" demand. Telling him she hadn't gotten the message in time had crossed her mind, but she decided that was not in her best interest. She had no idea if Myrna was ever coming back— Sydney still hadn't heard from her—which made Gareth the controller of her fate for the foreseeable future. Due to the circumstances around her hiring, *Cachet* would never fire her, but if she pissed Gareth off, he could keep sticking her with bullshit assignments like this one, which was, in a sense, almost as bad.

No, the sensible part of Sydney's brain told her. *Actually, it wasn't.* She made eight thousand dollars a month to talk to celebrities and, on occasion, go to parties like this one. She only needed to get a snapshot of the action and a few quotes from some boldface names. It wasn't that deep.

Starving African babies, starving African babies, starving African babies, she silently chanted, scrounging in her bag for a working pen.

Max was standing in his office with his bare shins pressed against the chrome frame of the daybed and his cock in Natasha's mouth. He generally found it difficult to come from oral sex, but Natasha had a way with her succulent Russian mouth that could bring him to satisfaction in six minutes flat. They were four minutes in when the sudden vibration of his iPhone in his jacket pocket threatened to break his concentration. He knew it was Remy summoning him downstairs, as she had been for the last hour, and he also knew that if he didn't respond this time, someone would come up to bang on his door and jeopardize his chances of crossing the finish line.

He felt like MacGyver as he retrieved the device with his unsteady right hand, keeping his left on Natasha's head, but he couldn't do anything but laugh when he saw Remy's message: "pls come now!" His laughter turned into a satisfied moan when, a moment later, he did just that.

The elevator pinged, and before Sydney could step aside, a herd of Muffies stampeded by, rushing toward the shoes as if they were at a sample sale and if they didn't hurry, all the good shit would be gone. (The way the registers were ringing, they were probably right.)

Last to exit was an older woman who wore a fur stole and her gray hair in an immaculate chignon. She didn't rush at all. She sauntered off and waited for Lulu to come to her.

"Mahhhvelous idea, having it here," she gushed after Lulu welcomed her with a double air kiss.

"Well," Lulu trilled, "this is the Park Avenue Princess's second home!"

"More like her third or fourth," the old woman (whose last name was probably Van der Something) quipped. Then she and Lulu strolled away, laughing the laugh of the insanely rich.

Disgusted though Sydney was by the exchange, it was a brilliantly ridiculous quote, and from the guest of honor herself. All she had to do now was get the full name of the fur-clad quipper, and one more juicy quote like that one, and she could be out.

But this was what she hated about party coverage, she thought, silently cursing Gareth. It put her in the position of being snubbed by people who didn't want to be quoted in the magazine. With celebrity profiles, she had some semblance of control. The subjects had to talk to her, and if someone threw her shade, she'd return the favor in print. At parties like this, any C-list nobody was free to brush her off if they didn't want to answer meaningless questions like "What makes a P. Diddy party so fabulous?" And it was always C-list nobodies (trying to act A-list) who pulled shit like that.

Surprisingly, in the two years she'd spent covering parties for *Cachet*, she'd never crossed paths with Lulu. Although she had come across plenty of self-important people whose orders she'd taken, phones she'd answered, complicated coffee orders she had once fetched. And they rarely recognized her. Granted, she was years older and many pounds lighter, but was that the reason someone she'd waited on twenty times could stare right in her face without a hint of recognition? She didn't think so. More likely it was because she had been just a minion then, an invisible worker bee. Landing the high-profile job with *Cachet* had given her entrée to this rarefied world and put her on more equal footing, but she clung to her outsider status like a coat of arms.

Feeling very Angelina Jolie in the jeans, leather jacket, and motorcycle boots she'd worn to subtly telegraph her contempt to the glammed-up crowd, she waded tentatively into the fray. She walked among them now. But she would never *be* one of them.

The first words out of Natasha's mouth after she finished wiping it were, "You know that red Luella bag you put on hold for me?"

Aside from the occasional blow job, Max hadn't slept with her in six months, but she was exempted from the discount demotion that applied to most of his former paramours. After they'd officially split, he hadn't made her pay for the first few things she'd asked him to put "on hold," and they now had a mutual understanding that "on hold" meant "free." It was no skin off his nose—technically he was supposed to pay the 50 percent cost of everything he charged to the house account, but he never did. (And there was no cap on the family account.) The bills got sucked into a black hole . . . or maybe Avery paid them? Max didn't ask, didn't care. He had better things to spend his money on. It certainly wasn't going to end up in Harvey's coffers.

And he felt an obligation to protect Natasha from herself. A guileless, twenty-five-year-old Russian living the American dream, she was incapable of seeing more than three months into the future. She didn't need to waste her money on overpriced bags and skin-care regimens. (And since she hadn't paid her taxes for two years and he'd had to "loan" her twelve thousand dollars—"loan" being a code word for "give"—to get the IRS to remove the lien from her bank account, he didn't trust that she'd keep proper receipts and write these things off on her taxes.) Five years from now the poor thing would probably be on the skids with nothing but a bunch of designer clothes and old magazine covers to comfort her. Unless she married some Eurotrash playboy, which, sadly, was her only hope of survival. So, for her, anything.

What she didn't need to know was that Max kept a treasure trove of waiting-list-only luxury handbags locked in a cabinet in his office, doling them out strategically like casino chips. This was a recently instituted policy after he'd discovered his unfettered access to luxury goods could score him bigger things than sex. His latest and greatest trade-off: three round-trip domestic flights on Marquis Jets in exchange for securing a nine thousand-dollar handbag for the CEO's wife. Remy kept track of the inventory in the Golden Cabinet, so Max had no idea whether this red Luella bag that Natasha was now asking for in brown was locked inside, and despite his warm postejaculatory feelings toward her, he wasn't about to fling open the doors and allow her access to his secret stash.

Instead, he led her out of his office, saying, "Let's go downstairs and check."

Most of the guests were society types Sydney wouldn't have known from a can of paint, but with the help of Lulu's book publicist, a heavyset, likable frump named Millicent—not to be confused with her personal publicist, a sleek, stylish gal named Sasha—she'd made the necessary identifications. Now she was waiting for Remy to return with an advance copy of Lulu's book. Sydney was confident it would be terrible, which was exactly why she'd jumped at the chance to acquire a copy without adding to Lulu's sales.

Though gloating over how bad it was wouldn't keep this book from becoming a bestseller like the others, she thought bitterly. The idle rich were the newest celebrities, and in the genre known as "chic lit," the quality of the writing didn't seem to matter. Sydney had been in stubborn denial about this unfortunate reality until the night she'd happened into Barnes & Noble Union Square and found a standing-room-only audience assembled to hear Lulu Merriwether read from her second piece of trash. Most appalling was that it was regular folks who'd come out (on a rainy night!) to worship at Lulu's altar. Didn't these women realize they were spending their hard-earned cash to make bestselling authors out of snobs who wouldn't deign to acknowledge them outside of a book signing? At least movie stars played characters. Lulu Merriwether was just telling tales about how much better than everyone else she and her friends thought they were. Sydney had skimmed some of the other books in the genre and they all seemed like one long condescension that said, "You wish you could wear what I wear, shop where I shop, live how I live, date who I date, but you never will, so give me your $23.95 and then be gone, you little peasant."

That night she'd watched in astonishment as a legion of frizzy-haired administrative assistants with promotional totes on their laps listened with rapt attention as Lulu, styled within an inch of her life, fielded questions about her writing routine ("Five days a week. No matter what!") and why she felt most creative at her beachfront Hamptons home ("The sound of the ocean is quite soothing"). Knowing that Lulu Merriwether had probably just regaled some underpaid hack with gossipy stories in lieu of writing her own book, Sydney stood in the back, fighting a violent urge to shout, "The empress has no clothes!"

It was like high school all over again, she'd thought. And she was looking at a room full of grown-up Tammi Silowitzes trying to bask in the reflection of the mean girl's superficial glow. Sydney hadn't thought about Tammi in years, or realized until that moment that it was her former classmate who had, in a roundabout way, jump-started her writing career. Before she began writing for Omnimedia, her one and only byline had appeared in the *Scarsdale High Gazette* on the scathing editorial she'd written in a fit of indignation following "the Tammi Silowitz incident." The news that Tammi had swallowed half a bottle of extra-strength Tylenol after being rejected by the cheerleading squad for the third year in a row hadn't come as such a shock to Sydney when she'd heard. Tammi had to be mental to think those pom-pom-shaking twats would allow a pockmarked chubster like her into their little sorority. Sydney wasn't really friends with Tammi, but they had honors calculus together and she'd witnessed Tammi's pitiful attempts to get noticed by the "in crowd." Sydney had taken that road but quickly abandoned it. Like around sixth grade. "If you can't join 'em, fuck 'em" was her way of looking at it. Sometimes she wanted to go up to Tammi and slap some sense into her. *Wake up, Tammi; you'll never be one of them!* She didn't bother, knowing it would be a waste of time. Tammi just didn't get it, as her half-assed suicide bid confirmed.

In high school, the general assumption that everyone wanted to be a cheerleader but only the chosen few were allowed the privilege annoyed Sydney to no end. She had no such aspirations. As she wrote in her editorial, she thought cheerleading was a pointless and degrading extracurricular activity. She furthermore suggested that the energies of the female population would be better expended *playing* on teams rather than cheering for them. The piece caused quite a stir, drawing the ire and harassment of the popular clique, which only elevated Sydney's martyr status among the voiceless, ignored masses who made up the other 98 percent of the school. It was a small personal victory that ultimately did nothing to disrupt the social hierarchy of the school, just as nothing Sydney could do would keep Lulu Merriwether off the bestseller list . . .

Deciding it would be best to accept that inconvenient truth, she made a beeline for the elevator, reminding herself that the opposite of love wasn't hate but indifference.

After locating Natasha's precious bag trapped in a locked display case and promising to "put it on hold" for her, Max put her in a cab and headed back inside to break bread with the person who was number one on the stalker list posted in the security office. (Number two was another slightly "off" woman he'd slept with once and could never bring himself to call again after she sent him a mushy e-mail in which she described herself as a "purest." Mitzi Berman was number three.) Security did a pretty good job of heading Lulu off before she could get up to Max's office, but outside of the store, he was defenseless. And now, in a perverse reversal of fortune, he found himself in concert with the woman.

Harvey's was a favorite of the old guard, but getting the society princess to anoint the store as a cool place for her generation went a long way in Avery's master plan of attracting the younger crowd. Max just wished Avery was here to run the show. But she wasn't, he thought spitefully, visions of Avery lying in bed with ankles swollen to the size of two-liter Coke bottles flashing in his head.

He slumped in the corner of the elevator, dreading the onslaught he was about to brave. Because it wasn't just Lulu with whom he could not deal. It was all of them. Her whole disgusting rich-girl posse. They were all up there, he thought. Waiting to pounce.

Just like stars were the biggest starfuckers, rich girls were the biggest golddiggers. And with him, the procurement of luxury goods was a favored flirting technique. "Max, there's a bag that I really want," they'd say with a seductive pout. "Can you bump me up the waiting list?" *Sure,* he always wanted to tell them. *Can you bump my dick with your surgically enhanced lips?* (He remembered a time when a society girl would never consider having obvious cosmetic surgery. Now most of them looked like Hollywood harlots and were desperately trying to land their own reality shows, a level of tackiness Max couldn't have imagined he'd see in his lifetime.) He never made the request because it was unlikely that any of them would have Natasha's skills, but if he had asked, it wasn't out of the question that one of them would drop to her knees and get to it. What a lot of people didn't understand—or maybe they did now, thanks to Paris Hilton—was that rich girls were the biggest freaks. They didn't have to worry about getting "a reputation" because if you were "of" the Basses or the Merriwethers you could do whatever you wanted, sexually or otherwise, and it wouldn't stick. You got a free pass. Every rich girl he dated at Brown was three-input. As was Lulu. He didn't care for the third, rarely used orifice, but it was nice to know he had the option. Irony was, the sex with Lulu wasn't that hot, but the limitless possibilities kept him going back.

They'd known each other for years, but they hooked up right after he'd finished his apartment, at a time when he was bored and restless. They were "together" for three months, two and a half of which he spent trying to ditch her. The fact that he didn't want their dalliance to continue was trumped by the fact that she did. After his usual fadeaway didn't work, he'd been forced to tell her, "Lulu, I don't want to be with you. Do not call me.

Do not come by the store looking for me. It's over between us and there is no chance of us ever having anything real." The next day he ran into one of her friends, who prodded him about how long their "trial separation" was going to last.

Their brief yet tumultuous fling had taught Max a valuable lesson: Stick to waitresses. There were a million cute waitresses in New York and none of them knew he was Harvey Cooper's son unless he told them. And he usually didn't. With them, he could just be Max. Or Coop, as a lot of his friends called him. He knew the "service girls" honestly found him funny or charming, that they were sleeping with him because he turned them on, not faking it because they were looking for a husband with the right pedigree and liquidity. And when it was over, he could disappear and never run into them again.

He'd be running into girls like Lulu for the rest of his life. It was amazing how he could be in London, Paris, Kenya and run into people he'd gone to school with on the Upper East Side. Maybe he should leave New York, he thought, each *ping* of the elevator sounding more ominous. Avery had been working on him to revamp the L.A. store. She and Harvey would be thrilled if he showed the slightest interest in doing that. He had a few friends out there. He could submerge himself in a whole new social world. He could surf . . .

The final *ping* sounded, snapping him back to reality, and he braced himself for what was sure to be a total clusterfuck.

CHAPTER TWENTY-NINE

Max stepped off the elevator and saw his latest crush heading straight for him. "Hey . . ." Disappointed that she whizzed right past and stabbed at the Lobby button as if it had done something to her, he slipped his arm through the closing doors and more forcefully repeated himself. "Hey!"

When she looked up, her grimace was replaced by a vague look of recognition. Not the greeting he was hoping for. "Hey . . ." She squinted at him as if she was trying to remember something.

Realizing what that something was, he said, "Max."

She nodded. "Right."

Annoyed that she didn't remember his name when he remembered hers, Max banged the closing doors back harder than he intended. "I didn't expect to see you here."

"I was working." She held up her notepad. "I had to cover it for *Cachet*."

"Cool," Max said. "So that's what you do. You're a writer?"

"Yeah," she said, dropping the pad into her bag. "Have they got you working this thing? I'd think this would be the last place you'd want to be after hours."

"It is," Max said. The doors began to close again, and this time when he banged them back, she was clearly annoyed. He felt he should come clean and explain that his work here did not involve opening doors—although he did not intend to tell her just yet that his family owned the store—and oh, what a laugh they would have! But just then he heard Remy's high-pitched chirp and turned to see her skidding across the marble floor. She practically threw a copy of Lulu's book at him, yammering something about his "saying a few words" and how late he was before she was intercepted by another woman from the events department who seemed to be in a comparable state of anxiety.

After they rushed off, Max turned back to Sydney, who said, "Well, see ya!" Max took that as a cue for him to let the doors go, but instead he checked to see if anyone was watching—no one was—and stepped inside. This didn't do anything to change the mild look of displeasure on her face. (She seemed to have a permanent "Who are you and why are you talking to me?" expression veiled across her otherwise lovely features.)

"You're leaving?" she said. "I thought you were working here."

"No, I'm not. I mean, well, I am . . ."

Before he could fess up, Sydney leaned toward him and whispered, "I don't blame you for skipping out. We're nothing but the help to these people."

The remark struck Max cold. *These people?*

"Frankly, I don't know how you can work here and deal with them every day. And *this* chick?" She pointed to the book he'd forgotten he was holding. "Vile."

"Lulu?" Max said, his body temperature rising now as he flushed with panic. "You know her?"

"Oh, sure. We *summer* together in the country every year," she said, mocking the verbal affectations almost every Hamptonite he knew used.

His head clouded by the turn their encounter had taken, Max said, "So you *don't* know her?"

"Of course I don't know her. You think I would associate with such a person?" The elevator doors opened, and Sydney marched out as if she were heading to an antiwar rally. "But I know enough about her to know I hate everything she represents!"

Max stood rooted to the spot, processing that statement for so long that the doors closed and he wound up on the lower level. He jumped out, leaped up the stairs two at a time, and caught Sydney halfway up the block. She seemed to have been ranting the whole time and hadn't noticed his disappearance.

"She's just some rich girl who has never worked a day in her life and who never *will* work a day in her life! But it's not good enough to be born rich. Oh no, now she has to pretend to have a career too!"

One step behind, Max nodded to himself. *If she only knew . . .*

Sydney reached the subway station on the corner and punctuated her rant with an exasperated huff. "Don't you hate people like that?"

Max blanked, then said the only thing he could say in that supremely awkward moment. "Loathe."

The perfect hostess, Lulu was smiling, air-kissing, waving across the room, all while managing to balance her tiara and hiss at Remy out of the side of her mouth. "Where the hell is Max? He's supposed to introduce me!"

Remy looked around. "He was just . . ." She did a full revolution, scanning the entire room. "He was just here."

"Find him!" Lulu snapped. She drifted away to greet a fashionably late A-list arrival and Remy scampered off in search of Max.

Waving the book wildly in the air, Sydney roared, "I could write a novel ten times better than this!"

Seated on the bench, Max smiled up at her. "Do you write fiction?"

Sydney sized him up with a look. It was as if he was trying to make date conversation. "I don't have the patience," she said. "Anyway, who says it's fiction? It's just gossip about her mean-girl clique. Anyone could spin that into a marketable book. It doesn't take any real skill."

"Hmm," Max said. "I suppose."

He supposed? Sydney walked to the edge of the platform and looked down the tunnel. When a distant light appeared, she stepped back to the wall. All the way back. One of her many fears was that a mental case would come out of nowhere and push her onto the tracks right as the train was coming. People always said she was paranoid, but that had happened to a girl in her high school (the train wasn't coming, but imagine the rats!), and it had happened last week to a woman in Brooklyn, so how was it paranoid to think it could happen to her? And she didn't really know this guy. He might be the crazy to do it.

"But let's say I did write a novel," she said, keeping her eye on him. "Do you suppose Random House would give me half a million dollars for it? Would *Vogue* do a three-page spread on me?"

Max got up and stood beside her. "Perhaps."

"Perhaps? No fucking way, José! And you know why?" The train rumbled into the station, which was perfect timing because Sydney felt like screaming, and now she had an excuse to do just that. "BECAUSE MY LAST NAME ISN'T MERRIWETHER!" The train came to a stop, and Sydney shook her head in disgust. "The rich get richer . . ."

"It's a travesty," Max said, and followed her through the opening doors.

"Where is he?" Lulu snapped, in a full-on snit.

Cowering beside her, Remy admitted, "I can't find him."

Lulu's friend Ashley sauntered by. "Can't find who?"

"Max," Lulu said distractedly.

"I called his cell," Remy said. "It went straight to voice mail."

"I think he left," Ashley said.

Trying to keep Lulu calm, Remy said, "No, no, he didn't leave. He's around here somewhere."

"I saw him get on the elevator with that girl," Ashley said.

Lulu turned to her. "What girl?"

"God, you didn't see her?" Ashley said. "I was wondering why she was even here."

Lulu was thinking the same thing about Ashley, a peripheral friend she'd met in college and had never managed to shake. "Obviously I didn't see her or I wouldn't be talking to you right now," she said, so secure in her superior position that she could be openly bitchy.

"That skank who screwed Carter!" Ashley screeched, sipping from her third glass of champagne.

Carter had screwed many skanks, so Lulu was forced to ask for clarification. She ushered Ashley over to the corner so Remy wouldn't hear. "Which one?"

"The one you got fired," Ashley said.

"From Saks?"

"No, the waitress."

"From Odeon?"

"No," Ashley said, putting her hand over her mouth as she hiccupped. "From Indochine. Remember?"

Lulu had a vague recollection. That was long ago, and with all the cheating Carter had done, details were sketchy.

"Her name is Sydney something," Ashley said. "She writes for *Cachet* now. I've seen her picture in there a few times." And then, because Lulu always treated her like a serf, she added, "She looks *good*."

"Who invited her?" Lulu demanded.

"How should I know? It's your party. Did you check the dressing rooms?" Champagne sloshed out of her glass as she gestured wildly toward the other side of the floor. "She's probably in there screwing him. HOOKER!"

Lulu's parents and several guests looked over from the middle of the room. "Shut up and go away," Lulu demanded. Ashley did as she was told, and Lulu waved for Remy to come to her. "Did you check the dressing rooms?"

"This is the shoe department," Remy said. "There are no dressing rooms on this floor."

"Then check the other floors!"

"All of them?"

"Yes!"

"Her name is Sydney Zamora." Even though Lulu and Ashley had turned their backs on her, Remy had heard every word. Neither of them realized how loudly they were talking. "She was covering the party for *Cachet*."

"Well, she didn't speak to me," Lulu said. "And it's my party! How does Max know her?"

"I don't know," Remy said, biting her lip. She had just radioed down to security and they said Max had left with a woman and hadn't come back. Why he would have done that, Remy didn't know, but she didn't want Lulunatic to have any more reason to be mad at him.

"Call his cell again," Lulu said.

Remy speed-dialed. "Straight to voice mail," she said. "But it's okay, Lulu. It's okay. I'll do it. I'll introduce you."

Lulu looked her up and down, revolted by her business-casual attire. "Not dressed like that you won't."

• • •

During their brief interaction at the gallery, Max had found Sydney to be funny and inviting. He'd thought about her a few times, wondered if she'd call. But it was this close-up glimpse of her judgmental, angry, snappish side that had him hooked. Difficult women were his specialty. He loved nothing more than a lioness that needed a good taming . . .

"So who else do you write for besides *Cachet*?" he said, making an effort not to invade her space, though her alluring scent was making it difficult. When they'd gotten on, the two-seater in the corner was empty, so he grabbed it. He was very happy to be squished in the subway version of a love seat with her. She clearly was not.

"I've written for a couple of other magazines," she said, leaning as far away from him as possible. "Now I'm on contract with *Cachet*."

"I read *Cachet* every month," he said, trying to tamp down his blatant interest. "The horoscopes are scarily accurate."

"Aren't they?" Forgetting herself, she leaned toward him with a big, bright smile on her face, then, realizing her lapse, backed away. "The guy who does them, Michael, he's a riot. He gives these talks once a month and he'll tell you what the planets are doing or whatever. You know, like 'Mercury's in retrograde. Don't leave your apartment until the twelfth.'" They both laughed. "And believe me, when he says that, I don't leave my apartment until the twelfth!"

Max laughed some more. And she was funny too.

She took the book from his lap and cracked open the cover. "Oh look, it's signed," she sniffed, noticing Lulu's loopy signature on the title page. "Maybe when she's dead it'll be worth something."

Max frowned. And they were having such a lovely time. "Why is it that you hate her so much? Just because she's rich?"

"Not just that she's rich," Sydney said. "She is undeserving of all that she has."

"How do you know?"

"How do I know? How do I know?" she screeched as if he had just said maybe Hitler wasn't such a bad guy.

"Okay," Max said. "I understand what you mean. But that's the family she was born into. What is she supposed to do?" Although this "Down with rich people" development had put him in quite a spot, he was interested to know what she thought. These were the things no one would ever tell him.

"She's supposed to not be a vapid, self-centered bitch. Do you know she infiltrated a charity that gives away baby clothes to welfare mothers just so she could steal their blueprint and start a rival charity with her name on it?"

"Yes," Max said. "I did hear something about that."

"Well, do you think she did that because she really cares about welfare mothers?"

"No, I don't think she's really thinking about what it will do for them. She's thinking about how it will make her look. But so be it if ultimately those women get what they need. Right?"

"Wrong," Sydney said emphatically. "The organization whose blueprint she stole has been around for fifty years. It's respected and well run. And Lulu's Helping fucking Hand is taking money and resources away from them. People are not going to donate to two charities that do the exact same thing. She gets more publicity and she has more pull on the social scene, which means she'll raise more money. She founded a *rival charity.* Before her that term didn't exist. Come on, Matt, that's fucked up!"

"Agreed. And it's Max."

"Right. Is that short for something?"

"Maximillian."

"Maximillian?" she repeated with a little laugh. "How white of you."

"What are you?" he said, scrutinizing her features. "Brazilian?"

"Brazilian? That's a new one," she said. "I'm a lot of things. Afro-Cuban, Portuguese, Irish . . . I get offended for everybody."

"Hmm, I can tell. But Irish? Very white of you."

"I'm multiracial," she said, suppressing a smile. "It's very dangerous to consider yourself white in a world that does not."

"I went to Rio earlier this year," he said, trying to picture her in one of those tiny bikinis the Brazilian girls wore. "Have you ever been?"

"No. But getting back to Lulu, whose profligate ways you seem to be defending . . ."

"I'm not defending her."

"It sure seems that way. I mean, if I had that much money, I would be doing all kinds of good things with it."

"Everyone is a product of their environment," Max snapped, the comment zeroing in on the ever-present shame he felt for living a life of inertia, loafing around because he could, never doing anything productive or meaningful.

"See, there you go again. Defending her."

"I'm *not* defending her," Max said too forcefully. The last thing he wanted to do was defend Lulu—although her family was ten times richer than his, which meant she was ten times more fucked up. He was defending himself now. "I'm just saying that if you had grown up with that much money, you wouldn't be you, Sydney. You would be her. Or someone like her. So you really don't know what you would do." That shut her up. Max knew he had pissed her off royally—he didn't think he'd ever seen a harder glare on a woman—but after years of hearing people talk this kind of hypothetical foolishness and biting his tongue because he was a member of "the oppressor class," spewing felt so damn good he couldn't stop. "And I am sick of hearing people talk about what they would do if they had 'that much money.' It doesn't take a billion dollars to help people, sweetheart. You can do that for free."

"I do help people," Sydney wailed, a jolt of indignation pushing her halfway off the seat. "I just gave four bags of clothing and accessories to Goodwill!"

"Really," Max replied coolly. "Were they last season?"

Mortally affronted, Sydney reeled back and banged her head on the pole. When Max reached out to see if she was okay, she jumped to her feet and swung around to face the door.

"Still four stops till Christopher Street," Max said, looking up at the electronic sign with confusion.

Sydney tightened her grip on the pole and stared at the door. "I'll stand."

The room looked like a *W* party page come to life, and Remy felt herself breaking out into a cold sweat. In school she always sat in the back of the class so the teacher would never call on her, and she would feign illness on the days of oral reports, such was her dread of public speaking. Why had she volunteered to do this? She must have been suffering from dementia brought on by the stress of dealing with Lulu all day. *Keep it simple,* she told herself. *Short and sweet.*

"Thank you all for coming tonight," she said, trying to keep the quiver out of her voice. She looked at The Donald and gulped. And Melania! She had never seen such big boobs on such a thin woman. Were they real? Was she? With proportions like that she couldn't possibly be human!

She felt her breathing grow shallow and her mind begin to wander. She had a cavity . . . she'd run out of toilet paper . . . she needed to change her sheets . . . the auction for the dress she wanted on eBay was ending tonight . . . her lease was coming up for renewal . . . if she didn't get away from her slutty drunken roommate . . . she hadn't had sex since . . . since . . .

Finish and get off, she told herself. *Short and sweet.* "And now a few words from our guest of honor, *New York Times* bestselling author Lulu Merriwether . . ."

To great applause, Lulu swarmed in front of Remy like Diana Ross showing up a replacement Supreme. Completely obscured by the billowing kimono sleeves of Lulu's silk tunic, Remy backed away, clapping softly, wearing Manolos a size too small and a plain black dress with a price tag hanging from the back.

At first Max thought it was cute that she'd gotten so angry. They were having their first fight. Then she ignored him for a full stop. And two more. The conductor had just announced Christopher Street coming up next. He didn't even have her number. If he wanted to get back into her good graces, he had to act fast. Or he might never hear from her again.

"I'll let you in on a little secret," he said, scooting across the seat to get closer to where she was standing.

Sydney glanced over, not bothering to turn her head all the way to look at him. "Yes, Maximillian?"

He waved the book in the air. "Lulu didn't really write this."

Sydney turned her head all the way and looked at him. "What do you mean?"

"She had a ghostwriter."

Her eyelids fluttering with excitement, she slid back into their little love seat, squealing, *"You lie!"*

"Nope."

Giddier by the second, she said, "I knew it!"

"You knew that?"

"Well, suspected. And I've tried to convince other people. Okay, tell me everything you know."

Feeling a rush from getting such a reaction out of her, Max said, "It's a collaboration of sorts. Lulu feeds the ghostwriter all these gossipy stories about her rich friends, and the ghostwriter outlines and writes the story. Lulu oversees the whole operation, but she doesn't write a word."

"Exactly as I imagined," she said. "I hope the ghostwriter got something out of it."

"Forty thousand dollars cash," Max said.

"Per book?"

"No, it was a four-book deal."

"Slave labor!" Sydney bit her lip, then, sotto voce, asked, "So who's the ghostwriter?"

With his index finger, Max motioned for her to come closer. When she did, he whispered into her ear, letting his lips softly graze her lobe. "I'm not at liberty to say."

The intimacy of the situation was broken when she pulled herself up on the pole, lost in her own private moment of celebration. "This is just too good," she mumbled. "Five days a week, my ass!"

Max wasn't sure what that meant, but watching her lick her luscious lips as if she'd just devoured a spoonful of chocolate mousse, her eyes a dreamy haze, he regretted his indiscretion. This chick was a celebrity reporter for Chrissake! She probably had "Page Six" on speed dial. Lulunatic would have his balls if this got out. And what a terrible position to put Remy in. Jesus, what was he thinking? "I told you that in confidence, by the way," he added—pointlessly, he knew. The damage was done.

"Don't worry," Sydney said. "I won't tell anyone . . . I heard it from you!" She cackled with delight, then as the train pulled into Christopher Street, she asked, "Hey, where do you live?"

"Brooklyn."

"Oh," she said as if offering a condolence. "So I guess I'll see you . . . later."

"Maybe at Joe's Pub," Max said. "Next Saturday?" She stared at him, not putting it together. "My band is playing. I gave you a flyer."

"Right," she said vaguely.

"Try to stop by. We go on around ten."

"I'll try," she said, putting on a smile. "Either way, I'm gonna call you about using that discount."

The doors opened and Max gave a quick wave. "Can't wait."

CHAPTER THIRTY

A spark crackled through the crowd as Brett Babcock, led by his immense bodyguard, Fats, staggered out of G-spot with a lit Newport dangling from his lips and a bottle of Johnnie Walker Black in his clutches. He was flanked by two rowdy buddies, Freddy and J-Dub, both of whom had bit parts in the cop drama Brett was currently shooting in the city, and close on their heels were three starstruck one-night-stands-in-the-making who looked like escapees from a *Girls Gone Wild* video. Last in line was Sydney, getting tossed around in the chaos.

Fats opened the door of the waiting SUV, a tricked-out, blacked-out Denali fit for a Jolie-Pitt, allowing Brett and his boys to jump in. When the three little chickadees tried to hop in behind them, Fats's beefy arm lowered like a tollbooth crossing.

"No room, girls!" Brett shouted.

"Awww, Brett!" they wailed.

Sydney pushed her way through the crowd with the help of Fats, who, the last time she'd hung out with Brett, had talked her ear off about the merits of Lap-Band versus gastric bypass surgery. He helped Sydney in, slammed the back door, then climbed into the front passenger seat, lowering the right side of the car with his girth. While blunt-rolling duties were handled by J-Dub, a small-time rapper who'd managed to carve out a decent career as an actor, Brett hung out of the open window, making a clownishly sad face at the girls.

"Why is there room for *her*?" whined the blonde Brett had been making out with for the last hour but whose name he did not know.

Brett took a swig of scotch from the fresh glass Freddy supplied him, dribbling a few drops on his white undershirt, and flicked his still-lit cigarette toward an approaching paparazzo. "Because she puts out!"

Up front, Fats and the driver shared a gut-busting laugh. In another zip code of the cavernous SUV, J-Dub chuckled while running his tongue along the edge of the blunt wrapper as if it were an envelope. Freddy, a no-talent who was being paid by the studio to accompany Brett everywhere and steer him away from trouble but who was ill equipped for such a Herculean task, leaned over Brett and laughed in the girls' faces. Even Sydney, who was scribbling the quote in her notebook, wondering how she could use it without bringing herself into the story, had to smile.

Nobody was prepared for the response that came from the quietest of the three girls when she took two steps forward and, like a dragon breathing fire, roared, "*I* PUT OUT!"

There was a brief, stunned silence, after which Brett, Freddy, and J-Dub fell to the floor of the car in drunken hysterics. Sydney watched them, piled all over one another like kids in a sandbox, and shook her head. She had hung out with Brett & Co. twice already, but tonight they were in rare form.

Brett crawled back up to the window, barely able to breathe from laughing, and between gasps said, "All right. Jump in a cab and follow us."

That ignited another laughing fit as the groupies ran off as if he'd just shot a gun at a track meet. Hanging halfway out of the window, Brett watched them trying to desperately flag down a taxi, then slid back inside, yelling, "Go! Go! Go! Go! Go!"

The driver peeled off and ran a red light, leaving the girls choking on exhaust fumes, and Sydney fastened her seat belt. (In this group, she was the only person who ever wore one.) She checked her watch. Half past one. At this hour, she was usually snuggled cozily in bed reading one of the five or six books she kept in the bottom of her nightstand. (*In Search of Bill Clinton: A Psychological Biography* was currently at the top of the pile.) But she knew this night had only just begun. She looked at Brett, trying to keep her expression blank so he wouldn't know just how over him she really was. "So where to now?"

Brett puffed, puffed, passed, then blew a long stream of smoke into her face. "Brooklyn."

• • •

Duke thought Max was a dilettante for DJing with an iPod system, but Max didn't care. Who wanted to spend the whole night digging in record crates and cuing up songs when you could make a playlist and press one button? Answer: Duke. He insisted on "keeping it old-school" so Max allowed him to store his turntables and records at his place (along with all the other junk Duke couldn't fit into his spartan East Village studio) and let him spin for an hour at a time at his frequent parties. DJing was about tailoring the music to your crowd, not yourself, Max had tried to explain. It didn't matter that they didn't like Beyoncé and Fergie. Girls did. And getting the girls to shake their cute little asses got guys to follow, and that made everyone happy. It was a pretty simple behavioral algorithm but one Duke continued to miscalculate. Tonight, as usual, his eclectic selections had cleared the dance floor, something Duke failed to notice—or at least care about—once he got lost in the little party that was always raging in his head.

Walking up to the workout area that overlooked the main floor of the loft, Max waved his arms to alert Duke that his time on the "one and twos" was over—even though his allotted hour wasn't up yet. Tapping the button that lit up his iSpinner (the whole thing could fit into one of Duke's milk crates), Max scrolled through the dozen or so playlists he had made, trying to decide which one would reenergize his guests now that Duke had sucked most of the life out of the party.

"Hey!" Duke shouted over the sounds of the Clash song that was playing. He looked over the railing, peering down at the crowd of partygoers lounging on the sprawling first floor of the converted firehouse Max called home. "Isn't that . . . ?"

"The klepto?" Max said, taking a look. A cute chick—like, really cute— had been nabbed at the store the other day with an astonishing number of pilfered goods stashed on her person, and security had invited Max down to the holding room for the interrogation. Max told her they wouldn't press charges as long as she promised not to return to the store, then, escorting her out, he invited her to his birthday party. A stupid move, he realized later, when he remembered he was having the party at his house.

"No," Duke said. "Brett Babcock."

. . .

Light-headed from a contact high, Sydney entered first and stood on the main floor, agog. *Who the hell lived here?*

She wasn't familiar with DUMBO, a neighborhood she knew mostly by its trendy reputation, and when they pulled up in front of the firehouse she thought it was one of those secret clubs that only a celebrity like Brett would know about. But it wasn't a club. It was somebody's home. A massive, meticulously decorated loft that looked like something out of *Elle Decor.*

People were dancing, drinking, shooting pool. There was picked-over food and the remnants of a birthday cake on a long table next to the open kitchen. She rarely went out to parties or clubs unless it was work-related, but she could put names to many of the faces. Models, actors, entertainment players, and one very pretty MTV VJ. "Scenesters," she wrote in her notebook. "People who never had to wait on line outside a club. Everyone 'a somebody' in their own universe."

She heard Brett staggering in and stepped back out into the vestibule to ask, "Whose party is this?"

He strolled past, posse two steps behind. "Who cares?"

Swept in with their rolling tide, Sydney carefully observed the room, interested to see the reaction Brett would get. The people at this party were the kind that did not get excited when they found themselves in the presence of celebrity. If Madonna had walked into the room, no one would have batted an eye (even though they would have been thinking, *Madonna's here!* and subtly tracking her every twitch to tell their friends about it the next day). But when Brett made his grand entrance he was hard to ignore. Waving his arms, one hand clutching his trusty bottle of whiskey, he stomped into the thick of the action with the swagger of someone used to being the coolest person in any room.

J-Dub began rhyming along to the Jay-Z song that was thumping, and Brett wrapped his arm around his boy's neck as they yelled, in unison, "Got ninety-nine problems but a bitch ain't one!"

If Max could have chosen a surprise guest it probably wouldn't have been Brett Babcock. The famous bad boy would undoubtedly absorb the attention of every woman in the room, thereby throwing the energy off balance. But after Duke's garbage spin, he figured the party could use a human B$_{12}$ shot. Max hadn't invited Brett—he'd never even met the guy—but that was what made his parties the shit. You never knew who might roll through. Max was about to get back to his playlists when he recognized the woman at Brett's side. His entire body snapping to attention like a dog in heat, he said, "That's her."

Getting his full hour of spin now that Max had been distracted (the Jay-Z song was the best he'd played all night), Duke pushed the headphone off one ear. "What?"

"That's her!"

"Who?" Duke said, flipping a White Stripes song onto the turntable. "The klepto?"

"No, Sydney!" Backing into the shadows when he saw her looking around at everything as if she were there as a prospective buyer, Max almost fell over one of Duke's crates.

"Sydney who?"

"The chick we met at the gallery."

"The one that was into me," Duke stated as if this was a verified fact. He glanced down at the action with renewed interest. "Where?"

"She's talking to Brett." Max stepped behind the iSpinner, where he felt safely hidden from view, his mind so jumbled he couldn't remember what he had on his various playlists. *What was Sydney doing with Brett Babcock?!* He randomly chose a playlist to put an immediate end to Duke's reign of terror and went back to clocking her movements.

Seeing her scribble in the same striped pad she'd been carrying at Lulu's party made him remember her saying something about profiling Brett. *Of course,* he thought, filled with relief. He would have lost all respect for her if she had been dating a famous tool like Brett Babcock! And that, he suddenly realized, was exactly how she was going to feel about him when she found out that he'd dated Lulu Merriwether.

"Did you know she was doing Brett Babcock?" Duke said.

"She's not *doing him,*" Max said, rising to her defense. "She's doing *a story* on him. She writes for *Cachet.*"

Duke pulled the crate over to the railing so he could have a bird's-eye view of what was going on. "So then go talk to her."

"I can't," Max grumbled. "I told you what she said."

"That she hates Lulu?" Duke shrugged, looking at records to play for his next spin session, which would never come. "So do a lot of people."

"I believe her exact words were 'I can't stand people like that,'" Max said, glad he had hidden all of his personal effects and locked the doors to the other rooms in anticipation of the klepto. "*I'm* people like that."

"No, you're not," Duke said. "Anyway, she said that in the hypothetical. If you go down there and say, 'Guess what? I'm not a doorman. I actually own the store. And this phat pad? It's all mine,' I bet she changes her tune."

"I don't own the store. Harvey does."

Duke threw his arms in the air and swayed to the music. "Technicalities!"

His eyes fixed on Sydney and Brett, Max said glumly, "You don't know her."

Duke stopped swaying. "And after one subway ride, you do?"

Sydney could tell everyone felt a little bit cooler even if they were trying not to show it. The appearance of Brett Babcock was confirmation that this was the place to be. It was good color for the piece, but she needed facts. Spotting Freddy heading back from the kitchen with a six-pack of soda and some red plastic cups, she sidled up to him. "Freddy, whose party is this?"

Freddy backed her into the middle of the makeshift dance floor, where Brett was grinding on a very tall girl who Sydney guessed had a twenty-five-inch waist. "Natasha's ex-boyfriend's."

Sydney stood there, not dancing, while Freddy tried to goad her with his ridiculous gyrations. Pressing her pen point against the pad, she said, "Natasha who?"

A hand that Sydney immediately recognized as Brett's reached over her shoulder (he had a ring of thorns tattooed on his middle finger over the name of the model who'd been too dumb or desperate—or both—to read the clear signs of impending doom when he chose that digit to display their "wedding band") and snatched the pad out of her hand. "Put down your fucking pad," he said, tossing the pad to J-Dub, who made no attempt to catch it. "And have some fun!"

Sydney spotted her notebook on the floor just as someone's stiletto ripped out one of the pages. She dove down to retrieve it, and when she stood up she saw that the stiletto belonged to Lulu Merriwether. As Lulu murmured a barely audible "Sorry," which was negated with a dirty look, Sydney turned the other cheek, thinking she really had ninety-nine problems tonight and this bitch was certainly one.

"I don't even know her!" Max shouted, more out of frustration that he was in hiding at his own birthday party—how pathetic!—than Lulu's petty harassment. She was towering over him as he sat crouched against the railing, watching Sydney and Brett like a peeping Tom. And he felt like one when he looked up and saw that Lulu wasn't wearing panties under her flippy minidress. He really hated shaved pussies. Women said it felt better, cleaner, but it wasn't natural. Fucking her made him feel as if he was molesting a child. "And don't bother to wish me a happy birthday," he added churlishly.

Lulu took him up on that offer, giving him a light kick instead. "You knew her well enough to run off from my book party with her when you were supposed to introduce me!"

Max looked up with concern and noticed that Lulu had purposely widened her stance. Remy had told him Lulu was pissed that he'd skipped out on the party, and Lulu had left him a message to tell him herself. Then she'd called Avery to complain, and Avery had left him a peeved voice mail. (And in her uncomfortably pregnant state, Avery's peevishness had reached new heights.) Since Lulunatic's psychotic anger could escalate to violence at any moment, it was disconcerting to know that she could identify Sydney on sight. "That's not what happened," Max lied, spinning an incoherent yarn about some emergency Harvey had called about that needed immediate attention.

"Well, you invited her to your party!"

"I didn't invite her," he said, wanting to point out that he hadn't invited Lulu or her minions either. He knew he should have hired security! "She's here with Brett."

"I see that," Lulu said. "Is she screwing him too?"

Max couldn't tell if that was contempt or envy in her voice, but he had a weird sense of déjà vu. Lulu's dislike of Sydney was very similar to the level of dislike Sydney had for her. And they had never even met. Girls were so weird. "She's doing a story on Brett," he said, just to set the record straight. "And I'm not sleeping with her. I told you I hardly know her. I haven't even said a word to her all night."

Lulu didn't know what to make of that, so she just flounced down the stairs and, Max hoped, out of the party.

"Nigga, that's the same shit you said last night," J-Dub shouted, so drunk that white boy Brett had suddenly become a "nigga."

Perched on the back of the couch, surrounded by a bevy of women, Brett howled. And when Brett howled, everyone howled. It was as if he brought his own personal laugh track with him everywhere he went. (And most of the things he said weren't remotely funny.) Sitting cross-legged on the floor with her chin in her hand, Sydney's mouth opened, but out came a yawn, not a laugh. It was almost three and she was desperate for sleep. She'd been at the gym at eight A.M. Thankfully, after Brett did a few slides down the brass fire pole, they were on the move.

"Back to the hotel, kids!" Brett said, standing in front of the open door of the Denali, waving random women in like a field trip chaperone. He patted the last girl on the butt. "That's right. Fill 'er up!"

"I have enough, Brett," Sydney said, standing at a safe distance before he shoved her in and forced her to join them for the after-after party. "I'm gonna head home."

Brett grabbed her by the arm and slurred, "We'll give you a ride."

"Thank you," she said, pulling away. "I'll be fine."

"Oh no you don't!" He pulled her back. "Party's not over till The Babcock says it's over."

"Lemme go," she said as Brett, just as she feared, tried to push her into the car.

Fats saw them tussling from the other side of the truck and hurried around to keep Brett from getting into another front-page fiasco. Slowed by his excess weight, he waddled up too late to stop Brett from grabbing Sydney's face and planting a sloppy kiss on her mouth. Brett made an exaggerated sucking noise as he pulled away, then smiled. "Who loves ya, baby?"

"Fuck," Fats muttered.

• • •

After his initial shock wore off, Max pulled himself away from the window and made a mad dash toward the front door.

"Fight!" Duke yelled, scrambling behind him. "Fight!"

Outside, Sydney was frozen, but as Brett put one wobbly leg into the truck, his raucous laughter punctuated by hiccups, she snapped back to attention. "Wow, Brett," she said. "For a minute there I thought you were going to rough me up like you did Nicolette."

Brett whipped around as fast as he could with that much alcohol in his system, looking like a bull ready to gore. "I NEVER TOUCHED THAT COKE FIEND!" Sydney broke out into a jubilant smile and pulled out her pad. "SHE ASSAULTED"—the rotund bodyguard shoved Brett into the truck and slammed the door, but a second later, he popped out of the sunroof, wild-eyed—"ME! I'M GONNA COUNTERSUE!"

The car zoomed off and Brett knocked around in the sunroof, looking as if he might hurl, while Sydney stood on the sidewalk, looking happier than a pig in shit. When she finished scribbling, she stretched her arm high in the air and yelled at the top of her lungs, "WHO LOVES YA, BAY-BEEEE!"

A yellow cab, which was hard to come by in Brooklyn at that hour, dropped some people off at the building across the street, and Sydney merrily skipped over and grabbed it.

Max and Duke were left standing in the vestibule, front door ajar, riveted by the scene they had just witnessed. Max had envisioned himself charging to her rescue, and even though he had never hit anyone in his life, that vision included knocking badass Brett out with one punch. Sydney would look at him, shocked, and say, "Max! What are you doing here?" And he'd grab her and say, "Don't worry about me. Are you all right?" And she'd look at him dreamily and say, "I am now." And they'd kiss passionately, breaking apart only when Brett got up, rubbing his chin, and said, "Quite a punch you've got there."

That would have been the coolest scenario, Max thought. Unfortunately, it hadn't played out that way, because his pretty girl didn't need rescuing after all.

CHAPTER THIRTY-ONE

Sydney was sitting on a bench in the lobby of Country Day, thinking that was an odd name for a school on the Upper West Side of Manhattan. While Caleigh reclined in the Bugaboo next to her, a herd of preschoolers suddenly rushed past into the waiting arms of their nannies of color. With her similar complexion Sydney thought she fit right in, but the one mother she'd spotted—identified because she was blond, well-dressed (and tressed), and wearing a sizable rock—was clocking her as if she was there to pull off an abduction.

The last time Sydney had come here with Liz she'd been eyed with similar suspicion. Standing on the curb while Liz went inside to get Ben, she'd said hello to a cute little girl she'd met at Ben's birthday party in the Hamptons and the girl's black stay-at-home gay dad had swooped in like a hawk: "Do we know you?" *Rich people,* Sydney thought, smoothing Caleigh's silky hair. Didn't matter if they were black, white, gay, straight. They were a breed unto themselves. Uptight. Annoying. Rude (while claiming everyone else was). Rich Mommy probably didn't have anything better to do than fantasize about implausible kidnapping scenarios. That was something Liz did on a regular basis, when she wasn't wondering if a mole was cancerous, if her housekeeper was stealing her bras, if the organic muffins at Whole Foods were really gluten-free . . .

But who was Sydney to talk? Being a contract writer at *Cachet* meant she only had to write ten features a year, and since the average three-pager like the one she'd recently done on Fergie never took more than a day or so to write, she worked fewer than twenty hours most weeks. Some weeks she didn't work at all. She was very likely the only New Yorker who had time to answer text messages in full, grammatically correct sentences. Though she never did. Just as she never made plans with anyone, except Jeffrey, with less than a week's notice. Staying busy was like a competitive sport in New York. Let everyone who was so "crazy at work" think she was crazier! Although the truth was, with her obsessive working out, determined bargain hunting, and endless running of pointless errands, her day-to-day reality was not very much different from that of Liz or Rich Mommy. Except they had a purpose: their kids.

"Where's Mommy?"

Sydney turned and saw Ben standing a foot away. "Hello to you too." Sydney smiled at his never-far-behind buddy. "Hi, Noah."

"Where's Mom?" Ben whined. (Another problem a man around the house might solve.)

"Dentist. Her tooth cracked. Let's go."

"Wait," Ben said, tugging the wrinkled hem of Sydney's "Beyotch" tee, which, Sydney suddenly realized, was probably the reason Rich Mommy was staring. Accepting that she was the only adult available to answer the question he obviously wanted answered, Ben took a breath and fired away. "Do you know what my moms were gonna name me if they hadn't named me Ben?"

Strapping Caleigh in, Sydney glanced back at Noah, who was just staring at her. What a bizarre but fabulous time they were living in, she thought, when a kid could say something like "my moms" and no one batted a fucking eyelash. The correct answer was "Toby," but bragging rights were obviously riding on this. Hoping to win some brownie points, she said, "Anakin?"

"See!" Ben turned and jabbed his finger in Noah's face. "Told you!"

"But they didn't name you Anakin," Noah said, the black side of his biracial heritage surfacing in the form of a ghetto neck roll. "They named you Benjamin!"

When Caleigh slipped the bottle out of her mouth and busted out with, "Uh-oh!" Noah and Sydney looked at her, then each other, and cracked up. That was the only phrase Caleigh knew, but homegirl's timing was impeccable!

Humiliated, Ben shot back, "Anakin is my *middle* name!"

"Ben," Sydney said with a scolding look. "Quit while you're ahead."

"Yeah," Noah said, giving Sydney the warm smile she had been expecting from Ben before he trotted off.

"Uh-oh, uh-oh," Ben said, turning his frustration on the one person he knew wouldn't fight back. He slapped his hands on his forehead. "Oh brother! That's all I ever hear from this kid!"

Walking to the corner, he quickly recovered from the dissing, getting so much love from his female classmates that Sydney felt as if she was back to shadowing Brett Babcock. "Where's Lily?" she said, keeping an eye out for the cutie he'd been exchanging Valentines with since kindergarten.

"Ga-stod," Ben said.

Sydney was as disturbed as she was amused by that answer. "Gstaad, you mean."

"Yeah," Ben said, trying to pronounce it the way she had. "It's in Switzerland."

"Yes," Sydney said. "I know." She shook her head, wondering if it was possible to raise a levelheaded kid when everyone he knew had two homes and jetted off to ritzy places like Ga-stod. Private schools in New York were more expensive than most colleges, and the competition to get your two-year-old into one started before he or she was conceived! Which really was just vanity and insecurity on the part of the parents since study after study had proven that the best determinant of a person's chances in life was self-esteem. Children who believed they were capable of doing great things would do them whether they went to Harvard or City College. Sydney couldn't imagine raising a child in a sheltered world where kids were picked up from school and taken to the park by nannies when their mothers, like Liz, had the luxury of not working. Getting a nanny or a housekeeper to clean the house or do the laundry, grunt work that no one except obsessive-compulsives wanted to do, was one thing. But if you didn't want to take your own kids to the park, what the hell did you want to do with them?

Of course, Sydney had just told Ben they couldn't stop at the park on the way home, but that was only because she was crazy tired and, not being a mother herself, she didn't have the constitution to handle spur-of-the moment forays with more than one child. She was jonesing for a nap, but since Liz still wasn't back (contrary to what the bumbling doorman, who still thought Liz and Joyce were "roommates," had told them), she steered them toward the next best thing: TV. Specifically *The Empire Strikes Back,* a DVD that could put Ben into a near coma after an astonishing number of viewings and that seemed to overwhelm Caleigh's limited sensory perceptions as well. (To be on the safe side, Sydney also handed Caleigh her favorite musical toy.)

Reclined on the massive sofa between her two charges, feet kicked up on an ottoman, she was preparing to rest her weary head when she noticed the message icon on her cell phone. She'd turned the ringer off last night before she went to bed to make sure she could sleep late in peace, a maneuver Liz circumvented by ringing her rarely used home phone until Sydney got up and angrily answered, "WHAT?" She was sure the message was from Liz, calling to make sure everything had gone okay at the school, but the name she saw listed multiple times when she clicked "Missed Calls" was Gareth's.

"Sorry," she said the moment he picked up. "My ringer was off."

"Didn't I tell you not to do that?" he said, Sydney's preemptive apology seeming only to anger him more. "Keep the volume on High! What if we'd gotten the call from The Raven?"

"Did you?" Sydney said, snapping at Ben to lower the volume on the TV.

"Not yet. But I did get a call this morning from Paula Fox."

"From 'Page Six'?" Sydney asked, coming out of her slouch. She wasn't questioning whether Paula Fox worked at the gossip column—everyone in the media world knew who she was—but why her calling Gareth would make him call *Sydney* six times in four hours. She wasn't above reading "Page Six," just like she wasn't above reading tabloids. The boldface names they chronicled were like sitcom characters whose lives were unfurling episodically for the entertainment of the general public. Celebrities liked to rail about the invasion of their privacy, but what would Jessica Simpson do if there wasn't a cadre of paparazzi waiting to snap her wobbling out of Koi on vertiginous heels? If *People* didn't want to shoot her in soft lighting for a cover story about how she found true love with Nick, John, Tony, et al? In the minds of the public, and her own probably, she'd cease to exist. And then she wouldn't be able to reap millions selling makeup and clothing and hair extensions. Far from invading her privacy, the readers of *Us Weekly* were doing manufactured celebrities like Jessica Simpson a favor by keeping sales up. And anyone who sold baby pictures to *OK!* for millions forfeited the right to complain when paparazzi got free snaps of them coming out of the preschool parking lot. Sydney was familiar enough with the inner workings of celebrity life to know that most of those candids were as staged as a cover shoot. Publicists (or other low-level emissaries) tipped off gossip columns and paparazzi to the whereabouts of their clients all the time, hoping that the sighting would make it into print. A mention in "Page Six" was the best thing that could happen to some attention-starved people. For Sydney, it was the worst. Which was why she flopped forward as if she'd been punched in the gut when Gareth said, "She wants to know why you were making out with Brett Babcock."

Caleigh paused in her keyboard banging and looked over as Sydney swallowed a gulp of air. "Who told her that?"

"Is it true?"

Sydney sat up, grabbing at her stomach. "Okay, listen . . ."

"Is it true?" Gareth snapped. "I have to call her by five o'clock or she's going with what she has."

Sydney knew it was close to four so she stopped stalling. "Yes, it's true." She heard Gareth heave a disgusted sigh.

"But *he* kissed *me!*" Sydney had forgotten she was in the presence of children until Ben, riding the arm of the couch like a rocking horse, turned away from the fifty-two-inch plasma screen and looked at her as if she'd done something completely scandalous that he couldn't wait to tell his mother about. (Sydney would likely get a call from Liz by tomorrow afternoon, asking, "Who kissed you?") Caleigh banged away as if she was conducting a symphony that only she could hear, and Ben retaliated by pumping up the volume on the TV, causing Gareth to shout, "What is all that bloody noise?"

"Sorry, I'm babysitting." Sydney reached for the remote control and Ben pulled it away, leaving her no choice but to smack him on the leg. Then she walked to the kitchen, the fierceness in her voice channeled into a strained whisper. "He practically assaulted me."

"Tell me what happened."

Thinking Gareth was trying to pump her for salacious details for his own perverse pleasure, Sydney said, "There's nothing to tell. Call Paula and tell her it's not true."

"You just said it was," Gareth said in such a detached manner that Sydney pictured him kicked back at his desk, nibbling on a muffin.

"So lie and say it's not!" Ben looked over his shoulder and Sydney walked farther away. First she was kissing, now she was lying. He was going to have a field day relating this entire conversation to Liz the minute she walked through the door! "Wait, does Conrad know about this?" she said, flushing with embarrassment at the thought.

"Not yet. He's been out of the office all day. That's why you need to tell me exactly what happened," Gareth said, adding dramatically, "he needs to know the truth."

"Okay, he was crazy drunk," Sydney told him, thinking Gareth was right for once. Conrad needed to know the truth, not some thirdhand version of events that made her sound like a desperate groupie! "And when we were going our separate ways at about three A.M., he grabbed me suddenly and kissed me on the mouth. It only lasted a second. It was nothing. Really."

"If it was nothing, why didn't you tell me?"

Because I can't trust you and you'd probably try to use it against me. "Because I didn't want to turn a molehill into a mountain," Sydney said. "Now get her to kill it."

"Why didn't you dodge him when he went in for the kiss?"

"I don't know. It was three in the morning and I had a contact high. Maybe my reflexes were slow."

"You had a contact high?" Gareth said. Sydney could almost see him sit up straight, as if the story had just gotten good. "That's your excuse?"

"No," Sydney said. "And don't tell Conrad I said that. Now get her to kill it."

"Give me something juicier to offer her."

"Like a trade, you mean." She knew gossip columnists did this. They blackmailed you into throwing someone else under the bus, which Sydney would have done happily, but whom? "Don't you have anything?"

"Nothing that beats this," Gareth said, putting the onus back on her.

"And what I didn't get a chance to tell you was that I got him on the record about Nicolette." Sydney was going to let him read about it when she turned in the piece, but now that she was drowning in this gossip cesspool, she tossed it out there like a life preserver, hoping it would keep her afloat until she found a way to save herself.

"You did?" Gareth said, sounding cautiously interested. "What did he say?"

"He called her a coke fiend and said *she* assaulted *him*. Hey," Sydney said, spotting a shoreline in the distance. "Use that. Tease it to set up the piece. It's in the July issue, right?"

"No, it got pushed back because the movie's in reshoots. We can't tease it this early."

Yes, he could, Sydney thought. The useless asshole just wasn't willing to help her! "What about that aging supermodel who got drunk on the cover shoot because she couldn't fit into the bathing suit?"

"Boring," Gareth said. "And her husband is dying. Have some sympathy."

"Well, doesn't anyone in that office have anything on anybody?" Sydney snapped just as she heard a crash coming from the living room. She turned and saw Caleigh's colorful keyboard banging on the floor near the play area by the window and Ben's arm still extended in a Frisbee-tossing position.

"Go play it over there!" he shouted, and Caleigh raised up on her knees, pedaling her arms in the air, like a puppy trying to reach a doorknob. As she began to fall forward, Sydney dropped the phone and let out an earth-shattering scream as she ran to the couch, reaching over the back just as her precious little boo-boo tumbled head over heels onto the hardwood floor. WHY THE FUCK DIDN'T LIZ HAVE CARPETING?

"It wasn't my fault," Ben yelped, doing nothing to help his wailing sister.

Sydney scooped Caleigh off the floor and screamed back, "Yes, it was, you fucking brat!" Hearing the expletive, Ben gasped—in that house you weren't even allowed to say "stupid"—but Sydney was unrepentant. "That's right. I said 'Fuck'! You wanna tell your mother? Go right ahead, kid! She's not the boss of me!"

Ben gaped at her as if she had turned into a demon right before his eyes, and she grabbed the back of his T-shirt, pulling him off the sofa arm with one violent yank. Lovingly bouncing Caleigh in her right arm and dragging Ben toward his room with her left, she was reminded of the documentary she'd seen about the conjoined twins who each controlled one side of their body. "Six minutes!" she screamed, throwing the kitchen timer into Ben's room after she shoved him inside. "Do not show your face until that bell goes off. I'm serious!"

After she got Caleigh to calm down, she put the battery back in her phone and redialed Gareth, who in lieu of "Hello" said, "Are they still alive?"

Sydney was more worried about her own predicament. "Did you even ask around?"

"Excuse me?" Gareth said snottily.

"Did you ask around to see if anyone has any gossip we can trade?"

"What would you like me to do? Send out a mass e-mail?"

"Yes!"

"Then everyone will want to know why."

"Oh, right. Who else knows about this?"

"Only me," Gareth said, the conversation obviously boring him now.

"That means you and Kimberly."

"Well, sure."

Great, Sydney thought. If Kimberly knew, then everyone knew. She was a mass e-mail in human form. Noticing that Caleigh was on the floor (no more couch for her), eating out of a pot of Burt's Bees lip balm, she said, "Gareth, let me call you back."

Sydney had always considered herself a fun, responsible guardian, but kneeling to pick up the spilled contents of her purse, she wondered how she had suddenly become Michael Jackson. She was about to put Caleigh in the fenced-in play area, where the poor baby would be safe, but then she saw that her little pumpkin had struck gold.

"You're such a smart girl," she said, hitting Redial on her phone as Caleigh smeared her greasy hands all over the smiling author photo on the back of Lulu Merriwether's book. "Yes, you are."

CHAPTER THIRTY-TWO

R ory, honey," Mitzi said, trying to calm her latest head case. "I can lead a horse to water, but I can't make him drink if he wants Diet Coke."

"I can be Diet Coke!" Rory all but screamed, her anxious shrill piercing through Mitzi's Jawbone earpiece. "He just has to give me a chance! Tell me what he said! Exactly!"

He said he didn't like you. To be exact, he didn't like you at all. Because you came across as needy and desperate and you were dressed like a tramp.

As much as Mitzi wanted to say that, naturally she didn't. She believed in brutal honesty, but only when it would help someone. And Rory Applebaum, she now realized, was beyond help.

"He was vague," Mitzi said. She gripped the escalator's handrail, and looking at the fading color on her nails, wondered if the spa would be able to squeeze her in for a manicure after lunch. "Why don't you tell me what happened last night, Rory? Then maybe I can tell you what you did wrong."

"Wrong? He said I did something wrong?"

Mitzi bit the inside of her cheek to keep from screaming. This was the fourth time Rory had called her today to get a recap of last night's date, but this time she'd called from a restricted number and Mitzi had foolishly answered. And that's what bugged Mitzi. Rory was smart enough to do that. She was smart enough to graduate summa cum laude from Cornell. She was smart enough to run her own consulting business. But her emotional intelligence was evidently quite low. That's what so many women didn't understand. The drive and tenacity that served them well in college and the professional world could become a fatal liability when it came to romance. Most of them needed to take a chill pill. Rory Applebaum, who thanks to her fatal attraction to the negative would now be filed under "desperado" in Mitzi's database, needed to take two.

"Honey, you're just not his type," Mitzi told her, using the matchmaker's version of "It's not you, it's me."

Rory gasped. "He *said* that?"

"*I'm* saying that," Mitzi said. She stepped off the escalator on the third floor, did a quick scan of the deserted men's section, and continued on her ascent. "Are you coming to my talk next week?"

"You're having a talk? Next week?" Rory said, sounding as anxious about that as she did about her failed date. "No one told me!"

After that reaction, Mitzi was almost sorry she'd mentioned it now. "It's not a dinner party," she said, wondering if this girl would remain single forever, a very real possibility. "It's a seminar at the Y. And I need you to be there. You know why?"

"No . . ." Rory answered hesitantly, for once correctly reading the signs of trouble. "Why?"

"Because you're great-looking, you have a great education, a successful career . . . you're a perfect example of the woman who has everything going for her and lets it all go to waste."

At long last, Rory was quiet, and in that brief reprieve, Mitzi reminded herself that this was business, not personal. There was a time, back when she first started, when a hopeless singleton like Rory Applebaum would make her heart heavy and she'd spend fifteen minutes trying to counsel and console. Not anymore. Desperadoes made her look bad, they were bad for business, and Mitzi had learned to weed them out as soon as she identified them. Lovelorn women who wanted advice could buy her book, register for one of her seminars, or tell it to "Dear Abby."

"All the info is on my site," she said, reaching up to remove her earpiece. "Now I have to run." She could hear Rory pleading, "Just tell me what he sa—" as she clicked off, but Mitzi knew that if this pointless conversation continued for another second, there would be tears. And now was not the time to have her energy drained. She had a "simulated" in fifteen minutes.

Stepping off on the fourth floor, Mitzi quickly scanned the massive shoe department, always a good hunting ground for new girls. She saw a couple of prospects who looked promising from a distance, but they might be Monets. (Good from far but far from good.) But then she saw a familiar face and thought, *Speaking of women who don't get it* . . .

"She's here!" Remy shouted. "Hide!"

Max ducked under his desk, ordering Remy to "bolt the door and call security!"

Remy turned the latch on the door and reached for the phone, but Lulunatic was screaming bloody murder before she could dial. "Open up, Max! I know you're in there!"

Max peered out from under the desk. Why was he hiding? Lulu wasn't a locksmith. He looked around the office for a hiding spot, then pushed Remy toward the cabinet, motioning for her to help him move it away from the wall.

"I can't!" she cried, realizing what he was telling her to do. "I'm claustrophobic!"

"Shhh," Max said, putting a finger to his lips. Trying to think of another way out, he looked at the phone on his desk. Too close to the door. Lulu would hear. He reached into his pocket and pulled out his iPhone. "Okay," he said, sinking to the floor in the corner. "Let me call for backup."

Picking up her direct line on the first ring, Norma said, "Harvey wants to know what's going on down there."

Max cupped his hand over his mouth. "We're under siege. Call security!"

"Why can't you fight your own battles?"

"She might be armed!"

"With what? A wallet?"

Although Norma hung up without giving him any indication that security had been called, Max assumed that was the case. (When Harvey was in the office it was as if the pope was in town.) But after a few interminable minutes neither security nor Norma had come to their rescue. Trapped in his all-white office, listening to Remy repeat "Where are they?" over and over, like a barely audible distress signal, he felt as if he were locked in a padded cell with the Rain Man. Harvey hated commotion in the office, even if it was just harmless frivolity, but Max wouldn't put it past Norma to shut Harvey's door and not call security, just to make Max pay for whatever perceived misdeeds she was holding against him.

There had been brief moments of silence when they thought Lulu had left, but then she would start banging again. And she'd just yelled, "I know you're in there! I'm not leaving!" Seeing no other way out, Max nudged the cabinet away from the wall. "It'll only be a second," he said, coaxing Remy to slide behind it. "Don't make a sound."

With Remy safely hidden (but shaking like a leaf), Max went to the door and cracked it open a smidge. "Lulu," he said, as if he had no idea she was there. "'Sup?"

"I want that girl fired!"

Max responded in song. *"You can't always get what you want . . ."*

Lulu pushed her way in, waving a copy of the *New York Post* like a toreador's cape. "I know she's responsible for this!"

"She's not," Max said. "I guarantee you that."

Looking high and low for any sign of Remy, Lulu spun around, beaming her fury directly at Max. "Oh no? Then who is?"

Technically, he was, Max thought. He was a fool to have told Sydney about it, knowing how much she hated Lulu. She hadn't wasted any time in getting Lulu up on the crucifix, achieving quite a feat in getting Max to actually feel sorry for Lulu. But what really made him feel like a shitheel was the position he'd put Remy in. And he didn't mean behind the cabinet! She liked writing those stupid books for Lulu and, even worse, she liked being around Lulu, feeling needed by her. She considered Lulu a friend. Talk about delusional. She was Lulu's slave, and just as Sydney had said, was earning slave wages. Max wished she had let him negotiate her fees, but Lulu had contacted Remy without his knowledge, and though he knew this whole charade would blow up in Remy's face sooner or later, he had tried to stay out of it. And then, in the end, he'd been the idiot who detonated the bomb. He thought about telling Lulu the truth, but she already had it in for him simply for breaking up with her. Add this to her stewing pot of rage, something she had every right to be angry about, and there was no telling what she might do to exact revenge.

"I can tell you with full confidence that Remy is not responsible," he said. At this point, that was as far as he was prepared to go.

"Let her tell me that," Lulu said. "Where is she?"

"Why would she rat you out to the papers?" Max said, trying to reason with her.

Lulu whacked Max in the chest with the rolled-up paper. "Because she wants to be me! It's not enough that I pay her, that I let her stay in my homes. She wants credit too. She's trying to get a book deal out of this!"

"It's a blind item," Max said. "Big deal."

"'Which Park Avenue princess paid a ghostwriter ten thousand dollars to write each of the bestselling romans à clef for which she got paid millions' is not fucking blind!" she shrieked, reciting the item verbatim without looking at the paper. "Stevie Wonder could read between those lines!"

For lack of a comeback, Max said, "Please leave."

Lulu had no such intention, but then backup arrived—at last! The two security men stood in the doorway with their hands clasped behind their backs, and one of them said, rather meekly, "Ms. Merriwether, would you come with us, please?" There was protocol for dealing with VIPs—there were more shoplifters in that category than one would imagine—and Max knew there wasn't much more they could do or say to get rid of her unless she physically assaulted them. That was exactly why she was number one on the stalker list. Once she got past the first lines of defense, it was impossible to get rid of her!

They were definitely going to have a meeting about this security breach first thing tomorrow, Max thought, but right now all he cared about was Remy. If Lulu figured out she was back there—and now that an eerie silence had fallen over the room, he could hear Remy's labored breathing—Lulu was definitely not going to leave, and this fiasco was going to get ratcheted up to Def-Con 4! Max edged slowly toward the cabinet to place himself between the two women in case an altercation suddenly flared up and, feeling the need to create a diversion, began shouting. "Lulu, you're just some rich girl who has never worked a day in her life," he said, spewing Sydney's words as if she had taken possession of his body. "It's not enough that you were born rich. Oh no, you have to pretend to have a career too!"

Both security guys took a step back, as if to disassociate themselves from Max's statements, while Lulu fired back without hesitation: "You're one to talk!"

Max almost shoved her out of the office himself, but she did everyone a favor and vacated the premises of her own miffed accord. "Don't touch me!" she shouted at the security men, her supple blond tresses whipping one of them in the face on the way out.

A moment later, Norma appeared at Max's door, just in time to see him push the cabinet back and catch Remy as she collapsed into his arms.

Standing in front of a full-length mirror, Sydney turned to the right, then to the left, admiring the $795 Lanvin flats she'd been obsessing about for three months. She turned all the way around and peeked over her shoulder. From all angles, they looked as cute as she had imagined they would. And today, thanks to her new buddy, Maximillian, they would finally be hers.

On the verge of a shopping orgasm, she heard someone say, "These would do so much more for your legs." Thinking the salesgirl should really mind her own business, Sydney ripped her gaze away from her lovely Lanvins and there, standing behind her, was that horrible old woman.

Sydney looked at the strappy wedge heel swinging on Mitzi Berman's finger, then back down at her own feet. She had been dreaming of owning the Lanvins ever since she'd seen Elle Macpherson wearing them in *Star*, and the outfit Sydney had worn today, expressly for this shopping jaunt— straight-leg Hudson jeans (Art of Shopping sample sale), white V-neck tee (American Apparel), and gray pinstripe blazer (Banana Republic, final sale, many moons ago)—were cheap chic approximations of the "Oh, I just threw this on" ensemble Elle had been wearing. But Sydney would never be known as "The Body," so there was only so much she could emulate.

"I don't like to show leg," she said, thinking it was just like Mitzi Berman to call this shortcoming to mind. "I only wear pants, remember?" She took a seat on the leather bench, panicking when she noticed Mitzi's book was visible in her tote (Devi Kroell for Target, $29.99). She reached down to hide it but stopped herself. Maybe Mitzi hadn't seen it.

"It's gonna be number one on the nonfiction list next week," Mitzi reported proudly, joining Sydney on the bench.

"Good for you," Sydney said, kicking off the Lanvins. Her orgasm blown, she almost didn't feel like buying them anymore. She looked back toward the escalator. Where the hell was Max?

"Excuse me," Mitzi said, holding the wedge out to the approaching salesgirl. "Can we see these in a . . ." She looked at Sydney, who refused to answer. She didn't have to. Mitzi had chosen the same salesgirl who had just brought out the Lanvins, and most of the sales staff knew Sydney's size from all the times she came in to try on shoes and never bought anything.

"A nine," the salesgirl said, looking at Sydney for confirmation.

"Yes," Mitzi said, smiling. "Thank you." As the salesgirl retreated, Mitzi reached down to grab the book out of Sydney's bag. "Guess you haven't gotten to chapter nine. It's called, 'Save Your Flats for the Beach.'"

Sydney tried to grab the book first, feeling violated that Mitzi was touching her possessions. It didn't matter that Mitzi had written the book—it was hers now! Mitzi beat her to it, and when the fluorescent yellow highlighter pen that was stuck between the pages fell to the carpet, Sydney cringed.

"Highlighting, are we?" Mitzi said, delighted to have unexpectedly scored such a humiliating blow.

"I'm highlighting because I'm planning to write a story about this whole matchmaking business," Sydney said, making up the lie on the spot. "Blow the lid off the whole thing!"

Mitzi sat up at full attention, not at all bothered by the insinuation that an exposé was in the works. "For *Cachet*?"

"No," Sydney said. "Maybe for *Marie Claire*." God knows she didn't want anyone to know she had considered, however briefly, joining Mitzi's prostitution ring, but women's magazines liked stories that had some personal element. Writing under her Nancy O'Reilly alias would enable her to offer a first-person perspective. And in a magazine like *Marie Claire*, she could discuss the sociopolitical meaning of women offering themselves up like chattel in this day and age, a concept that definitely made for an interesting pitch.

"So you write for them too," Mitzi said.

Looking around for Max, Sydney mumbled, "On occasion."

"I'd prefer to see it in *Cachet*," Mitzi said. "*Marie Claire* has an all-female readership, and my clients are exclusively male. Well-to-do types who read *Cachet*. Their readers have an average annual income of one hundred and fifty thousand dollars."

Sydney was impressed that Mitzi knew her business so well. Carefully placing her Lanvins back into the box, she said, "Well, then maybe you should pitch it to *Cachet* yourself."

"We did!" Mitzi huffed.

Assuming that by "we" she meant whatever publicity firm she employed to feed her insatiable hunger for attention, Sydney said, "Didn't want you, huh?"

Mitzi slid toward Sydney, trying to get chummy. "Is it true they're profiling Samantha Roberts?"

Sydney scooted away an equal distance. "I have no idea."

"I gave that girl her start, you know! Why would they profile her when I taught her everything she knows?"

"Oh, I don't know," Sydney said. "Maybe because she has a hit reality show."

"I pitched that to Bravo three years ago," Mitzi raged. "It's ageism, if you ask me!"

Hearing that, Sydney felt a bit of sympathy for Mitzi. She hated to see a woman discriminated against because of her looks or age, and for Mitzi Berman, a woman whose neck looked ten years older than her face, those things seemed to be one and the same. "Could be," Sydney said, reminding herself that Mitzi Berman was not her friend and her feelings were therefore irrelevant. "But then again some of the pick-up lines in your book are pretty ridiculous."

"They work!"

"I'm sure you have all kinds of statistics to back that up," Sydney said as the salesgirl finally returned with the wedges. (Where had she been? In Italy, cobbling them herself?) "But I would never go up to a man and say, 'Hello, gorgeous!' And I don't know any self-respecting woman who would."

Sydney knew this dis would provoke a snappy comeback, which she welcomed. That was the only thing she liked about this old coot, she thought, bending down to fasten herself into the wedges. Fighting with her.

By the time she sat upright, Mitzi still had not responded, and Sydney wondered if perhaps she was having a stroke. She checked Mitzi's eyes for signs of conscious activity and saw that they were filled with steely determination as she canvassed the shoe department, finally zeroing in on a seriously good-looking guy loitering a few feet away.

"You must be shopping for your girlfriend," Mitzi called out. "With a sick body like that, you've got to have one."

The shiver of embarrassment that shot up Sydney's spine propelled her to her feet, and trying to make a quick escape in the wedges, she almost twisted her ankle. She managed to wobble over to the mirror unharmed, where she witnessed the hottie . . . laughing?

"My secre—" he began, quickly correcting himself. "Executive assistant." Sydney gave him a gold star for that and kept watching. "She put a note in my calendar that today was her birthday and that she's an eight."

Mitzi, who had obviously hit her internal coy button, looked up at him, batting her false eyelashes. "Smart girl."

He slid down onto the bench. "But do you think that means an eight in shoes or in clothes?"

"Well, let's see," Mitzi said. She swung her body in his direction, giving him her full attention, a maneuver Sydney recalled reading about in her book. "How much does she weigh?"

He looked around and pointed at Sydney. "She's about her size."

"I'm a four," Sydney nearly shouted, unable to resist making that statement out loud (and rounding down a bit). "She definitely meant shoes."

"Those are nice, I guess," Hottie said, pointing at the wedges as Sydney wobbled back to the bench. Looking up at her, he said, "You think she would like those?"

"How should I know?" Sydney sniffed. "I don't even know her."

Mitzi gave Sydney the evil eye, and Sydney collapsed onto the bench, hunching over like a scolded child. That was the first thought that had come to mind, but why had she let it come out of her mouth? And in such a dismissive tone? This guy was tall, dark, and handsome and sweet enough to spend time picking out an expensive birthday gift for the woman he knew not to call his secretary. God, she thought, was Mitzi right about her?

"Where do you work?" Mitzi said, picking up Sydney's fumble and running with it.

"I'm a lawyer at Cromwell, Whitney, Harrison—"

"Zinterhoffer and LeBoeuf?" Sydney said. "No way. I work for *Cachet*!"

"Great," Hottie said with a warm smile. "So we're in the same building."

A mischievous grin spread across Mitzi's tightly pulled face. "Whaddaya know?" When the hottie didn't immediately capitalize on this coincidence, she nudged, "I hear the cafeteria there is fabulous."

"Yeah, it's pretty good." He smiled at Sydney. "We should have lunch sometime."

"I work from home," Sydney said, her inherent standoffishness rearing its ugly head again. But this time, she recovered before Mitzi's evil eye could reach her. "But I'm at the office all the time." She smiled back at him and Mitzi nodded her approval.

"I'm Grant, by the way." He stretched out his hand (large and masculine, Sydney noted). Shaking it, Sydney felt as if her own internal coy button had been activated. She didn't think she had one!

"Sydney," she said, barely able to hold his warm gaze.

When he went to shake Mitzi's hand, she hit him with the business card she'd retrieved from her purse like a gunslinger pulling a pistol out of a holster. Grant gave it a look and said, "Professional matchmaker? I thought those were an urban myth!"

"Nope!" Mitzi stood up, slipped her purse over her wrist, and struck a beauty-pageant pose. "Here I am, in the flesh! So you're single?"

"Yes."

"How old?"

"Thirty-six."

"Well, I found you one beautiful girl," she said without acknowledging that Sydney was that person. "If this doesn't work out, call me. I have plenty more!"

Mortified by the implication that she was part of Mitzi Berman's stable, Sydney confided out of the side of her mouth, "I don't even know this woman."

"No," Mitzi said pointedly. "She's just writing an article on me." Shuffling off, she winked at Sydney. "Call me about that."

Grant slid closer, filling the space Mitzi had left, and Sydney said, "Okay, tell me a little bit about your assistant. First of all, how old is she?"

As Grant gave her the lowdown on his twenty-nine-year-old assistant, Sydney glanced over her shoulder and saw Mitzi completely turned around on the up escalator, watching her latest match unfold until the very last second. When she caught Sydney's eye, she smiled like a proud mother hen and mouthed, "You're welcome."

CHAPTER THIRTY-THREE

Sydney opened her front door wearing nothing but a short terry robe and her divine Lanvin flats. She stretched out her foot, pointing her toe like a ballerina. "Seventy. Percent. Off."

Jeffrey gasped. "Are you kidding?" Still gazing at her fancy footwear, he said, "Hold up . . . you licked his balls?"

Sydney took two steps back. "What?"

"To get the seventy percent!"

"I did no such thing," Sydney begged his pardon. "I don't think I've ever done that." She turned and walked into the living room. "Oh, wait . . ."

"You know you have," Jeffrey said. "You little freak."

"No sexual favors were exchanged." She sat on the couch and hugged her knees to her chest, letting her beautifully shod feet hang off the edge. It was pathetic that a material possession could make her feel this good, but the truth of the matter was, due to whatever emotional or psychological deficiency she had in her makeup, they did. She almost felt like twirling. "What can I tell you? He likes me."

When Max had finally arrived, he'd told her there was an extra 20 percent discount if you signed up for a Harvey's card *that day only.* How lucky was she? The salesgirl didn't seem to know anything about it, but after Max told her what to do, she did it, no questions asked. (Every female employee in the store seemed to have a crush on him.) Knowing she could only get the extra 20 off that day, Sydney decided to pull the trigger on two other purchases she'd been mulling: a Chloé blouse and a pair of J Brand jeans. And then, experiencing some kind of endorphin high, she'd decided to make a spree of it. She usually liked to shop alone, but Max, in addition to being ever so handy with the hookups, turned out to be quite a useful and fun shopping companion. He sat patiently outside the dressing room while she tried on a million things, telling her what looked good and what color might suit her better, and never once did she feel as if he was doing it to earn "pussy points." Such thoughtful fashion advice, combined with the lack of sexual overture, would have made her question his sexuality, but her gaydar was leaning more toward metrosexual than homosexual. Judging by his tense reaction when he saw her with Grant, he was definitely interested. And after the fun afternoon they'd had, Sydney didn't mind that he was.

That wasn't something she was about to admit to Jeffrey, who was just waiting for her to fall into bed with another useless slacker so he could say, "Told you so!" And she wasn't going to let him in on her full haul either. Jeffrey already had a wish list a mile long. If he knew how many things she'd bagged, he'd expect to get just as many. Looking enviously at her shoes, he was already whining, "When are you going to take me over there?"

"Soon," Sydney assured him. "Soon."

Jeffrey huffed—when it came to shopping, soon could never come soon enough for him—and carried his black makeup case over to the windowsill, where he began to line up products. Watching him, Sydney said, "Shouldn't we be in the bathroom?"

"First tip," he said, rolling her office chair to the window. "It's always best to work in natural light."

Sydney might have known that if she had actually read Jeffrey's bestselling how-to book, *Beauty for All,* but she'd only glanced at the photos. She didn't need makeup advice. For day, she usually swept a hint of bronzer across her cheeks and dabbed a coat of rosebud salve on her lips. At night, she might jazz things up by adding a light coat of mascara and some sheer lip gloss. She called her look natural. Jeffrey called it naked. When she'd told him earlier that she wanted to be made up, not over, he'd threatened, "Tonight calls for some drama, and you're gonna bring it whether you like it or not!" She could see that she was going to have to fight him every step of the way to keep her look as minimal as possible, but better to fight with Jeffrey than the unknown glam squad Mitzi Berman had threatened to sic on her.

Sydney had capitulated and told Mitzi Berman that she'd be open to trying a fix-up after Mitzi's embarrassingly aggressive tactics had borne fruit and scored Sydney a lunch date with Grant, a looker who hadn't lived up to his star billing. (They'd had lunch at the Omnimedia cafeteria, then dinner two nights later, after which Sydney discovered, during the course of heavy petting, that he had a needle dick, giving her no choice but to leave immediately and delete his number from her phone on the way out of his building.) Although the thought of seriously playing the dating game was exhausting, she figured that the more darts she launched, the quicker she'd hit her target. And then she could be done with dating. She just wanted to find one person, the *right* person, with whom she could settle into a nice, comfortable, drama-free relationship that would produce children in a timely fashion so she could get out of this romantic limbo and move forward with her fucking life. Was that so much to ask?

"But I'm only doing this for the purpose of writing the article," she'd stressed to Mitzi, telling herself the same story to get through these Lucille Ball–esque hijinks without being asphyxiated with shame. Mitzi's attitude seemed to be "Yeah, whatever." Whether Sydney hooked up with one of her guys or wrote an article about her for a national magazine, it was a win-win for her. But when Mitzi insisted Sydney use her glam squad in order to write about the full experience of working with Mitzi Berman Serious Matchmaking, Inc.—"date preparation" services were five hundred dollars extra, but Sydney would get them for free—Sydney realized she'd backed herself into a corner. She wasn't about to take a chance on Mitzi's team of beautifiers, but thinking fast, she told Mitzi that Jeffrey-James Eliot was a close friend of hers and he would act as her one-man glam squad. Pleased that a celebrity makeup artist would be part of her article, Mitzi finally let her be. She knew Sydney would be in good hands with Jeffrey, but looking at the ridiculous number of makeup products and cosmetic utensils he'd unpacked—he was like a magician pulling a never-ending scarf out of a black hat!—Sydney wasn't as sure.

"Remember," she said, rolling the chair over to her computer so she could cue up her "work it out" gym mix on iTunes, "I want it natural."

"Then call Bobbi Brown," Jeffrey said. He turned toward her with an Evian atomizer in hand and said, "Close your eyes."

After a quick burst of water sprayed Sydney's face, her eyes blinked open. "What's that for?"

"We need you to look dewy," Jeffrey said. "Like you're still in your child-bearing years."

Used to Jeffrey's sarcasm, Sydney merely smirked, bunching up her robe to cover her bare breasts. There were trees blocking the view of the brownstones across the street and there probably weren't too many people home at six in the evening, but simply wearing open-toed shoes made her feel exposed.

"So what do we know about this moneybags?" Jeffrey said, spackling some kind of primer all over her face.

"His name is Gregory."

"Like Peck. Good start." He took out a makeup sponge and began spreading the primer coat around, giving her another tip while he was at it. "Blending is the key to flawless makeup."

"I'll be sure to remember that."

"So," he said, blending like a maniac, "what else?"

"Nothing more to tell. Mitzi's stingy with the information to prevent Googling."

He took a step back and tossed the used sponge in the wastebasket under Sydney's desk. "Should we practice?"

Sydney looked him up and down. "You want me to practice for a date?"

"Couldn't hurt."

Sydney sat there for a moment, refusing to dignify that rude suggestion with a response. She knew she needed help getting ready for this date. That was why Jeffrey was here. She thought her own personal style, when she put the effort in, was rather fly, but as anyone could plainly see, it wasn't necessarily man-catching. Her casual tomboy-meets-boho look attracted stunted adolescents like Kyle, and that was what she needed to get away from. But she wasn't sure how she would dress for a date—a real date, not Chipotle and a movie—with the kind of successful grown-up that Mitzi would set her up with.

She had always been defiantly unsexy because sexy and feminine were characteristics she associated with women who were weak, not in control.

Women who had to get over on their beauty because their brains couldn't get the job done. Women who needed constant validation from men. But wearing a dress and a pair of heels wouldn't change who she was. And she had always secretly envied women who could put on stilettos and a slinky dress and own it. The J. Los of the world. There was power in being unapologetically sexy, and sometimes she wondered what that would feel like. And where was the harm as long as she made sure these wife-hungry bachelors knew she wasn't some "Yes, dear" submissive looking to be rescued? She'd been there, done that, never again. But life was different now. She had a career and her own money.

The problem was that men liked women to be dependent on them. Dependent but not needy. That was the little "gotcha." If you were too needy, they didn't want you. But if you were too independent, they didn't want you either. The secret was to appear somewhat independent but still make them feel useful by acting docile and helpless in some sense but not actually *be* helpless because then they wouldn't respect you and they'd treat you like the doormat you were. It really was some tricky shit.

So, yes, she knew she needed help in navigating these new choppy waters. The fact that Jeffrey was here and, after three years, finally getting his wish to glam her up was an open admission of that. But *practice for a date*? Them was fightin' words!

"Hold up," she said, rolling the chair away as he came at her holding a skinny makeup brush. "You don't think I can do this."

Jeffrey went to work applying what she assumed was concealer because he was dabbing it on the dark circles under her eyes. "Did I say that?"

"Well, yeah, you did," Sydney said, rolling back again to separate her face from his brush. "Why else would you want me to practice for a date? You don't think I can do this!"

"Look," Jeffrey said, resting his blending hand on his hip. " 'Me, Myself and I' is your favorite song for a reason. Now along comes Mitzi Berman. She wants your favorite song to be 'Cater to You.' How's that gonna work?"

"First of all," Sydney said, " 'Me, Myself and I' is not my favorite song!"

"One of 'em," Jeffrey said, holding the back of the chair steady as he blended the concealer. "Anyway, you know what I'm getting at."

"You think I can't get a normal, successful man to be interested in me?"

"Of course you can. You're smart, you're pretty, you're funny. Why wouldn't a guy be interested in you? The question is, are you gonna be interested in him?" He stepped back and began searching for yet another product on the windowsill. "I'm not sure why you're doing this."

When he turned around, Sydney was on her feet. "You told me to do it!"

Jeffrey pushed her back into the chair. "Bitch, please. We don't have time for this."

CHAPTER THIRTY-FOUR

As Jeffrey dug through her closet, searching for a heel higher than three inches, Sydney stared into the mirror, marveling at her makeover.

It was far from natural, but she kinda loved it! He'd put contour on the sides of her nose and somehow transformed it into the one she'd always dreamed of having. The smoky eyes were, as promised, fabulous. The faint darkness under her eyes was gone. The sheer pinkish gloss—Petal, it was called—gave her lips just the right amount of pucker. He'd strong-armed her into the false eyelashes, straddling the chair and taking her by force, and that was her one regret. Every time she blinked she felt like two sticky black fans were trying to attack her eyeballs!

"Don't you have one pair of stilettos in here just in case?" he said, throwing sneakers, flats, chunky boots, and more sneakers out of the closet onto a discarded heap on the bedroom floor.

Just in case what? She needed to hit the street and turn some tricks? She got an emergency call to walk the runway during Fashion Week? "I don't wear stilettos, Jeffrey," she told him. "You know that."

And still he continued to dig, giving up only when he reached into the back corner and came up with a dust bunny. "You have such a good foundation," he sighed, scooting out of the closet and leaning back on his elbows to rest. "Pretty face, great body." He raised up a bit. "Which you worked very hard for, I might add."

As if Sydney needed him to tell her that? She was the one sweating it out in the gym six days a week and wrestling constantly with her overwhelming desire to binge on bread.

"Do you know how many women would kill to have what you have?" Giving his bloated stomach a pat, he added, "Men too. But you . . ." He pushed himself up off the floor and wiped away the traces of dust. "You refuse to work it to the best of your ability!"

Sydney rolled her eyes. Gay men were forever talking about bringing out somebody's "inner diva." What Jeffrey never seemed to get was that his idea of sexy was her idea of slutty. The body-hugging clothes, hair extensions, and, from now on, fake eyelashes, she'd leave to the Carmen Electras and Amanda Lepores of the world.

"You know who we need?" he finally said.

"Who?" Sydney was forced to ask when, being all dramatic, he refused to answer his own rhetorical question. "Who do we need, Jeffrey? Tell me."

"That ho from next door!" He grabbed Sydney's wrist and, despite her violent protestations, dragged her out into the hallway.

This solution was far scarier than any she could have imagined, but hating to hear another woman unfairly maligned in such a way, she forgot about her own predicament for a second and rose to her neighbor's defense. "She's not a ho. She's an *exotic dancer.*"

"Her name is Candi with an *i,*" Jeffrey said, as if that were the equivalent of having a ho certificate.

"Her name is Cand*ace,*" Sydney said, lowering her voice as a signal to Jeffrey that he should do the same. "People just call her Candi."

"Yeah, people who stick dollar bills up her twat!"

"Omigod," Sydney whispered, trying her damnedest not to laugh. "Shut. Up."

He yanked Sydney the last few feet to Candi's door. "And look where all your hard work has gotten you. I bet you and this hooker are about the same size."

When he let go of her wrist to knock, Sydney made a mad dash back to her apartment, but Jeffrey was undeterred. He stood there, waiting for Candi to answer, while Sydney stood by her door in her bathrobe, hoping she wouldn't. "Let's just go to Intermix!" she yelled out of desperation. Then she heard the latch on Candi's door turn. *Oh God . . .*

It wasn't that she didn't like Candi. She did. In a bizarre way, Sydney respected her, even. She wasn't a hooker or a ho. She was, as the plaque on her bedroom wall proudly attested, the top earner at Scores. She probably made as much money as Sydney and worked similarly light hours. Their apartments were the only two on the top floor of the building, and because they were both home during the day, they had become unlikely friends. That was probably why Sydney got so defensive when Jeffrey made merciless fun of the poor girl. Sydney knew she had tacitly encouraged his derisiveness by acting as if she and Candi were simply neighbors who interacted for the sake of convenience. In actuality, they hung out more than Jeffrey knew because, disturbingly, they had quite a lot in common. They both hit the gym a lot. They liked to watch the same shows—*American Idol, Keeping Up with the Kardashians,* and *Lost* (although Sydney had to spend an extra hour explaining to Candi what had just happened in every episode). And they both were attracted to sorry-ass men. (Since Kyle was in a class above the brutes Candi dated, Sydney had passed along his number and told Candi they'd make a cute couple.) And now that Sydney was alone every night, she had begun to welcome the *Three's Company*–like intrusions of her own personal Chrissy Snow, an embarrassing commentary on her social life (or lack thereof). But while Candi wasn't, in any literal sense, a ho, Sydney didn't want to belabor the point because the girl sure as hell dressed like one.

Standing in front of the mirror in Candi's frilly bedroom wearing a clingy gray jersey minidress and four-inch platform heels that would surely be the death of her, Sydney said, "I don't think so."

Reclined on Candi's four-poster bed, Jeffrey pulled a pink feather boa from the bedpost and snaked it around his neck, noting, "Those look exactly like the platforms Louboutin did last spring." He wriggled his eyebrows, trying to alert Sydney to the Scores plaque on the wall, and Sydney gave him a look that said, *Behave!* Candi had been so excited to take part in the makeover, and all Jeffrey had done the whole time was mock her. What was even meaner was that he did it to her face because she was too dumb to realize it.

"Hey Candi," he said, flicking the end of the boa against the back of her toned leg—she was wearing a pink Juicy couture short set and, fittingly, Candie's—as she rummaged through her dresser drawer. "Where'd you get those?"

Candi looked back, tossing her thick, tackily streaked tresses over her artificially tanned shoulder. "The shoes? Pink Pussycat. I get a discount there!"

"I bet you do," Jeffrey murmured, caressing himself with the boa.

Candi found what she was searching for and click-clacked over to Sydney. "Here," she said, handing her a black satin Wonderbra. "Put this on and you'll be all set!"

"Thank you," Sydney said, eyeing the sexy undergarment warily. (She only wore all-cotton, and she preferred racerbacks.) "But we definitely don't wear the same size."

"We did before the surgery," Candi said, cupping her enlarged pups. They heard the buzzer ringing in Sydney's apartment, and when Sydney said it was probably the car, Candi click-clacked over to the window and looked out. "Awww, he sent a car for you! That's so romantic."

Jeffrey rolled his eyes and at least had the decency to mumble his final insult: "Hos have such low expectations."

Five minutes later, Sydney carefully took her first steps down the stairs like a toddler just getting her footing as Jeffrey and Candi stood by the railing that stretched between the two apartments, beaming like proud parents sending their baby off to her first prom.

When the unexpected flash of Candi's camera threw Sydney off balance, Jeffrey cautioned, "Careful!"

"Well, don't do that!" Sydney shouted, never taking her eyes off her wobbly feet.

"Let's see a smile," Jeffrey said.

"I'll smile when I get there!"

"Nice attitude," he muttered as Sydney struggled to stay focused on her descent, which would have been easier without tips from the dating coaching duo of Jeffrey & Candi raining down upon her.

"Laugh at his jokes," Jeffrey said.

"Yeah!" Candi chimed in. "Even if they aren't funny!"

Sydney wondered if they had been reading Mitzi's book. She tried to recall some of the tips she'd picked up, but her mind drew a blank. Maybe she and Jeffrey should have practiced!

"Show interest in Gregory's work," Jeffrey advised.

"Even if it's totally boring!" Candi added.

Another tip ripped from Mitzi's playbook, Sydney thought. They should write their own dating manual. Who knew what men wanted better than a gay man and a stripper?

"Oh oh oh," Candi began to yip just as Sydney made it to the halfway mark of the first flight of stairs. Sounding as though she'd just remembered the most important tip of all, she yelled, "Remember to stick your tits out!"

That ho-ish helpful hint caused Sydney's head to whip around, and she caught a brief glimpse of Jeffrey staring at a grinning Candi with the same perplexed look that crossed Sydney's face before her feet came out from under her. It took a few seconds for her to realize she was airborne. That no part of her body—not her hands, her feet, her butt—was making contact with the staircase. Next thing she knew, she was splattered, facedown, on the third-floor landing. She lay there, dazed, hearing high-pitched screams of "Oh my God!" and "Call 911!," both Jeffrey's and Candi's Southern accents so intensified in the moment of panic that she couldn't distinguish one from the other.

Candi pushed Sydney onto her back and cradled her head, while Jeffrey, the son of a bitch, went straight for Candi's shoe. It was only at that moment that Sydney realized it was no longer attached to her foot. As he fiddled with the broken strap, Candi stroked Sydney's face, and for an instant, Sydney felt all the maternal affection she had never known as a child. "Are you okay?" Candi kept saying with genuine concern until Sydney realized the answer was no. She was not okay.

"I'm bleeding," she cried, patting the wetness spilling across her chest. That got Jeffrey to look over, but his hands were still going on the strap.

"No," Candi said, pulling down the front of the dress. "It's the bra. I think it sprung a leak."

Sydney struggled to push herself up. "What?"

"There's water in it," Candi said, pointing at the busted balloon peeking out of the ripped seam.

Hearing two quick beeps from the town car outside, Sydney laid her head back on the linoleum, her chest soaked. "Jeffrey," she whimpered. "I can't. I can't do this."

Half an hour later, she limped into Il Cantinori wearing kitten heels and the basic black shift dress she saved for mandatory social functions, a nasty purple bruise the size of a dinner plate forming on the back of her thigh. The hostess directed her to the bar, where Gregory, an okay-looking white guy in his mid-forties, was waiting. Going on autopilot, Sydney pushed out a smile along with her hand, which now sported a jaggedly chipped nail. "Hi, I'm Sydney."

"No," Gregory said, his eyes lighting up as if he'd just won a million dollars from a scratch-off lottery ticket he only expected would yield a hundred at best. "You're stunning!"

"Don't objectify me," Sydney said, and the date when downhill from there.

CHAPTER THIRTY-FIVE

Buzzzzz.

Sydney slapped the snooze button and rolled over, smushing her smiling mug into the pillow, the melody of her new favorite song playing in her head. There had been plenty of songs that would make her pump the volume and shout, "This is my song!" but it had always been her fantasy that someone would actually pen a song for her. And finally someone had.

She'd been in a cab, fleeing the scene of her Mitzi Berman–arranged disaster, when she remembered the text Max had sent earlier, reminding her of his gig. By that hour, her head was throbbing as insistently as the bruise on the back of her thigh, and she wasn't sure if she should tell the cabbie to detour to Joe's Pub or the hospital. All Mitzi Berman cared about—all anyone seemed to care about—was her finding a man. Well, what if she had a concussion? And because she'd gone on this disastrous date instead of going to the hospital, she went to sleep and never woke up? This date could have literally been the death of her!

Since all she wanted to do was sleep, she figured the only way to *not* become Heath Ledger was to go to Max's gig. Her interest in actually hearing his band was minimal, but they were so good, she stayed for the whole set, grooving so vigorously on her bar stool that it took a stab of pain to remind her of her injuries. Max's weirdo friend Duke was the lead singer, and he had an amazing voice that Sydney couldn't believe was coming out of that body. Max was on bass; from his vantage point at the back of the small stage, he couldn't see her, but Sydney knew he expected to. When she'd shown up at the door her name was at the top of the band's list, a placement that indicated a higher level of romantic interest than he was letting on. Unfortunately, he'd caught Sydney at the inopportune moment when she was determined to break her addiction to slackers. Otherwise his "I'm only interested in being friends" reverse psychology would have netted him a piece by now.

Especially after he'd written a song about her. No wonder he kept nudging her to come to his show! What was he supposed to say? "Hey, I wrote a song about you. It's called 'Infatuation'?" Duke had earned a laugh from the crowd with his intro. "This next one is brand-new, written by our bass player. It's about a chick who wants nothing to do with him."

Beep. Beep. Beep.

Sydney rolled over and, hazily noting the time, realized it had been her phone buzzing, not the clock. And whoever was calling her at a quarter past eight had just left a message. Knowing that unless something calamitous had happened to one of her family members, it could only be one person, she closed her eyes and tried to take a moment before she listened to the . . .

Buzzzzzzzz.

"Mitzi," she answered groggily. "Let me explain."

" 'Don't objectify me'?" Mitzi barked, way too ferocious for the ungodly hour. "Are you insane?"

Sydney stacked some pillows against the wall behind her bed and rested against them. "Are you insane?" was one of Myrna's favorite rhetorical jabs, one of the clearest examples of projection Sydney had ever encountered, and hearing it now from Mitzi Berman summoned up a host of unpleasant associations that put Sydney in a worse frame of mind than being woken up before nine already had. If she hadn't quit smoking, she'd be reaching for a Marlboro Light right now.

"You told him you thought all politicians are liars?"

"How was I supposed to know he wanted to run for mayor?"

"You don't need to know. Don't talk politics on a first date! Basic rule!"

"Okay, but listen, things were going badly before I got there. I fell down the stairs . . ."

"What does that have to do with him?"

Sydney fiddled with the coverlet. "Nothing, I guess."

"Finally, you guess right," Mitzi said. "You said you read my book, but you probably skimmed it. If you had read it, you'd know that it doesn't matter what happens ten minutes or ten years before the date. Check your baggage at the door, girlfriend!"

Quietly, Sydney said, "I know, Mitzi."

"No, you don't! If you knew anything, you wouldn't have told him about running into your ex."

"I know," Sydney said, thinking, *God, what did this guy do? Give Mitzi a transcript?* This was like being graded on a date! And she was flunking! Trying to prove that she had read the book, she quoted one of Mitzi's rules back to her. "'If he tries to bring up a past relationship, "Next!"'"

"He didn't bring it up," Mitzi said. "*You* brought it up!"

"I know," Sydney said, sliding down onto her back.

"Stop saying you know. You obviously know nothing. You violated all the rules!"

"I know," Sydney said. Again. Then, trying to offer a reasonable excuse, she said, "I guess I . . . forgot?"

"You're hopeless," Mitzi said, heaving a disgusted sigh. "You really are. I can't believe he actually wants to see you again."

Sydney pushed herself back up to a sitting position. "He does?"

"He's a masochist!"

"Yeah, well, I don't see that happening," Sydney said, realizing she was fully awake now and might be able to make the early Yogilates class.

"Excuse me?"

"There was just something about him."

"Like what?"

"I can't put my finger on it. His cologne? It was very off-putting. It was the cologne of a man who thinks too much of himself."

"Are you sure that wasn't your own natural scent you were smelling?"

Sydney couldn't help smiling. When it came to deadpan delivery, Mitzi Berman was the master. "Look, I'm sorry," she said, thinking they could write the whole thing off as a fluke. "Better luck next time, right?"

"Next time?" Mitzi snapped. "Get a clue. You are so out of my database it isn't even funny!"

Click!

CHAPTER THIRTY-SIX

When Fiona walked into the second bedroom of the chintz-filled Upper East Side apartment that doubled as Mitzi Berman's home office and nervously informed her that Sydney Zamora was there to see her, Mitzi growled, "Get rid of her!"

"Too late," Sydney said, pushing past Fiona. Sydney could only imagine what kind of monstrous image the girl had of her thanks to Mitzi's unforgiving brush, but thankfully Fiona didn't have the backbone to dismiss her at the door as Mitzi was surely wishing she had.

Mitzi said, "I'll call you back" into her headset, flicked the arm away from her mouth, and gave Fiona a visual signal that the police needn't be called.

"For you," Sydney said, placing a Harvey's box on Mitzi's desk and herself in the chair in front of it.

Mitzi eyed the box warily, then opened it as though it might contain a bomb. "Goyard," she said flatly when she pulled back the tissue.

"I brought it as a peace offering," Sydney said, putting on her best smile.

Without taking the bag out for closer inspection, Mitzi dropped the box on the floor and gave it a swift kick with the rounded toe of her Chanel spectator pump. "Thanks. Now get out."

Watching the box slide into the corner like a hockey puck, Sydney said, "Um, do you know how much that cost?" It was completely tacky to mention price when giving a gift, and given this one's shady origins, how dead wrong was she to bring it up? (After pricing real ones at Harvey's and deciding Mitzi wasn't worth the money, even with Max's discount, she'd left the store with a shopping bag and an empty box and headed down to Canal Street, where she copped this $150 replica.) But that was exactly why she was there, she thought. She was always doing and saying dumb shit. She needed help.

"You cannot put a price on the embarrassment you've caused me," Mitzi said coldly.

"I know," Sydney said, her hands clasped solemnly on her lap. "My behavior was inexcusable. That's why I came here. To apologize." She let her head bow, but only a little bit. She wasn't going to grovel! "And I thought you could use a new bag." She looked at Mitzi's old one, discarded on the love seat like a used-up hooker. "That one's jacked!"

Sydney was hoping to infuse the room with some levity, but Mitzi looked ready to stab her. "Thanks. Again. But you're not getting back into my database." She flicked her hand as if Sydney were a buzzing insect. "Now be on your way."

"Mitzi, look . . ." Sydney leaned forward, and seeing that she had no intention of leaving, Mitzi turned her head away, groaning audibly. "Maybe you were a little bit right about me."

Mitzi turned back. "A little bit?"

"Come on, Mitzi! I'm not some horrible person."

"No one said you were."

"Then stop treating me like the creature from the Black Lagoon!"

"You get what you give."

"And that's why I'm here," Sydney said, splaying her hands open. "Giving humility. Giving you your due. I mean, look at me!" She stood up and stepped away from the desk so Mitzi could get a load of her outfit. Flippy little tweed skirt. Fitted cardigan. Her Lanvin flats. She'd even tried to blow out her own hair (then pushed it back with a skinny headband when it didn't come out so great). "I feel like a chicer version of Doris Day. And what, no props?"

Mitzi groaned again when Sydney reclaimed the seat she had never been offered in the first place. "I don't know what you're talking about and I don't care about this little costume you put on. What I do know is that I'm through with you."

"Mitzi, please," Sydney said, wringing her hands. "I genuinely apologize a million times over."

"I don't do second chances."

"I don't know why I acted that way."

"That's something you should delve into," Mitzi said. "In therapy."

"I *am* in therapy," Sydney said, which was only partly true since she'd basically reduced Liessel to a pill pusher. "But I'm going to start going more often." That was an outright lie, and she compounded it by adding, "I promise. Just give me another chance."

Mitzi look up from the papers she was pretending to be interested in and gave Sydney a long, hard look. "Do you realize there are women who come in here who are in their forties, never married, sloppy fat, with terrible skin, awful perms, and no sense of style? Women who would *kill* to be you. Because you've already cleared the biggest hurdle. You're beautiful. You have it all. Looks, brains, a great career, personality. And what do you do? You squander it!"

"You think I have a good personality?"

"I didn't say good," Mitzi snapped. "But you have spark. And I suspect there might be a more pleasant personality buried underneath all that aggression. But after how you treated Gregory, I can't trust you to be alone with one of my guys again. You are a danger to yourself and others."

"I don't want to pretend to be something I'm not."

"Neither do I," Mitzi said, offended at the insinuation. "Neither does the guy across the table. That's the number-one complaint my guys have. 'She acted one way on the first few dates and then she became a different person.'"

"Exactly."

"No one's asking you to put on a petticoat, Sydney. I'm saying put on some makeup, a nice dress. Be you. You at your best. I know this tough girl, 'I don't need anybody' persona isn't you. It's a front you put up."

"It's not a front I put up, Mitzi. It's just . . ." Sydney let out a frustrated grunt. "It's something that comes out when I'm in a datelike situation. I can't help it. I get competitive. I don't know what it is."

"I do," Mitzi said. "It's called feminism."

Sydney raised her eyebrows. "Feminism?"

Mitzi nodded. "Yup. I deal with women all day long, and a lot of them are like you. I mean, you're an extreme case. You're very, very challenged socially, but it all stems from the same thing. Women of your generation grew up believing they could do everything a man could do. And I'm the last person to say a woman is not a man's equal. We are equals. But we're different, Sydney. Different doesn't mean lesser. It means different. He's an apple, you're an orange. Both delicious. And once you accept that, maybe you'll stop competing and just be."

Sydney felt her eyes welling up as she sat there, biting her lip and hating herself. "I don't think I know how to do that," she said, quickly wiping under her eye before a tear dared to escape. "Just be?"

Mitzi plucked a tissue out of the floral ceramic holder on her antiquey reproduction of a desk and handed it over. The fact that she showed no emotion in doing this gave Sydney the impression that women cried in her office every day, which somehow made her feel pathetically common but also like less of a loser.

"I don't know why you have this need to self-destruct," Mitzi said. "Why you can't let your guard down. But I'll tell you this: If you don't make some radical changes in your behavior, you will die alone." She tapped the mouthpiece of her headset back to conversational position. "Now, if you'll excuse me."

Sydney sat hunched over in the chair, dabbing at her damp cheek, muttering, "You're right, Mitzi. You're right." Deciding it was best to leave before she said something else that got her back into hot water, she stood before Mitzi, keeping her head and eyes lowered. "Thank you, Mitzi. Thank you for giving me another chance."

Mitzi's eyes flicked up. "Another chance?"

"I promise," Sydney said, heading for the door. "I won't let you down next time."

"No, you won't," Mitzi said. "Because there isn't going to be a next time."

CHAPTER THIRTY-SEVEN

Following the pretty hostess into the private room at Chinatown Brasserie where Lorelei Murphy was having a dinner to celebrate her thirtieth (supposedly) birthday, Max felt like a wild animal who'd been unwittingly ensnared in a game hunter's net. Despite his lineage, the fashion world wasn't really his scene, and normally he would have Natasha by his side to act as a buffer at such a gathering. But thanks to Lorelei's skills as a booker, Natasha was in Turks and Caicos getting twice her day rate to act as a standby, literally, in case the severely anorexic model of the moment who'd been booked to shoot the prestigious Pirelli swimsuit calendar collapsed from malnourishment under the beating sun. Max had been planning to sample the food at the newly opened brasserie anyway so he decided to go it alone, thinking he could grab a bite and quickly pay his respects. When he found a cozy dozen gathered around a long table and all twelve faces swiveled in his direction, smiling as he entered, he realized he was stuck there for the duration, bufferless.

Had he known there was going to be arranged seating, he would have thought twice about cavalierly showing up alone. Dinner parties were enjoyable only if you were seated next to hot, available women or, barring that, men with something interesting to say. The woman to Max's left wasn't even lukewarm (she was married, besides), and suspecting that Lorelei had stacked the (place)cards to give the André Leon Talley wannabe heading Max's way an opportunity to work him for a store discount, he briefly considered going to the bathroom and disappearing into the night. Ducking out would have been the height of rudeness, but Lorelei had instantly forgiven the fashion divo's late arrival when he handed over his gift—a small, flat box that was instantly recognizable, from its signature orange color, as being from Hermès. Why should she care about Max's early departure when *his* box (containing a beautiful Margiela dress) was already safely stacked on her luxurious pile?

Max hated to be so cynical, but he'd once been at a party where the hostess got drunk and announced that she'd invited him primarily because of the caliber of gift he would bring. Everyone shared a knowing laugh at his expense—too knowing, he felt—and what should have been an inconsequential moment that faded quickly from memory had instead left an indelible mark on his psyche. *Ha-ha, so funny, so fucking funny,* he'd thought, more angry at himself than anyone for not being able to shrug it off. His anger dissolved like a match in the wind when he made an early exit, revoked gift in hand, and bestowed the $595 pashmina on a homeless woman he almost tripped over coming out of the building, someone who needed it a helluva lot more than that drunk bitch ever did. *He who laughs last laughs the loudest,* he'd thought, smiling the whole cab ride home.

Lorelei was not that caliber of user, but seeing her point in his direction while whispering to her fabulously dressed friend (his black leather trench and enormous snakeskin satchel had Max's gaydar pinging off the charts), Max felt unfairly targeted. And that, in his mind, justified an early exit. How he was going to manage this was his most pressing concern until he thought to look at the name scribbled on the little cardboard tent propped in front of the seat to his right. Just as his eyes focused in the dimness, the man himself spoke up.

"Jeffrey-James Eliot," he said, triggering in Max a sense of déjà vu. "The makeup artist."

Max gave his name hesitantly, watching the increasingly perplexed expression on Jeffrey's clean-shaved (and lightly made-up?) face. He had indeed been tipped off to his true identity, Max thought, a dozen questions and no plausible answers knocking around like pinballs in his head.

"Please don't say anything," he pleaded, trying to do damage control before Jeffrey could piece it all together and come to his own conclusion. "I'm going to tell her. I am."

"And when you do," Jeffrey said, examining the assortment of appetizers laid out on the table, "she's gonna throw up the deuces faster than you can say good golly Miss Molly."

As Jeffrey picked up a dumpling and popped it in his mouth, Max stared at him in confusion. He'd always considered himself to be pretty hip, but this ghetto-meets-gay dialect was unfamiliar to him. "She's going to *what*?"

Jeffrey seemed annoyed that Max was distracting him from sampling the buffet. "Throw up the deuces," he said, putting up two fingers in the shape of a vee. "Peace you out, kick you to the curb . . ."

"Oh," Max said. "Yes. I got that feeling. That's why I haven't said anything."

"I've seen it happen many a time," Jeffrey said, separating his chopsticks with a quick snap. "It ain't pretty."

Max was relieved that he and Jeffrey were on the same page until it dawned on him that this was not a good thing. "So wait," he said. "You really think that if I tell her the truth, she's never going to speak to me again?"

Wolfing down two dumplings in rapid succession, Jeffrey mumbled, "Um-hmm."

"Come on," Max said. "Not if I plead my case. Right?"

Jeffrey tilted his head and listened patiently while using his tongue to dislodge remnants of dumpling that were wedged in his back molars.

"I mean, none of this was done with malicious intent," Max said. "No one got hurt. It's just a harmless misunderstanding that went too far."

Jeffrey stared at Max as though he were a child asking to have ice cream for breakfast. As if he was naive to the point of silliness. "You have no idea who you're dealing with, do you?" Max wasn't sure what to make of that question, and he became more confounded as Jeffrey's eyes narrowed and his voice dropped to an ominous whisper more fitting for conjuring spirits over a Ouija board. "There are people Sydney has known for years and years and then one day"—he snapped his fingers—"they're gone."

"You mean people she's fallen out with?"

"Not always." Jeffrey reached for a spring roll. "And it's not even like a 'You're dead to me!' thing. Because people still reminisce about the dead, you know?" He turned to Max but looked past him as if he was trying to make sense of it himself. "It's like they *never existed*. Their names never cross her lips again."

Max tried to probe for further insight, but Jeffrey waved him off with the chopsticks, claiming, "I've said too much."

"Don't leave me hanging, Jeffrey! You obviously know her much better than I do." Holding his wineglass out so the waiter could refill it, Jeffrey nodded. "So steer me in the right direction," Max said. "Help me out here!"

"Why should I?" Jeffrey said, turning his (surgically slimmed?) nose up haughtily. "The only thing I know about you, besides the fact that your father owns Harvey's, is that you're a liar."

"That's a bit harsh," Max said, although he knew, for this queen, it was probably tame. "I never told her I was the doorman. It was a misunderstanding that I didn't clear up. It's a sin of omission."

"A sin nonetheless," Jeffrey noted.

Max saw him eying the last dumpling and laid claim to it in retaliation. Then he mushed it up on his plate, sulking until Jeffrey took pity on him.

"Okay, listen," Jeffrey said, stabbing the chopsticks at Max for emphasis. "You can never ever tell her I told you this." He waited for Max to show some sign of agreement, as if he needed to have a binding oral contract before he could divulge the information. Max nodded and he divulged. "I loooove that chile to death," he said, patting a hand against the hairy patch of collarbone exposed at the neck of his unbuttoned paisley shirt. "Lord knows I do." His bosom heaved. "But the truth is she can be somewhat self-defeating in matters of the heart. She's quite commitmentphobic."

"Aren't we all?"

Jeffrey reared up. "What *the hell* you mean by that? You tryin' to hit it and quit it?"

Thrown off balance by Jeffrey's ability to go from effete to aggressive in the space of five seconds, Max jiggled his head from side to side as if there were water clogging his ear. *"What?"*

"Fuck her and flee," Jeffrey said, each sharply enunciated word an indictment.

"No!" Max said. Then he mumbled, "At least not the flee part."

"What?" Jeffrey said, cupping his manicured fingers—even with the ambient lighting Max detected the shimmer of clear polish—around his diamond-studded ear. "What was that?"

"I said I'm not planning to flee," Max told him. "I'm interested in her romantically, okay? I admit that."

Jeffrey seemed both surprised and impressed by Max's candor. "Okay. All right. It's all good." He settled back into his chair and turned his attention back to the smorgasbord on the table. "At least we know you're not gay. That came up."

"Mmm, yes," Max said, making sure his tone didn't betray any offense. "I've heard that before."

Jeffrey gave him the side-eye. "But I know one when I see one."

Max saw the waiters coming around with the second course and realized he hadn't yet sampled the first. He took a bite of the dumpling on his plate. It was cold.

"So . . ." Jeffrey placed his interlocked fingers under his chin, regarding Max pensively. "What are your intentions?"

Max looked around in confusion. "Pardon?"

"You heard me."

A waiter stuck his arm between them to grab an emptied tray, and Max used the interruption to consider his response. How did one respond to a question like that? What were they going to talk next? Dowries?

Jeffrey crossed one thick leg over the other and reached for his wineglass. "I imagine a rich, good-looking boy like you has girls lining up to give you anything you want," he said before taking a sip.

Max glanced around, checking to see if anyone else was listening. When he saw that the guests nearest to them were all engaged in their own conversations, he felt safe that no one would call his bluff when he answered, "It's not like that." His player tendencies were not a subject he wanted to delve into further, so he went on the offensive, adroitly moving the conversation along. "Anyway, you're kind of jumping the gun here, don't you think? We haven't even been on a proper date yet."

"So you haven't," Jeffrey conceded. "Do you have a problem with monogamy?"

Max swallowed a groan. This wasn't a conversation, he thought. It was an interrogation. Although he had to admit, the challenge of conquering Mount Sydney seemed more exciting every time the difficulty level jumped up a notch. This overly inquisitive queen was only the latest obstacle to fall in his path. And after coming this far, he couldn't turn back now.

"I have no problems with monogamy," he said, and that was the truth. And not a cleaned-up version of the truth, the kind he often told. He dated around plenty, but when he was in a committed relationship he was faithful. That wasn't really saying much since he'd never been in a relationship that lasted more than a year. His marriage hadn't even lasted that long. But the fact that he'd even *been* married was proof that he was comfortable with the idea of long-term commitment. That brief, ill-fated union was something he rarely discussed, but in this unusual situation, he thought, admitting he was divorced might actually shore up his image. So he did.

"*You?*" Jeffrey said, frowning suspiciously. "Married?"

"Yes," Max said, somewhat affronted by his reaction. "Why should that surprise you?"

"I don't know," Jeffrey said. "Rich, handsome boy like you, gettin' all this ass . . ."

"Did I say that?"

"Didn't have to," Jeffrey said with an accusing glance. "I know what goes on. Why would you want to settle down?"

"Because I was in love," Max said, to which Jeffrey responded, "Touching."

"She moved back to Europe," Max told him to make it clear that she was completely out of the picture. "Haven't seen her in years."

Jeffrey scooped a spoonful of sautéed vegetables onto his plate, then passed the serving dish to Max, casually asking, "So you cheated on her?"

"No!" Max said, accidentally spitting a bit of dumpling onto the vegetables.

Jeffrey nodded toward the defiled piece of broccoli. "Please take that."

Max dumped a heap of vegetables onto his plate. "Why are you so intent on believing the worst about me?"

"It's not about you in particular," Jeffrey said. "Don't take it personally."

"How else am I supposed to take it?"

"Men, in general, are pigs," Jeffrey said matter-of-factly. "No one knows that better than a gay man. In my book, they're all guilty until proven innocent."

"Jeffrey, I think it's very sweet that you're so protective of Sydney," Max said, thinking he sounded a little "sweet" for choosing to use that word in regard to another man. "But I'm not a pig. I assure you of that."

"Time will tell," Jeffrey said. "So what happened with your wife?"

"Long story short, she turned out to be a money-hungry bitch."

"Ah," Jeffrey said, buying that answer without hesitation. "Well, that's one thing I can assure you that Sydney is not."

"I know," Max said. It was one of the things he liked about her. This was the first time in his life that he was worried that a woman *wouldn't* like him because of the family he came from.

Jeffrey savored a sip of wine, then surprised Max by saying, "I have a good feeling about you."

Max perked up. He wasn't expecting to gain an ally. The most he had hoped for was not being ratted out. "You do?"

"Yes," Jeffrey said. "So I'm going to help you out." He hesitated. "That is, if you want my advice."

"Of course," Max said. "What do you suggest?"

"Don't tell her."

That was the last thing Max was expecting to hear. Not sure he understood correctly, he repeated Jeffrey's suggestion in the form of a question. "*Don't* tell her?"

"Get her to fall for you," Jeffrey said. "*Then* tell her. It's the only way."

Max considered this to be highly questionable advice bordering on lunacy. "Don't you think the longer I wait, the angrier she'll be?"

"No," Jeffrey said confidently. "I think the more attached to you she is, the harder it will be for her to dismiss you."

"I see your point," Max said.

"Trust me. I know this bitch better than she knows herself."

"But it feels so sleazy, lying to her," Max said. "And it's hard keeping everything straight. I'm starting to feel like one of those con men you see on *Dateline* who marry five different women and bilk them all of their life savings!"

"Go on, then," Jeffrey said, insulted that his word was not being taken as gospel. "Tell her. It's your life."

Imagining how that conversation might go, Max realized that Jeffrey's advice made sense. He thought about how angry Sydney could get, how her eyes contorted with rage whenever she talked about . . . *Oh God,* he thought. *Lulu!* He hadn't even thought that far ahead. Sydney might be willing to give him a chance, but once she found out he'd stuck his dick into Lulunatic, it was going to be all over for him. Recognizing the need for Jeffrey's sage counsel, Max admitted, "There's another problem."

"What's that?" Jeffrey said, blotting his mouth with the napkin.

"I, very briefly, dated Lulu Merriwether."

Letting his chin fall against his hairy chest patch, Jeffrey moaned in exasperation. "You really want to make this difficult."

"Sydney detests her. I know," Max said. "What's the deal with that anyway?"

"Lulu Merriwether got Sydney fired from Indochine," Jeffrey told him. "Like, seven years ago. I can understand why Sydney doesn't like her, but it's not healthy to carry a grudge around for that long."

No, it wasn't, Max thought. But it did bode well for him. Sydney didn't just hate Lulu for what she represented. She had a legitimate beef with her. Still, knowing she could be angry about it so many years later, coupled with the knowledge that she could summarily erase people out of her life without so much as a second thought, made him wonder if his infatuation was blinding him to some seriously dysfunctional tendencies that would come back to bite him in the ass later. Maybe he should get out now when he had a chance.

"So," Jeffrey said. "What are you going to do?"

"I will continue with this insane charade and let it lead where it may," Max said, making the decision as he spoke it.

"Trust me," Jeffrey said. "It's for her own good."

"But this was your idea, Jeffrey! If the shit hits the fan, you have to back me up."

"I got you," Jeffrey said, raising a fist in some kind of black or gay gesture that Max didn't really get. "Just know that your secret's out now, playa. Get outta line . . ." He leaned toward Max threateningly but trailed off when a hush fell over the room. They both looked up and saw one of the waiters walking slowly toward Lorelei with his hand sheltering the lit candle stuck in the center of her birthday cupcake. After he passed and everyone's eyes were focused on the birthday girl, Jeffrey finished making his threat. "Get outta line," he whispered into Max's ear, "and I will blow your shit up with a quickness. Believe that."

"Duly noted," Max whispered back. Then they began to sing.

CHAPTER THIRTY-EIGHT

After examining his expensive handiwork from all angles, Christian Michel twisted Sydney around to face the mirror and said, *"Voilà!"* Standing tall, Sydney looked at her new weave from the front, then from the side. She shook her head and watched the glossy black tips swish against the back pockets of her jeans. When Christian's sycophantic underlings crowded around, praising him to the heavens, Sydney felt that was her cue to start belting out, "I got you, babe."

Christian didn't ask her if she liked it. He liked it. His "people" like it. That was what mattered. And Sydney was happy . . . that it was over. It had taken five hours to lay these tracks, and after reading every magazine in the Christian Michel salon—or looking at the pics, since half of them were in French—she'd gotten so bored she'd started doing algebra problems for fun. If Christian Michel was being paid fourteen thousand dollars to sew three tracks of human hair into her head and each measured three feet in length, how much was he getting per foot?

Since *Cachet* was paying the astronomical $1,500-per-foot fee, it was most important that Conrad approved and, unbeknownst to Sydney, he'd been invited to get a look-see. Christian shooed the assistants away; and in the mirror, Sydney could see Gareth and Conrad heading straight for her, walking in lockstep with cell phones glued to their ears.

There were air kisses all around and Sydney thought how weird it was to see three men kissing one another like that. Christian was French, so that was his standard greeting. Gareth was gay. But what was Conrad's excuse? Oh, right, she thought. He was weird. Or rather, "eccentric," which was what weird became in higher tax brackets.

For Sydney, Conrad had a single cheek-to-cheek brush, a perimeter violation she had learned to tolerate since he was technically her boss, while Gareth barely acknowledged her. Wearing his trademark green Crocs and khakis, with his paunch straining his white button-down shirt, Conrad proceeded to walk a slow semicircle around her, as if her hair was Christian's final exam and he was checking it for errors. He pressed his palms on the crown of Sydney's head (serious violation!), to see if he could feel the tracks, Sydney presumed, then ran his hands down the length of her mane, giving the ends a congratulatory flip.

"Magnifique!" he cheered, causing Christian's knees to buckle with joy as if he had just been named America's Next Top Model. Gareth, the Miss J of this scenario, gave a light, fey clap.

A short debate ensued about whether "the hair," as they objectively referred to it, should be trimmed or cut into a style (they decided to leave it long and straight). Then a joyful round of farewell kisses was exchanged and *Cachet*'s two top dogs made a beeline for the elevator as though they were heads of state whose day was scheduled down to the minute. They'd departed so abruptly, Sydney hadn't had the chance to bring up the matter she'd wanted to discuss with Conrad. It was really something that should be addressed to Gareth now that Myrna was gone, so calling Conrad directly wouldn't have made sense. She was planning to "bump into him" at the office and bring it up casually, like "Oh, you know, I wasn't sure about . . ." but she didn't have a reason to go to the office anymore. So it was now or never.

She hated that Gareth, who was sure to fuck this up for her, was around, but she got lucky. The moment she called Conrad back, his British lapdog sat down by the front desk to take a call on his pretentious little European phone. *Good,* Sydney thought. *Stay there.*

"Oh, Conrad," she said as he walked toward her. "I wasn't sure what to do about my new contract." Sydney began gathering her things, acting as though she too had more important things to get to. (In truth, she was heading home to watch a recorded episode of today's *Oprah*. Kirstie Alley was on.) She hitched the bag over her shoulder and looked at the mirror, smoothing her horse hair. "It said one twenty-five."

It was a well-known fact that Conrad did not like to deal with the mundane details of running the magazine. He left that to Myrna while he focused on glamorous aspects of the top spot like picking covers, organizing his annual Oscar party, and courting young, nubile starlets (whom he landed because of his exalted position despite being a tubby, middle-aged man). Gambling that Conrad had only a vague recollection of the exact dollar amount of her new contract, Sydney said, "Myrna told me I was getting bumped up."

"Right, right. Of course," Conrad said, clearly befuddled but nodding vigorously. "You're getting bumped up to . . ."

As his clipped voice trailed off, Sydney flipped her mane over her shoulder and smiled serenely. Myrna had told her she was getting one twenty-five, as the contract correctly stated, with a promise of one fifty next year, but there was no chance Conrad was going to give Myrna a ring to confirm that. The poor woman was probably in an insane asylum somewhere under lock and key. And Chad, the little shit, was already up to two seventy-five and optioning his bullshit stories left and right. DreamWorks had just optioned his piece about an eighty-year-old Bosnian cobbler. *Where the hell was the movie in that?* Sure, Chad was forty-five and had been in the game much longer than Sydney, but she wasn't asking for two seventy-five. Although maybe she should. After all, Conrad had just handed her a blank check.

He stared at her, awaiting a number, and Sydney tried to think fast. For the last two weeks, she had been scheming on how she could get an audience with him to have this conversation. Why hadn't she decided on a figure? After the tongue-lashing she'd gotten from Myrna during her first "contract negotiation," you'd think she'd have been prepared!

But that was the problem, Sydney thought. Being Myrna's protégée meant never having to fight her own battles. She didn't know how to approach Conrad on a business level because she'd never had to. Forty-eight and trying to stay relevant, Conrad only wanted to hear about movies she'd seen, music she'd downloaded, new designers she'd discovered, blogs she'd RSSed, apps she'd added on Facebook . . . anything hot happening hip new now.

All work-related issues were addressed to Myrna, who'd always find a swift resolution. And the harder-won the victory, the better. Myrna lived to battle. But as much as Sydney wished Myrna was here to do her dirty work, she was hating her all the same because Myrna was the reason Sydney hadn't gotten a raise in two years!

Around the time her first yearlong contract was coming up for renewal, Myrna told Sydney the magazine was giving her another two-year contract at the same rate. She'd mentioned it casually on the way to their weekly lunch and Sydney agreed without hesitation, thinking it was a done deal. But when was anything ever simple with Myrna?

"You're not supposed to just say yes!" Myrna had screamed. "Negotiate!"

Negotiate? They were in Harvey's picking up Myrna's hair gel. Sydney didn't know she was expected to enter contract negotiations in front of the Kiehl's counter! Flustered, she'd explained that she was just so grateful to Myrna for all she had done for her. That was before she'd realized flattery always made Myrna suspicious.

"Grateful? To me?" Myrna had scoffed. "Are you insane?" When the salesgirl told Myrna they were out of her beloved hair gel, Myrna berated the girl thoroughly, then stormed off to the elevator, seamlessly segueing back into berating Sydney. "The money isn't being siphoned out of my personal bank account, dummy. Omnimedia is signing your checks. They're a multibillion-dollar corporation! And you're only in this position so they can prove they're not perpetuating institutionalized racism and sexism, which we know they are!" Sydney could still picture Myrna jumping up and down in the elevator (in front of a woman and her child, who began to cry), yelling, "STICK IT TO THEM! STICK IT TO THEM!"

Sydney didn't work for Myrna directly—officially she was an independent contractor—but once Myrna took on the role of mentor, the professional boundaries had become blurred. Myrna told her so many personal things, Sydney thought it was okay to do the same. That day she'd realized she was wrong. But that was only after she'd made a bigger error in judgment. Seated at their usual godfather table in the back room at Binky's, she confessed to Myrna that she didn't really feel deserving of more money since she was only writing ten stories a year, and measly ones at that.

Myrna had gone apeshit.

"Men don't think about how much they deserve," she'd hissed. "They think about how much they can get! That basketball player, Le-something, got ninety million dollars from Nike before he ever stepped on an NBA court. He was in *fucking high school!* Do you think he feels guilty? King James, they call him. Do you think when King James lays his head on the pillow at night, he wonders if he really deserves his crown?"

He might, Sydney thought. But she kept quiet. By that point, she knew Myrna was off on one of her legendary mouth-frothing tirades, so she settled in and took it.

"Jesus, when are you stupid women gonna get a fucking clue and realize it's not about deserving it?" she'd said, between savage gulps of her martini. "It's about determining your own market value." When a hint of confusion rippled across Sydney's face—*market value?*—Myrna said, "Did you really get into Princeton early admission?" A City College dropout, Myrna always liked to throw that in her face. And like clockwork came the inevitable slight: "Right, but you didn't graduate."

Sydney had developed a coping mechanism for the times Myrna went off on her, and fleeing was not an option. She cast her mind elsewhere, imagining she was on a sunny beach, on a date with Benjamin Bratt, pushing her nephew on a swing . . . That day it was difficult to transport herself to calmer environs since Myrna was sitting directly in front of her, jabbing a toothpick at Sydney as if she were aiming a dart at her eye.

"Look," she said, slightly calmer, popping the olive into her mouth. "If you applied for a job as a receptionist, you would have to take whatever salary was being offered. If they said it paid twenty thousand a year, you couldn't come back and say, 'Well, I was thinking more like twenty-four.' Because there are a million high school dropouts who can answer a phone, and they'll do it for twenty. They have no choice. They have no leverage. You do." Myrna almost sounded supportive, and Sydney found herself listening appreciatively. "Omnimedia will be battling this lawsuit for years. They wouldn't let you go unless you decapitated old Mo Gubelman." She cackled at the idea, which Sydney imagined she fantasized about regularly although she had probably never met the reclusive Omnimedia chairman. "You have these motherfuckers by the balls! And yet here you are, bending over to let them fuck you in the ass." They were having a late lunch and no one was within earshot so Myrna let the vulgarities rip freely while Sydney tried to make her way back to the beach. "Is being sodomized some kind of turn-on for you?" she said, leaning across the table to lock onto Sydney's wandering eyes. "Is that your thing? Do you want me to get you a big fat dildo for Christmas?" She sat back and laughed, too busy getting her jollies to touch her food. "Do you realize that when Warhol started painting soup cans, people thought he was nuts? A few years later a Warhol was worth a million dollars, and last year one sold for ninety-five million. Why? Because art is about perception. It's speculative. It's *ether!*" Her hands grabbed at the air as if she might catch an invisible Warhol floating by. "In this situation, you are Warhol! You are King James! You are Nicole fucking Kidman! Stop thinking like a goddamned receptionist!"

Sydney had tried not to listen because she hated the messenger and the delivery, but the message was invaluable. And she was in an even better position now because *Cachet* desperately wanted this Raven story and she was the only Cherokee-resembling reporter they could send to do the job. So what that she hadn't been working for twenty years like Chad. It's not about deserving it, she told herself. It was about determining her own market value.

But if she asked for too much, Conrad might say no, she thought, feeling droplets of sweat form on the nape of her neck under the weight of The Hair. But what was so bad about that? So he'd say no. Then they'd negotiate. And Conrad would be negotiable. Gareth, whom she saw heading toward them, wouldn't.

"Two hundred," she said evenly, thinking she'd start high and work her way back to something more reasonable.

Sydney watched Conrad's gray eyebrows crinkle, and then his head turned, almost imperceptibly, in Gareth's direction. Sydney's heartbeat quickened to an alarming rate but, channeling her inner Myrna, she held her gaze steady, hoping to shame an answer out of him before he realized Gareth was right behind him. *Was he the boss or not?*

She didn't expect him to haggle with her as HR had done—a man of Conrad Drake's stature didn't haggle—but she sensed he might come back with a lower number, not as the beginning of a negotiation but as a final verdict. One sixty? One seventy-five? Either of those would do, she thought.

But when he spoke, it wasn't a number. It was a single, astonishing word that blew into Sydney's face like a gloriously cold gust of air on a hot summer's day. "Fine."

As thrilled as she was, Sydney didn't allow herself to get caught up in the ecstasy of the moment. Doing Myrna proud, she upped her gangsta and added, "For two years."

CHAPTER THIRTY-NINE

Max had asked Jeffrey to meet him at Binky's to discuss his covert wooing of Sydney, but after listening to the gruesome retelling of events, Jeffrey lost his appetite.

They went rock climbing and Sydney rang the bell before Max got halfway up the eighteen-foot wall. This happened three times.

They went to the batting cages and Sydney whacked the ball like Barry Bonds. On steroids. Max set a strikeout record.

They went bowling and Sydney scored six strikes, spinning around and yelling, "Sucka!" in Max's face every time, as well as each of the seven times he rolled a gutter ball.

They played pool at her neighborhood bar, and this being something Max was good at, he suggested they put a wager on the game. Sydney sharked him out of fifty bucks, then another hundred when she challenged him to a "double or nothing" rematch. And she still made him pay for the beer.

They went to Scrabble Night at Pete's Candy Store in Williamsburg and Sydney bingoed twice in the heated match she'd gotten into with Moby after she'd abandoned her game with Max, deeming him an unworthy opponent. ("You don't even know all the two-letter words!") After she narrowly beat Moby, a known Scrabble aficionado and the event's reigning champ, while trash-talking mercilessly, the famed musician invited her back for a rematch the following week. (Sydney told him she was busy.)

She wanted to go horseback riding in Prospect Park, but fearing another humiliation, Max told her he was allergic.

"Good," Jeffrey said, stirring Splenda into his coffee. "You can't take another hit." Trying to stay positive, he added, "You're spending a lot of time together. That's a plus."

"We also went to a kickboxing class and I did pretty well in that," Max said, desperate not to look like a total loser.

"But there's no clear winner in a kickboxing class," Jeffrey said. He took a sip of coffee to test the temperature, then set the cup on the table to cool. "And Sydney is a woman who views things in absolutes."

It seemed Jeffrey might be the only one to benefit from Max's masochistic tendencies. Now maybe Sydney would stop asking him to do all that stuff. What about *gay* didn't she understand? But watching the lines of distress spread across Max's sharp, white-person features—his face looked like a sunburst with his aquiline nose at the center—Jeffrey felt like a failure in his role as romantic adviser. "It's good that you let her beat you," he said, going into full spin mode. "It is. Really. That's a turn-on for her. Overpowering a man."

Max perked up, and Jeffrey could tell he was imagining an overpowering of a different kind. Once the reverie passed, he fell back into a defeated slump. "I don't let her beat me," Max said. "She just does."

That was clear, but Jeffrey had chosen his words to encourage. It was okay for Sydney to beat him at a few recreational sports, but Maximillian (as Jeffrey preferred to call him) was letting her beat him down. That wasn't doing anyone a damn bit of good. Once Sydney smelled fear, it was going to be over for him! And if she cut him loose, Jeffrey was never going to get the fully financed shopping spree that had been promised him. Finding his coffee cooled, Jeffrey took a long sip to give himself a moment to do the same. But when he spoke, his question still didn't come out right. "Isn't there *anything* you can do?"

"Yes!" Max said, his body jerking upright as if controlled by a puppeteer's string. "There are lots of things I can do!"

Touchy, Jeffrey thought. *Must be a sore spot for him.* For a grown man who was destined to spend his whole life working for his father—in a capacity, it was becoming clear, that didn't require any real skill—Jeffrey imagined it would be. Not that he wouldn't trade places with Maximillian in a sprinter's heartbeat.

"I meant things that you can beat her at," Jeffrey clarified, adopting a tone usually reserved for his sensitive six-year-old niece. Max began to nod, but after the beatings Max had taken, Jeffrey didn't think he understood how much he had to prove. "Can you *kick her ass* at it?"

"Yes," Max said confidently. "Yes!"

Afraid that the sport in which Max hoped to claim victory would be something completely queer like ice skating, Jeffrey refrained from probing further. Instead, he just said, "Good. Show her you ain't no punk."

Sydney stood over Max, holding her racket at her hip. "Get up, pussy!"

"Sydney, I can't," he said, writhing in pain. "My knee." He writhed some more. "My knee!"

"Stop faking!" was Sydney's response to his anguished cry. He'd been bragging about what a great tennis player he was, how he could have been captain of his college team (except he didn't want the responsibility). And now that she, a relatively novice player—a girl!—had rallied back from a forty–love deficit to win the second set, something had happened to his knee? At match point? Puh-leeze. If he hadn't gotten so down on himself, cursing after every missed point when things started going her way, he wouldn't have found himself in a situation that called for such desperate theatrics. He was a better player by far than she was, and a much better server. But she'd hung tough, willing herself back into the game. *Mind over matter, baby.* That's what she wanted to tell him, and she would if he ever stopped whining.

"Please," he said, propping himself up on his elbow. "Help me up." Sydney went to grab his hand, but then he said, "Help me to the bench."

"The bench?" Sydney's hand dropped back to her side. "Game's not over."

"Sydney, my knee popped out!"

"Pop it back in."

"I can't," he said, reaching up to her like a beggar in Calcutta. "I can't stand up. I need you to help me to the bench. And then get my phone from the locker room. I might have to call my doctor."

"What's wrong with your left leg?"

He squinted up at her. "What?"

"Stand on your left leg and finish the game. Then I'll help you to the bench." Before he could quibble and moan some more, she turned, trotted back to her side of the court, and, while he was contorted in a position that made him look like he was playing a solo game of Twister, went ahead and served her final ace. "I win," she shouted, raising her arms victoriously.

Then she rushed the net, hurdled over, and, although Max didn't look like he wanted her help anymore, she offered it anyway.

"This isn't *Pretty Woman*," Max said when he found Jeffrey waiting in the men's department, holding a wish list three pages long. He'd earned the spree, but glancing at the numbered list, Max caught sight of a number *twenty-four* (Armani coat with fur). And that was only page two! Max was so appalled that he almost had Jeffrey thrown out of the store. Only a woman who had been fucking him—and fucking him well—for quite some time was going to accumulate that much merch on the Cooper family dime! "Pick your top five items," he said sharply. "I've only got half an hour."

Watching as Jeffrey quickly flipped through his stapled pages as if he were cramming for the LSAT, Max smiled to himself. Jeffrey would get his five things (even if they had to call another store), but Max had come to see that if he needed to show anyone he "wasn't no punk," it was Jeffrey. It was a real issue for him, this punk thing. "I may be gay, but I ain't no punk," he'd say at the most random times, apropos of nothing. One time he'd flexed on Max as he said it. Max almost gave him the name of a therapist he knew who specialized in GLBT issues, but he worried that having this woman's number in his phone might throw his own sexuality into question. And telling Jeffrey the truth—that he'd dated the sexy doc a few times—would open the door to a different line of questioning.

It made perfect sense that Jeffrey would be sensitive about his masculinity (if one could even apply that term to a man who never went out in public without a light coat of makeup). All his life, Jeffrey had probably been made to prove his toughness in ways Max couldn't even begin to imagine. But Max wasn't gay. Some might classify him as a metrosexual, but that didn't bother him one bit. He had a sense of style, he was well groomed. Where was the shame in that? He was comfortable with the man he was, and he had never worried that anyone, male or female, would think he was a wuss. Until Jeffrey put the idea in his head. Now he had a complex about it!

"So the tennis thing really blew up in my face," he said, following Jeffrey as he beelined to the Y-3 section.

Jeffrey glanced back at him. "I heard."

"Match point," Max groused, reliving the humiliating incident in his mind as he'd been doing obsessively for the last two days. "I had her. Jeffrey, I swear, I had her!"

Jeffrey grabbed a size large track suit and made a sharp left toward the Lucien Pellat-Finet cashmeres. "What's done is done."

"So what's my next move? I'm kinda stuck here." Max could plainly see that Jeffrey was more interested in reaping his reward than in helping him, and when Jeffrey looked past Max toward a table piled with hundred-dollar T-shirts, Max almost called off the whole spree!

But then Jeffrey answered him. "Fight with her." He picked up a tee that read "Talentless but Connected" and showed it to Max, laughing. "You should get this one!"

Max ripped the shirt from Jeffrey's grip and tossed it back on the table. "I already have two." (They were both gifts and he'd never worn them. He liked the irony, but it hit a little too close to home.) "Listen to me, Jeffrey. Or the spree's canceled!" Jeffrey straightened up like a private saluting his colonel and Max asked for clarification. "What do you mean by 'fight with her'?"

"Start an argument with her and win it," Jeffrey advised. "You can't dominate her physically, so overpower her mentally. She'll respect that."

Listening to another of Jeffrey's counterintuitive suggestions, Max felt unsure. He didn't like fighting with people. He fought plenty with the people in his life—Avery, his father, Norma, Duke, Mitzi Berman, Lulu, even Remy a little now that they spent so much time together. So, yes, okay, he basically fought—or bickered, if you will—with everyone in his life. But not on purpose!

Although he wouldn't have to go out of his way to pick a fight with Sydney. She was always just a misread comment away from being up in arms about something that ultimately didn't matter. (She'd told Max she was taking Xanax, and sometimes he wanted to suggest she up the dosage.) She had such a hair-trigger temper that one never knew when a spat would escalate into a I'm-never-speaking-to-you-again deal breaker.

"Here's my concern," he told Jeffrey. "What if I take it too far and she banishes me like you said she's known to do?"

"You've got me on your side," Jeffrey said. "I'll make sure you don't get a one-way ticket to Siberia. Anyway, I've been putting little bugs in her ear about you. Good things."

Max was surprised to hear this. "You have?"

"The way you've been performing, you need the backup," Jeffrey said, picking through the T-shirts. "And, look, that's what you like about her, isn't it? She's combative, she's unpredictable, she's infuriating sometimes . . . never dull." He looked up and laughed. "Hell, that's what I like about her!"

He was right, Max thought. That was exactly what he liked about Sydney. After he'd been weighed down with the drudgery of his new position, she'd brought some excitement and spontaneity into his life. He loved the fact that she didn't have a nine-to-five job and made her own schedule. Her sense of entitlement about her "me time" had emboldened him to cut out of work early and meet her for the odd weekday matinee whenever he was lucky enough to get her call. (Although he still told Remy and Norma that he was going to physical rehab.) And while he continued to sneak quick naps in his locked office in the afternoon, it was a source of great shame! Not for Sydney. She'd often yawn when they were on the phone, then say, "Gotta go. Nap time!" She was, in many ways, Max's hero.

"Thank you, Jeffrey," Max said, giving him an appreciative pat on the shoulder. Who would have thought that beneath that shallow facade lay such a wise soul? He almost gave him the green light for another five items, but there was no need to open *that* can of worms.

"No problem," Jeffrey said. "So the next time you hang out, really get into it with her. Go at her hard. Hit her where it hurts," he practically growled, the sexual overtones of his passionate delivery making Max quite uncomfortable. "That kind of shit turns her on." He pulled a blue T-shirt out of the pile, then clutched it to his chest, thinking. "Maybe you should prepare your argument beforehand. Like a debate. 'Cause I'll tell you, honey, I'm not sure you can hold your own wingin' it."

Ignoring the fact that Jeffrey had just called him *honey*—it wasn't the first time—Max nodded, warming to the idea. "Prepare my remarks," he said. "Good idea, Jeffrey."

"Talk politics, any kind of women's issue," Jeffrey said. "Maybe something that raises a class issue. You know how she likes to get all Norma

Rae." He rolled his eyes. "But stay away from race. Go outta bounds on that one, you might lose her and me too."

Max gave a heartfelt nod. "Gotcha."

Spotting another T-shirt on the table, Jeffrey broke out into a big grin. "And for your big debate, I know exactly what you should wear."

When Sydney saw Max waiting for her outside the Film Forum, she rushed up to him and brushed his cheek with her own, a perimeter violation she didn't realize she was committing until it was too late. She had never greeted him that way before, had never even had the impulse to do that, but seeing him in that tee had her so tickled she'd momentarily lost her head. It was navy blue washed cotton, vintage looking, and it had one word printed in mustard yellow on the front in big block letters. "Feminist."

"Where'd you get that?" she said, touching the hem to get the feel of the cotton.

"The store. It's Rogan."

"Omigod, I'm so all about Rogan," she gushed, hating that she sounded like a "character" on *The Hills*. "I have to get one!"

"Never fear, my fair feminist." Max reached into the murse he sometimes carried—it was beat-up brown leather, a messenger bag really, not gay at all—and pulled out another tee in red. "Size small?"

Sydney grabbed it. That was what she loved about wearing men's clothing—she could pretend she actually wore a small. "And I like the red better too," she said, holding it up to herself. "Good choice."

She could tell it was making Max so happy to do something that made her happy, and suddenly she had the impulse to kiss him. On the mouth. With tongue. But she couldn't do that, could she? He was a doorman/musician. She was through with slackers, done with slashes! Allowing herself to become involved with him would be going backward. She needed to find a real man, a provider for her kids, a head-of-the-household type (who knew that she was really going to be the boss).

But it hadn't felt so bad to give him that air kiss. And this T-shirt, she thought. What a lovely, thoughtful gesture. It was too bad that he didn't have a real job. Or else they'd be fucking right now instead of going to see the Lagerfeld documentary.

But such a sweet gift deserved an appropriate thank-you, so Sydney made a conscious decision to violate her perimeter again. She pressed her lips against Max's cheek, letting them linger a second longer than necessary, then she pulled back and tried to smile with her eyes the way Tyra was always telling the girls on *Top Model* to do. "You did good, Max," she said, stroking his arm. "Real good."

CHAPTER FORTY

After the movie they'd taken a long, meandering walk, which was becoming a frequent occurrence, their circuitous route usually determined by the many people Sydney had to dodge. The city seemed to be filled with Omnimedia employees she didn't want to have to chitchat with (Max understood), friends she'd dropped (most, it seemed, because they had the nerve to get married or pregnant), and a shockingly long list of people she'd dated once and never called again. (The fact that her ex list was as long as his struck Max as both impressive and unnerving). These sudden avoidance maneuvers were constant reminders that Max might very well be one of the people she'd be dodging in a month's time. As it was, he never knew when she might abruptly say she "had to go" and not say where. Now that he knew she routinely expelled people from her life as a matter of course, every moment they spent together felt as if it might be their last. And there was something kind of wonderful about that.

And today, strolling through Union Square, enjoying the glorious weather while sipping their smoothies, had been especially wonderful. The last thing Max wanted to do was start a fight. But at this point, he trusted Jeffrey's instincts more than he trusted his own. He literally wasn't himself with Sydney. Being known for his last name and store connections had always been his personal bête noire, but he hadn't realized how much he relied on those things until he'd been stripped of them. He never put emphasis on who he was or what he had, and he hated when anyone else did, but those things were always there, helping him in myriad ways nonetheless. He could see that now.

But as eye-opening as this improbable little charade had been, showing him things about himself that he never would have understood otherwise, he'd grown tired of it. The voice inside his head that periodically screamed, *TELL HER!* was growing more insistent, and today he was *thisclose* to confessing all. But then, as they entered Barnes & Noble, the perfect argument starter appeared, like a sign from Jeffrey to stick to the game plan.

"Oh, look," Max had said, pointing to the display touting Lulu's upcoming appearance. "Tomorrow night. Wanna go?"

He was sure that was going to set Sydney off on a profanity-laced tirade, but she only gave the poster a passing glance and headed over to the new-releases wall. They proceeded to wander around the store for an hour, checking out books and magazines, and after trying diligently to bring the conversation back to Lulu, Max was beginning to feel like a contestant on an early episode of *Survivor*. He kept rubbing sticks together, but he couldn't get the fire to catch. But then when they stopped in the café for a nibble, Sydney got on one of her rants—about *Sex and the City*, of all things—and soon Max started to smell smoke.

"A sequel to the movie?" she said, making a leap from some seemingly unrelated topic. "Please! *Sex and the City* had its time, but we've moved on. We've gone green. We've lived through Katrina and seven years of a pointless war. The Rich Cabal That Controls All wasn't able to steal another election, as I feared they would, and now we have a biracial, multicultural president who is the embodiment of everything we, as a nation, and we, as its citizens, should strive to be. And a First Lady who shops online at J.Crew! The whole 'happiness means being rich and fabulous and wearing Manolos' thing is waaaaaaay over. That's what your pal Lulu Merriwether is riding on," she said, making another sudden leap that made Max sit up at attention. "*That* fucking wave. And I, for one, am ready to see the bitch drown."

Finally, Max thought. Seeing a clear entry point, he proceeded full steam ahead with his planned provocation. "Sydney, has it ever occurred to you that to my housekeeper—"

She dusted banana bread crumbs from her hands. "You have a housekeeper?"

"Yes," Max answered, and tried to get back into the flow of his argument. "And has it ever . . ."

"Why would you have a housekeeper? You live in some shitty little apartment in Brooklyn!"

"I said I live in Brooklyn. I didn't say my apartment was shitty."

Sydney held her chin in her hand and regarded him for a long moment. "You come from a rich family, don't you?"

Max nervously crossed and uncrossed his legs. He and Jeffrey hadn't discussed what to do in the event of an emergency! "What makes you say that?"

"Well, come on, Max, you graduated from Brown and now you work as a doorman."

Max wasn't sure how those two pieces fit together in the backstory she'd been building for his "character" so he waited, offering nothing. Letting her fill in the blanks as she wished made him feel less guilty than fabricating things outright, and the little details she invented often told him more about her than the person she thought he might be.

"Only a rich kid goes to a school like Brown and then does nothing with that education. And a doorman of all things? I mean, really." She swigged some water. "That's not to say I don't admire you in a way."

Max got a little excited. Sydney admired him? Really? Then he realized it wasn't him she admired, it was the person she thought he was. Doorman Guy. *Tell her!* the voice screamed. *Just tell her!*

"You're obviously smart," she said. "You enunciate more clearly than anyone I've ever met. You've got that rich-kid, privately schooled vibe. You could have a well-paying job doing anything you set your mind to, but you *choose* to have this no-pressure job because it gives you the flexibility to focus on your music. Why should you give all your time and energy to The Man?"

Max smiled. Doorman Guy really wasn't that different from him. He was like the Clark Kent to his Superman!

"You probably live in Williamsburg."

Close, Max thought, sipping his water.

"Yeah, Williamsburg," she said, continuing her character sketch without any input from him. "And you own your place, right?"

Max kept sipping.

"Sure. Because your parents helped you buy it. Lucky you. But it can't be that big. You're so lazy you can't clean up your own mess? You make some poor immigrant wash your floors?"

"Sydney, this is what I'm getting at," Max said, breathing easy that he'd made it through the rough patch unscathed. "Hildy, my housekeeper, has a job because of me." And his Christmas bonus paid for her eldest son's freshman year at John Jay. "I'm not oppressing her. I'm employing her."

Max felt a great deal of satisfaction when Sydney lowered her eyes, chastened, and said, "Yes, that's true. You're right." She started cleaning away the refuse that had accumulated on the table. "I was thinking of getting a housekeeper. Because I'm too lazy to clean my own mess, I guess." She laughed as though this was a source of shame. "Does Hildy work Manhattan?"

Max was sure she would, but he would never allow Sydney to get near her. Hildy knew too much. "Don't know," he said, annoyed that Sydney got up and started walking to the trash can just when he was about to deliver his big line! He waited until they were on the escalator, where he could better hold her attention, and then he pulled the pin out of the grenade, spitting the words out quickly before she interrupted him again. "Has it ever occurred to you that to my housekeeper, who lives in a two-bedroom apartment in Far Rockaway with her three children, you *are* Lulu Merriwether?"

Sydney whipped around, and when the escalator stairs disappeared under her feet, she tripped backward onto the second-floor landing, slackjawed. When the shock of Max's accusation wore off, she shouted, "How DARE you!"

Max had the urge to backpedal, to acquiesce in the face of her fiery wrath, but he heard Jeffrey's voice willing him forward like some kind of gay Yoda: *Show her you ain't no punk.*

"Sydney, you go to Ranjit Sagoo," he said, hurrying to the next leg of their descent as if he'd just stolen something. "I know how expensive that guy is." (Because he'd gone to him many years ago. Total rip-off.) "Paying someone thousands of dollars to tell you what to eat is a luxury most people can't afford."

"I don't pay Ranjit!" Sydney said, stomping behind Max as he made a quick U-turn onto the escalator. "I did a story on him. He offered me his services for free!"

He'd done the same for Max. Ranjit did that for a lot of people. A few months of free coddling and people became so codependent they'd pay (and he'd charge) anything. "For how long?"

"Well, I just started paying him," Sydney mumbled, turning away. "But I really need him! I used to be fat, you know!"

Max ran his eyes over her tall, toned frame. He couldn't imagine her being fat, and her quickly averted gaze told him that wasn't an admission she'd intended to make. She was rattled, he thought. The plan was working! Launching another dart he knew couldn't miss, he said, "Sydney, you're wearing fourteen thousand dollars' worth of human hair on your head. That's someone's college tuition."

"It's for work!" she shouted, and as she leaped off the escalator after him, a chunk of weave unfurled, Rapunzel-like, from the tight bun she kept it wrapped in and slapped her across the face.

"If you say so, Cher," Max murmured before drawing her attention to one last bit of incriminating evidence. "And let's not forget you're wearing eight-hundred-dollar shoes."

Sydney gaped down at her beloved Lanvins, and when she looked up, Max was on the sidewalk. "I got these for seventy percent off," she yelled, two long, furious strides putting her back at his side. "And you damn well know that!"

"Right," Max said. "So they were only three hundred dollars. And that Balenciaga, with discount, was only what? Four fifty? And isn't that the Anna Sui top we picked out? That was only about two hundred and something . . ."

Max tried not to laugh as Sydney clutched the bag over the top and then pressed her arms over it, trying to cover it all, as if her precious designer spoils had rendered her naked in the middle of Union Square. When she began to hem and haw, it gave Max so much pleasure after all the incendiary crap he'd listened to that he laughed in her face.

"I . . . I . . . I . . . ," she stammered. "I never buy myself anything! I shop at Forever 21," she said, pointing to the store across the park. "I shop at H&M. I shop the Harvey's warehouse sale. So what if I want to splurge on myself every once in a while! I'm entitled!"

"Exactly," Max said, filled with a deeper sense of satisfaction than he expected this moment of victory would bring. "You *are* entitled." Exposing Sydney's faux proletariat leanings was quite a triumph, but seeing her so upset made it bittersweet. "For you," Max said, speaking gently, "splurging means buying a thousand-dollar purse that you won't use next year. For Hildy, and people like her, it means buying a lottery ticket." He gave Sydney's hands an affectionate squeeze, then spontaneously decided to inject her with an extra dose of her own medicine. "Now I have to go."

He ambled through the farmers' market, smiling to himself, until he heard her anxiously call out to him. "Wait, are we still going to Costco tomorrow?"

"Pick you up at twelve," he shouted over his shoulder. Then he speed-dialed his gay Yoda, thinking, *Who's the punk now?*

CHAPTER FORTY-ONE

After picking up her latest must-have item, a pair of knee-high lace-up Michael Kors boots, Sydney and Max were rushing out of the store to catch a foreign film playing downtown at Sunshine Cinema. Had they bumped into anyone else, a friend of hers or his, they both would have done the same thing—pretended they didn't see the person or, if that was not an option, said a quick hello. But when Sydney spotted Jeffrey swanning past the Marc Jacobs counter on the first floor, she made a sharp detour and stepped to him as if he'd insulted her mama (or at least, someone she actually liked). "Where *the hell* have you been?"

Jeffrey looked around and, noting Sydney's presence, answered blandly, "I left you three voice mails."

"You left me two. And both were at, like, eight in the morning. You know I don't pick up my phone before ten."

"Well," Jeffrey said with a dismissive swirl of the hand. "What can I tell you?"

"You can tell me why you also didn't respond to my e-mail."

"E-mail?" Jeffrey said, peering into the glass case at a red leather wallet. "I didn't get any e-mail."

Sydney had the distinct feeling that he had been trying to blow her off, and she wanted to openly make that accusation, but she realized he actually might be telling the truth. "I sent it from my new e-mail, feministareigns at Gmail."

"Ooh chile, was that you?" he said, still considering the wallet. "I thought that was a virus. I deleted that immediately."

"I resent it twice!"

"I thought it was a virulent strain."

Virulent? Sydney thought. Since when did Jeffrey use words like *virulent?* When the little Spanish man who had been speaking to the saleswoman turned and began openly listening to their conversation, hanging territorially at Jeffrey's side, Sydney realized he wasn't just a random shopper. Regarding him as if he were an autograph hound approaching her with a Sharpie and an unflattering photograph, she said, "And who is *this?*"

"This," Jeffrey said, his pause the equivalent of a conversational drumroll, "is Hector."

"Hector?" Sydney said as if the name itself was laughable. She looked at Max. "Max, you remember my friend Jeffrey, don't you?" Max smiled politely, and her own smile turned into a smirk. "I haven't seen or heard from him in so long, I can hardly remember him myself. And this is Jeffrey's new friend," she said, giving the boy toy a good looking over. "Hector."

"Boyfriend," the boy toy took it upon himself to clarify.

"Ha!" Sydney loudly scoffed, shifting her accusatory gaze to Jeffrey. "I don't speak to you for two weeks and you have a boyfriend? Named Hector?"

Jeffrey stepped away from his diminutive lover, grabbed Sydney by the elbow, and dragged her over to Goyard. "Yes, okay?"

"Yes and . . . what else? Who is this person? How did you meet him?" She peered around Jeffrey and saw Max watching them while Lil Hector fondled a Marc Jacobs murse. "I mean, how can you have a boyfriend if I don't know about it!"

"You've been spending a lot of time with Max," Jeffrey growled hoarsely, pushing her up against a glass counter as though he were about to either fuck her or mug her (and knowing Jeffrey's proclivities, only the latter was likely). "Do I complain about that?"

"Because I still have time for you!"

"I've been working a lot too." He took a step back and glanced over his shoulder to check on his boo. "Jessica was in town."

"Alba?" Sydney said, smiling. "Did you see the baby?"

"Yeah," Jeffrey said distractedly. "Very cute."

"See, Jeffrey, this is what I'm talking about. That's the kind of thing you need to tell me immediately. Like, as soon as you leave her hotel. And you used to. But now I have to hear it way after the fact when I bump into you and your Latin lover shopping for murses at Harvey's!" Sydney shook her head as if the indignity was too much to bear. "I don't know if I like what this guy is doing to you."

"What he's doing to me?" Jeffrey repeated incredulously. "He's making me happy so, yes, I guess you would have a problem with that."

"Jeffrey!" Sydney said, swayed by the gale force of his viciousness. "What is that supposed to mean?"

Jeffrey looked past her to check on Hector. "Look, I really have to go."

Sydney grabbed his coat sleeve. "You can't leave his side for two minutes? What is he, an infant?"

"I can't do this right now," Jeffrey said, yanking his arm away. "I'll give you a call later."

Sydney stepped in front of him. "I want you to take back what you just said."

"What did I just say?"

"That of course I would have a problem with someone making you happy."

"Why should I take it back?"

"Because you don't really believe that!"

"Yes," Jeffrey said. "I do."

"Well, that's just . . ." Sydney's mouth stayed open long enough for another ten words to come out, but none did.

"That's real talk, baby. That's what that is." Jeffrey backed her against the counter again. "You can't find a man and you want me to be alone like you. Misery loves company."

Max approached, tapping his watch. "Sydney, the movie."

Hector was two steps behind, swinging a Harvey's shopping bag. "Jeffrey, the dog."

"Yes," Jeffrey said, tossing off a "honey" that Sydney knew was just for her benefit. "Let's skedaddle."

Sydney hated listening to Jeffrey go on about his damn dog, the incredulously named Dolce von Eliot, but feeling like an outsider to his life now, she inquired about the ugly mutt as if she actually gave a shit. "Dolce? Is he okay?"

"No," Hector said, taking Jeffrey's hand. "Our new dog."

Sydney felt her eyebrows rise almost to her hairline. "New dog?"

Hector smiled. "Frida."

Sydney looked at Max, her eyebrows stuck in their crazily arched position. "They have a new dog." Then she turned and spoke directly to Jeffrey as though Little Latin Lover Boy had vanished. "Named Frida?"

The happy couple answered as one. "Yes."

"Frida von Eliot?"

"Frida von Eliot-Rodriguez," Hector said. "Hyphenated. Like Jolie-Pitt."

Sydney threw up her hands in surrender (before she actually threw up). She needed to walk away now before they announced their plans to adopt a third-world baby. "Okay, we really have to run," she said, grabbing Max by the arm. "Call me whenever you find the time."

"Will do," Jeffrey said, and Hector joined him in a wave.

CHAPTER FORTY-TWO

This is some good shit," Max said, inspecting the expertly rolled joint. "You roll this?"

"Me?" Sydney coughed. "Nah." She expelled smoke from her lungs. "That came prerolled."

Max took a long pull. "I need to get the number of your guy. Does he deliver?"

"This is Manhattan. Of course my guy delivers."

Max expelled the smoke from his lungs and leaned his head back on Sydney's couch, smiling up at the ceiling. The Hector bit had been another stroke of devious brilliance from Jeffrey-James Eliot, modern-day courtier. Rehearsing the whole thing beforehand, Max thought the "misery loves company" line was too harsh, but Jeffrey decided to go with it. And proving once again that when it came to Sydney, Jeffrey knew best, the ruse had worked like a charm.

All the way downtown to the movie (and all throughout dinner afterward) Sydney had railed against the union of Jeffrey and the friendly dog groomer she believed to be his besotted lover: "They got a dog together? Max, don't you realize that's the gay equivalent of marriage? And they've only known each other for two weeks? That's like running off to Vegas! And the hyphenation? Frida von Eliot-Rodriguez? Too ridiculous to even process!"

After dinner she had invited Max back to her place to watch a movie—an exciting development he had to immediately (but surreptitiously) text

Jeffrey about—and though the voice that screamed, *Tell her!* was giving him a headache tonight, Max had managed to silence it, sensing sex (or at the very least, intentional skin-to-skin contact) was in the offing.

"Oh no, wait," Sydney said, turning to the program guide, which didn't have much to offer at one A.M. "I didn't get this from my guy. I stole this from Brett Babcock."

The only response Max could manage was "Whaaa . . . ?"

"He won't miss it," Sydney said. "Those guys had so much weed on them at all times, if they ever got caught, they'd be doing ten to twenty."

"I'd think someone like Brett would be more"—Max stared up at a chipped piece of plaster until he remembered what he was going to say—"careful."

"There is no correlation between the words *Brett Babcock* and *careful.*" Sydney pushed herself up on her knees and leaned over Max to take the joint that was dangling dangerously near her couch. "Anyway, he doesn't have to be. He makes the studios fly him private so he can carry his own stash."

Max went to take another pull and saw that his fingers were pressed together but nothing was between them. His head lolled to the side and he peered at Sydney. "I wanted to kill him when he . . ."

They listened to half a song playing on her laptop until she unknowingly completed his thought. "He kissed me, you know."

Not yet so out of his head that he couldn't recognize an opportunity to encourage the intimacy of the situation, Max said, "Did you like it?"

Sydney responded to his flirtatious question by laughing until her eyes watered. Max wasn't sure if it was the smoke, his clumsy attempt at flirtation, or something else that had set her off until she said, "I find Brett Babcock completely grotesque. He's a chauvinist! The kind of man who thinks women are objects that exist only for his pleasure. And we didn't kiss. That's how my editor tried to make it sound. Brett was drunk and he kissed me. You see the difference? I was the passive object of his drunken lust! I could have pressed charges." She took another pull and coughed, "I should have!"

"Okay, you know what?" Max said as a new song began to play. "I'm going to make you a playlist. How much Mariah Carey must we endure? You're obsessed with her!"

"I'm not. Maybe iTunes is." Sydney's heavy eyes drifted away from the computer toward nothing in particular. "Do you ever notice how it shuffles to the same songs a lot? And it doesn't shuffle to certain songs at all. Even if you keep pressing forward and shuffle through the whole list."

Max snuggled up to the pillow. "Weird."

"You know what song I do kinda want? That one you sang at your show. The one you wrote."

Sensing a compliment coming his way, Max managed to lift his head, and he saw that Sydney was looking at him strangely. "Which one?"

" 'Infatuation,' " she said. "That was my favorite song."

Max laid his head back on the pillow and let his eyes close. "Lotta people say that."

"You must have been really inspired when you wrote that," he heard Sydney say, noticing somewhere in the background of his muddled consciousness that her voice sounded . . . different.

"Inspired by this chick who turned out to be a total skank. That's what sucks. Every time we perform it, I have to think about—" Before Max could finish the sentence, he had a pillow slammed in his face.

"I thought you wrote that about me!"

Max squinted at her, scratching his head. Then he began to laugh. And laugh. And laugh.

"Get out!" Sydney said, pointing to the door.

"I'll write you a song," Max said, raising his arm protectively as she went in for another pillow slam. "I promise. What should I call it? 'Taming of the Shrew'?"

That earned him a swift kick in the leg. "What's so terrible about Mariah Carey, anyway?"

Max hadn't been in a fully upright position in two hours, but that question forced him to sit up straight and plant his bare feet on Sydney's floor. "What's so terrible about Mariah Carey? Do you hear yourself?"

"Look, I'm not in the Mariah Carey butterflies and rainbows fan club or anything, but she does have more number-one singles than Elvis." She waved a lighter's flame over the end of the roach. "Or something like that."

"She's a tacky, screeching horror!"

"Max, you're a songwriter. How many number-one singles have you written?"

"I haven't tried to write any."

"And what are you, proud of that? Like you could if you tried!"

"Yeah, but . . ."

"Yeah but nothing! Give MC her due. The hardest thing in the world is to make something look easy. You know as well as I do that writing a number-one pop song is as hard as composing a symphony!"

His mind becoming very fuzzy, Max mumbled, "Do I know that?"

"And the woman escaped an oppressive marriage! She stood up to the patriarchy! Mimi emancipated herself!" Sydney tried to stand on the couch cushions as she gave her little "You go, girl" speech, but she wobbled and fell back onto her ass, pulling her sweats halfway down in the process. "Stop hating!"

"I'm not," Max said.

"Yes, you are. Because you know none of your odes to skanks are gonna land on the top of the charts. Or on the bottom, even."

"You just said that was your favorite song!"

"Well, it ain't anymore!" Sydney looked at Max, and they both burst out laughing. "You're lucky Jeffrey's not here," she said, trying to keep the argument going. "Mariah is his girl. If he heard you say some blasphemous shit like that, he'd cut you." She swung her feet back onto the couch and positioned them in the space Max's limbs weren't already occupying. "Can you believe him?"

"Believe who?" Max said absently, pulling Sydney's Mac onto his lap to give her iTunes library a closer look.

"Jeffrey!" Sydney gave him a little kick as if Jeffrey, the person she was really angry at, might feel it. "With that Hector person. I mean, he was short! Jeffrey hates short guys!"

"Yeah, well," Max mumbled, raising the laptop screen higher with his bent knees to obscure his loopy grin. He could tell Sydney was waiting for him to join in the Hector bashing or the Jeffrey bashing or just say something negative about the situation, but the great thing about Sydney was that she could have an argument all by herself.

"And the way Jeffrey was catering to him. It was just sad. He couldn't leave his side for two minutes to talk to me? I mean, I expect women to toss me aside the minute they find a man . . ." Max tilted his head to look around the screen when he heard her voice turn sad. "I guess I always thought Jeffrey would be alone and I would have him all to myself. So I would never be alone. But now I am."

Max lowered the music. "You have me."

Sydney turned and stared at him, still holding the clicker, then ruined the moment by bringing up the one subject that was guaranteed to make his dick *soft.* "I need to know more about this starter marriage of yours. Like where did you meet her? Did you know right away you were in love with her? What made you want to propose?" She pulled her knees up into her chest, as if she was curling up for story time. "And *how* did you propose? Was it super romantic? Were you on bended knee?"

Max realized she had a much higher marijuana tolerance than he, because while she was able to give voice to that litany of questions, he could barely remember who'd starred in the Judd Apatow bromance they'd just watched an hour ago. (And wasn't it always the same five people?) "Did my publicist schedule this interview with you?" he said, deflecting. "Because nobody told me."

Sydney's laughter momentarily lifted her chin from her knee, then she tucked back into her cozy curl, waiting to hear the whole sordid saga. "No, really."

"What about you?"

"Me?" she said, stretching her legs out.

"I've already told you a little about my ex-wife," Max said, wishing there wasn't a layer of stiff denim preventing her bare toes from grazing his balls. "I'm assuming you've never been married." Sydney shook her head, confirming this. "But have you ever been close? You've made it clear that this guy you just broke up with didn't mean anything. Hasn't there ever been someone who has?"

"I could be married right now," Sydney said, smirking. "Or I'd probably be divorced by now. Like you."

"Really?" Max said, perking up. "What happened?"

"We had a spectacular breakup, it was a very traumatic time in my life and I've put it behind me." She took the television off Mute, and the braying sounds of the guy hawking ShamWows filled the room. "That's all I can say about it."

As soon as she set the clicker on the table, Max reached up and hit the Mute button. "What are you, under a gag order?"

"You could say that. Self-imposed."

"Maybe you should talk about it."

"I have a shrink. And I don't even talk to her about it."

"Oh, come on, Sydney! You can't say 'spectacular breakup' and then leave it at that."

"So you want me to tell you my most humiliating story, then you'll tell me yours? Is that the game we're playing now, Max?"

Max slouched down at his end of the couch, getting comfortable. That was exactly the game they were playing. And thinking they'd both probably be passed out by the time it was his turn, he insisted, "You first."

CHAPTER FORTY-THREE

Sydney hadn't even wanted to go to the game. Trevor had Knicks season tickets, and in an effort to be a supportive girlfriend she'd tried, she really had, to get into the spirit. That was difficult when Trevor only took her to games against shitty opponents. The games were usually blowouts or just plain boring, and Trevor had banned her from doing the one thing that kept her entertained: talking about how the other team's uniforms could be redesigned. Sometimes, when she wanted to get back at him for some insensitive thing he'd said or done that week (there was always something), she'd point out which guys were sexy, who had the most defined arms or the best tattoos. That drove him insane. He was a Neanderthal that way.

For the season's most hotly anticipated games, it was his Wall Street buddies who enjoyed the privilege of using his extra seat. So when Trevor called that afternoon with the great news that she'd be allowed to attend the sold-out Knicks–Heat game because the intended guest had been poisoned by some bad sushi, Sydney was less than thrilled. She was a fill-in. What a privilege.

Though the game had been close throughout the first half, she couldn't work up enough interest to care, and she'd spent the last ten seconds before the halftime buzzer plotting her route to the bathroom. All she wanted to do was pee. Instead, she wound up starring in the halftime sideshow.

"Good luck," she heard Trevor say, and when she turned around all she saw was his back as someone whisked him away. In the space of four minutes, the announcer had called her seat number as the grand-prize winner of courtside seats to the upcoming Lakers game and Trevor had dragged her down the aisle to the court, whooping it up in a mortifying fan frenzy. But she thought they were just coming down to pick up the winning tickets. Where was he going? And good luck? With what?

Before she could ask any questions, the guy who had been talking to Trevor took out a black strip of cloth, stepped behind Sydney, and threw it over her head. She whipped around and addressed him in the same outraged tone she'd used with the pervert who pressed himself into her ass on the subway last week: *"What are you doing?"*

"I'm putting on the blindfold," he said matter-of-factly. As if she was his S and M partner and they'd done this a million times!

"Blindfold? *What blindfold?* Where's Trevor?" Her eyes zigzagged around the court. There were cameramen, players, team personnel, and cheerleaders forming a ring around the rectangular playing area and security guards stationed at all four points. No sign of Trevor.

"He's over there," the blindfolder said, not indicating where "over there" was. He took hold of Sydney's shoulders, turned her around, and tried once again to get the blindfold on.

"Why are you doing this to me?" she cried. "I don't understand."

"I just told you," he said patiently. "You have to go out on the court and find the mascot." He pointed to the huge Knicks-outfitted bear waving at the crowd from under one of the baskets.

"Blindfolded?"

"Yes," he said. "The crowd is going to help you."

He helpfully repeated what Sydney figured was the same thing he had just told Trevor while she was watching Billy Baldwin chomp on a fully loaded hot dog (that had been brought to him by a half-dressed attendant who looked like she was about to start peeling off what little there was of her cheerleader's outfit). Watching the blindfolder closely this time, Sydney realized he was just a boy, really, maybe twenty, but he looked even younger, with apple cheeks and a face so smooth he probably only had to shave once a week, if ever. He had that collegiate "anything is possible" spark that she had lost after a few years of wading around in the muck of the real world. He was probably an intern. And this was one of his duties. Blindfold the halftime contestants.

"When they yell 'Hot!' you're going in the right direction. When they yell 'Cold!' you're going in the wrong direction," he said. "Don't worry. It'll be fun!"

You can't be fucking serious, she thought, and just that quickly he had roped her into the blindfold, whipping it around as handily as a cowboy worked a lasso. "I thought I already won the tickets!" she screeched, hysteria overtaking her.

Then he was pulling her out into open territory. *Omigod,* she thought. *This is not happening.* She heard the crowd hoot and holler. *Omigod, it is!*

"Why can't Trevor do it?" she said, feeling her chest rise and fall as he pulled her along, a lamb to the slaughter.

"Hey, what's your name?"

She did not want to participate in this any more than she already had, but she heard herself say, "Sydney." *Where had that come from?* They stopped walking, then he tapped her on the shoulder and chirped, "Good luck!"

Just walk away, she told herself. *You don't have to do this!* But God, Trevor really wanted those tickets. If she blew this chance to get them, he'd be so mad.

So what? her better instincts were screaming. *You should be mad. Where is he? Why isn't he saving you?*

"Let's hear it for Sydney," the announcer boomed through the PA system, and it was like hearing God speak her name.

The crowd sent up a thunderous roar. That was not what it sounded like from section 201. The collective sound of their voices was amplified, massive and overwhelming, the effect of which made her sway back slightly. She no longer felt nervous or embarrassed. She felt sheer terror. *This is what people feel like when a plane is going down,* she thought hysterically. And suddenly she thought of her father and she felt the tears coming. How had he felt in those last seconds, seeing the headlights coming straight for him? The blindfold was so tight the tears didn't fall; the water pooled under her eyes and soaked into the fabric.

How could that have happened to her daddy, she thought, still unwilling to believe it *had* happened. He was the best father she could have ever asked for, a damn good mother too after Vera went AWOL, and had she ever once gone with Liz to the cemetery to visit him?

It was all so FUCKED, she thought. Everything. Her entire life. Including this moment! *Somebody make it stooooooooop!*

"Sydney, you have fifteen seconds to find the mascot," the announcer said. "Okay, on your mark . . ."

Trevor, that piece of shit! He probably thought this was just the greatest, funniest thing ever. And he'd probably spend the third quarter calling all his friends to tell them that not only had he scored courtside seats but that they "wouldn't believe what Sydney did to get them!" Half the time Trevor didn't have a clue. He made loads of money, but he had the emotional intelligence of a thumbtack. Oh yeah, this was fucking *hilarious*. For him!

"Get set . . ."

Forget him, she thought. *Save yourself!* But she couldn't. She was completely paralyzed. It was worse than those awful nightmares where you just want to run but you can't move. This was lucid dreaming in reverse. The other night she'd dreamed an unseen assailant was chasing her, but in the midst of her terror she'd thought, *This is a dream. I can wake up. I can make this stop. I'm in control.* And she woke up. Now she was awake wishing she was safe in her lumpy bed just having a nightmare. She was the "somebody" who needed to stop this. So why couldn't she? What was wrong with her?

When the announcer finally said, "Go!" she started walking around with her arms outstretched like a mummy's. It was as if she had no mind of her own and someone was steering her by remote control.

"And she's off," the announcer said, as if she were an entrant in the Kentucky Derby.

There wasn't even a sliver of light. All she could see were kaleidoscopes spinning behind her eyelids. She'd always heard that blind people's other senses were more acute, but after only a few minutes of temporary blindness she was surprised to hear cries of "Go, Sydney!" and "Sell me the tickets!" as loud and clear as music came through her headphones, and the intermingled smells of hot dogs and popcorn and beer became so strong, she felt her stomach lurch.

"She's running around. Let's hear it, Knicks fans," the announcer instructed. "Is she hot or cold?"

"COLD!" the capacity crowd shouted.

Who cares if Trevor gets mad? she thought, wobbling and groping at the air. *He's moving to London!* His bank had offered him a position in their

London office, and he was leaning toward accepting it. He told her they could have a long-distance relationship, and it was so like him to assume that she wanted one. She was praying that he'd take the position so she'd be rid of him because she didn't have the willpower to just break up with him like she should have done a long time ago.

Even though she told him she loved him all the time (and had almost convinced herself that she meant it), she didn't. She was beginning to think she really hated the bastard. But was it him she hated or the fact that she needed him so much? That was what confused her. And until she clarified that for herself, what was the point in giving up all the good stuff that came with this otherwise suffocating relationship? Being with Trevor meant she could eat at nice restaurants and go on wonderful vacations without worrying about the cost. She could have the clothes or expensive (to her) beauty treatments she'd never waste her Indochine tips on. At thirty, Trevor was only four years older than she was, but it was the crucial period when young adults turned into full-fledged adults, when they stopped sleeping on futons in shared hovels and got real beds, with matching sheet sets, that sat in the bedrooms of apartments rented without guarantors. After six years of struggling on her own, Trevor was like a rest stop, and despite the increasing emotional and psychological tax she had to pay for the comforts he offered, she couldn't seem to force herself to get back out there on the road alone again.

"Warmer," the crowd chanted, and Sydney imagined that word flashing on the scoreboard because it was too unified. She staggered forward, and as much as she hated Trevor at that moment—and she was going to kick his ass when she got ahold of him—she hated herself more. Why couldn't she just say no? To Trevor, to this stupid contest, to anyone? Twice a week she found herself spending money she didn't have to go to a bar with people she didn't care about one way or the other instead of simply saying, "I'm busy." She forwarded chain e-mails, she tipped 20 percent when she got bad service, she couldn't hang up on telemarketers, and just about every time she went to Bloomie Nails for the cheapest, no-frills manicure, she'd smudge her polish on the way out and never once had she asked the woman to fix it!

Those were things only she knew. Most people considered her confident, capable, and sometimes abrasive, because she talked a good game—even to herself—but when it came down to it, she was all bark and no bite. She probably wouldn't kick Trevor's ass for this later. She'd probably just whine and pout.

She let him bully her into so many things it was just pathetic. How had it gotten to the point where he decided what television shows they watched, which DVDs they rented, where they went on vacation, which parties they went to and how long they stayed, sometimes even what she ate ("No bread for you!"). In the beginning she spoke up for herself, told him off when he got out of line. Now he won every argument because she didn't put up much of a fight. Somehow, sometime, the power had shifted, and their relationship had fallen into a rhythm she didn't know how to change.

Sometimes she thought her compliance was what Trevor liked best about her. She gave in to everything and expected not much in return. My God, it hadn't occurred to her until just this second, as she felt herself going haywire, moving in multiple directions as some people yelled "Hot" and some yelled "Cold," that she was just like his last two girlfriends! The little pieces of information he doled out made his exes sound like wounded birds whose helplessness he subtly encouraged. His last girlfriend had never had a job and she was twenty-nine! She'd been supported by her parents and then basically by Trevor, and it didn't sound as if anyone had ever encouraged her to support herself.

And Trevor had no time for women like her friend Melanie, whom he called a "loud bitch" when she was simply an assertive woman. To Melanie's face, though, he was as sweet as could be. He always took great pains to come across as Mr. Nice Guy, and Sydney had become the silent coconspirator, helping to keep the facade in place. She hated herself for it, but most of the time it was so much easier to give in. Just last night he kept pestering her for sex, poking her in the back with his dick. Finally, she just let him, the whole time thinking, *Get it over with!* She had the same thought now. Except tonight she was being molested by thousands.

"She needs help," the announcer said. "Is she hot or cold?"

"Hot!" she heard people yelling from her right, her left, overhead. She thought she was walking straight forward, but she wasn't sure. She'd lost her bearings. She stopped and turned slowly to the left and angry taunts of "Colder" rained down on her. She turned to the right and she instantly heard a thunderous, unified chant of "WARMER!"

"Ten seconds," the announcer boomed.

Ten seconds? She felt as if she'd been out there for ten days! The darkness was making her feel claustrophobic. The crowd was closing in on her. This mob was going to descend on her at any second. "Help me," she gasped, a hostage to her own passivity. "Please help me."

The chants of "HOTTER!" became frantic, but Sydney put her hand up to her eyes, clawing at the blindfold. She was going to rip this thing off and twenty thousand people were going to boo her for not going through with this game, but she didn't care anymore.

Move to London, Trevor! And don't ever come back! See if I fucking care!

Then she heard some guy yell, in a thick Brooklyn accent, "Baby, you're so hot you're on motherfuckin' fire!" and she lunged forward. When she felt the synthetic fur in one hand and the nylon of the Knicks jersey in the other, her whole body went limp. It was over, she thought, clinging to the mascot. There was applause, cheers, whistles, and then, when she buried her face in his furry chest, the sound of laughter.

"Congratulations, Sydney," the announcer boomed, "you've just won two courtside seats to the Knicks' next home game against the Los Angeles La-kers!"

Thank God, she thought, letting go of the mascot. It was over. She tugged the blindfold down and squeezed her eyes open and closed to readjust them to the light. Through the haze she saw Spike Lee in a Knicks jersey that fell past his knees, clapping. The cheerleaders were under one basket, shaking their pom-poms. The TNT guys seated at the press table were oblivious, staring at notes. One of them was having his makeup touched up.

She was sure the worst was over. That is, until the announcer came back on and said, "Sydneeeee, we have another surprise for you." It was only then that she knew true fear. The mascot dragged her back out to center court, holding her arm high in the air, and she seriously questioned whether she had died and gone to hell.

A cameraman appeared beside her, tilting a camera up to her face, and she flinched, shuffling backward. She had not signed any release for this, and she wondered if she could sue MSG for the emotional damage being inflicted upon her. And then, as if everything that had just occurred hadn't been strange enough, something truly bizarre happened. The mascot took his head off.

Sydney looked at him, having the same odd sensation she'd experienced the week before when she'd seen a familiar-looking guy in Hudson News and then right before she went up to him, she realized it wasn't someone she knew personally—it was a B-list TV star whose picture she'd seen a hundred times in *People*. She probably blinked ten times before it sunk in that she was looking at Trevor.

As two guys appeared at his sides and helped to unzip him out of the costume, she heard a few whistles. Then nothing but a steady soothing hum, like the sound of an air conditioner. She saw nothing except Trevor. He looked as if he was on a darkened stage and there was a spotlight just on his face. When he got down on one knee and held up a small black box near his chin, Sydney's hand rushed up to her mouth, which opened to form a little O. She didn't feel her eyes well up, just two rivers of tears gushing down her face. Taking this as a good sign, Trevor flashed a smile. And when she frantically shook her head from side to side, he evidently interpreted this gesture to mean, *Oh, honey, I can't believe this day has finally come!*, because he smiled wider and nodded his head as if to say, *Oh yes, yes it has.*

Sydney couldn't hear anything, but as his mouth began to move in slow motion, she could clearly read his lips. "Will . . . you . . . marry . . . me?"

Marry him? She wished she had a hunting knife so she could stab him repeatedly and leave him to bleed to death on the Garden floor. In three years, did he know absolutely nothing about her? How could he even think that she would want a proposal like this? Or that gaudy ring?! But maybe that was his plan. In this position, how could she say no? Sad thing was, she had given him every reason to believe such a demented scheme would work. She closed her eyes to make his face disappear, and the air conditioner hum faded out, her breathing slowed, and she hoped she was fainting.

Then she heard the distant sound of birds chirping. She saw a house. A large white house with a picket fence. The door was opening. A woman was standing there. A woman with thin, pale eyebrows who looked like . . . her? Yes, it was. But her hair was almost blond, styled in a 1950s bouffant, held back with a thin pink headband and too much hair spray. She had on little white earrings that looked like rosebuds. Her nails were a shade of cotton-candy pink that matched the headband and the pink polka-dot belt around her waist, which was . . . tiny? She was curtsying now. Why? And why on earth was she wearing a hoop skirt? And a goddamn gingham apron!

This is a nightmare. This is all a nightmare. You can make it stop . . .

She was opening the door for a man who faintly resembled Trevor but looked more like a Ken doll. He was standing on the welcome mat in a starched gray suit, his short brown hair immaculate, handing her his leather briefcase. In the living room, there were kids, a gaggle of kids. Boys, lots of playful little boys, in navy blue shorts and white shirts with Peter Pan collars. And a few girls in white eyelet dresses with pink bows in their hair, trailing behind with bowed heads.

You're in control. Wake up, now! Wake up . . .

She was in the kitchen. A pristine white kitchen with shiny stainless-steel appliances. She put on two gingham oven mitts that perfectly matched the apron. She opened the stove and pulled out a succulent pot roast. She placed it on a large silver serving tray and walked into the dining room, where the entire brood was gathered, banging their knives and forks on the oak table. Like savages.

"Dinner!" she sang.

Her eyes popped open and there she was again, in the Garden, in front of everyone. She saw angry faces, laughing faces, shocked faces with slack mouths. And Trevor looking up at her with a frozen smile.

Then one drunken voice pierced through the cacophony of screams and whistles. And it said, "RUN!"

Her hand came down from her gaping mouth, clenching into a fist at her side. Then the fist was in front of her face and she caught a glimpse of the bracelet Trevor had given her for Valentine's Day sliding down her wrist. Up came her left fist and then her right, then her left . . . The shouts and whistles faded into a low indecipherable murmuring and she felt the breeze against her face as she sprinted across the court. She heard the words of the Heat players ("What the fuck!") whip past her ("Holy shit!") like wind ("Where's she going?") as she headed for the tunnel. The security guard was waiting, blocking the entrance with his arms spread out like one of the Knicks on defense. He went left. She went right. His voice echoed behind her. "You can't go down theeeeere!" She rounded the corner and bumped into a man so tall she bounced off his stomach. She sidestepped him and kept going, dodging the next guy and then picking up speed as the rest of the men, startled, stepped back against the wall, giving her clear passage. She spotted the red letters of the exit sign glowing down at the end. "Heeeey," the security guards were shouting behind her. "Stooooop!" The tunnel stretched out, and every step she took, the exit got farther away. She couldn't make it. She couldn't breathe. And then, all of a sudden, there was the door. She barreled through and kept running, hearing the alarm blare. There were cars, rows and rows of parked cars, but blessedly no people. She ducked between two hulking SUVs, letting the darkness swallow her up, crouching into a squat against the wall. Then she closed her eyes and let out a long ecstatic moan as she soaked her jeans, while inside, as she would later learn from the back page of the *New York Post,* Trevor staggered off the court, dazed and confused, the scoreboard answering his question in front of the national media and twenty thousand stunned fans: "GUESS THAT'S A NO!"

CHAPTER FORTY-FOUR

When his BlackBerry began to vibrate across his desk and Sydney's name flashed on the screen, Max picked up immediately. "Hey," he said, the softness in his voice giving away too much to Remy.

It sounded as though she was already in a conversation with someone else, a heated conversation, and Max was catching the tail end of what she was saying: "The motherfucker jinxed me!"

He put a finger up to Remy to let her know he'd be a moment. "Hey, um, who are you talking to?"

"You, idiot!" she screamed. "You!"

Idiot? Max thought. *Me?* When he'd left her yesterday morning, he thought they were finally moving in the right direction. He had even violated his own two-day rule and asked if he could see her again last night. After she said she had to write her Brett Babcock story (hadn't she turned that in already?), he thought about dropping by anyway, but he played it cool. He'd forgotten how enjoyable it was to have a woman seduce him. To not have to be in control, to be taken by surprise. And because of this little charade that Jeffrey had convinced him to prolong, she had fallen for him. Not for an idea of who he was, not for what he had or what he could get her . . . Well, yes, taking her to Harvey's twice a week and coming up with a reason that she could get 70 percent off had helped. But she was getting that without sleeping with him!

Seduce wasn't even the word. She'd *jumped* him! All this time she had been trying to act as if she wasn't interested, but she wanted him. She wanted him bad. And it wasn't even the sex (twice) that assured him she was hooked. It was that horribly humiliating story that she had never told anyone. Except him. After he'd heard that, he'd wanted to tell her everything, but her sudden demand for sex had prevented him from doing that. Then, at four A.M. she'd thrown him out because she said she couldn't fall asleep in the same bed with a "stranger." They'd just done everything short of swinging from a chandelier (though very little kissing on the mouth, which she kept avoiding) and then all of a sudden he was a *stranger*? Max had never been so insulted in all his life! But who was he to complain when he'd been lying to her all this time? So he'd just left, pissed.

But he planned to tell her everything tonight. Now that they had taken it to the next level, it was imperative that he come clean, and until a moment ago, he hadn't had any fears that she would reject him. He'd been floating on a cloud all day, unable to think about anything other than when he would see her again, but now he felt as if the clouds had parted and he was hurtling to earth at a hundred miles per hour. To escape Remy's prying eyes, he spun around in his chair and said, "Why am I an idiot?"

"Ever since I ran into him all this bad stuff has been happening to me," she said, riled up to the point of breathlessness.

It took Max a second to figure out that they were no longer talking about him, the idiot, but rather the aforementioned motherfucker. And that was . . . "Who?"

"Trevor, idiot! Trevor!"

Max was much more interested in finding out how he had suddenly become an idiot than in what her ex had done, but he listened, using the time to get his strength up for whatever residual anger she was obviously about to lay on him. "Trevor, your ex," he said patiently. "Right." He glanced over his shoulder and saw that Remy was still waiting to get back to her boring task list, which almost seemed a more appealing option now. Pulling the phone away from his mouth, Max told her he needed a minute alone, then got back to Sydney. "So you think Trevor jinxed you. Now what does that even mean?"

"First, Gristedes stopped carrying Bran Buds . . ."

"Brand what?" With all the background noise, he could barely hear her, even though she was speaking with more intensity than usual. "Where are you?"

"Walking down Fourteenth," she said quickly. "Bran Buds is my favorite cereal. Well, not favorite . . . it's necessary. I need to eat it every day to stay regular. It's like my medicine. And last week Gristedes stopped carrying it."

"Regularity" was a topic of discussion more appropriate for couples that had been married thirty years, Max thought. It wasn't something he expected, or wanted, someone he was sleeping with to bring up. Ever. "Is that the only place you can get it?"

"No, but it's the most convenient!"

"And this constitutes a jinx?" He saw Remy pass by his door and tried to call her back in. The sooner they got through the daily task list, the sooner he could go home.

"That was just the first thing," Sydney said. "Then two of my favorite restaurants closed. Mekong and Thai Grill! Just shut down. No warning. Nothing! I ordered from Mekong three times a week. It'd been open for, like, twenty years!"

"Coincidence," Max said. Realizing she was quite serious about this jinx, Max wondered if she was more unstable than he had initially surmised. He'd tangled with his fair share of crazy chicks and learned the hard way that they were only exciting up to a point.

"Yeah, well, how do you explain the fact that yesterday my masseure, Ethan, tells me he's not going to be working at Clay anymore? And I'm like, 'Okay, where are you going?' 'Cause I'm thinking he's just going to another gym or a spa. No big deal. The worst thing is I might have to pay a little more, but he's my guy, he's worth it, right?"

Max waved Remy into his office. "Yeah, and . . ."

"And he tells me he's not gonna be doing massage anymore. At all. Because he's moving to a commune!" Max laughed and Sydney said, "Exactly! I start cracking up. That's gotta be a joke, right? I had fucking tears in my eyes. And he's just looking at me. And then he goes, 'Sydney, I'm not kidding. I'm really moving to a commune.' Can you imagine? I mean, what the fuck, man! And so I'm like, 'Okay, massage me at the commune!' But it's four hours upstate!"

"I'll give you the name of my girl," Max said as Remy stared in his face. "But let me call you later. I'm in . . ." He was about to say "a meeting" but caught himself. "I'm at work."

"Yeah, well, I'm not finished," Sydney said. "You know how I know for sure that Trevor jinxed me?"

Max could tell she was ramping up to a heavy-duty anger dump, and he now wished he hadn't picked up the call in the first place. Sighing, he asked, "How?"

"Because you gave me herpes, motherfucker!"

Max pulled the phone away from his ear as her shrieking voice pierced his brain, and only after a few seconds was he able to process the words rattling in his ear canal. *Herpes?* He shooed Remy back out of the office, praying she had not been able to hear that, and shut the door behind her. "What are you talking about?"

"You heard me, you herpes-infecting son of a bitch!"

The intensity of her anger disturbed Max. He pictured her stomping down Fourteenth Street in the midday rush, bellowing up to the heavens as if she'd just been visited by a biblical plague. It wasn't that deep, but . . . Christ! Suddenly, his balls were itching. "You have genital herpes?"

"Eeeew," she moaned. "Don't even say that. Wait, why did you say that? Do you?"

"No! You just said you did."

"Not genital, idiot. On my lip!"

Max collapsed on the daybed and exhaled, only then realizing he had been holding his breath for the last thirty seconds. "That's not the end of the world."

"You haven't seen my lip, bitch!"

He sat upright and took a breath. "Sydney, I'm sorry this happened to you, but please stop calling me names."

"Excuse me, Maximillian," she said, mocking his polite tone, "but this didn't just *happen* to me. You *did* it to me. I think I've earned the right to call you a few names. Dickhead! Asshole! Disease spreader!"

"Stop it!" Max shouted, trying to remember when a woman had angered him to this extreme. "You have no right to call me anything because I didn't give it to you." He held the phone in front of his mouth and yelled, "I don't have herpes." Then, out of spite, he added, "You do."

"What are you trying to imply?" Max could just see her head pulling back and her mouth falling open the way it did whenever anyone dared point out an inconvenient truth to her. "That I've been hoing around?"

Accustomed to her bullying tactics, Max answered calmly. "Of course not. But—"

"You're the only person I've had skin-to-skin contact with in the last seven to ten days, faggot! Trust, it was you."

"*Faggot?* Sydney, listen to yourself! What's wrong with you?"

"I have herpes. That's what's wrong with me! This shit doesn't go away. Not ever, ever, ever! Making the mistake of touching you has changed my life forever. For the worst! I knew I should have stayed away from you. I'm so stupid, stupid, stupid!"

"You didn't get it from me," Max shouted back, angry and appalled. "I don't have it!"

"It was an asymptomatic transmission, asshole!"

Max jumped to his feet and began pacing back and forth in his office, gripping the phone like a vise. "Asymptomatic transmission from skin-to-skin contact means you could have gotten it from anyone, sweetheart. Anyone who gave you an air kiss. A friend, your sister . . ."

"My sister doesn't have herpes, you little prick! She's a lesbian!"

"What the fuck does that have to do with anything?" Max said, looking at his iPhone as if *it* were crazy. Remy knocked on the door and he snapped, "I need a second, girl!"

"Who's that?" Sydney said and Max blurted, "My assistant."

"Assistant for what?"

Shit! "A *sales* assistant. I'm on a break. All I'm trying to say is have a little perspective. It could be a lot worse."

"That's easy for you to say, Patient Zero! And I hate when people say that. Of course it could be worse. Unless you're an illiterate HIV-positive Sudanese orphan it could always be fucking worse! That doesn't change the fact that I have a festering cold sore on my lip the size of a motherfucking raisin!"

Shaking off the shiver of disgust that image produced, Max yelled back, "Well it's not my fault, b—"

"I *know* you didn't just fix your mouth to call me a bitch!" Sydney huffed, escalating to a new level of outrage.

"No, no, no," Max said. "I was going to say *baby*." A weak cover, but it was all he had.

"No you were not!" After that furious reply, she didn't sound angry anymore. She sounded like she was about to pass out. "You gave me herpes," she whimpered. "And you don't even care. I was so wrong about you." There was a brief pause, then the strength came back into her voice. *"You're a monster!"*

Max had never been thought of as monstrous, and for a second, he felt quite powerful. So much so that he was going to strike back and tell her exactly how ridiculous she was being and that if this was how she was going to behave, then maybe they should just put an end to things right now and save themselves the bother. But then he heard her voice crack. He couldn't even make out what she was saying, and he realized her anger was masking serious emotional distress.

"Look, Sydney," he said, feeling like all (or some) of the things she was calling him for allowing his own feelings to come before hers. "I know this sucks. I'm sorry . . . this happened to you." He heard himself trying to defend his position, still thinking about himself. "Maybe I *did* give it to you," he said, sacrificing himself. "Maybe I *am* an asymptomatic carrier. There's no way of knowing. But you weren't wrong about me, so please don't think that." He waited for her to answer, hoping the response would be positive, but all he heard was shallow breathing. "I was going to make dinner reservations tonight, but you probably don't want to go out now. Why don't I come by after work and we can order in?"

"We can't order in," she whimpered. "All my favorite restaurants are closed."

"I know a great Thai place," he said. "I'll pick something up and bring it over. Anything you want. Pad thai? You like pad thai, right? Hold the peanuts?"

"This is what I get," Max heard her muttering through the sounds of horns honking and the faraway blare of an ambulance siren. "This is what I get for allowing him inside my perimeter . . ."

"Sydney," he said. "Can you hear me? I said I'll come over later with dinner. Do you need anything else?"

"Yes," she said, her voice clear, strong, and furious again. "I need you to stay the fuck away from me."

ACT THREE

The fairy tale isn't having a rich, handsome prince
sweep you off your feet. It's having someone see
you and love you, flaws and all.

—MIRIAM BERMAN

CHAPTER FORTY-FIVE

S ydney spied something funky going on inside Jerome Bailey's mouth the moment she saw him waiting at the bar. Now, as he burst into a full, hearty laugh and his fleshy lips opened wider, she got a good look at the ample space between his top two front teeth. Then she spotted a *gold* tooth hidden off to the side. Who had Mitzi set her up with? A rapper? A drug dealer? *Suge Knight?*

After her first disastrous date and Mitzi's vow that she would never deal with her again, Sydney was shocked when Mitzi called to give her a second chance. "I need you to be on your best behavior," Mitzi had said. "Study my book, meditate, whatever you need to do. Don't blow this!" Sydney promised she wouldn't and, intent on keeping that promise, she had gone out of her way to prepare. She'd had her nails done, bought a fancy new dress from Bergdorf's (after the Max debacle, she was avoiding Harvey's, and it killed her to pay full price), and, with Jeffrey out of town on a job, done her own makeup, fake eyelashes and all, using the step-by-step instructions he'd e-mailed her. She'd even taken Mitzi's advice and meditated this afternoon (in the chair while she was having her hair blown out). Mitzi had been right about her. She had a wall up, and if she didn't want to be childless and alone for the rest of her life, it had to come down.

She arrived at The Palm a few minutes before eight feeling confident that she could knock this date out of the park, but uproarious laughter was not the response she was expecting to the Mitzi-sanctioned opener, "So, what do you do?" Sitting across from Jerome, she nibbled on a piece of buttered bread (*Forgive me, Ranjit*), waiting to be let in on the joke. Normally, she tried not to ask what someone did for a living unless it came up naturally in conversation. It was a very New York question, a way for people to categorize you, to stick you in a box that would be filed away on an arbitrarily devised scale of importance. Were you someone they needed to know? Could you possibly do something for them? Might you introduce them to someone they needed to know because *that* person might be able to do something for them? The kind of horribly elitist bullshit Gareth Ogle*prick* engaged in on a regular basis. (Sydney had once mentioned her friend Mira in passing and he said, "Who is she?" Sydney told him she was a friend from her college days. "No," Gareth said. "Who *is* she? Where does she *work*? What does she *do*?") Sydney had only posed the question to Jerome the moment they were seated because she was going by the book! Successful men loved to talk about their work, Mitzi said, and no matter how boring the answer, listen and stay engaged. But Mitzi hadn't mentioned what to do if your date laughed in your face.

"I'm sorry," Sydney said, the natural impatience she had tried to meditate away rising to the surface. "Did I say something funny?"

"No, no," Jerome said, catching his breath. "*I'm* sorry. Really. I'm not laughing at you. It's just that I rarely get asked that question."

Must not be from New York, then, Sydney thought. The suit was another giveaway that he wasn't a city boy. It was a simple, dark gray three-button, which was fine, but it had a slight *sheen*. He was so large, though, he was probably forced to shop at Rochester Big & Tall, and Sydney couldn't imagine their suit selection was very good.

"And when women ask," Jerome said, peering into the bread basket, "it's usually because they're trying to pretend they don't know." He hunched over, trying to smell the bread. "But I can tell you really don't."

Sydney tilted the basket toward him. "Would you like a piece? It's very good."

He threw up his massive hands and backed away. "I can't. My nutritionist would kill me!"

"Mine too!" Sydney said, glad to have him as a partner in nutritional crime. She picked up the bread basket and held it up close to his nose, tempting him. "Go on. Have some. You know you want to."

Jerome examined each piece of bread before selecting the smallest hunk.

Sydney set the basket down and slid the butter dish his way. "No butter," he said. "No butter!"

She smiled. It was funny—but odd—that such a huge guy would be so worried about his weight. Putting it together, she said, "Are you an athlete?" She'd had that thought the moment she saw him but kept it to herself. What if he owned a computer software company or something? She didn't want to insult him.

"I'm sorry," Jerome said, nodding as he swallowed a small piece of bread. "I never answered your question. Yes. I'm a football player."

"That's nice," Sydney said, buttering another piece of bread. Her last! "You mean, like, professionally?"

"In the NFL," he said. "Yes."

While the bread transported him into a momentary state of rapture, Sydney took the opportunity to really examine his face. He had a potato head that was as massive as his hands, a wide, flat nose, an extraordinarily muscular neck, and ears that seemed tiny in comparison to everything else. Nothing about him seemed familiar. "So what are you, famous or something?"

Jerome finished gulping his water and placed the glass—which looked like a shot glass in his hand—on the table. "Yes."

Sydney liked that response. No hemming and hawing, no false modesty. Just stated as fact. *Yes, I'm famous.* Still, she couldn't let that go without some teasing. "Well, you can't be that famous because I've never heard of you!"

"Apparently, you don't follow football," Jerome said, staring lustfully at the remaining piece of bread.

"Wanna split—" Before Sydney had finished asking, Jerome had torn it in half and handed her the bigger piece. "And you're right," she said after they had both quietly enjoyed the indulgence. "I've never watched a football game in my life. But if you were as famous as you claim, I'd know who you were anyway. I don't watch hockey, but I know who Wayne Gretzky is."

"Okay, hold on," Jerome said, and Sydney could almost feel the spirit of Mitzi Berman fly over the table on a broomstick. She had offended him. She was falling back into her old snippy self. *Be agreeable,* she thought. *Flatter him.* "I never claimed to be Wayne Gretzky famous." He was definitely offended. "And I bet you can't name one football player." He gave her a long look, clearly issuing a challenge, then added, "Someone currently playing. Don't say O.J."

Sydney bit her lip and tried to hold back her smile. That was exactly who she was about to say! She thought for a second until a name came to her. "Tom Brady."

"Guurrl, you only know him cause he's married to Gisele Bündchen!"

Sydney let out a little whoop of delight. "You're so right!"

"Okay, that doesn't count." Jerome slapped the table as if calling a penalty. "Gimme another one!"

"Okay, okay," Sydney said, feeling the tide turn for Jerome. There was nothing more seductive than a man with a good sense of humor. And with that one comment he'd gained back most of the ground he'd lost due to his massiveness, his potato head, the gap, the gold tooth, the suit. First, for knowing exactly what she was thinking and calling her on it. Second, for calling her *guurrl,* which was just the cutest. Lastly, for his impeccable pronunciation of Bündchen!

The waiter brought their appetizers, and after Jerome did what looked to be a little prayer over his salad, he said, "Drawing a blank?"

"No, it's coming to me." Sydney tapped her finger on her forehead until she had something to offer. "Derwin . . . Davis."

"Derwin Davis? Who the hell . . . ?" Jerome stared at her in confusion, then sucked his teeth. "Wait a second. Isn't that a character on *The Game*?"

Trying not to spit any salad dressing at him, Sydney reached up to cover her mouth with the napkin. "I love that show."

"Me too," he said, and Sydney ticked off another thing they had in common. The Game, *a sense of humor, cheating on their diets, being up on celebrity couplings* . . . "But how you remember the last name of a television character? You must got a real good memory."

The "you must got a" made Sydney wonder if he'd finished college or dropped out early to go pro. If he was a big star, then he probably hadn't even studied or gone to class. He might be rich, famous, and illiterate, she thought. Which was not good for the gene pool. She had dated a few guys like that. They weren't completely illiterate—they didn't have to sign their name with an X or anything—but damn near. There was a music producer once, an actor, a low-level drug dealer . . . Roughnecks who had no real education but had become moderately successful using their ghetto street wisdom. She had great respect for anyone who could do that, and she (sorta) put herself in that category since she had dropped out of college after her freshman year. The difference was that she read all the time on her own, and she'd taken continuing-ed classes at the New School over the years in whatever subjects caught her fancy. She'd just signed up for a weekend screenwriting seminar through Mediabistro. And she'd gotten into Princeton and every other school she'd applied to; she'd gotten 1310 on her SATs. Her intelligence was not in question. How much wisdom did you need to be a football player? When was the last time Jerome Bailey cracked open a book? Did he read the paper? Did he go to the theater? He was funny, but was he just *another dumb jock*?

"Put this in context for me," Sydney said, trying to figure out how to work the conversation back to his grades or some other evidence of his mental capacity. "Have you ever been in the Super Bowl?"

"What do you think this is?" He stretched his hand across the table. His hands were the size of baseball mitts, but after the disappointment of Mitzi's first, unofficial fix-up, Big Hand/Little Dick Grant, she didn't want to read too much into that.

"A Super Bowl ring," Sydney said. He nodded and she inspected the engraving further. "You were the MVP?" He nodded again. "Well done, Jerome." As he pulled his hand away, she added, "It's kinda tacky, though."

Stop it, she heard Mitzi's voice say, but Jerome just smiled, taking it all in stride, and she liked him even more for not holding her irrepressible bitchiness against her. "It's a sign of achievement," he said. "It's not really for the look."

"So have you ever been in a commercial?"

"A couple."

"On a Wheaties box?"

He nodded. "After the Super Bowl." After the waiter removed their appetizer plates, Jerome said, "I won the Heisman in '92. That's like an MVP for college players. I left college in my junior year to go pro. I signed endorsement deals with Adidas, Gatorade, and Duracell, to name a few. I played with the Cowboys for seven years, and after we won the Super Bowl, I got to say, 'I'm going to Disney World' in the commercial. I'd go on, but it'd probably be easier if you just Googled all this later." He sat back, and the waiter placed their entrées on the table. "Anything else, Miss Journalist?"

Sydney had been smiling the whole time she was listening to him, but now, watching him dip a piece of lobster into the dish of melted butter, trying to get just the tiniest bit, she let out a (rather unfeminine) snort of laughter. "How'd you know I was a journalist?"

"Mitzi told me."

"She didn't give me any information about you. Except your first name."

"That's because I'm the client."

"Yeah, so what's the deal with that anyway? You're Mr. Super Bowl MVP, decent-looking guy. Why do you need Mitzi Berman to find you a woman?"

"Decent-looking?" Jerome said, looking up from his plate. "Gotta work to get a compliment outta you, I see."

"Come on," Sydney said, thinking "decent-looking" *was* a compliment for him! "You're a big, tough football player. Do you really care if I think you're *hot*?"

"Of course I do. You think guys don't have feelings?"

"You don't even know me."

"I wanna get to know you."

"You are," Sydney said. "Now you know I'm a hard person to get compliments from."

She smiled and Jerome smiled back. "See, you wanna stereotype me," he said. "But you're the tough cookie. Don't judge a book by its cover, baby."

Sydney wasn't as fond of *baby* as she was of *guurrl,* but she let it go. Their banter had gotten off to a bumpy start, but there seemed to be a rhythm to the conversation now and she wanted to keep it going. "I'm not a tough cookie," she said. "Not by choice. I'm just a single woman living in New York."

"I feel you. But don't you care what a man thinks about you, if he finds you attractive?"

"Not really," Sydney said. "If one guy doesn't find me attractive, another will. You know what they say. There's someone for everybody. And I'm reminded of that every time I take the subway and see two madly-in-love toothless crackheads or the full-bodied tattoo couple or the uptight white couple in matching khakis." Jerome didn't seem to relate, and it occurred to her that he probably never took the subway. "I may think a person is as unsexy as can be, but that's just my opinion, so who cares? He probably thinks the same about me."

"About you? Never!"

Sydney smiled, thinking this dude really did have a great sense of humor. "The opinion I value most is my own. If I think my outfit or my hair or my body looks all right, then I'm good."

"Great attitude," Jerome said. "And attitude is everything."

"And some guys, you don't want them to find you attractive, you know? 'Cause they like slutty chicks!"

"You just described our whole front line."

"And you know what it is too? If a woman comes up to me and says, 'I love your outfit,' that's the ultimate compliment because you know it's genuine. But when a guy tells you you're beautiful or whatever, you dismiss it because you know he just wants the panties."

Jerome stuck his fork into what Sydney couldn't believe was the last bit of lobster on his plate—she had barely gotten started—and said, "True."

"Jerome!" she said, laughing. "You're not supposed to say, 'True.' You're supposed to say, 'Nah, sometimes I just wanna say something nice. It's not always about getting the panties.'"

He reached over with his fork and pointed at the sautéed potatoes on her plate. "Can I try these?"

"Sure," she said, realizing how much food she still had left on her plate. She was talking too much. Mitzi had warned her about that.

"And what you mean I'm 'sposed to say? If you're a man and you're straight, you see an attractive woman . . . It is what it is. You were speaking the truth." He dabbed his mouth with the napkin. "I agreed."

"Okay, fine. I like to be right."

"I can tell. And for the record, this man finds you very attractive." Making direct eye contact, he added, "In every way. Interpret that however you like."

"Well, thank you, Jerome," Sydney said, proud that she was able to simply accept the compliment without making a smart-alecky comment.

"You're very welcome, Sydney." He reached over and grabbed another forkful of potatoes. "So what are you, ethnically speaking?"

"My father was Afro-Cuban—"

"Was?"

"He died. When I was about eighteen."

"I'm sorry," Jerome said.

"Don't be. You didn't kill him. My mother is French, Portuguese, and Irish."

"Quite a mix you have going on there." He raised his sparse eyebrows appreciatively. "It suits you."

Sydney could almost feel herself blushing. "I think the only reason I haven't been kicked out of Mitzi's database is because I'm on the affirmative action program. She mentioned something about being light in the exotic category."

"Kick you out? Why would she do that?"

"She thinks I'm a ballbuster."

Sydney was sort of hoping he'd look surprised, like *Ballbuster? You?*, but he just gave a shrug and said, "Some guys like that."

"Please tell her that," Sydney said.

"But you're right about her not having a lotta women of color. I told her that's what I was looking for and she been sending me Persian, Indian, Chinese . . . Those wasn't the colors I was talking 'bout. One time she sent me this Greek chick. I mean, she was real tan and she had a big ass and everything, but Greek ain't colored!" Sydney cracked up. "Yeah, me and your girl Mitzi had to huddle after that."

Sydney couldn't stop smiling, partly because she was thinking how strange it was that when Gareth used the word *colored* she was outraged and when Jerome used it she was touched. The fact that he'd make a joke like that was a signal that he considered her from the same tribe. And after a lifetime of not being white enough or black enough or Latina enough, it was always nice when someone just accepted her for who she was and said, "You can be on my team." Her warm feelings for Jerome reaching a full simmer, she leaned toward him and said, "So I'm more your speed?"

"Yeah," he said, giving his full stomach a satisfied pat. "This time Mitzi was on point."

"I think that's cool," Sydney said. "That you want a woman of color. Big-time football player and everything . . . I'd think you'd be into white women."

"I am," he said, getting the waiter's attention. "I just don't wanna marry one."

"Wait a second," Sydney said. "What does that—" She paused when the waiter appeared to take their dessert order, and then they were interrupted again when the maître d' came over and whispered something in Jerome's ear. When they finally had some privacy, she leaned across the table and, feeling comfortable enough to inject a little sexual innuendo into their banter, whispered, "What does that mean? You *smashed* the Greek chick?"

Smiling wide enough to expose his gap, probably because her phrasing was confirmation that they *were* from the same tribe, Jerome turned his head sideways and rubbed the back of his thick neck. "We can't discuss that with children present."

"What children?" Sydney started looking around, more for comic effect than anything, but then she saw the child. A little boy being ushered up to the table by the maître d' with his father following closely behind. This, she thought, must have been what the whispering was about.

The boy, who was probably about eight, handed Jerome a pen and a fresh cocktail napkin that had a little palm tree imprinted in the corner. "Hey, little fella," Jerome said easily, as if he were filming a commercial and this was take ninety-six. "What's your name?"

"Tyson," the boy, who seemed to have his eyes glued open, said.

"You play sports, Tyson?" Jerome asked, scribbling.

Tyson gulped hard and his eyes opened wider. "Football."

Jerome handed him the autographed napkin and the pen. "You get good grades?"

"Yes, sir," Tyson said, and Sydney thought, *Sir?* This kid had to be a tourist. Jerome looked to his equally starstruck father for confirmation and the man nodded vigorously. Definitely tourists, Sydney thought, disdainfully noting that he and his eight-year-old son were wearing the same outfit (Dockers, light blue oxford, navy blazer, and loafers—with tassels!)

"Well, how would you like . . ." Jerome paused, pointing his thick finger down at the little boy like a schoolmarm. "But understand I'm only making this offer because you get good grades." Tyson nodded obediently and then Jerome hit him with the offer. "How would you like to be my guest at the first game of the season?"

"Your guest? The first game?" Tyson's big brown eyes rolled around like dropped marbles and he put his hands next to his ears as though he might have to catch brain matter when his head exploded from the intense ecstasy of it all. He looked back at his ecstatic father, who managed to stammer, "We're . . . we're . . . we're from Georgia, but we'll come back. *Of course we'll come back!*" Sydney thought he was going jump in the air and click his heels. Even the maître d', who had struck Sydney as somewhat aloof—although not to NFL great Jerome Bailey—seemed touched to have facilitated this once-in-a-lifetime Hallmark moment for little Tyson from Georgia.

After Jerome gave them the number for "Sherri in the ticket office," father and son were ushered away. "Thank you so much, Mr. Bailey," the father said, bowing and shuffling backward as if leaving the presence of a Japanese dignitary. "Thank you so much."

The little boy, too stunned after the ticket offer to say anything, was walking in a daze at his father's side until he suddenly broke away as if he were running a scripted play in the middle of The Palm and doubled back to the table. "Thank you, Mr. Bailey," he said, overflowing with preadolescent earnestness. "You are my hero." And then, to the delight of everyone watching, he turned and scampered back to his table.

Sydney slapped her hand to her chest, verklempt. "Oh my God! Was that the cutest thing you've ever seen in your whole life?"

"No," Jerome said, feeding her a spoonful of crème brûlée. "You are."

CHAPTER FORTY-SIX

They'd driven back downtown in Jerome's Bentley, which Sydney thought was kind of ostentatious. She'd seen enough E! specials on the fabulous lives of hip-hop stars to know a car like that cost hundreds of thousands of dollars. *Hundreds of thousands of dollars.* For a car! She found herself wondering how many African villages could be fed with such an expense, not to mention all the gas it must guzzle. Forget about Jerome's big hands. His carbon footprint was probably enormous!

But she wasn't going to hold it against him. He was a big guy, an NFL player. A big car like that suited him. He probably couldn't fit in a Prius! And his car wasn't all tricked out or some tacky color. If he'd been driving a powder-blue Bentley like the one she'd seen Puffy tooling down Ocean Drive in on the E! special (top down, rims spinning), that would have been a clear sign of a deeper, as-yet-unseen ignorance she probably couldn't have tolerated in the long run. Thankfully, Jerome's car was an elegant gunmetal gray. It purred like a kitten and drove like it was on a cloud. The seat was so comfortable that when they stopped at a light and Jerome was going through the seven-CD changer looking for the right mood music, she almost fell asleep! She got a second wind when the supple sounds of his R & B mix began seeping out of a high-tech surround-sound speaker system that made Sydney feel as if she was relaxing in an ergonomic pod at NASA! There was a little Mary, a dash of Sade, a totally random Tamia song she used to love. "Share

My World" came on and he started crooning, "'Share my world . . . Ooh la la la'" and he really got into it, singing all the riffs, bumping those big shoulders, bobbing that potato head? *Say whaaaat?* Sydney almost told him to pull over and get his dick out! She wanted him to impregnate her right then and there!

She could get used to riding around in a car like this, she thought. *Ooh la la la.* With a guy like him. *Ooh la la la.* And as her macho side told her, *If you were a really rich, single, thirty-six-year-old black man who'd grown up poor, you would be riding around in a car like that.* Women bought clothes and beauty products all the time. Men made big purchases, cars and electronic equipment, every once in a while. In the end, it all added up to the same thing. They were all conspicuous consumers. No one, except the freegans, was innocent! And Jerome was no Lulu Merriwether. He worked for his money, supported his whole family, and had his own charity, which helped disadvantaged kids back in North Carolina, where he'd grown up. Besides, he'd scored a lot of points at dinner. And banked a hundred more with the impromptu Mary J. serenade. He had a few to give.

Instead of dropping her at her front door, he'd parked a few blocks away and said, "It's a nice night. Let's walk." Sydney wanted to invite him up and get busy, but then all her strategic date work would be for naught. Although if Jerome grabbed her and overpowered her with his intoxicating masculinity, as she was imagining right now that he would, she might not be able to resist. She'd bedded plenty of guys after just meeting them, but those were guys who were only good for bedding. Jerome Bailey was grade-A husband and father material. Panties couldn't come off until the third date at least. But there was nothing wrong with a good-night kiss, she thought. That was all she could think about, although he had finally gotten around to explaining why he was using a professional matchmaker, something she wanted to hear.

"Probably for the same reason as any other successful guy. You don't have time to look."

"So hiring Mitzi is the same as having a personal shopper," Sydney said, counting the number of buildings until they got to hers. "She shows you the goods and you say, 'I like this' or 'I don't like that.'"

"Right . . ." Jerome said hesitantly. "But for the record, you equated women with 'goods.' Don't put that in my mouth."

Sydney had been grinning most of the night—she couldn't stop—but that made her grin blossom into a full, Kool-Aid smile. Jerome was funny, smart (street or book was still to be determined), decent, compassionate, sane. But that remark showed that he *got* her. And wasn't that the most important thing? How many people in her life could she say that about? Her mother and sister certainly didn't get her. *She* didn't get all the women she'd once called friends who'd given up their careers to spend their days in the kiddie park and now had no personal ambition whatsoever. Even Jeffrey, who was her closest confidant and "got" a lot of her quirks, still said and did things sometimes that made her feel like he didn't understand the first thing about her.

And if anyone were to really get her, she'd expect it to be a gay man. A gay man trapped in a woman's body was what Jeffrey and her other gays always said she was, but gay men liked to dress up, they liked to decorate. Most of the time, Sydney felt more like an emotional hermaphrodite. One half of her was a raging feminist shouting, "Anything the boys can do, I can do better!" The other was a macho man shouting back, "Oh, shut up, bitch!" And neither of those people was as feminine as Jeffrey. That was a level of emotional complexity that Jeffrey, as down for her as he could be, would never comprehend. But Jerome had made several comments tonight that made her feel like somehow he might. Everything he'd said and done made her feel like he liked her for who she was, he wasn't at all intimidated by her, and unlike Mitzi (and her mother and Liz and, it seemed, a whole lot of people), he wouldn't want her to change a single thing about herself. Sure, she'd been working the tools she'd picked up from Mitzi's book, but most of it had come naturally. It had all been there inside of her, she thought. She just hadn't given it a chance to come out! She never would have imagined that Mitzi Berman would turn out to be the fairy godmother who unleashed her womanly wiles or that a professional football player would be the guy to "get" her, but however implausibly this all had happened, it felt nice. To be gotten.

"And I just got traded to the Giants last season," Jerome said, casually taking her hand as if they'd been dating for years. "You move to a new city, you don't know anyone except your teammates. I travel all the time." He shrugged. "It's hard to meet women. Except the ones who go out of their way to meet you."

"Groupies, you mean?"

"You don't wanna mess with them." Jerome shook his head at the skank-iness of it all. "And there's a whole network of people who work with profes-sional athletes, you know. When you move, there's someone to find you a house, set it up, do everything and anything you have the money but not the time to do. A lot of the guys use Mitzi."

Sydney's body fell away from his as she turned and looked up at him, shocked. *"A lot of the guys use Mitzi?"*

He gripped her hand and pulled her back closer. "Why is that weird?"

"Because!" She felt warm and tingly inside, charged up with sexual en-ergy as though his hand were a power cord and hers were a USB port. "Those guys want to get married?"

"Sydney, do you think because we play professional sports we're all sav-ages?"

Kinda, she was thinking.

"Everyone wants to fall in love, get married, have kids," Jerome said, sounding borderline offended that he had to defend the civility of his football-playing brethren. "These are all basic, human desires. Niggas want to spread their seed!"

After Sydney stopped cracking up, she squinted up at him. He was so big and tall, he made her feel as waifish as Kate Moss, which she just loooooooved. "I thought you said the whole front line liked slutty chicks."

"Yeah, but those are the younger guys," he admitted. "Those guys just want ass and mo' ass."

"Were you like that?" Sydney asked, watching his face closely to catch his first, honest reaction.

"Did I get a lotta ass?" he repeated, wisely giving himself a moment to consider his answer. "Yeah, sure, my fair share." He let go of Sydney's hand, wrapped his arm around her, and pulled her in for a quick, reassuring hug. "But all my tests came back negative, so don't you worry about that, my darling."

Overcome by his huggy-bear cuteness, Sydney wrapped herself around his beefy arm and nuzzled her face into his shoulder, giggling uncontrolla-bly while hoping her heavier-than-normal makeup didn't rub off on his suit jacket. But then she heard him say, "So what about you?" and her relaxed body went stiff. What was he asking? Did she get a lot of ass in her younger days? It was okay for *her* to ask because it was okay for a guy to admit that he had. It made him *look good*, even. Like, *Yeah, I got a lot of ass because I was cool and chicks wanted to give it to me, and being the virile, red-blooded heterosexual male that I am, I welcomed it gladly.* Saying "I got my fair share" and jokingly adding "But all my tests came back negative" was actually the *perfect* answer to that question.

For a woman, there was no perfect answer. Sydney wasn't ashamed to admit how many people she'd slept with. Nineteen, at last count. She'd lost her virginity at sixteen (to a graduating senior she'd carefully chosen because she knew he had sexual experience and he'd be off to college and out of her hair after their summer fling). That averaged out to 1.2 guys a year over the last seventeen years. Which, in her mind, made her quite chaste. But she'd had guys react with horror at her "number," even when they'd slept with twice as many people. Such completely sexist overreactions never made her feel like a slut—it was their madonna-whore complex, let them deal with it—but she had, on occasion, used it as an excuse to stop sleeping with the guys who'd made the mistake of trying to run that double standard on her. But her number was not something she was going to discuss on a first, blind date with a man who had, in the last three hours, shot to the top of her "potential baby daddies" list. He shouldn't feel comfortable enough to ask her that, Sydney thought. She must be doing something wrong. Because if he was asking, that meant he thought there was a chance that the answer might be yes!

"So," he said, noticing that she was no longer nuzzling his arm but squeezing it tightly. "What about you? Why would a beautiful, intelligent, funny woman like yourself need Mitzi Berman to hook *you* up?"

Sydney's body collapsed with relief. *That* was what he wanted to know? She let go of his arm, snaked her hand down his sleeve, and slid it back into his warm, massive grip. Thinking more about what his kiss was going to be like than her answer—her building was only three doors away; she had to get ready—she blurted, "Oh, I'm writing an article on her."

Mistake, and she knew it immediately. Using Mitzi's services was one of the things they had in common. They were in this together, she thought. By saying that, she had just abandoned ship. She could see he was looking at her with concern, thinking maybe he'd been duped, so she quickly followed up, "I mean, that's how I met her. I approached her to do a piece on this whole professional matchmaking craze. And she really sold me on the idea. You know that Mitzi. Persuasive!"

"She sure is," Jerome agreed. But he was still frowning. "So are you going to write about this date for a magazine?"

Sydney nuzzled his arm again and looked up at him, batting her now partially detached fake eyelashes. "Only good things."

"Seriously," he said, letting her hand slip from his grip. "Are you?"

Even that was sexy, Sydney thought. The way he was demanding a straight answer. She almost didn't want to give him one just to see if he'd get rough with her. She'd never been with such a big guy. He could flip her around and do things to her that none of her puny boy toys would ever dare. And she wanted him to do those things. Like, now. Would it really be so terrible if they went upstairs and fooled around with all their clothes on? Yes, she thought, pausing the sex scene playing in her mind. Who was she kidding? Once things got started they weren't going to stop.

"I might do a profile on Mitzi," she told Jerome truthfully. "But I wouldn't write about you or this date." Then she looked into his eyes and took a calculated risk. "I wouldn't write about *us*." She knew Mitzi wouldn't approve of an "us" reference on a first date, but Sydney didn't care. She didn't have time to play games anymore. She wasn't looking for a boyfriend. She was ready for something serious. And she wanted Jerome to know unequivocally that she was feeling him in a major way. So fuck the rule book. She was going for hers!

"Us," Jerome noted, smiling to himself, and Sydney felt as if she were walking on air. They came up to her building, and she could feel the butterflies fluttering in her stomach. She couldn't remember the last time she'd been this nervous on a date. Had she ever? Was that a sign of true love? She was back to imagining what his huge (had to be) dick would feel like at the moment of entry when she saw some movement in the front yard of the brownstone next door. She slowed almost to a stop, squinting into the darkness.

After taking a few steps without her, Jerome looked back. "Hey," he said. "I thought you said this one." He pointed at her building. "Fifty-two?"

Sydney motioned for him to come back. The kiss could wait.

CHAPTER FORTY-SEVEN

Sydney watched the shadowy figure shifting in the corner, facing the darkened ground-floor window of the brownstone next door. At first, she thought it was the owner putting out the trash, but she looked around and saw three trash cans bearing the house number lined up by the curb. Hmmm.

She had just finished reading *The Gift of Fear* by Gavin De Becker, a security expert she'd seen on *Oprah,* and she had the sudden, electrifying realization that she was, at that moment, being visited by the gift. The crux of the book was that women, raised to be nice and agreeable, are often too nice and agreeable to say, "Leave me alone" when all their instincts tell them they should. As a result, they wind up raped or abducted or killed all because they didn't want some strange man they didn't know from a hole in the wall to think they were being a bitch. Sydney was used to being called a bitch, so she was a step ahead in that regard, but she discounted her intuition, in small ways, all the time. After reading *The Gift of Fear,* she'd been making a concerted effort to stop doing that, to listen to her inner voice more keenly. Feeling her senses going on high alert, she realized that her first thought was not that this might be the owner putting out the trash. That was the thought that had tried to explain away her first instinct: *Something ain't right here.*

She knew the guy who owned this brownstone. He was in his fifties. A fuddy duddy. He wouldn't be wearing a hooded sweatshirt and jeans that sagged like that. And at eleven o'clock, he'd probably be in bed. Fast asleep.

Her intuition was telling her that something sinister was going on here, and suddenly remembering about the Perry Street pervert—had they ever caught that guy?—she had cause to investigate further.

"Excuse me," she called out, loud and strong. There had been a community meeting down at the precinct months ago that she hadn't gone to, but she'd seen flyers posted along the street. All she could remember was that this perv had been sighted several times jerking off in people's yards on and around Perry Street, which was two blocks over.

"*Excuse me,*" she called out, louder and stronger, when the guy just stood there, facing the window, like a statue. He'd heard them talking. Was he hoping they'd walk by and not notice him?

Keeping her eyes on him, she rooted around in her clutch until she felt her keys. She pulled them out, holding tight on to the rape whistle that dangled from the chain. The suspect also began fumbling around, still with his back to them. Was he reaching for something? A weapon? The question was answered when Sydney heard something that, with her heightened awareness, sounded like it was being projected through a loudspeaker: the zip of his pants. That was all the evidence she needed. She stuck the whistle between her lips and blew hard. Too hard, apparently, because it only made a hollow squeaking sound. She tried again with the same result. Dammit! *Was there some technique to whistle blowing?*

"What the fuck are you doing?" the suspect said, rushing out of the shadows. He got a glimpse of Jerome, who was looking at Sydney like he wanted to ask the same question, and instantly backed away.

"Don't you think I should be asking you that, pervert?" Sydney saw him inching closer to the gate, so she walked up to it, blocking his passage.

"*Pervert?*" he said, aggrieved. "I was taking a piss!"

"Where is it?" Sydney demanded, leaning over the gate to peer into the corner where he'd been standing.

"Where is what?" he snapped, his eyes jumping nervously from her cocked whistle to Jerome hulking behind her.

"The piss, asshole! The piss!" If this was the guy, she thought, he was shit out of luck tonight. There was no way he was getting by her and Jerome Bailey! "I don't see it!" Her head bobbed and weaved as she tried to catch sight of any liquid reflection glistening on the concrete. "And why are you pissing on people's property anyway?"

He reached for the gate, mumbling, "You're crazy, lady."

Sydney raised the whistle to her lips. "Back the fuck up or I blow." She should have started blowing and asked questions after everyone on the block, who'd gotten similar whistles at the community meeting (she'd always had her own), was out there to back her up. But what if she was wrong? What if he really was taking a piss and she got a lynch mob out here to attack him? Holding tight onto the fluorescent yellow whistle—it had the pervert so scared it was like holding a gun—she told Jerome, "Watch him while I check for the piss." Why prematurely get the entire block involved when she had Jerome? He was all the backup she needed.

"Sydney, come on," Jerome said, and she recognized the sound of exasperation and embarrassment in his voice. That was what Kyle sounded like the night she'd tried to stick him with the bill at Quo. "He was just taking a . . ."

"We'll see," she said, opening the gate. Jerome didn't know there was a pervert on the loose who liked to jerk off in people's yards. A white or Hispanic male, five foot seven, in his late twenties, with dark hair, last seen wearing jeans and a blue hooded sweatshirt. (Suddenly she could see the flyer in her mind's eye as clear as a digital image.) With the perv right there, she couldn't clue Jerome in that, with the exception of the color of the sweatshirt, this creep accurately fit the fucking description!

But Jerome didn't need all those facts. He was a man's man. A Super Bowl MVP. He could knock this scrawny twerp's lights out with one tackle, and Sydney knew he would if the perv tried anything fishy. Feeling confident with Jerome covering her, she looked right into the perv's face as she passed him on her way to the piss search. Fit the description *and* he looked like the sketch!

Just as she suspected, the corner turned up dry. She was about to shout, "Call the cops!" when she looked through the ground-floor window and saw that the two little girls who lived there were asleep, curled up on the couch in the den, illuminated only by the flicker of the flat-screen TV, which was still playing *Shrek*.

This guy wasn't a pervert, Sydney thought, her entire body shaking with rage. He was a pedophile! She turned and, lunging at him with the abandon of a beach volleyball player, shrieked, "Motherfucker!!!"

Before he swung the gate open and bolted down the street, Sydney managed to scratch his face, and as her bare knees slammed onto the concrete (*This is why I always wear pants, Mitzi!*), she looked at her bloody fingers, proudly thinking, *You can run but you can't hide. I've got your DNA, babyfucker!* Her senses were heightened to such bionic proportions that as she rolled into the flower bed, she kept her triumphant hand raised to save the evidence from contamination.

"Sydney!" Jerome shouted, kneeling beside her in the dirt. "You're bleeding!"

"So what!" Sydney shrieked, pushing him back. "Go after him, idiot! He's getting away!" Deducing that he had no survival skills—did he need a fucking playbook to know what to do?—she scrambled to her feet, scooped her whistle out of the dirt, kicked off her heels, ripped the impaled hem of her Diane von Furstenberg dress off the gate, and took off. "Call 911!" she shouted at Jerome as she dashed into the street. "Call 911!"

The perv was already halfway down the block, but like the idiot he had to be, he was running in the middle of the street, and under the streetlights, that white sweatshirt looked like a neon sign. Carried on pure adrenaline, Sydney raced after him, barefoot, making better time than a Kenyan marathon runner, her blown-out tresses and shredded chiffon dress flapping behind her. When she stuck the soiled whistle in her mouth, her instinctual memory reminded her of what she'd done wrong before and this time it emitted a clear, high-pitched SOS. "Perry Street Pervert!" she screamed when she came up for air. She saw lights flicking on, windows being raised. "Perry Street Pervert! Perry Street Pervert!" Then she took another gulp of air and went back to blowing.

Just as the perv hung a left and headed toward Perry Street, a guy ran down the stairs of the house on the corner wearing a bathrobe and carrying a bat. "That way!" Sydney said, pointing the vigilante in the right direction. Then she stooped over and rested her hands on her bloodied knees, as if she and the guy were running a relay race and she had just handed him the baton. Adrenaline could carry her only so far, and she wanted to plop down right there in the street to take a breather, but Babe Ruth, who looked like he'd just woken up and wasn't sure if he was sleepwalking or not, couldn't be trusted. She dragged herself to the corner and watched him, gathering enough lung power to shout, "White sweatshirt!"

She saw him tackle the perv from behind the way Jerome should have done, and then they began wrestling on the ground. A few other guys who couldn't have had any idea what was going on seemed to appear out of nowhere, having picked up the scent of violence, and joined in the beatdown. One picked up the vigilante's bat and started randomly hitting people with it.

"Are you all right?" Sydney heard a man's voice say, and feeling his hand on her shoulder, she flinched. It was a guy she recognized from her building, and she saw other familiar faces from the block surrounding her, all staring uncomfortably as though she might be in need of a rape kit, but no one wanted to know for sure. Trying to gather strength just to speak, she fell against the closest car, setting off a piercing alarm, which, under normal circumstances, would have made her jump out of her skin. Now, with police sirens drawing closer and the melee raging out of control, it just added another layer to the frenzied atmosphere and, completely drained, she had no reaction at all. Limply lifting her arm, she motioned toward the pile of fighting men and, between gasps, said, "Go . . . get him . . . the one . . . in the robe." Then she spotted the bat-wielding vigilante squirming at the bottom of the pile, his robe splayed open. He was naked underneath. "Wait," she tried to yell, pushing away the woman who stayed behind to tend to her. "He's not . . ." Her voice faded to a strangled whisper. ". . . the perv."

The cop cars screeched up, causing the brawlers to scatter, and Sydney saw Jerome walking toward her, looking no worse for the wear (other than his dirty trousers). He scooped her up in his big, strong arms like some kind of action hero and carried her to the nearest stoop, where he cradled her like a baby, brushing tangled strands of hair out of her sweaty, makeup-smeared face.

"Now," he said in the softest voice imaginable, "you're *my* hero."

CHAPTER FORTY-EIGHT

He didn't know, Sydney kept telling herself. Jerome had no idea that a pervert was on the loose in the neighborhood. If he'd had any idea, he would have come to her rescue, no question. *This is what you do,* she told herself. *You find reasons to write people off.* Friends sometimes, but mostly men. She didn't even have a clear idea why, really. To ditch them before they had a chance to ditch her? Because she found relationships so emotionally taxing? Whatever the reason, she couldn't do it this time. Not to Jerome. He was everything she'd said she wanted. She just prayed that he still wanted her.

After he'd told her that she was his hero (a line she wasn't buying), she'd managed a small smile, but she really wanted to cry. Their wonderful, joyous, perfect night had come to such a bizarre end, she didn't know if she'd ever see him again. (That sweet moment with little Tyson from Georgia, when it felt like everything was going to work out and work out perfectly, seemed to have happened a decade ago.) He'd waited while the EMS people cleaned up her bruises, but she could tell he was itching to get out of there. Especially after the EMS guy asked to take a picture with him on his camera phone. And the moment they were done bandaging her, he made tracks. He didn't want to have his name in the papers, he said, which Sydney understood because neither did she. But as the only eyewitness, she had to go to the precinct and file a report to make sure the pig got locked up. That was all the reward she wanted, so to deflect attention from herself, she had given most of the credit to the bat-wielding vigilante, who was more than happy to take it. The guy, as it turned out, was perfectly cast for the role of the hero. (His name was Rob Benedetto and he was a twenty-eight-year-old kickboxing instructor at Crunch.) After all the preening and exaggerating he'd done down at the station, Sydney was sure posing for the cover of tomorrow's *Post* wearing his blood-soaked bathrobe with his splintered bat cocked over his shoulder would be the high point of an otherwise uneventful life. Though, unlike most men who liked to think they were capable of heroics but never had to put that theory to the test, Rob Benedetto had actually answered the call and come out swinging. He'd earned his moment in the sun, Sydney thought. And intent on letting him have it all to himself, she snuck out of the back of the precinct after a kind lady cop tipped her off that the photogs camped out front really wanted a picture of *the woman* who'd nabbed the Perry Street pervert.

Then, at 2:35 A.M., just as she was slipping into a cab, her phone rang and the name Mitzi Berman flashed on the screen. Jesus, she thought. As if she hadn't been through enough for one night? The last thing Jerome had said to her was "I'll call you." (She was sitting in the back of the ambulance and he was heading back to his Bentley, the stark symbolism of which said it all, she'd thought.) And now look what he'd gone and done. He'd called Mitzi instead. (That or Mitzi had a police scanner.)

Filled with a sense of foreboding, Sydney watched Mitzi's name flashing on the screen, thinking how rare it was to recognize a life-changing moment as it happened. Did Jerome think she was a psycho? *Probably.* Had he been totally, unforgivably, humiliated? *Hopefully not.* Would he ever want to see her again? *Please, please, please, please . . .* She was going to have to face the truth sooner or later, so she clicked Talk feeling like she was ripping a Band-Aid off fast.

"Well, thank you," Mitzi said.

Thank you? That unexpectedly fortuitous opening caused Sydney's hopes to soar, and for a moment she stopped thinking about how quickly she could get her hands on some Vicodin. Jerome *did* think she was a she-ro! He was in love with her. He wanted to marry her and father her children! Then the part of her brain that was always on the lookout for catastrophe made her ask, "Thank you for what?"

"Jerome told me to find him a white woman!" Mitzi crowed, as if she was delivering the punch line to a dirty joke.

Sydney didn't remember opening her mouth or her hand—for a second everything faded to black—but she must have done both because she heard an ear-rattling wail of "Nooooo!" echo through the cab, and when she looked down, her phone was hitting the dirty rubber floor mat.

"Everything all right?" the driver said, turning halfway around. "You okay?"

"No!" she screamed again, at him, ducking down to pick up the phone. "I am not okay!" Before she got the phone to her ear, she could hear Mitzi squawking. ". . . chased a pervert down the street? Barefoot? Are you deranged?" Then she said, "Don't answer that."

"What was I supposed to do?" Sydney wailed. "Let him get away?"

"YES!" Mitzi barked, that singular response packed with more fury than Sydney had ever heard from her (and she'd heard plenty). "It was either Jerome Bailey or the pervert, and you chose the pervert." She stopped yelling and dialed down to her normal level of snarkiness. "When he gets out, I hope you two are very happy together."

"Please, Mitzi," Sydney pleaded, her battered body trembling from the cumulative physical, emotional, and psychological trauma of the whole night. "Please. You have to help me."

"You need help," Mitzi said. "But not any that I can give."

"We were perfect for each other," Sydney said, rubbing her nose on the front of her ruined dress, which was now no better than a paper towel. "We *are* perfect for each other. I know we are! We're gonna share our world! He promised to be here!" She began to sob so hard she could barely breathe, her words coming out in incoherent burps. "Whenever . . . leave never . . . ooh . . . la . . . la . . ." She sobbed for a few seconds then, like a car puttering out of gas, muttered a final, defeated "La."

"Now I don't even know what you're talking about," Mitzi said. "Not that I ever did. This is what I'm saying. You need help. Do the world a favor and get some."

Thinking about how excited she'd been three hours ago to call Mitzi and report back on how great everything had gone (up to that point), Sydney realized how much Mitzi's approval meant, and she felt more pathetic for even caring. "Every . . . every . . . everything," she said, not sure if a word or vomit was going to come out after each gasp, "was going great until . . ."

"Until you decided to *emasculate* him," Mitzi snapped, completely unsympathetic to Sydney's fragile emotional state. "And how you managed to do that to an NFL linebacker is one for the books. You should call Guinness!"

Mitzi's flippancy did Sydney the favor of turning her overwhelming despair into anger, an emotion she handled like a soft, fragrant security blanket. "I'm gonna call *him*!" she threatened, pissed that Mitzi had gotten her into this mess and was now hanging her out to dry.

"You have his number?"

"Um, no," Sydney said, rethinking her tone. "But you do."

"Ha!" Mitzi scoffed. "Last place you're gonna get it!"

"Give it to me," Sydney said evenly.

"You had him," Mitzi said. "You had him on the hook and you threw him back."

"He said that? He said he was hooked?" Grasping for any sign of redemption, Sydney pleaded, "Tell me exactly what he said!"

"That he wants a white woman!" Mitzi told her again, driving the stake deeper into Sydney's shattering heart. "So thanks again for that. Makes my life a whole lot easier. I'll have him engaged to a white woman before sundown!"

"No! Don't! Stop!" Sydney said, reduced to desperate, monosyllabic utterances.

"Hey," Mitzi said. "I can lead a horse to café au lait, but I can't make him drink if he wants whole milk!"

This woman was cold-blooded, Sydney thought, listening to Mitzi's demented cackle. She wished she could just hang up on her and never speak to her again, but that would mean giving up on Jerome, something she wasn't prepared to do.

"Hold on a sec," Sydney said, trying to sound friendly in her jacked-up state. "I'm pulling up to my building." She pressed the phone against her shoulder as she rummaged through her clutch for money, wincing when she found a new sore spot. "Actually, lemme call you right back."

"It's three o'clock in the morning," Mitzi said. "Don't call me back tonight. Don't call me back *ever*. And don't try to call Jerome Bailey either. Call a psychiatrist. You need one. Desperately."

Mitzi hung up, and Sydney sat in the cab with one bare, bandaged leg hanging out of the open door, the sobs coming in tidal waves, until the driver helped her out, pried the twenty out of her hand, and left her on the stoop, where she sobbed and sobbed and sobbed until Candi came home from a long, lucrative night of stripping and helped her upstairs.

CHAPTER FORTY-NINE

Jerome was the perfect man for her. Jerome was her soul mate. She could quit working because Jerome made enough money to support them comfortably. Forever. And if your work wasn't your passion and money was no object, what was the point? She'd sign a prenup. She'd insist on it. She didn't want his money. That needed to be clear. She'd even have a wedding. She'd do that. For Jerome. She'd make that sacrifice. She'd had dreams about him. Carrying her over the threshold. Then ripping her dress off and fucking the shit out of her. She'd masturbated thinking about him. What his huge, black NFL cock would feel like inside of her. She could never be an NFL wife, but Jerome was retiring next year. It was all so perfect. They'd have time to travel. That's why work was out and kids would have to wait. They needed time to be alone. As a couple. She'd always wanted to go on safari. There was a great one in Johannesburg. Maybe for the honeymoon? Jerome traveled constantly for work. He'd be a good travel companion. And with him taking care of things, she could invest the little nest egg she'd been saving to buy an apartment. She wouldn't need one now. Jerome lived in New Jersey. Saddle River. In a huge house. Five bedrooms. Great place to raise kids. And she could do the suburban thing. She preferred it to city pretensions. She'd rather chow down on a table full of nibbles at the Cheesecake Factory than nibble on a twenty-eight-dollar quarter-sized crab cake at Quo. But she'd learn how to cook, play wifey. That would endear her to the family. They'd be country for sure, but they were in North Carolina, so that could be tolerated. They'd accept her because she was "of color," because she had full lips and hips, because she had a good job (for now) and good hair. And she knew how to hang, how to *talk the talk,* when she got around some folks. If she was forced to visit, she'd bring Jeffrey. And she'd keep everyone far, far away from her mother. What had happened wasn't Jerome's fault. It was her fault. Completely. She'd make it up to him. Anyhow, any way. Now all she had to do was get his number. Mitzi hadn't returned any of her calls. Should she call his agent and leave a message? It had only been a few weeks. Maybe he'd call her. Maybe he'd been thinking about it; maybe he wanted to. But he'd have to get her number from Mitzi. Then Mitzi would talk him out of calling her. *Cockblocking bitch!* That's why she needed to call his agent and leave her number! So if he wanted to call her, he could.

"Okay, we need to stop."

"Oh, already?" Sydney glanced at her watch. "I wanted to talk about freezing my eggs, but I guess—"

"Sydney, I'm very glad to hear that you made a connection with someone," Liessel said. "But it was only one date."

"It was a *perfect* date," Sydney said, bristling. "I mean, you hear people all the time say, 'The first time I met him, I just knew.'" Liessel didn't offer any gesture of acknowledgment, so Sydney said, "You *have* heard people say that, haven't you?" Liessel nodded. "Well, now I'm one of those people!"

"Didn't you say you were sleeping with someone else?"

"*Who?*"

"I don't know. Matt? Was that his name?"

"Max?" Sydney asked, as though she wasn't quite sure herself.

"Yes," Liessel said. "Where does Max fit into this?"

"He doesn't."

"So you slept with him because . . ."

"He was around. But he gave me herpes. I told you that, right?"

"Herpes?" Liessel said, recoiling as if it were airborne.

"On my lip," Sydney said dismissively. "It went away. It was horrible, though." She stared at her restlessly tapping foot for a few seconds. "And it might have been possible that I actually got it from my stripper next-door neighbor because the day after I accused him of giving it to me I saw some shady shit on her lip and a tube of Abreva in her bag . . . but whatever. He's nobody!"

"Well," Liessel said, setting aside her yellow legal pad. "I think this is a real breakthrough for you."

Sydney reached down for her bag. "You do?"

"Yes. You called to make a real appointment. To talk, not just for pills. You signed up with this matchmaker, which really took you outside your comfort zone. And then something wonderful came of it. You met a man you really liked, a man who allowed you to get in touch with things you've been avoiding."

"Avoiding?" Sydney said. "Things like what?"

"Like your deep need to be taken care of. To be vulnerable." Liessel bent forward, resting her forearms on her thighs. "And I think this man, Jerome, because he's a famous football player, a man who dwarfs you physically, who outearns you tenfold, because he's a . . ." Liessel swirled her hand in the air, searching for the right phrasing. "A *paragon of masculinity* of almost mythical proportions, a man young boys worship as a hero . . ." She went deeper into her Freudian crouch and gave Sydney that deep, soul-searching shrink look. "I think that allowed you to feel girlish for once. And I think you liked it. I think you liked it a lot."

While listening to that succinct analysis, Sydney had frowned, she'd cringed, she'd smirked. Now she was nodding. Maybe Liessel wasn't so useless after all. Where had all this insight been for the last few years?

"So whether or not you ever see this man again, I think the experience has done wonders for you." Liessel picked up a business card that was on the end table next to her. "You should continue this discussion." She raised up from her leather armchair, handing the card to Sydney. "With Dr. Fieve."

She sat back down and placed both forearms on the chair's armrests as though she was preparing for turbulence. "He's taking my patient load."

Patient load? Sydney didn't like the way that sounded. Were Liessel's patients a pile of shit this Dr. Fieve person was being made to clean up? "Where are you going?" Sydney said, fingering the card. "I mean, what are we even talking about here?"

"I'm taking an extended hiatus."

Sydney stared at Liessel, trying to decode that purposely ambiguous statement, but she'd need more to go on than that. "What for? You're not that old. You can't be retiring."

"It's a personal matter."

"What are you, sick?"

"No, no, no," Liessel said, quick to shoot that down.

"So you're dumping me?" After two years of badgering, she finally decided to open up to this stupid twat, and that's it, *sayonara?*

"It's not like that," Liessel said, sliding forward in her chair to get all "But I care about you, I do." "I'm not seeing *any* patients anymore."

Sydney knew it wasn't like that. She'd just said that to make the bitch feel guilty. And watching Liessel twist in her chair, it was obvious she had succeeded. If she was going to have this conversation with every one of her patients, you'd think she would have a better speech prepared.

"What personal matter?" Sydney pressed. "Now that you're not my doctor anymore you can tell me, right?"

"I'd rather not." Liessel pulled out an invoice from underneath her legal pad and held it out toward Sydney. "Your insurance pays eighty percent, but you still have a balance due."

Sydney touched the paper and it was as if Liessel's big secret was transmitted to her through a flash of kinetic energy. "Omigod," she gasped, her free hand rushing to cover her mouth. "You're marrying him!"

"Well . . ." Liessel said, but she couldn't even come out with it. She just made a reluctant admission with a shrug.

Sydney blasted to her feet. "How could you!"

"Sydney, what do you mean?" Liessel said, suppressing nervous laughter. "This is my life. Dr. Fieve is very—"

"Leave Fieve out of it! This is about you." She glanced absently at the invoice. "So this is what you do, huh? Take the money and run?"

"You don't owe very much, Sydney, but it's your responsibility—"

Sydney ripped the invoice in half, then into fourths, and tossed the torn shards into the air like jumbo pieces of confetti. "I'm not talking about the invoice, lady. I'm talking about you marrying that pig!"

Liessel watched the paper float down to the beige carpet. "Wait, you're not . . ." She looked up at Sydney. "You're not going to pay that?"

"Get your fucking sugar daddy to pay it!" She stood in front of Liessel with her hands on her hips, her chest heaving with outrage. "You do realize his second wife was institutionalized for a year after she left him. And I don't know what the statute of limitations is for murder, but I'm not buying that the first wife died under mysterious circumstances. As far as I'm concerned, he's still a suspect!"

"Sydney," Liessel sighed. "That's just . . ."

Sydney bent down and yelled in her face. "It's all in *Vanity Fair,* baby! *It's all in* Vanity Fair!"

"This is a personal decision I've made," Liessel said, speaking to Sydney's back as she paced toward the window. "And the balance due is your responsibility."

Sydney spun around and wagged her finger at her forty-something, Harvard-educated, billionaire-betrothed psychiatrist as if the woman were a disobedient child. "You have *some nerve* talking to me about responsibility. Where's your responsibility? To your fucking patients!"

"This has nothing to do with you or how I feel about my patients."

"It has everything to do with us!" Sydney bellowed, her arms flying up as though she were riding a roller coaster at Six Flags. "You spend all this time and money going to Harvard! So you can help people. Then you throw it all away for the first rich slob that comes along?" She paced back to the window and stared down onto Fifth Avenue, rambling to herself in a pained whisper. "I mean, I read 'Page Six.' I knew you were dating this asshole. But then I hadn't heard anything. I thought maybe you'd broken up. I hoped you had." She turned back to Liessel, voicing her accusation clearly. "I gave you the benefit of the doubt. You're supposed to be a blank slate. Do you think people feel comfortable talking to you about their mundane money problems when they know you spend the holidays in Saint Barth's hobnobbing with celebrities on your billionaire boyfriend's yacht?" Sydney fell back into the chair. "Do you?"

"Well, I think—"

"They don't!" Liessel was not only betraying her patients, she was betraying her own womanhood! But there was a silver lining to this, Sydney thought. She was bound to quit seeing Liessel sooner or later, but this turn of events allowed her to say everything she'd been wanting to say since she'd seen that first item in "Page Six." And since this was the end-all session, Liessel was going to hear it whether she wanted to or not! "Do you think women feel comfortable taking advice from you when they know you're screwing a ruthless pig who had armed guards throw his fourth wife out of her house five days before the prenup expired?"

"I'd say there are a lot of people who come to me for exactly that reason."

That comment gave Sydney pause. Was Liessel actually trying to defend her indefensible position? "Oh, so you're saying rich people come to you because you can feel their pain?"

"Something like that."

"Then why not continue seeing your rich, screwed-up patients? Why quit?"

"Because . . ."

Sydney pounced on Liessel's hesitation and finished the sentence for her. "He wants you to."

Liessel looked down at the carpet, and Sydney settled back into the chair, happily thinking, *I win*. She'd spoken up for all the patients this weak excuse for a woman was abandoning, emotional invalids who probably wanted to say exactly what she'd said but wouldn't dare. And looking at Liessel, hunched over, broken, and ashamed—as she should be for whoring herself out to a man she'd have to hope would only emotionally and verbally abuse her but not kill her like he had his first wife (allegedly)—Sydney felt more sorry for the woman than anything.

But as she reached into her bag to grab her checkbook and be done with her once and for all, Sydney realized she'd claimed victory too soon. Glancing up, she was startled (and somewhat frightened) to see that Liessel's usual mask of detached politeness had been reconfigured into an expression that eerily resembled that of a crazed Chucky doll.

"Believe whatever you need to believe," she said, headshrinking to the bitter end. "But we only hate in others what we hate in ourselves."

CHAPTER FIFTY

S ydney was baffled as to how she'd wound up at Nobu on a date with a sixty-three-year-old man who said he'd been divorced after thirty-three years, the same length of time she had been alive. Then Bachelor Number Three told her his full name, and when she put this together with his earlier statement that he was "in retail," the full understanding of who this man was, in the larger context of the world, momentarily rendered her speechless.

"Harvey Cooper," she said after she'd sucked the beans out of two pieces of edamame and thrown the lifeless shells in the bowl on the table. "As in . . ."

It was evidently a query he was used to answering. "Yes," he said evenly.

"Well," Sydney said, rearranging her napkin. She almost said "Wow," which was what she was thinking, but she didn't want him to think she was impressed by money and social status. (She was annoyed that she'd even *thought* "Wow" because that was clear evidence to the contrary.)

She knew something fishy was going on the moment Fiona called and told her that Mitzi had decided to give her another chance. But this would be her third time at bat.

And hadn't Mitzi been adamant that she didn't even do seconds? Je-rome was clearly an affirmative action setup, but Harvey Cooper didn't seem like the type who'd request "an exotic." (And if he was, that was seri-ously suspect.)

Sydney wanted to tell Fiona to permanently delete her from Mitzi's database because she honestly didn't want another shot. Contracting that disgusting herpes sore after letting Max touch her one time couldn't have been a bigger hint from the universe that she needed to fall back and regroup. And that was what she'd decided to do. She was through with men! She was done with dating! She'd taken a vow of celibacy!

But who could pass up an invitation to devour Nobu's creamy rock shrimp and melt-in-your mouth black cod, especially on someone else's dime? It wasn't like she had anything better to do this Saturday night. Max had been permanently jettisoned, she wasn't speaking to Jeffrey or Liz at the moment, her secondary gays were prepping for the Pride Parade, her useless therapist had dropped her, Dr. Fieve turned out to be a dick, and she was still on indefinite hold for The Big Interview with the crazy tranny so she didn't even have any pointless celebrity fluff pieces to fill her lonely days and nights. She'd become so desperate for companionship that she'd spent the whole day yesterday on her couch with Stripper Candi watching a marathon of *I Love New York 2*, a second-generation wack reality show that was only slightly more pathetic than her life (if one could call it that) in its current incarnation.

When she'd arrived at Nobu 57, wearing a simply chic black dress, discounted Mizrahi slingbacks, and a basic makeup job (no mascara), she asked the gentleman at the table she was sent to if there had been some mistake. It wasn't that he was a total geezer. He was moderately attractive, with a full head of only slightly graying brown hair. From what she could see in his seated position, he was relatively fit. Not too wrinkly. His dark suit was impeccably tailored (but knowing what she knew now, that made sense). If she'd had an older guy fantasy, he'd do. Too bad she didn't.

In an effort to clear up the confusion, he had explained that he'd asked to be set up with women "in a certain age range," as he put it. "Women who still wanted to have children," he'd said awkwardly. "Maybe that explains it?"

Sure, Sydney thought. That explained everything. From his end. Despite his careful wording, what he was really looking for was a woman who "could" have a family. Women with viable wombs. Breeders. There were plenty of forty- or fifty-year-old women who "wanted" children, but it would be difficult if not impossible to do that naturally. And if you were paying good money, why get defective merchandise? She almost leaned across the table and screamed, "My womb's not for sale, Grandpa!" but she was so glad she hadn't lost her cool. Because there was a story here, she realized. And Harvey Cooper was the ultimate "get."

"So are you a customer?" he said between bites of the rock shrimp, which he managed to eat without smearing the creamy sauce all over his mouth the way Sydney always did.

Something about being referred to as one of his "customers" made this already awkward arrangement even more so. It was as if he were a hooker asking to "service" her. But deciding to suck up to him a little before she made her interview request, Sydney said, "Frequent as of late. I know a doorman who works there."

"Really? Who is that?"

"He's just a doorman. You wouldn't know him."

"Every employee is important in his or her unique capacity," he said as if he was quoting from an employee manual that had "Harveys is an equal opportunity employer" printed on the back. "I make it a point to know my employees by name. Tony?"

"No, um . . ." Realizing whatever unsavory practices Max used to get her 70 percent off would probably get him fired, she caught herself before she implicated him. "Someone else." And then she quickly got off the subject. "So when is that new women's floor going to be open?"

"Next month. We're very excited about it. Are you?"

"Me?" Sydney said, distracted by thoughts of how green with envy Chad, that pompous fuck, would be when the *Cachet* exposé she wrote about the loony matchmaker who supplied wives to powerful men, including a very well-known (but in the piece, unnamed) retail chairman, was optioned by Paramount *for millions*!

"You said you were a customer," Harvey said, slicing his yellowtail. "I always like to hear from my customers."

Sydney had plenty to say about how the store could be improved; she'd had a long discussion with Max about that not too long ago. And knowing that she was not trying to date Harvey Cooper but rather to score an interview with him, she felt freed from the coquettish shackles Mitzi had somehow brainwashed her into thinking she needed to win a man over. "Well, you know how the women's department is going to be on the top floor? And you have all the luxury accessories on the ground floor?"

Harvey nodded. "Yes."

"Well, that placement is completely backward. I mean really, just all wrong!"

"Is it?" Harvey said, taken aback. "Tell me why."

"It bags are like crack for the fashionable lady of means."

"Crack," Harvey repeated, either because he wasn't familiar with such a low-class drug or because he didn't like his merch being compared to it. Or both?

"Hard drugs," Sydney said. "It bags are like an addiction. And an addict will go anywhere to score."

"Right," Harvey said, ignoring his yellowtail as he tried to understand where this was going.

"Your store," Sydney said, thinking that sounded more deferential than saying "Harvey's," "is one of the few places where I can get an authentic Marc Jacobs. But if that's what I'm there to get, I want to get in and out. In and out!"

"Why is that?" Harvey said with genuine concern. "Wouldn't you browse?"

"Browse?" What a silly question, Sydney thought. And a perfect example of how out of touch CEOs were with the masses and why they were all begging for bailouts! Realizing she was going to have to lay this out for the old man in detail, she took a breath and tried to keep it simple. "I don't browse, Harvey, because we're in a depression."

"Yes," Harvey said gravely, receiving those words like a cancer diagnosis. "Of course."

"Even if I have a grand to spare, who the hell do I think I am to spend it on *a purse*? What kind of person does that make me? Forget about *buying* it. I'm disgusted with myself for even *wanting* it. I shouldn't be within a hundred blocks of your store. But I am."

"Because you're an addict."

Sydney smiled. "You got it."

"But this is a recent phenomenon," Harvey ventured hopefully as Sydney took a break from their lesson to inhale her yellowtail.

"Well, I think most women feel that way now because the situation is so dire and we keep hearing about it everywhere. Did you see that *Times* piece last week about women asking for plain shopping bags when they buy things at expensive stores?"

Harvey nodded. "We might go that route. Temporarily."

"You should. Budget is the new black. But I've always felt guilty about buying expensive things for myself. I think a lot of women do."

Harvey pushed his plate aside and leaned toward Sydney. "But why? You work hard for your money."

"Okay, let me stop you right there," Sydney said. "Just hearing you *say* that makes me feel guilty because, in my case, it's not true. I *don't* work hard for my money. I got my job writing for *Cachet* because they were about to get hit with a huge discrimination suit. I'm sure you've heard about it. And I could write those stories in my sleep. So, for me, that's part of it."

"But it's not as if you're stealing the money," Harvey said.

"Feels that way sometimes. But that's just me."

"But why do women feel guilty for spending the money they've earned?"

"Because women are socialized to give, not get." The black cod arrived and, taking her first bite, Sydney almost forgot Harvey was there. She wanted to have another immediately, but Harvey was staring at her, ignoring his food, forcing her to do the same for the moment. "And, look, I know I've been brainwashed to believe that I need *things* to be happy. Expensive things that I see fetishized in magazines, in ads, in movies, everywhere I look. It's all a trick. I know it's a trick. Still, I fall for it. After a while it starts to feel like a trick I'm playing on myself. And why, Harvey? *Why?*"

"Because this is America. We're consumers. That's what we do. We consume."

"And look where it's gotten us," Sydney said. "This is as good a time as any for us to question what we consume and why. I mean, every year I clean out my closets and give bags of stuff, half of it unworn, to Goodwill. And then I go back and buy more. It's an addiction. That's my point."

"Would I be an enabler if I asked you to finish telling me why our product placement is totally backward? I don't think we ever got to that."

"An enabler? Harvey, you're the main supplier! You're the kingpin!" Harvey smiled and Sydney smiled back because she could tell she had this interview in the bag and her exposé was going to be fire! *Take that, Chad!* "But, yes, I'll lay it out for you anyway. I'll tell you how you can get me completely strung out."

"Superb."

"Okay, by putting the it bags by the door, you're letting me get away. You've gotta get me up to nine, Harvey!"

"So you're suggesting we put luxury bags on nine?" Harvey said, suddenly sounding miffed. "We can't do that."

Trying to gauge how far she should push this, Sydney asked, "Why is that?"

"High-end handbags, scarves, jewelry, items that can be easily and elegantly displayed, leave a visceral impression. We're a luxury store. Those items signify luxury. As soon as a customer walks in, that's what she should see."

"Fine. Keep those things there," Sydney said, as if the decision were up to her. "But maybe you put some of the bags up on nine. The ones that are most in demand. Because if I'm jonesing for a Jacobs, I'll go up to nine and crawl on the floor of a dusty stockroom if I have to. And once I'm up there, I'll see the other, lower-priced merch and wind up buying something else. Guaranteed."

"But you're already feeling so guilty about your splurge. Might you go for a lower-priced bag instead of the Jacobs?"

"Instead of? Never. In addition to? Probably."

"Really . . ."

"An addict is an addict. I still need my fix."

"But that means you're spending more money."

"Does an addict think straight? But I also wouldn't rock my MJ on a daily basis."

"No?"

"Nah. I save that for when I have a whole look together."

"So how many bags do you use? In a week's time, say."

"I usually have three or four in heavy rotation. All serving different purposes. I wouldn't carry suede if it looks like rain. I have a jumbo Devi Kroell for Target tote that I use for carrying my laptop. A small black Balenciaga"— that she'd never admit to a luxury goods purveyor was a fake—"if I'm traveling light. And I have a bunch of ninety-nine-cent reusable totes that I use until they fall apart. Whole Foods really changed the game with that."

Harvey gave that a ponder. "Huh."

"So why don't you test it out?" Sydney said. "Put some of the most sought-after bags up on nine." Struck by a new twist on her idea, Sydney leaned across the table and used one of the moves she'd read about in Mitzi's book: the tap. She pressed her fingers, lightly and quickly, on top of Harvey's hand and said, "I know! Maybe there's a secret room. And when women come asking for the bag, that's where they go. It'll make people feel like they're in a very chic little club!" Harvey pondered too long this time and Sydney thought she'd lost him. "So what do you think?"

"I think we should discuss this further," Harvey said. "Next Saturday? Are you free?"

CHAPTER FIFTY-ONE

The gay roundtable was convened at Cafeteria for a long-overdue brunch, and as soon as Billy, a MAC salesclerk by day, a cabaret performer known as Miss Billie by night, sat down, he jumped headlong into the gossip session already in progress. "It's so Michael Douglas/Catherine Zeta-Jones!"

"It's so Donald/Melania," said Andre J., the famed cross-dresser whom Sydney had met at Sacred Center, Liz's gay church, the same month he'd appeared on the cover of French *Vogue*.

"It's so Rupert Murdoch/Wendi Deng," Raphael, a style expert who'd just gotten his own makeover show on Oxygen, chimed in.

"It's so Jack Nicholson/Lara Flynn Boyle," said Phillipe, a gorge graphic designer.

Sydney paused midchew, mumbling, "You really pulled that one outta your ass!"

"I know," Rafe said, looking miffed that his longtime partner had played the worst hand in their little parlor game. "Isn't one of them *dead*?"

"Okay," Phillipe said. "It's so . . . Jack Nicholson/Rebecca Broussard."

Billy looked around with confusion. "Rebecca who?"

"The baby mama," Sydney said, giving Phillipe a high five for citing that obscure celebrity coupling. "Nice one!"

Realizing the round robin had circled back to him, Billy said, "It's so Harrison/Calista."

Then Rafe cracked everyone up with the best "It's so" yet. "It's so Ashton/Demi!"

When the laughter died down and Sydney had wiped away the bit of egg she'd spit on Phillipe's plate, he pressed for specifics. "What did you talk about?"

"The store," Sydney said. "I laid out, in detail, how he could better capitalize on women's twisted relationship to luxury goods. He was enthralled."

That was the only part of this conversation that was based in any reality, but she was letting the boys make their own inferences. Although the date-turned-marketing meeting seemed to be a turn-on for old Harvey (who was clearly a workaholic with limited social skills and almost no dating experience, certainly not in any recent millennium), the only thing Sydney wanted from him was an interview. But she loved seeing her gays gag over the idea that she was dating a rich, powerful retail magnate. So let them. The public humiliations she'd suffered at the hands of Mitzi Berman had allowed her to see how romantically challenged everyone really thought she was. And she didn't like being seen as a failure at anything. Even love. This unexpected hookup with Harvey Cooper (Mitzi's motives were still murky) was doing wonders to shore up her image, and within a day this beneficial morsel of gossip would have filtered through the entire downtown gay community (which was where all juicy New York gossip ultimately sourced back to). And then in a few weeks or so Sydney would convene another brunch to announce that she'd *dumped* Harvey Cooper and she'd forever be known as a legendary feminista fatale!

"So," Rafe asked excitedly, "are you going to see him again?"

"Saturday," Sydney triumphantly announced.

"Saturday?" Andre scoffed. "Doesn't he know that's the night you stay in?"

"He's sixty-three," Sydney said. "He was married for over thirty years. He knows nothing about current social mores."

"Hold on," Rafe said, looking around. "Where's Jeffrey?"

"Jeffrey and I aren't speaking right now," Sydney said, getting the full attention of the scandal-craving table.

"Uh-oh," Phillipe said. "What happened?"

"Nothing," Sydney said, salting her eggs. "He doesn't have time for me anymore. He's too busy with Hector. And Frida."

Andre came back to the conversation after he'd gotten up to take a picture with two "fans." "Wait," he said, his huge blaxploitation-era Afro shimmying like Jell-O, "what are we talking about?"

"Jeffrey and Sydney aren't speaking," Rafe reported before looking back down to Sydney's end of the table. "Now, who is Hector? And who else did you say? Fifi?"

"Frida! Their new dog. Jeffrey and his Latin lover of two weeks got a dog together. It's outrageous!"

"Hector?" Phillipe said. "That's Jeffrey's dog groomer. We use him too."

Pushing the bread away, Sydney showed little interest in the profession of the man for whom she'd been dumped. "Oh, is that what he does?"

"They're dating?" Phillipe said. "He doesn't seem like Jeffrey's type."

"I know, right?" Sydney said, now *very* interested in the topic. "He's so short. *So* not Jeffrey's type. But they got a dog together. It must be love."

"Wait a second," Billy said. "So you didn't invite Jeffrey to brunch just because he has a new boyfriend? Um, hi, hater!"

"I didn't invite him," Sydney shot back, "because he never calls me anymore." She waved her fork at him. "Bye, hater!"

"Who cares if Jeffrey dumped you," Rafe said. "You've got Harvey now, girl!"

"Think of all the goodies that could be yours," Andre, the biggest fashion hound of the bunch, swooned.

"Okay, forget about Harvey and Jeffrey for a moment," Billy said. "What's the deal with The Raven?"

"Still waiting for the call." Sydney stood up, removed the newsboy cap she was wearing to hide her horse hair, and let it spill out for the full amusement and worship of her gays. "But I got my Cherokee look down!"

Andre screamed, alarming the people at the next table, and ran over to pet it. "Extensions by Christian!"

Sydney squirmed under his grasping touch. "How did you know?"

"I'd know his work anywhere," Andre said. "Can I have them when he takes them out?"

"They're yours," Sydney said, thinking that seemed kind of gross. She plopped the hat back on as a sign to Andre that he should go back to his seat and stop stroking her. "It's like having an unwanted pet. Who sleeps on your head. All day."

"Whose phone is that?" Phillipe said, looking annoyed. "It's so loud!"

Sydney heard the annoying salsa ring that she'd assigned to the most annoying person in her life and pulled the phone from her coat pocket. "It's Gareth," she said. "Calling me on a Sunday. That can only mean one thing . . ."

"Aw, shit," Andre said. "It's on!"

CHAPTER FIFTY-TWO

Tall and incredibly lithe, The Raven had almost no bodily hair other than a sumptuous black mane that looked very much like the two pounds of costly weave Sydney was toting around (except The Raven's wasn't matted). When she'd gotten her first up-close glimpse of the artist formerly known as Randy Lee, Sydney was stunned to see the subtle "work" that had transformed him into a stunning female diva as beautifully groomed as any. And a diva (s)he was.

For the first four days, the subject of Sydney's in-depth cover story had only communicated with her through Anya, her publicist intermediary, and none of the terse, whispered communications mentioned when the interview was going to go down. Sydney couldn't fathom why Anya would agree to such a punishing tour of duty (unless her salary was in the millions) because, despite what Sydney had been misled to believe, Burning Feathers was not a "holistic spa." It was a fucking prison camp.

On the fifth night of her sentence, Sydney had been fast asleep on her cot, fully clothed in her sweats, sneakers, and Polartec fleece (who knew it could get that cold in the desert?), when Anya unzipped her teepee, peeked her head in, and whispered the magic words: "She's ready."

Sydney didn't care that she had survived the boot camp and made it to the reward round. All she wanted to do was go back to dreaming of Krispy Kremes (which she wasn't even allowed to have in her waking life)! But she pushed herself up on her elbows, realizing she had no idea what time it was.

Nine P.M.? Three A.M.? Close to sunrise? After waking at a predawn hour for the past four days, being forced to go on progressively longer hikes each morning, walking over hot coals last night (all in her mind, *her ass*—there were blisters on her feet!), and subsisting on clear broth, raw vegetables, and fresh-squeezed juices, her circadian rhythm was all fucked up! She couldn't even do a simple time check because all the electronic devices she would have normally referred to—phone, laptop, digital recorder—had been confiscated when she arrived at Burning Feathers. Because that's what happened when you went to prison, Sydney thought, stomping out of the teepee behind Anya. They confiscated your shit!

The revoked digital recorder was the device Sydney had been fretting about the most. How was she supposed to accurately record quotes by hand? She wasn't a fucking stenographer! But it turned out that even the pad and pen were unnecessary. After all the hype leading up to this epic interview, The Raven, sitting cross-legged in front of a gas lantern in the sweatbox from which Sydney had gone running the night before after what seemed to be an endless "cycle" of intense chanting around a blazing bonfire, had said only four words to Sydney: "I'm in the now." (She'd said those words eight or nine times, but only those words, sometimes accompanied by a dismissive wave.)

"You know, Raven," Sydney said, deciding to go the provocative route once she realized none of her questions about The Raven's colorful past were going to be answered. "I find it hard to believe you'd *choose* to be a woman. Life is so much easier when you have a penis."

Whether The Raven had had the 'ol snip snip was one of the crucial questions that Gareth wanted answered—he was obsessed with the specifics of The Raven's current genitalia—and Sydney thought throwing "penis" out early would help them ease into discussing it. Getting only a creepy stare in response, Sydney followed that sociopolitical grenade toss with a little rapid-fire extolling all the ways manhood trumped womanhood, basically denouncing The Raven's whole existence. But the sharp-tongued, attacking style that had worked wonders on Brett Babcock had the opposite effect on The Raven. Instead of jumping in to defend herself, as Sydney was expecting, The Raven eventually jumped up and hurried out of the sweatbox, her fast-stepping turning into a desperate trot as Sydney, low on blood sugar and sleep, chased her back to the reservation, decrying womanhood like a bad spoken-word artist.

"If I were a man, I wouldn't have wasted the better part of the last two decades obsessing about my weight," she ranted on the run, her interview strategy manifesting more like a form of dementia. "If I were a man, I'd have a whole bunch of kids because I'd never have to push them out of a small orifice in my body, I'd never get stretch marks, and I could dump the majority of domestic and child-rearing responsibilities on my dutiful wife! If I were a man, I could admit that I wanted to make a shitload of money and everyone would applaud me! I would never have to worry that some multiple sex offender released from jail after a ridiculously light sentence would jump out of the shadows and do unspeakable things to me from which I would never recover! I would come ALL THE TIME and it would be EE-EEEEEEEASY!"

When The Raven finally made it back to the safety of Anya's paid embrace, she was a six-foot-two-inch quivering, tranny mess. But she finally had something else to say. To Anya. "Get her away from me!"

CHAPTER FIFTY-THREE

Rolling around on the thick beige wall-to-wall carpeting, her arms and legs flailing in the air, Myrna looked like an insect that was about to get sprayed with Raid. "Wish I could've seen that!" she whooped. "You go, girl!"

Hunched on Myrna's couch in the throes of despair, her black extensions tangled into a waist-length mess, Sydney moaned, "'You go, girl'? Myrna, they FIRED ME!"

She clamped her hands over her ears, pained by the evil echo of those words. *FIRED ME! FIRED ME! FIRED ME!* And all because of that diva pseudobitch! This cover story was supposed to be the highlight of her career. Instead, it had ended it! Yes, she had slurred The Raven's gender identity. Yes, she had completely lost it! But how could anyone expect her to be in good form after spending four days in a teepee in the desert with no solid food, little sleep, and no Internet access? Couldn't they have just given her a warning or something?

"It was only a matter of time," Myrna said, doing a Cro-Magnon walk/crawl over to her wet bar. "I told you."

Sydney stared mindlessly at the television. *The View* was on Mute. She didn't want to be lectured by Myrna. She wanted to be consoled. Myrna was the only person who would really empathize with her situation, which was why she had come to Myrna's place straight from the airport. In a cab. She hadn't even been able to take a company town car! From Newark, it was eighty dollars plus tolls and tip! Now that she was unemployed, that felt like a fucking fortune! But after sobbing the entire ride, literally feeling as though her body was going to break apart, she sure enough snapped out of her fog when the cabdriver didn't give her the correct change, and demanded that extra dollar. (She was broken, she'd thought, but at least her basic survival skills were still intact.)

Listening to Myrna rail against the evil Omnimedia empire only somewhat quelled her misery because she knew Myrna would pounce on any reason to rail against any form of patriarchy. And whatever sympathy Sydney was receiving was nullified by the joy Myrna was clearly taking in having someone join her in exile. It was no coincidence that the first time she'd returned one of Sydney's many messages was after Sydney had left one saying she'd been fired. And after hearing the whole story of Sydney's careerending desert freakout, was rolling around on the floor with glee an appropriate reaction? (But then, there was no such thing as an appropriate reaction in the Myrnasphere.)

Myrna's living conditions were so depressing, Sydney almost wished she hadn't come. She'd realized the Midtown address Myrna had given her was a building for corporate housing when she overheard a broker in the elevator trying to sell an obviously out-of-town suit on the amenities (business center, gym, twenty-four-hour concierge, FedEx drop box in the lobby). Sydney was hoping that Myrna had found a way to scam living expenses from Omnimedia, but it turned out Myrna was living in a cookie-cutter fourteenthfloor studio (that had been furnished to look like a Ramada Inn) of her own free will and on her own dime. When she told Sydney she'd been living there for about a year, switching apartments every few months when she needed a change, Sydney felt that she was finally seeing Myrna Bell for who she really was. Howard Hughes. Without the fortune or influence.

"The men upstairs wanted any reminder of me gone. And they got their wish." Myrna set the second hard drink that Sydney had seen her swig (but which might have been the tail end of an all-night binge) on the glass coffee table and pulled out a large vision board for her new magazine, which she had bizarrely stowed under the couch. "But you can always come work for me."

Sydney didn't respond to that predictably narcissistic lunacy in words or expression. She'd gone numb.

"You have time to figure out your next move," Myrna said, looking at the jumble of torn magazine images that seemed to have nothing to do with one another. Watching her tack a clipping of a woman in a yoga pose onto another part of the board next to a picture of a woman on a motorcycle as if she was making some brilliant chess move, Sydney imagined this was Myrna's crazy mind writ large. "You should go traveling for a few months," Myrna said, rocking back and forth on her knees over the Crazy Board. "Get your head together. Let this whole thing with the trannies blow over."

"Oh God," Sydney moaned, the reminder of the tranny brouhaha plunging her into deeper despair. Her dissing of The Raven's chosen gender had made the papers, and the transgender community was threatening to boycott *Cachet* (which gave Gareth a perfect excuse to do what he'd been wanting to do for a long time: fire her troublemaking ass). There was nothing she'd like more than to just run away, especially after spending fifteen deeply depressing minutes with Myrna, but the idea of going home and finding a bunch of cross-dressers picketing on her doorstep kept her from leaving this undisclosed location. "I can't just run away until I know I have some other income," she said, thinking about that piece she wanted to do on Mitzi Berman. She really needed to get serious about that now. "I'm not rich, you know."

Myrna's head jerked up, and a chunk of her wet slick flopped on her forehead, making her look like Elvis in the boozy years. "What do you mean?"

"Unless I can get somebody else to take over my apartment for a few months," she said, thinking out loud. It was a great place; it'd be easy to rent. But could she illegally sublet an illegal sublet?

"What the fuck are you talking about?" Myrna said, her abrasive side making its inevitable appearance. "You should have a year's salary coming to you."

"Myrna, they fired me!"

"Are you retarded? They got rid of you, but you have a contract with Omnimedia that they are obligated to fulfill."

"Are you serious?"

"Fuck, yeah," Myrna said, polishing off her drink.

"Omigod, I didn't even tell you, Myrna! I shook Conrad down for two hundred thousand for two years! You would have been so proud of me."

Myrna went to the bar, returning with a freshly mixed drink, which she foisted on Sydney. "We should be celebrating."

"So you mean they'd have to pay me the whole four hundred thousand for doing nothing?"

"Think of it as severance," Myrna said, patting her wet palms on her men's pajama bottoms.

"Wait a second," Sydney said. "So you got your salary after they fired you?"

"How do you think I can live like this?" Myrna swept her arm around her depressing single-room abode as if it were a mansion to die for. "I got two years' salary and severance. I'm sittin' on millions, sister."

Sydney punched the sofa and yelped, "What?" She thought Myrna was down-and-out! Like her! But she was sitting on millions? Jesus, she really was Howard Hughes! Sydney had only a moment to puzzle over that before a truly heart-stopping thought gripped hold. "Omigod, the contract . . ." Had Max mailed it? She'd been carrying it around in her bag for more than a week, forgetting to remail it with a forty-two cent stamp after the thirty-nine-cent-stamped envelope was returned for insufficient postage. She paid all her bills online; no one sent letters anymore—getting the right stamp and mailing the damn thing turned into such an ordeal! Then she'd fished it out of her bag—it was all smudged and penmarked by then—when she was paying for something at Harvey's and Max told her he would drop it in the mail room for her. And she'd given it to him, thinking how nice it was to have him around, how he was always doing nice things for her, things that made her life easier, how he was just so useful. But had he mailed the damn thing?

When Sydney didn't answer, Myrna paused in her pointlessly rearranging of torn magazine images. "What?"

"I gave it to . . . this guy to mail," Sydney said, feeling like an idiot for leaving something that seemed inconsequential but had now turned out to be of vital importance in the hands of a useless slacker like Max. She didn't want to call him. Maybe she'd just text him?

"Why'd you do that?"

"Long story."

"Hmm . . . long story." Myrna peered at Sydney suspiciously as she shook the ice around in her glass. "You fuckin' this guy? Gettin' any dick these days?"

Myrna loved to live vicariously through other people's sex lives since she had none of her own, but was this really the time? Was it ever? "Myrna, please," Sydney said, feeling her energy rapidly depleting.

Myrna turned back to her board, hunching over in concentration. "Call Mary Ellen."

"In Business Affairs?"

"She'll tell you if they got it. She's cool." Myrna tossed Sydney her cell. "Her number's in there."

Thinking about the possible windfall this call might confirm, Sydney fell back on the couch and smiled for the first time in days. "So as long as they got the signed contract . . ."

"No, so long as they *executed* the signed contract," Myrna corrected. "And mailed a copy back to you."

Pressing the Talk button on Myrna's phone, Sydney could see her hand shaking. This might be the most important phone call of her life, she thought. She was scared that Mary Ellen wouldn't pick up, and then as her line rang a second time, more scared that she would. This could be the perfect out that she'd been looking for. Maybe this had all happened for a reason. Maybe this had been the divine plan all along. Please let Max have mailed that envelope, she thought. Please let Conrad have signed it. Please let it be in her mailbox right now!

"Oh, Sydney," Mary Ellen said. "I heard what happened." *Awkward!* "I wish I had better news for you, but we never got the contract back from you. I e-mailed you about it the other day before, you know, everything happened."

Of course they hadn't gotten it, Sydney thought, sliding down to the carpet, gulping the disgusting alcohol-heavy concoction Myrna had brewed as if it were medicinal. Of course she couldn't rely on Max to do one simple thing for her. She thought he was so useful, but he was useless, just like all the rest!

"Tough break," Myrna said, not even emotionally intelligent enough to look away from the Crazy Board.

Slumped against Myrna's couch with her legs spread, tangled weave draped over her shoulders, Sydney caught sight of herself in the tacky mirror next to the wet bar. She looked like an abandoned Bratz doll. But there was some greater plan at work here, she thought, sucking back the last of her drink. She wanted to get completely blotto and forget everything about her jinxed life, and somehow she'd found herself in the perfect place, with the perfect person, to do it. She slammed her empty glass on the carpet and demanded, "Another!"

CHAPTER FIFTY-FOUR

Oh God, what am I going to do?" Sydney wailed, flopping against the supple leather interior of Harvey Cooper's Mercedes as both he and his driver, Akil, listened uncomfortably.

She had totally forgotten they had a "date" planned for tonight until Harvey called earlier to confirm. She called him back with the intention of canceling, but in the process of telling him what had happened, she'd started sobbing again and he'd insisted on meeting at a place near her house. After going home to take a quick shower and lop off her extensions, she'd shown up at Extra Virgin wearing her boyfriend jeans, a hoodie, no makeup except for the unnatural redness around her puffy eyes, and a stubby sumo ponytail sticking out of the back of her head.

If Mitzi Berman had seen her, she would have dropped dead on the spot.

Harvey was wearing one of his impeccably tailored suits when Sydney found him ensconced at a table in a darkened back corner, which Sydney suspected he had requested because he knew tears were likely and he was trying to save them both the embarrassment. But there was no preventing that! Despite being massively hungover at eight P.M., Sydney ordered a shot of Patrón straightaway. She felt like the biggest loser on the planet—fired from her cush job, out of four hundred grand because she couldn't get it together to put a stamp on an envelope, enemy of the transgender community. She just wanted to drown her sorrows in alcohol until she was comatose.

"It's okay," Harvey kept saying (with as much compassion as a proctologist). "It was only a job. You'll find another."

Hearing that "this too shall pass" sentiment for the umpteenth time as Akil pulled up to her building, Sydney finally snapped: "That's easy for you to say!" The bitter, out-of-control sound of her voice made her realize she needed to get out of the car pronto. All she had to do was open the door and go inside before she ruined her chances of scoring the now all-important interview, which might be her only way of supporting herself until she found gainful employment!

As uncomfortable as her hysterics had made Harvey, it was clear that the geezer was attracted to her naked vulnerability. And that realization made Sydney feel at once disgusted, offended, depressed, and not a little bit opportunistic.

He was attractive enough. He was a nice man. And he wanted more kids. Someone had to give him some. In exchange, he would take care of her. Forever. This frantic worrying about finding another job would be gone. Just like that. She'd never have to get another stupid job. She'd never have to kowtow to The Man, just this one man. She could take up photography as a hobby like she'd always wanted to do. She could learn to cook. She could help Harvey with the store. The possibilities were endless.

And if she wanted to "go there," she had an opening. He'd been intrigued when she was forthright and assertive in telling him how to update the store, but it was this unexpected turn as the damsel in distress that had gotten the blood flowing in his old pecker. She could practically see him calling dibs on her womb!

Dabbing at her eyes with the monogrammed handkerchief he'd given her (the ultimate old-fogy accessory), she said, "Well, thank you for listening, Harvey. I'm a mess right now. But I'll be fine." The time wasn't right to mention the interview, and if she decided to start taking this completely improbable coupling seriously, she might not mention it at all. But keeping all roads open, she said, "Can I call you next week?"

"Sure, my dear," he said, causing Sydney to throw up a little in her mouth. *My dear?* Who was he now, *George Burns?*

She quickly pushed the bile back down when she realized he was making a move toward her. After sobbing openly everywhere and anywhere for the last twenty-four hours—on the security line at the airport, on the plane, in the cab to Myrna's, at Myrna's, in front of Harvey and his driver, in a crowded restaurant that people she knew frequented—her emotional barriers had all but dissolved and she did not fear a perimeter breach. She welcomed it. Before she realized Harvey was only intending to give her a "buck up" pat on the back, she decided to give him a chaste farewell kiss, so grateful was she to have someone to listen to her kvetching, which sounded beyond lame, even to her own ears.

Would it really be so wrong if they had a real date? she wondered as her lips gravitated toward his jowly cheek. So what that she'd never be in love with him? She was a thirty-three-year-old woman who had never been in love with anyone, and given her problems with emotional connection, who was to say she'd ever be? And so what that she'd never be hot for him physically? Passion only lasted so long. The kind of stability a man like Harvey Cooper could provide would last for generations. And that had a lot more value than any mind-blowing orgasm.

This all sounded so very logical looping around Sydney's battered psyche that her lips veered slightly off course and instead of landing on Harvey's cheek, they hit another target. She felt her lips pucker as his retreated and suddenly the crazed desperation of what she had just done hit her full force and Liessel's puzzling final analysis became crystal clear. She was no better than Melania. *We hate in others what we hate in ourselves.* She was no better than Wendi Deng. *We hate in others what we hate in ourselves.* She was no better than Liessel. And then the most chilling thought of all. She had, in that shameful moment, become . . . HER MOTHER!

Nooooooooooooooooooooooooooooooooooooooooooooo!

She separated her lips from Harvey's reddened face and slumped forward, clutching her gut, hoping she didn't hurl all over his pristine luxury vehicle, just as an aggressive knocking rocked the car. Harvey (or maybe Akil) put the back window down and there was Max, peering into the car with an expression of pained confusion.

He tilted his head sideways to get a look at Sydney in her crash-landing position. "Sydney?"

She sat up straight, squinting at him. "Max?"

He stuck his head through the window, squinting at Harvey. "Dad?"

For reasons she couldn't fathom in that *Twilight Zone* moment, Sydney turned not to Max or to Harvey but to Akil, as if *he* owed her an explanation. "DAD?"

CHAPTER FIFTY-FIVE

He's sixty-*two!*"

"He's sixty-*three*," Sydney corrected, stomping across the street after Max as Harvey and Akil watched from the car. "And I'd think you'd know that since you're . . . HIS SON!"

Max stopped at the curb and spun around, enraged. "Don't blame me because he's my father. You were kissing him!"

Reeling back as though that was the most preposterous accusation she had ever heard (even though she could still taste the red wine that Harvey had had at dinner on her lips), Sydney shouted back, "I was not!"

"Then what were you doing?"

"A story on him!"

"Oh, right," Max said. "I forgot. That's what you do when you profile people. You make out with them!"

Sydney fell back against the stone ledge in front of her building, horrified. *Well, she never!* "I'm writing an exposé on Mitzi Berman. I'm blowing the lid off the whole thing!"

After her words rung out, loudly, on her quiet, tree-lined street, Sydney looked toward Harvey's car—she probably wasn't going to get an interview with him after he'd heard that!—and saw it taking off down the street. *Shit!* She scooted up on the cold, pebbly ledge, pulled the hood of her sweatshirt over her head, and curled into herself, wishing she could just disappear.

"I wasn't kissing him, okay? He was . . . he was . . . consoling me. I lost my job, you know!"

"Yes, I do know. Jeffrey told me what happened. That's why I've been waiting here for two hours. He said you were hysterical. But now that you've been adequately consoled by my father, I guess I'll leave."

"Wait a second," she said, pushing her hood back. "Since when are you and Jeffrey all chummy? I just spoke to him a couple of hours ago. Then he immediately calls you?"

"We ran into each other at a dinner party a few weeks ago. And we became . . . friends."

"So . . . you've been talking about me behind my back?"

"Not in a bad way."

"Wait, so Jeffrey knew about all this? He knew and he didn't tell me?"

"Jeffrey was the one who told me not to tell you."

"And what was the reasoning behind that?"

"He said if you knew who I really was that you'd dismiss me."

"He's right. Now I know." Sydney hopped off the wall and let him talk to the hand. "You're dismissed."

"Sydney, please don't be like this," Max said, grabbing her arm as she began to walk away. "Let me explain."

"Yeah, I wanna hear this." She spun around and hopped back up on the ledge, her expression daring him to win her over. "Give it your best shot!"

Max rested against the ledge and took Sydney's hand. "I didn't mean for any of this to happen. I saw you that night at the gallery and you introduced me as the doorman and I just ran with it. It was just a joke."

"Yeah. On me."

"No, not like that. It was more of a . . . social experiment."

"A social experiment conducted by you and Jeffrey?"

"Jeffrey was only doing what he thought was best for you. He really looks out for you."

"I see," Sydney said. "So you were lying to me for my own good?"

"Well, Jeffrey was also in it for the free clothes."

"Free clothes?" Sydney said, reclaiming her hand. "You've been giving Jeffrey free clothes?" She leaned away. "And I only got seventy off?" She leaned back some more, almost falling backward over the recycling bin. "You were *my* connect!"

"Well, Jeffrey's been very helpful."

Sydney hopped off the wall. "I had sex with you!"

"Well, yeah, after that you would have gotten bumped up to full discount status, but you cut me off."

Sydney was already disgusted by every aspect of this conversation—the insinuation that she was trying to fuck a geriatric (it was a temporary moment of insanity!), the shameless deception, the exchange of goods for services (sexual, in her case)—but now Max had reminded her of the most disgusting part of this pointless charade. "I cut you off because you gave me herpes."

"Not true," Max said. "And you know it."

"Fine, maybe it was Candi," Sydney admitted, not sure if Jeffrey, the double-crosser, had tipped him off about that too. "I cut you off because I don't give a shit about you, Max. Is that what you wanna hear?"

"That's not true either," he said, using the soft voice Sydney realized she missed. "It was all just . . ." He took her hand again and held on when she tried to pull it away. "Remember when you asked me what happened with my ex-wife?"

"Is that even true?"

"Yes, that's true. I was married very briefly. Her name really is Eliana. I met her at Oxford. But you asked me what happened, why we broke up, and I couldn't really tell you then without telling you everything. We broke up because we came back to New York and she got to see me for who I really was. I mean, not me as a person. But she got to see me in the context of who my family was. And it ruined our relationship."

"How? Why?" Sydney said, the words coming out in angry, staccato bursts.

"Because at Oxford we were living in a bubble. She had never been to the States. She had no idea what Harvey's was. She just took me for who I was with her. And until that happened it had never even occurred to me that something like that was even possible."

"That what was possible?"

"That I could get out from under the burden of being the son and grandson of both Harvey Coopers. That has nothing to do with who I am as a person. But that's the first thing, sometimes the only thing, people see."

"Max, your grandfather founded one of the most well-known stores in America. There are people walking around with black bags that have your father's name on it. Don't tell me that has nothing to do with who you are." She yanked her hand from Max's grip. "It has to inform who you are in some way."

"You're right," Max admitted. "Of course it does, but—"

"And there are a lot of people who wouldn't think of that as a burden. I wish I had a father to burden me, but I don't. My father's dead. And my grandfather was killed by Castro!"

Max stood up very straight. *Your grandfather was killed by Castro?*"

"Well, figuratively," Sydney mumbled, getting quickly back to scolding him. "I'm sure there's a downside to being Harvey's son, but most people would suffer the bad to get the good."

"Because most people think it's all good. And that's because most people don't have to walk in my shoes."

"Excuse me if I don't feel any sympathy for you."

"I'm not asking you to. I'm just trying to explain why this got so out of hand."

"Yeah, well, I still don't understand."

"After a while I didn't want to tell you the truth because I realized I was feeling for you what I felt for Eliana in the beginning. That was the best time of my life. And I found that again. With you."

Sydney felt her stiff upper lip relaxing and stiffened it up again. "What are you talking about?"

"Because you got to know me for who I really was, the same way Eliana did."

"No I didn't, Max! You're Harvey Cooper's son. That's who you are. Whether you like it or not. Saying that has nothing to do with who you are is like me saying my father coming over here on a fucking dinghy has nothing to do with who I am. The person I got to know doesn't exist. That was some part you were playing, and now I don't know what's real and what's fake. You're not the doorman, but do you have a real job? Are you living off a trust fund? Did you really go to Brown? Are you and Jeffrey, like, besties now?" Before he could answer she added, "And if you are, that's *totally* gay."

"Jeffrey and I have spent more time together in the past few weeks than I would have liked," Max admitted, tackling the gay taunt first. "And it does make me somewhat uncomfortable when he calls me *honey*. But I deal with it."

Sydney smiled but looked away so Max couldn't share in the moment. "Great," she said, kicking her bitchy back up to high. "So you *are* besties."

"Syd, listen . . ." Max placed his hands on her shoulders and tried to lock on her wandering eyes. "I know this is completely weird. It's a lot to take in. I don't blame you for being mad. I'm just asking that you give us a chance to get to know each other for real and put all this weirdness behind us. Then if you want to write me off, you can."

"I *am* trying to get to know the real you," Sydney said, walking over to her stoop to get out of his reach. "Did you really go to Brown?"

Max sat next to her on the steps. "Yes. And I've been creative director at the store for the last four years, but I'm going to have to find other means of support because I'm no longer employed there."

"What do you mean? Since when?"

"Last week," Max reported calmly. "Harvey fired me."

"Your father fired you?"

"We were having a party for the opening of the new floor," Max said quickly, as if his firing had little relevance to the conversation. "And my sister, who's really in charge of things, was on maternity leave. I was filling in for her, and I let the invitations go out with the wrong date."

"And Harvey fired you for that?"

Max smiled. "Yes."

"What are you going to do now?"

"Anything I want. That's why I'm smiling."

"Okay, this," Sydney said, pointing back and forth between them as if the Grand Canyon could fit in those few inches, "is the difference between you and me. I just got fired from my job and I'm freaking out. You're celebrating. Must be nice to have a trust fund."

"Oh, right, we didn't address that one," Max said. "I blew most of the money I got from my mother and grandmother and Harvey doesn't believe in bequeathing assets to human beings, only institutions of betterment. Most of my income came from my job."

"You keep saying *most*," Sydney said, frowning at him. "That means you still have money somewhere. All rich people do."

"I took a big hit when the market crashed. Had to fire my broker."

"What a pity."

"Most of my money is tied up in my house."

"Right, the place you own in Williamsburg."

"DUMBO."

"You told me you lived in Williamsburg!"

"No, you told yourself that," Max said. "I just didn't correct you."

"Is that how you've been justifying all this? Because you're starting to sound like James Frey."

"And I'm starting to feel like I'm on *Oprah*," Max grumbled. "But I'm trying to be completely honest here. Remember when you went to that party with Brett Babcock? When he kissed you?"

"How could I forget?"

"That was my place."

Sydney's mouth fell open. "Noooo. That place? Was your place?" Her mouth fell open wider. "Nooooo!"

"I was watching you the whole time from up in the DJ booth." He bumped his shoulder against hers. "You're welcome to come over any time."

Sydney slid away. "I can't think about that now. I have to focus on getting another job. I'm completely fucked right now."

"Are you? Or is that what you're telling yourself?"

Sydney frowned over at him. "What is this, a Buddhist koan? I am!"

"Sydney, all you ever did was complain about how much you hated that job. And all I ever did was complain about mine."

"What's the correlation between those two things? We're not in the same boat, Max."

"In a way, maybe we are."

"We're not. I don't have stocks or a multimillion-dollar apartment I could sell in a pinch."

"Sending out the wrong invites, having people show up on the wrong date when construction was still going on, was a huge fuckup. And it took a fuckup that huge for Harvey to fire me. But maybe that's what I wanted all along. Maybe that's why I let it happen."

"Wait, are you trying to say that I did the same thing with The Raven?"

Max shrugged. "Jeffrey told me how you got the job and that they'd probably never fire you. You were sort of in the same boat as me. But you found a way to free yourself. Look at it that way."

Sydney jumped up. "I can't look at it that way! Do you realize I was a temp at Omnimedia before I lucked into that job?"

"I think Jeffrey mentioned that."

"And that I basically extorted a two hundred thousand a year contract out of Conrad Drake last month? Everyone in the publishing world knows how I got that job. No one else is going to pay me that kind of money. No one!"

"So get another job that you like, Sydney. Follow your heart."

"Oh man, you really don't fucking get it," Sydney said, pacing up and down the stairs. "I needed the security of that job. And the reason you don't get that is because you were born with a deeper sense of security than most people will ever know. Losing your job is liberating because there will always be money somewhere. You'll never be broke, you'll never be homeless. Those are the burdens most people carry around. You can take a leap of faith because you were born with a net. I wasn't."

"Well," Max said, chastised almost to the point of speechlessness. "You have *some* savings, don't you?"

"I would have a lot more if that envelope I asked you to mail had gotten where it was supposed to go!"

"The envelope?"

"Yes, Max. The envelope." She put one foot up on the step next to him and leaned on her knee, like a prosecutor about to grill a witness. "What happened with that?"

"Okay," Max said, becoming visibly nervous. "I said I was going to be completely honest with you from now on, so in all honesty, I don't really know."

"What does that mean? Did you mail it or not?"

"Well, I put it in the out-box in my office."

"Your office?" Looking dizzy, Sydney plopped down on the stoop, a few steps above him. "Okay, I have to get used to this. I keep picturing you standing by the door. But go on."

"Wait, why does this even matter? You said it was your *Cachet* contract. But you got fired."

"It matters because they would have been contractually obligated to pay me the full value of the contract if it had been executed. Four hundred grand. But according to a reliable source in Business Affairs, they never got it."

"Oh God," Max said, going ashen. He put his hand down on the step to steady himself and blurted, "Lulu stole it!"

Sydney grimaced at him, confusion coming before anger. "Lulu Merriwether?"

"I put it in the out-box," Max said, doubling over as though he were having an appendicitis attack. "But when I came back from lunch, I didn't see it there. And I didn't really think anything of it. But Norma said Lulu had come by looking for me. She could have seen your name on it and taken it. I don't know."

"Why would she be looking for you?"

Apparently forgetting in his panic-stricken state that this sensitive bit of his personal history—the worst bit—hadn't yet been divulged, Max answered as if it was public knowledge. "We dated."

"You fucked Lulu Merriwether?"

"That would be more accurate," he said. "Yes, I fucked her. A few times. It meant nothing."

"Okay, forget about that," Sydney said, back to pacing up the steps. "You think she took the envelope?"

"Well, she hates you, so she had motive."

Sydney ran back down to Max's step. "Hates me? What have I ever done to that cunt?"

"You got my attention. And you did rat her out to 'Page Six.' I'm sure that didn't help."

"How would she know that? *You told her?*"

"I didn't, but I'm sure someone did," Max said, glancing up to make sure he was not at risk of physical violence. "You think 'Page Six' is going to keep your secrets? That put me in quite a spot, by the way, and it almost got Remy killed."

"Remy?" Sydney jumped down to the sidewalk and started pacing there. "Who the fuck is Remy?"

"My assistant," Max said. "And Lulu's former ghostwriter. So you weren't the only one affected. If Lulu even took the envelope. We don't know that. Maybe the mail-room guy came and got it."

"Was there other mail in the out-box?"

"Yes."

"And was it still there when you came back from lunch?"

"Yes."

"Then she swiped it, you idiot!" Sydney leaned toward Max as if she was about to strangle him, then pulled back and started moaning to herself. "What an asshole! What an asshole!"

"Sydney, I'm sorry."

"Shut up, asshole!"

"Don't call me that," Max said, standing up to leave.

Sydney watched him walk past her and slip between the parked cars, looking up the street for a cab. "So that's it? You're sorry? I'm unemployed and soon to be broke and you're just going to go home, happily unemployed, to your multimillion-dollar loft and strum your guitar?"

"What other choice do I have?" Max said, a touch sarcastically.

"You can write me a check for four hundred grand," Sydney answered without any sarcasm at all.

"Sydney, I'm going to give you some time to cool off," Max said, staring up the street though there was nary a cab in sight. "You have my number. If you feel so inclined, use it."

"I'm serious," Sydney said, grabbing a fistful of his suede jacket. "Give me my fucking money."

"Are you extorting me?" Max said, shaking her off. "Is that what this is? An extortion attempt? Because you sound crazy."

"Well, you dated Lulunatic, didn't you? You like crazy chicks."

"And you let Mitzi Berman whore you out to anyone willing to pony up fifty grand!"

After a shocked moment of paralysis, Sydney raised her hand to slap his face (she'd always wanted to do that), but then she chickened out and clapped her hand over her gaping mouth instead.

"Are you going to tell me you were interviewing the other two guys Mitzi set you up with too?"

Through her fingers, Sydney mumbled, "Who said—"

"Jeffrey," Max replied coldly. "We're besties. We tell each other everything."

"Yes, I was interviewing them," Sydney claimed. "I'm working under-cover!"

Waving frantically at an off-duty cab, Max said, "Whatever."

"Is this the part where I beg you, my rich Prince Charming, not to leave?"

"No," Max said, slipping inside the taxi without giving her another look. "This is the part where we say good-bye."

CHAPTER FIFTY-SIX

Sydney buzzed in the FedEx guy, wondering why this one was willing to walk up three flights of stairs when none of the others ever would. She got her answer when she saw that the voice that had insisted, "I need a signature" through the scratchy intercom belonged not to an employee of FedEx, but to the CEO of Mitzi Berman Serious Matchmaking, Inc.

"Had to live on the fourth floor," Mitzi said, hoofing it up the last flight. "Everything about you is difficult." She gave Sydney a crabby look as she trudged, uninvited, into her apartment. "You can't return a phone call?"

"There's a reason I haven't called you back," Sydney said, letting the door slam. "I don't want to talk to you."

Mitzi plopped down on the sofa and set the Harvey's shopping bag she was toting at her feet. "Sure, I'd love a glass of water," she said when Sydney didn't offer. "After that hike, I'm parched." Sydney held a glass under the tap and Mitzi peered toward the kitchen. "Is that filtered?"

"No," Sydney said, handing it to her. "And I'm out of ice."

Mitzi looked around at the half-packed boxes and black Hefty bags full of clothes. "Going somewhere?"

"Moving," Sydney said, getting back down on her knees to continue separating a pile of clothes.

"Can't afford the place, huh? Now that you got canned."

"Well, yes, that's a concern," Sydney admitted bitterly. "And then after I had my huge blowup with Max and lost my interview with Harvey, I came upstairs to find the woman I've been illegally subletting from for three years sitting on the same couch where you're currently taking up space."

"Whoa," Mitzi said. "What happened?"

"She left her husband. She needs the place back."

"Divorcée, eh? Have her call me."

"Do you ever think of anything other than drumming up business?"

"Bringing people together for a lifetime of love and happiness is a gift, not a business."

"Then why don't you do it for free?"

"Gotta eat."

When Mitzi took off her coat and made herself comfortable, Sydney stopped separating clothes to ask, "Why are you here?"

"You won't return a call. You've been through some tough breaks. I wanted to make sure you weren't swinging from a rope."

"Damn," Sydney said, grimacing. "That's the most macabre attempt at consolation I've ever heard. But since you're here and you're obviously not going to leave, tell me this. Why did you set me up with Harvey? He's sixty-three, Mitzi. What would we have in common?"

"Apparently, a lot more than I thought," Mitzi said. "I couldn't believe it when he said you were going out on a second date. I thought after one dinner with you, he'd coming running back to me for someone more . . . appropriate." Sydney gave her a confused look and she said, "That's what I do when a sixty-year-old guy comes to me yapping about how he wants to start a second family. How he messed up the first time and wants to get it right."

"You send him a younger woman who's drama?"

"Ding, ding, ding!" Mitzi looked toward the bedroom as if she was expecting a game show host to appear. "What do we have for her, Bob?" Then she pulled a compact out of her purse (which Sydney noticed was a bigger version of the Goyard tote she'd given her) and began talking to the mirror as she blotted her shiny face with a powder puff. "He just became a grandfather of twins. He has two beautiful babies to bounce on his lap. Harvey's too hard on himself. He thinks because both of his boys turned out to be failures—"

"There's another one?"

Mitzi pulled the compact aside and whispered, "Druggie." She went back to powdering. "And Max isn't a failure just because he doesn't want to join the family business. He marches to his own beat. What's so wrong with that? And he doesn't give a crap because he knows Harvey already has an heir to the throne. It just happens to be his daughter, not one of his sons as he'd always imagined." She snapped the compact closed and slipped it back into her purse. "He's misguided and it's my job to show him the light. And you helped me do that. So thank you."

"Again I helped you?" Sydney said, wondering if she should inquire about Jerome.

"After all that drama you dumped on the poor man? Lucky he didn't have a coronary. But he came running back, asking for a mature woman, so it all worked out for the best."

"Was that your plan with Jerome too?" Sydney asked, honestly curious to know but also hoping Mitzi would let some info about him slip. "To get me to scare him into wanting a white woman?"

"No," Mitzi said. "That was just a lucky break."

"Well, make sure you hit me off with a percentage of your marriage bonus when both of them get hitched."

"Sure," Mitzi said. "Where should I send it?"

"Send it to my sister," Sydney said, dragging a Hefty bag to the door. "I'm sure you have her contact info."

"So that's it? Coupla bad breaks and you go into hiding?"

"A couple of bad breaks? Mitzi, my life is in ruins! My deepest, darkest fear has been realized. I'm homeless, soon to be destitute, and alone."

"You're not alone," Mitzi said. "Max still wants you."

"You spoke to him?"

"Briefly."

"What does everyone do? Come to you to confess their sins?"

"You should try it." Mitzi leaned back on the couch as if about to take a nap. "Might make you feel better."

"What did he say? Not that I even care. But since you won't leave . . ."

"Of course you don't care," Mitzi said. "You don't care about anyone. You don't need anyone."

"I care about Caleigh and Ben."

"Who are they?"

"My niece and nephew."

"Children," Mitzi said. "Okay, at least we know you're not a total Tin Man. Are you going to leave *them* a forwarding address at least?"

"What did Max say?" Sydney demanded. "Tell me or leave."

"He said he doesn't know how to deal with you. He said you infuriate him. He wishes he could quit you . . ."

"'Quit' me?" Sydney burst out laughing, the first time that had happened in more than a week. "That's what he said? What are we? Gay lovers who only meet on Brokeback Mountain?"

"Well, he actually didn't tell me," Mitzi admitted. "I'm paraphrasing. He told Harvey and Harvey told me. That's another good thing you've done. Got those two talking. I suspect they haven't had a heart-to-heart in years."

"Funny how I manage to bring happiness to everyone but myself," Sydney said, angrily throwing clothes into a garbage bag as though they belonged to an old lover and she was preparing them for incineration.

"Ponder that when you get to wherever you're going," Mitzi said, gathering her things.

"Yeah, well, I can't leave until Mercury's out of retrograde."

"With your attitude, Mercury's never going to be out of retrograde."

Seeing Mitzi shuffling toward the door, Sydney got up off the floor and, giving in to her frustration, finally admitted, "Look, I like him, okay?"

Mitzi stopped shuffling. "Okay . . ."

"But Max has grown up in this family where he's never had to work, never had to take responsibility for anything. He had a strong mother, a superwoman of a sister."

Mitzi cocked a smudged eyebrow. "What do you know about it?"

"You think I didn't Google the whole clan? I know plenty!"

"Well, the sister *is* a dynamo," Mitzi said. "The mother too, on the social circuit. But that's why he's comfortable with strong women."

"More like he's looking for a strong woman to take care of him."

"What's so wrong with that?"

"What's so wrong is that he doesn't want to grow up. He doesn't want to be an adult. Mitzi, can't you see he's the same guy I've been dating, just in a different form? It's like a sickness with me!"

"Hmmm," Mitzi said. "That's probably the most insightful thing I've ever heard you say. Surprising."

"I love how you can always find a way to make a compliment sound like an insult."

"It's a talent we share."

"Well, I want to have a baby, Mitzi. Not raise a fully grown one."

"You make some valid points," Mitzi conceded. "But you haven't gotten to really know him. The real Max. And you can't make a character assessment based on things you read on the Internet, Sydney!"

"Yeah, well, there's also one other little glitch."

"Excuses, excuses."

"Mitzi, *I kissed his father!*"

"Was there tongue?"

"Ewwww," Sydney said. "No!"

"Forget it ever happened."

"You think Max is going to let me forget?" Sydney said, following Mitzi as she continued to shuffle toward the door. "And then he dated Lulu. He doesn't have a job. I don't have a job. The whole thing is a raging hot mess!"

Mitzi yanked the door open, shouting, "Hon, love is a battlefield!"

"Okay, seriously, Mitzi, if you start singing Pat Benatar, I swear to God I'll throw you down these steps myself!"

"Take it from someone who knows," Mitzi said. "The fairy tale isn't having a rich, handsome prince sweep you off your feet. Having someone see you and love you, flaws and all, *that's* the fairy tale. Wasn't that what you were blubbering about in my office? 'I want someone to love me the way I am!' Well, you got him."

Sydney stood in the doorway, biting her lip to keep from blubbering now. Every time she saw this woman, she wound up crying. Not this time!

"But you, my darling, want a happily ever after about as much as I want this." Mitzi handed over the Harvey's bag, which contained the faux Goyard Sydney had tried to pass off on her. Then she looked down at the stairs and sighed, "At least I won't have to go to the gym today."

CHAPTER FIFTY-SEVEN

S o this is it, huh?"

Sydney slammed the door of the red Mini Cooper she'd rented and
looked up and down the block. It looked clean, quiet, and residential
like any other. There was nothing that screamed, *Commune!*

"This is it!" When Ethan smiled proudly as though he'd built every
modest house on the block with his own hands, Sydney wondered if this
reflected a sense of communal ownership.

"I can see communal living is serving you well," Sydney said. She gave
him a quick embrace, but judging by the new and improved looks of him, it
might not be long before she was giving him more than that. His floppy
curls had been replaced by a cleaner cut, he had a healthy summer glow, and
he was wearing basic black drawstring pants with his plain tee instead of the
horrible bike shorts and massage oil holster he always used to wear.

"Come on," he said cheerily. "I'll take you to your house." He glanced at
the trunk. "Anything you need me to carry?"

"No, just this," Sydney said, tugging the strap of the weekend bag over
her shoulder. "I FedExed all my stuff."

"Yeah, we were wondering what was in all of those boxes . . ."

"Wow, I shipped them ground. Trying to watch my pennies, you know?
You got them already?"

"Yes, we did," Ethan said.

"Good," Sydney mumbled, wondering if this insistent use of "we" (she'd shipped them to Ethan specifically) was a sign of cultish behavior. *Shades of Jonestown?*

"We put them in your room," Ethan said, again speaking as a collective. "But you know it's not that big."

Of course she knew that. She'd clicked and read through every link on the Web site, including every one of the FAQs and most of the threads on the forum. There hadn't been any mention of storage, but she assumed that since the room was the size of a jail cell, there was some!

"I can put stuff under my bed," she said, wondering if every house they passed was going to be her new home. "Or the basement?"

"There's no basement in your house," Ethan told her. "And you can't really store many personal belongings in the shared spaces."

"In my house?" Sydney grabbed his arm, as though they might get separated walking down the completely empty street. "So we're not in the same house? What if I don't like the people in my house? Can I put in for a transfer?" Ethan just looked at her strangely and she was embarrassed to have said the wrong thing (though she didn't really know what).

"This isn't camp," he said. "You don't have to pal around with the people in your house. Everyone has their own life."

"Oh yeah," Sydney said. "Right. I knew that."

Natasha looked up at Max. "What's wrong?"

"Just forget it." He rolled onto his side, clutching his eight-hundred-thread-count sheets.

Natasha crawled up toward the headboard. "Is it me?"

Max reached around and gave her scrawny, bare leg a pat. "Definitely not."

They lay there for an uncomfortable moment, Natasha trying to spoon while Max curled into himself, until Natasha said, "You know that Mulberry bag you got me in black . . . ?"

At the end of a perfectly calm and uneventful day, Sydney was doing her daily straighten at the commune's thrift shop when a trio of fashionistas wandered in. Sydney couldn't imagine what they were doing in that unglamorous neck of the woods. Passing through on a road trip? Shooting a J.Crew catalog? Lost?

The tall blonde was immediately drawn to Sydney's old Lanvins as though she was equipped with a designer-detecting homing device. "Wow, look! I couldn't find these anywhere."

"They're pretty worn," sniffed the brunette.

Blondie turned them over and looked at the soles. "But they're my size! And they're only thirty bucks!"

"Get 'em," the brunette said.

You don't deserve them, Sydney thought, tracking their every move while she stood behind the counter trying to look busy. She'd brought all her designer clothes to the thrift shop after she'd discovered there was only a small bureau in her room and she didn't need more than a few pairs of jeans and tees since that was all she (or anyone else) ever wore. But her precious Lanvins . . . why had she given those up? Even if she wasn't going to wear them, she should have kept them just because.

Although, on second thought, what would be the point of that? Or, on third thought, wasn't giving them away the whole point? The disgust she felt watching these Carrie Bradshaw wannabes, with their LV bags, too-high-for-daytime heels, and dermatologically treated faces, only confirmed that moving to the commune was the best decision she'd ever made. After a brief adjustment period, she had fallen into the groove of communal living and even made connections with a few people she would already call friends. It was like living on a college campus with mature, enlightened students, but there were no tests, only optional meditation and yoga classes.

Max had been right about one thing, she thought, watching the fashionistas ooh and aah over all the worldly possessions she had renounced. In her previous existence, how had she been any better than someone like Lulu Merriwether? She couldn't believe she used to regularly spend eighty dollars for a pedicure, a hundred dollars on dinner, three hundred (after a 70 percent discount) on the shoes Blondie had just dumped into her beat-up plastic basket. She'd been telling anyone who would listen that she never wanted to go back to her former life, so why was she trying to hold on to this little piece of it?

Giving silent thanks to Eckhart Tolle for making her aware of these feelings (and to Ethan, who'd been running the *New Earth* workshop), she surrendered her ego-driven attachment to this useless material possession and rung up Blondie's transaction wearing her new favorite accessory: a grateful smile.

Max slapped a forty-thousand-dollar check on Mitzi's desk. Now that he was unemployed, it was a tremendous outlay of cash, but you only live once.

"Told you my prices were going up," Mitzi said, enjoying what was clearly a moment of sheer desperation. "The standard package starts at fifty."

"I don't want the standard package," Max said. "I want you to find Sydney and tell me what I need to do to get her back."

"I'm impressed," Mitzi said. "This is quite a commitment you're making." She swiveled toward her computer screen, pink nails clicking against the keyboard. After a moment, Max heard the sound of the printer whirring and she said, "Grab that for me, will ya?"

Max wanted to say, "Do I look like your secretary?" but he wasn't in the position to be his usual facetious self. He took the paper out of the printer, and when he tried to hand it to her, Mitzi said, "That's for you."

Max looked down and saw that he was holding MapQuest directions to a location in upstate New York. "What is this?"

"Directions," Mitzi told him. "She's at a commune."

Max stared down at the paper. Then he looked up, squinting at Mitzi in disbelief. "Come on."

"I shit you not."

"Are you sure?" No one knew where Sydney was—not Jeffrey or her sister—and they'd all gotten the same text from her the day she left: "Leave me alone." "She told you this?"

The un-Botoxed parts of Mitzi's face wrinkled in annoyed confusion. "Course not. Not very forthcoming, that one. But I went over to her place and saw the Web site on her laptop. And there was an e-mail from some guy . . . Ethan, I think." She shrugged, adding, "I wasn't snooping. It was just right there out in the open."

Max hated road-tripping alone, and looking at the estimated driving time—four hours and twenty-eight minutes—he said, "Are you sure?"

"No, I'm not," Mitzi said. "But if you had any better leads, you wouldn't be here."

With a deeper sense of gratitude than he thought it possible to feel for Mitzi Berman, Max said, "Thank you." He looked down at the check on her desk. "So I guess I can, uh, just take this back?"

Mitzi grabbed it before he could. Then she tore it in half, got up, and pushed him out of her office. "Now go!"

CHAPTER FIFTY-EIGHT

For the Friday-night potluck, chairs were arranged in a circle in the living room of 204, the largest house, and everyone (the twenty or so who usually showed) chatted amiably while eating dinner off of cheap plastic plates balanced on their laps. Around dessert time, someone would stand up to "share," and tonight Sydney had promised Ethan that she would be one of them.

After a full month in residence, she was planning to tell everyone how much she had come to appreciate living there, how welcomed she'd felt by every single person ("I appreciate you" was a much bandied-about saying), but they were already on the fourth share, and all of Ethan's nudging hadn't gotten Sydney to budge. She really did want to thank everyone, but public speaking always gave her anxiety. And now that she'd traded her Xanax for meditation and *The Power of Now,* she needed to guard fiercely against unnecessary disruptions of her equilibrium. What if she wound up crying in front of everybody as she made her sappy declaration? They'd gotten tight, but not that tight!

And so Sydney sat there, nibbling on a sugar-free madeleine, as Soraya droned on about not loving herself enough, which sounded pretty whiny on the heels of Tessa's fierce vagina monologue about sacrificing for her art, a word she'd used interchangeably with *heart.* Her attention drifting, Sydney tuned in to the music playing outside, and when it got so loud that other heads turned curiously toward the door, she realized it wasn't just a passing car. Jumping at the opportunity to stall, she went to the window as Soraya droned to a close, planning to stand there (no matter what she saw) until someone else claimed the floor.

Still unable to see the blaster from the window, she quietly slipped outside and inched toward the street until she laid eyes on a truly headscratching sight. At the end of the block, a black Range Rover was parked in the middle of the street and there was a guy in a trench coat standing on top with an iPod boom box raised over his head, *Say Anything*–style.

Thinking it was one of the crazy townies pulling a prank, Sydney rushed toward him, her feet slipping out of her felt clogs, until she saw that it wasn't a crazy townie. It was her crazy *up*townie (socially speaking, despite his Brooklyn address)! And he was blasting the Mariah song "We Belong Together"! Omigod, she thought deliriously. He'd come to rescue her!

"Max!" she gasped, mortified by the time she reached him and noticed a few other residents dotting the sidewalk, watching curiously. "What are you doing? Get down from there!"

After he turned off the music, set the box on the roof, and almost busted his ass during a shaky dismount, he said, with a straight face, "I'm here to rescue you."

The smile that was bursting to come out turned into a scowl and then, dismissing the perfect synchronicity of their thoughts, Sydney screeched, "I don't need rescuing!"

"Did I say 'rescue'?" Max scratched his head, then moved on to the two days' worth of stubble on his chin. He looked like a vagrant who'd just woken up over a grate. "I didn't mean rescue. I had eight cups of coffee on the drive up here. Whooo . . . I'm wired!"

Sydney laughed, but recognizing about eight different "jilted lover kills ex" behaviors she'd read about in *The Gift of Fear,* she took another step back as a precautionary measure. She needed to humor him and slowly make her way back to group safety, but her own survival lost out to her uncontrollable need to provoke. "The pampered prince drove? I'd think you'd take the plane. It's only a thirty-minute flight."

"Jesus," Max said, banging himself in the head. "Why didn't Mitzi tell me that?"

"Mitzi told you I was here?" Sydney said, let down that the pamperedprince jab hadn't connected. "How did she know?"

Max's whole body went slack, and he collapsed onto a clean strip of curb. "She knows everything."

"Well, you can't leave your car blocking the street," Sydney said, staring down at him as a dozen people lingered on both sides of the street watching them. "And you interrupted Friday-night potluck. Maybe you should just go wait in my room until I'm ready to deal with you. Stop making a spectacle of yourself!"

Max jumped up. "Stop telling me what to do!"

Taking two quick leaps backward, Sydney said, "Oh, right, you're not the doorman anymore. No one tells Maximillian Cooper what to do!"

"Sydney, look," Max said. "I just drove five hours up here to see if you were okay. Jeffrey and your sister think you joined a cult, you know."

"And this is the cavalry they sent? You and an iPod boom box?"

Max angrily pulled off his *Say Anything* trench coat, dumping it in a bunch on the curb, and Sydney spotted a Harvey's tag (that said $885 . . . or $1,885?) hanging out of the sleeve. Whatever the ridiculous price (that he hadn't had to pay), he was still wearing a costume, she thought. Still playing games. Like a child.

"No one's heard from you," he said, beyond his breaking point. "Your phone's cut off. You don't return anyone's e-mails. We're all worried sick about you, Sydney! Don't you ever think about what running off like this does to everyone else? To the people who . . ." His voice caught suddenly and the rest of his declaration escaped in a strangled whisper. ". . . who love you."

The unplanned release of the love bomb caused Max to glance down at his Adidas and sudden tears to well up in Sydney's eyes. She wanted to jump into his arms and shout, "I love you too!" and then zoom off in his shiny car and not look back. She hated that lumpy bed! She hated sharing the bathroom! With men! She'd hated Ethan ever since she caught him making googly eyes at Tessa when she performed at the Coffee House! She hated not being able to quiet her mind chatter during meditation! She hated tofu and sugar-free desserts and all the macrobiotic shit everyone cooked! And she really, really hated how much she really, really missed Max!

But instead of telling him that, it was like some bitter, hateful cunt took control of her vocal cords and made her say, "If you came all the way up here to tell me you love me, Max, then at least look at me when you say it. Don't be a wimp!"

"Don't call me a wimp!" Max shouted, almost lunging at her. "You've beaten me at tennis, at pool, at poker, at Scrabble. You've tried to emasculate me in every way possible, but I'm still here!" He punched a fist in the air as though he'd just made it to the top of Mount Everest after losing his sherpa halfway up, and spun around, bellowing at the curious onlookers who'd clumped together in front of 204 to watch the drama unfold as a communal experience. *"I'm still fucking here!"* Then he clamped his hands around Sydney's head and planted a forceful kiss on her mouth. "I love you," he said, releasing her from his grip. "There. Was that *manly* enough for you?"

Sydney wanted to say "Yes!" She wanted to surrender. She wanted to accept her good fortune and allow her life to be easy for once. But that wasn't going to happen until she exorcised the hateful cunt. "NO!"

"Why the hell not?" Max shouted back.

"Because love *doesn't* conquer all!" Sydney gave him a poke in the chest, and detecting the silkiness of a cotton tee that probably cost a hundred dollars, she was reminded of why it was never going to work between them! "Maybe in your little fairy-tale world it does. But not in the real world where I live."

Max looked around as though a spaceship had just deposited him on another planet. "Real world? You're hiding out at a commune in a town that has a population of two thousand. There were more people than that in my high school! How is this the real world?"

"It's realer than the world you've been living in all your life!"

"Sydney, you don't know what my world is like because you won't take the time to get to know me. You just make these totally off-base assumptions and then you run. Just like you did with your ex. He wanted a commitment and you ran!"

Sydney gasped. She'd only told him that story because she was sky-high on Babcock's stash. How dare he throw that in her face! That was seven years ago. She was a completely different person now. She was a completely different person than she was *a month ago*. She'd tackled a lot of issues, shed a lot of ego in a month! She was a spiritual, ego-shedding being now! And he was just some . . . trustafarian. With no trust fund! And no job! Who was he to tell her *anything*?

"Well . . . well . . . well . . ." she practically hiccupped, trying to come up with a biting retort. "Well, maybe every decision I make isn't about a man! So don't flatter yourself, honey. I didn't come here to get away from you. I came here because I realized I didn't need to find a husband or any guy. I needed to find myself."

"So have you done that?" Max said, stifling a groan. "Can we leave now?"

"If I leave, I'll leave of my own volition. I'm not gonna leave to be with you! Because I don't want to be with someone I can beat at everything. I'm sick of being stronger, smarter, more capable. I want someone to open doors for me and carry my bags at the airport and fix my fucking modem when it's broken. I want someone to take care of me! I want to be *the girl*!" Sydney stopped abruptly, realizing what she'd just said, how many people had heard it, and that her face was wet with tears. "There!" she said, roughly wiping her nose with the back of her hand. "You broke me down. I said it! Happy?"

"Yes," Max said softly so only she would hear. "I can take care of you, Sydney. I want to. Just give me a chance."

Sydney backed away when he tried to embrace her, still fuming. "How are you going to take care of me when you can't fend for yourself, Max? You got fired from the only job you ever had. By your father! But you still stroll through life without a care in the world because you've got it like that. I wish I had it that easy."

"No, you don't," Max said, calmly interrupting her.

"Excuse me?"

"You don't want it easy," Max said, looking at her like she had finally come into focus. "You *want* to feel like everyone is against you. And where there are no enemies or problems, you create them. Maybe that's why having that cushy job made you so uncomfortable. Maybe that's why you did something to get yourself fired. And maybe that's why you don't want to be with me. Because I'm a great fucking guy, sweetheart, who women on both coasts are dying to be with. Ask Mitzi Berman. But those are women who want to be happy. And it's become very clear to me that you don't. So you know what? God bless and fuck you very much!"

He turned to walk back to his car, and Sydney followed him, shouting angrily. "You think being Harvey's son is such a burden, but at least you have a father." She grabbed his arm and forced him to look at her. "Where's my daddy, Max? *Dead,* that's where! Killed by some sixteen-year-old punk drunk driving his rich daddy's BMW! And you got away with it! *You got away with it!*"

Through her web of tears, Sydney saw Max's stricken face and, from 204, she heard gasps. Then she heard the echo of her own voice. Had she just said "you got away with it"?

"Oh, Sydney," Max said, wiping away her tears. "I'm not him." Hugging her tight, he kept repeating, "I'm not him. I'm not him."

Sydney didn't quite understand what had just happened, but she knew she was in Max's arms, crying her eyes out, and aside from glimpsing Ethan and Tessa sharing a bag of microwave popcorn, she felt happier than she had in a long time.

It was the next moment, when she'd have to explain to everyone watching what had just happened, that she couldn't bear. But if she left right this second, she thought, she wouldn't have to. Raising her lips to Max's ear, she whispered, "Meet me around the corner. In front of the thrift shop. In five!"

As she ran down the block, she looked back and saw Max jump back into the Rover and pull off, sending the iPod boom box he'd forgotten was still on the roof crashing to the street. When he pulled up in front of the shop around the corner, Sydney was dashing out with a pink neoprene laptop case under one arm and a Whole Foods tote over the other.

"What the hell are we doing?" he said, tossing empty Starbucks cups into the backseat.

Sydney looked out of the back window like they were filming a remake of *Thelma & Louise*. "Escaping!"

"Don't you need to go back to the house? Don't you need to get anything?"

"Like what? My yoga mat? I renounced all my worldly possessions!"

Max put his hand on the gearshift, shaking his head. "Sydney, you're nuts!"

"But that's why you love me." She leaned over and give him a smoochy, wet kiss. "Thanks for coming to my rescue." Starved for affection, Max slipped his hand around her neck, ready for a full makeout session, but Sydney turned to look out the back window. Seeing a stampede of Birks and Crocs coming around the corner, she slapped her hand over his and shifted the gear into drive. "Hit it!"

CHAPTER FIFTY-NINE

She refused to be involved in the planning. She'd shown up for dress fittings, handed in her guest list, come to the rehearsal dinner and obviously the ceremony. But that was it. She let Mitzi deal with the rest.

Now, taking her first steps down the aisle, Sydney wondered if that had been a mistake. Everything looked beautiful; the flowers must have cost a fortune. But who were all of these people? Mitzi told her it was going to be one hundred and fifty. It had to be twice that. Three hundred strangers all pointing digital cameras at her.

She'd told Max she wanted no part of this public spectacle and he said he didn't either, really, but what could they do? They had an obligation to the family. Sydney wasn't used to being obligated to anyone but herself. She'd never understood how liberating it was to not be close to your family until she had to be around Coopers all the time.

That wasn't to say she didn't like being co—creative director of the store, especially since Simon, her "work husband," had been wooed back. But at every other job she'd had, she couldn't have cared less what her coworkers thought of her because she knew she was just there for a spell and once she was gone, who gave a shit? She *had* to care what Harvey and Avery thought of her. She was marrying into their family.

When Harvey had first offered her the job, Sydney was conflicted about joining The Establishment, but Joyce had convinced her that the only way to change The Establishment was from the inside. And Joyce was right. On the creative end Sydney had been able to push her idea of affordable luxury and to highlight young emerging designers (there was a Senegalese girl she'd discovered who'd blown up like crazy), and she was also able to stay in Avery's ear about promoting a more female-friendly work environment. (The new flex-time program earned Avery a glowing piece in *Fortune*.) The small, contemporary boutiques they were rolling out in several cities to compete with Victor had been Sydney's idea, and getting Max to be in charge of their design had been a perfect way to pull him back into the fold and heal the rift that his firing had created. It turned out to be the perfect job for him, combining his talent and love for design with his need for constantly changing stimuli. Sometimes he'd hit three sites a week in three different cities, which removed him from the office drama and afforded them both the personal space they needed to keep from feeling bored or suffocated in the relationship. (Frequent romps in limos to and from the airport helped to keep things interesting too.)

Sydney didn't mind being in the office every day because there was always a lot going on and there was never any cattiness like at *Cachet*, despite Myrna's presence. Sydney had brought her in to edit the quarterly catalog, and she was doing a bang-up job. She still threw the occasional tantrum, and when that happened Sydney made sure she was taking her mood stabilizers. Although Myrna knew not to push it too far. Sydney was her boss now, something Sydney delighted in reminding her, and Myrna knew she'd fire her ass if she had to.

Thinking about the gratifying role reversal, Sydney smiled at Myrna, who was stuck in a back row, holding the adorable Chinese baby she'd adopted (God help that child). Spotting Jerome two rows ahead, Sydney's smile blossomed to a wattage that was probably inappropriate given her current situation. But what could she say? She still had a soft spot for him. That could not be said of Candi, whom Sydney saw peeking out from behind Jerome's enormous shoulders. Apparently, Jerome had tried to contact Sydney a few weeks after the Perry Street pervert incident and, in an attempt to circumvent Mitzi, he'd called *Cachet*. When he was told Sydney no longer worked there, he went to her apartment, where he'd learned, from Candi, that Sydney had moved and left no forwarding address. And now Jerome Bailey and the white-trash stripper were married. And expecting. *Lucky slut*, Sydney thought, turning to check out the who's who to her left.

The first face she saw was Lulu Merriwether's, and she quickly turned back to her right, her plastered smile faltering just as the official wedding photographer zoomed in for a close-up. Yes, she had gotten Max in the end and it was rumored that all Lulu and Brett Babcock ever did was fight (about his cheating), but Lulu had swiped that envelope. There was no hard evidence that she was the culprit, but Sydney knew, in an ESP kind of way, that she was guilty. She wasn't hurting for money now at all—it was weird how something that had consumed her for so many years no longer rated as a concern—but a girl could always use a healthy nest egg. And thanks to Lulunatic, Sydney had to start hers from scratch instead of with a first deposit of four hundred thousand dollars!

She was pissed that Lulu and Brett, who already looked drunk at three in the afternoon, were even invited, but thank God Remy was safe on the opposite side of the aisle. Sydney had taken Remy under her wing, and seeing her protégée's hair done up in soft curls, her makeup tastefully applied, her simple shift dress meeting the event's chic standards, Sydney swelled with pride. It was like looking at Melanie Griffith at the end of *Working Girl*. That was exactly the plotline Remy had stolen for her first novel (written under her own name), and Sydney couldn't have been more proud to see it hit the bestseller list if she had birthed that girl herself. It was an added bonus that Remy's little "working-class girl made good" chick lit had been optioned and rushed into production, while Lulu's rich bitch confessional had been shelved indefinitely because, as *Variety* noted, "In the current economic climate, the premise strikes an obscene note."

Now that Remy was involved in a serious relationship with the unlikeliest of celebrities—Duke, whose solo album had made him an indie rock god—she was doing better than Lulu in the man department as well. Sydney was happy for them, but she hoped they were using reliable contraception while road-tripping all over the country on Duke's tour bus. Max was always dropping hints about kids, and if Duke had one, Sydney knew he'd demand to have one too. Her need to breed didn't seem so urgent now that she'd settled down with her guy and one squirt of ejaculate could change the whole game. She liked having time alone, sleeping late on weekends, and going on spur-of-the-moment vacations where she and Max did nothing but lay on the beach, overeat, and get toasted every night. You couldn't do any of those things when you had kids (unless you wanted to be an ambivalent parent). So why not wait another year? Or two? Or, now that she finally had the body she wanted, *five*?

She'd advised Jeffrey not to rush into anything when Hector started getting all broody. They'd already adopted three dogs together. Did they need a baby too? Even though she'd grown to like Lil Hector (as she still privately called him), it annoyed her that she was the reason they'd gotten together. It wasn't that she didn't want Jeffrey to be happy—she just wanted him to be happy with someone she could tolerate over brunch.

Turning away as Lil Hector tried to snap her picture, Sydney saw that a seating snafu had placed Joyce just a Liz away from Vera (when those two needed at least ten feet of distance minimum). Sydney tried to telegraph a look of sympathy to her sister-in-law before beaming brightly at Dr. Wu, who always looked genuinely happy no matter what, and how he managed that while being married to Vera was unfathomable.

Struck by the sudden realization that people might be thinking the same thing about Max after he'd been with *her* for ten years, Sydney turned and looked at him standing at the top of the aisle. She'd never understood what a catch Max was considered to be until Jezebel ranked him number five on their DILF (Dudes I'd Like to Fuck) list. And then dozens of commenters agreed that Sydney was not good enough for him!

"How dare they!" Max had joked when Sydney made him look at it. Then he'd registered under the user name watchyoback and posted inflammatory statements that shamed the haters and praised Sydney to the heavens (she helped him word it). Thinking about that now, Sydney looked at him standing under the huppah, then glanced down at the beautiful engagement ring he'd given to her on a Thai beach, along with a certificate that it was a nonconflict diamond, and blinked back tears.

She almost walked over and kissed him until she remembered that was not part of the script. This wasn't *their* big day. They were merely supporting players in Mitzi's never-ending melodrama. Just having minimal involvement in this over-the-top extravaganza had confirmed Sydney's belief that eloping was the only way to go. That was the route Harvey was probably wishing he had taken. The poor man looked ready to soil his beautiful Armani suit.

Harvey's jitters visibly intensified when the bridal march sounded and everyone's attention turned to the door. Mitzi had demanded that all the guests wear white, and when she made her grand entrance, everyone saw why. She was sheathed in a blood-red couture gown, designed by Galliano himself. The dress was hot, very fashion-forward for an old broad like Mitzi, but as she proceeded down the aisle, surrounded by a sea of white-clad guests, it looked as though she was bleeding down a snow embankment.

Sydney couldn't control her tittering, and that set Max off. Much to Mitzi's dismay, they continued to titter together all through the sappy ceremony and then, fueled by champagne, during the even sappier toasts, the happy couple's first slow waltz . . .

None of it was really that funny, but knowing that Mitzi Berman-Cooper had found a way to permanently insert herself into both of their lives, that they'd have to spend every major holiday in her company, that she'd try to force them to have an even grander wedding, that she'd be nagging them about when they were going to have kids and nagging them about how they were raising them once they did, that she was already nagging them to call her "Mom" . . .

Knowing they'd never be rid of her, till death (or divorce, which Mitzi would never allow because it was bad for business) did they part, Max and Sydney had to laugh.

To keep from crying.